NORTHERN
STARS

Tor Anthologies edited by David G. Hartwell

NORTHERN STARS

The Anthology of Canadian Science Fiction

Edited by
David G. Hartwell and Glenn Grant

TOR

A Tom Doherty Associates Book
New York

For Ian and Toni Grant, my parents
(one could not ask for better).

—*Glenn Grant*

To Alison and Geoff, my stars. And to ConCept,
a small convention in Montreal with big ideas.

—*David G. Hartwell*

NORTHERN STARS: THE ANTHOLOGY OF CANADIAN SCIENCE FICTION

This book is printed on acid-free paper.

A Tor Book
Published by Tom Doherty Associates, Inc.
175 Fifth Avenue
New York, N.Y. 10010

Tor ® is a registered trademark of Tom Doherty Associates, Inc.

Design by Lynn Newmark

Library of Congress Cataloging-in-Publication Data

Northern Stars/David G. Hartwell and Glenn Grant, editors.
p. cm.
"A Tom Doherty Associates Book."

1. Science fiction, Canadian.   2. Canadian fiction—20th century.
I. Hartwell, David G.   II. Grant, Glenn.
PR9197.35.S33N67   1994   94-12918
813'.0876208971—dc20   CIP

Printed in the United States of America

ACKNOWLEDGMENTS

In selecting the stories for *Northern Stars*, David and I benefited greatly from the good judgment and hard work of many other editors and publishers. Gerry Truscott and Beach Holme Publishers (formerly Press Porcépic) of Victoria are the creative forces behind the excellent *Tesseracts* anthology series, brilliantly edited by Judith Merril, Phyllis Gotlieb, Douglas Barbour, Candas Jane Dorsey, Lorna Toolis, and Michael Skeet. This series was an important catalyst during the mid-eighties flowering of the Canadian SF field, especially through its many translations of the works of Francophone writers, which provided necessary windows onto the lively SF scene in Quebec. (The four stories originally written in French that appear in *Northern Stars* were all translated for the *Tesseracts* series.) In addition, Porcépic/Beach Holme publishes a strong line of original SF novels and single-author collections, including books by Andrew Weiner, Candas Jane Dorsey, Élisabeth Vonarburg, and Heather Spears. Outstanding anthologies and collections of English Canadian SF were also produced by Lesley Choyce of Pottersfield Press in Nova Scotia, particularly the spectacular *Ark of Ice: Canadian Futurefiction*. Meanwhile, the Copper Pig Writers' Society of Edmonton has been making great strides in the magazine field, publishing *On Spec*, the first national journal of Canadian speculative writing in English. In Quebec the active Francophone SF scene is served by the magazines *Solaris* and *imagine . . .*, and by several hardworking book publishers, including (among others) Préambule, Québec/Amérique, and Ianus.

David and I were assisted in our researches by the bilingual newsletters of the Canadian Science Fiction and Fantasy Association, *Communiqué* and *Top Secret*, produced by selflessly dedicated editors Jean-Louis Trudel, Aaron V. Humphrey, and Dale Sproule (with help from many other capable hands). For information on membership, or nonmember subscriptions to *Communiqué*, contact: SF Canada, 10523, 100th Avenue, Edmonton, Alberta, T5J 0A8 (E-mail: 71165.2152@compuserve.com).

Many thanks to everyone who so graciously provided their valuable time, suggestions, books, magazines, and references; in particular, we wish to thank Jean-Louis Trudel, Robert Sawyer, David Ketterer, Mark Shainblum, Dennis Mullen, Karl Shroeder, Donald Kingsbury, Edo Van Belkom, William Barrett, Joy Jones, Claude Lalumière, the friendly staff of the Merril

Collection of the Toronto Public Library, and the organizers of Montreal's ConCept '93 convention.

Special thanks to Kathryn Cramer, Emru Townsend, and James Bailie for graciously providing E-mail services.

Contents

10   CONTENTS

INTRODUCTION

Glenn Grant

Ever seen the movie *Blade Runner*? Great film; one of the very few that can be considered to be true science fiction (as opposed to some fool-headed Hollywood simulacrum of the genre). Unfortunately, the Denver test audiences didn't care for its unresolved closure, so the brainless producers chose to meddle with Ridley Scott's masterpiece, tacking on a silly happy ending. In the original director's cut, we last see Decker and the replicant, Rachel, as they board an elevator, then the doors shut. The End. Maybe they live happily ever after; probably not. But in the producer's cut, we see them smiling in Decker's sunlit car as they fly away, over an incongruously pristine mountain landscape.

Where, in their depleted, toxified world, could a retired Blade Runner and his rogue android lover go to find safety and freedom? Earlier in the film, Rachel suggested that she might try to escape by flying north. Of course: to the north, away from the urbanized and desertified wastelands of California, north to primeval Canada. That nice aerial footage of majestic, forested mountains? I'm told that's an outtake from the title sequence of *The Shining*, shot by Stanley Kubrick in Alberta.

Where else would one go to escape the hyperurban hell of the American future, but across the world's longest undefended border, into the vast, uncharted and untouched wilderness that is Canada. Out of the Future, into the Past. Sure. Everyone knows there's nothing up here but a few billion pine trees, some caribou, a quaint village or two, and the odd snowbound igloo. Everyone knows that the future will never come to Canada, if in fact the present should ever arrive. . . .

Poor Rachel and Decker. They're in for the shock of their lives.

Flying up the West Coast and crossing the 49th parallel, they come under the influence of the Northern Stars. Heads full of all those Hollywood misconceptions—smiling Mounties, roving Eskimo, unbroken expanses of driven snow—they suddenly find themselves immersed in the homegrown Canadian visions collected here in this book. . . .

First, Decker's air-car settles down among the close-crowded spires of "Couverville," the twenty-first-century Vancouver of William Gibson's "The Winter Market," cleaner perhaps but in some ways too disturbingly similar to the megalopolitan Los Angeles they've left behind. So they veer east, into the forested interior of British Columbia, only to find endless

clearcuts and the hotly contested ecological war zone of Claude-Michel Prévost's "Happy Days in Old Chernobyl." Barely escaping with their lives,
they cross the Rockies and traverse the Great Midwestern Dustbowl, perhaps flying over the technomadic instant city of my own story, "Memetic
Drift." Robert Charles Wilson's western roadhouse, in "Ballads in 3/4
Time" seems as if it should offer our travelers some sanctuary, but artificial
people such as Rachel are not yet emancipated here.

They continue on, then, and come to the postindustrial cities of Ontario,
including the Toronto of Candas Jane Dorsey's "(Learning About) Machine
Sex." Too corporate-dominated for comfort; perhaps Ottawa or Montreal
will be different? According to Jean-Louis Trudel's "Remember, the Dead
Say," these cities are different indeed, maddened by war, and caught in the
harsh political pincers of an unexpectedly violent future. Dodging a few
missiles, our refugees fly on, east to the Maritime Provinces. Here, like the
narrator of Spider Robinson's "User Friendly," they face some unpleasant
truths about the arrogance of alien invaders. Farther east, Garfield Reeves-
Stevens offers them similar cautions in the icebound waters of his "Outport."

But there are many worlds under these Northern Stars, so perhaps our
Blade Runner and replicant will climb aboard an outbound colony ship, to
discover the diverse alien worlds envisioned by Lesley Choyce, Terence
Green, Yves Meynard, Donald Kingsbury, and others collected here. I know
that somewhere among these stars they will find solace. Certainly they will
never be bored.

As coeditors of *Northern Stars*, David Hartwell and I are confident that you,
too, will be thrilled and enthralled by what you find in this anthology of the
best contemporary Canadian science fiction. Of course, no single book could
possibly contain *all* of the best stories in print, but we have striven for a representative cross section of the excellent work being done by Canadian SF
authors. (Our definition of "Canadian authors," by the way, is: Canadian
citizens who write here, or those that have only recently moved abroad, or
landed immigrants writing in Canada.)

We were motivated to do this book by the prospect of an imminent Ca-
nadian-hosted World Science Fiction Convention, Conadian, to be held in
Winnipeg in September of 1994. Only the third Worldcon to be hosted by
this country, it seemed a perfect opportunity to expose the work of Canadian SF writers to new and larger audiences. *Northern Stars* is the first anthology of contemporary Canadian science fiction to be published in
hardcover—although we must not forget to mention John Robert
Colombo's pioneering anthology, *Other Canadas* (McGraw-Hill Ryerson,
1979), an important historical overview of Canadian fantastic literature.
Compendious as it was, that book did not contain much science fiction, and
little contemporary writing.

We chose to limit ourselves to contemporary stories (written within the last twenty years) because we wanted to show the world what's going on in Canada today, to let everybody know that a vibrant SF scene has been bubbling along here for quite some time, and which, in the last ten years, has really started to put on steam. To this end we've gathered together the work of twenty-eight of Canada's best SF authors: twenty-five short stories—five of them translated from the French and two by Francophones writing in English—and two novel excerpts (one of them a work-in-progress), as well as two essays on the history and present condition of Canadian speculative literature. In addition, we've included a useful reference list of all the winners of the major Canadian SF and fantasy awards—which we compiled when we realized that such a listing had never been published.

Add it all up and we think you'll find that the result is a solid book, full of high-quality fiction. It doesn't surprise me at all that Canada is now producing such a wide array of top-notch science fiction writers—many more than David and I could possibly squeeze into this book. What seems strange to me is that it has taken so long to happen. As Judith Merril explains in her essay, this talented Canadian wave is a recent phenomenon; prior to the late 1970's, there probably weren't enough SF writers working in Canada to fill a book such as this one.

Thus, as I grew up, nearly all of the science fiction I read was written by American and British authors. It eventually began to bother me that the futures they envisioned never seemed to include Canada, as if Canada simply did not exist in the future. Indeed, if this country was mentioned at all, it was usually assumed to have broken up (always due to the secession of Quebec), or it was seen to have become part of the United States. The worldwide perception seems to be that it is the common desire of every Canadian to cease to be a Canadian.

True, the breakup of Canada is a real possibility, but hardly a foregone conclusion, or even the most likely scenario. (Note that, among all the stories in this volume, only one mentions an independent Quebec.) And the idea that we are all destined to become Americans is merely a long-standing pipe dream among our friendly neighbors to the south.

Exploring the possible futures open to us is one of science fiction's most important functions, and it's not a good idea to leave the job entirely to someone else. Thus it is heartening to see that Canadian SF has finally found its voice—or *voices*, I should say. For while I believe that our SF writing does share certain common characteristics that distinguish it from American and British SF, these commonalities are obscured by distinctive *regional* differences. Variations in geography, climate, and urban density have an even greater impact on the style and tenor of our writing than that other major factor, the languages in which we write.

As for those distinctive national qualities I mentioned: Douglas Barbour says (in *Tesseracts* [2]) that our best writers often "challenge certain assumptions and conventions of the traditional (read: American) paradigm" and that, "especially in the case of some women writers . . . the cast of the narrative, the weave of the story, resists the siren call of plot for something more subtle and finally more rewarding." In a similar vein, Candas Jane Dorsey tells me that Canadian SF "has more to do with progress toward understanding than with conflict resolution." We have a penchant for "mood pieces" that some conflict-obsessed American editors have been known to reject as "nonstories" in which "nothing happens."

Since *Northern Stars* is a science fiction anthology (and David and I have clear ideas about what constitutes a science fiction story), this book does not display quite as broad a range of styles as most previous Canadian SF anthologies. In Canada, even more than in Britain, "SF" more often means "speculative fiction" than "science fiction," and the former is a much wider catchall than the latter, including as it does magic realism, surrealism, and most other forms of the fantastic. The term "speculative fiction" does not recognize any academically imposed distinction between SF and "real literature," and thus many Canadian writers, even some of our Big Names, are quite comfortable to drift between the mainstream and the various genres. We are happy to be surfers of the Slipstream.

While hardworking small presses such as Beach Holme and Pottersfield have been busy publishing Canadian SF, unfortunately our major publishing houses have shown little enthusiasm for this aspect of our culture. The fact that this anthology is being produced by an American publisher speaks for itself.

Canadians should be natural SF writers, I think, because this country has been shaped, from its inception, by the kind of utopian dreams one encounters only in the most visionary scientific romances. Consider the Hudson's Bay Company, a megacorporation that once virtually owned a vast swath of North America. Consider the national railroad that stitched together this obviously impossible confederation; the huge locks and canals of the St. Lawrence Seaway; the Fuller domes of the Distant Early Warning radar web; the insanely oversized James Bay hydroelectric projects in northern Quebec; the very expensive exploitation of Alberta's tar sands and Newfoundland's Hibernia offshore oil fields; the ludicrously endless shopping-and-amusement complex known as the West Edmonton Mall . . .

In short, Canada itself is a continent-spanning megaproject on a truly science-fictional scale. Perhaps Canada *is* a work of science fiction.

WE HAVE MET THE ALIEN (AND IT IS US)

Judith Merril

Judith Merril is one of the central figures in the science fiction field. Both as a writer from the 1940's to the 1970's of such classic stories as "That Only a Mother" (1948), and as a leading reviewer of the 1950's and 1960's, she had a major impact. But it was as perhaps the most important anthologist of the 1950's and 1960's that she most influenced the development of modern science fiction, particularly the ten annual volumes of *Best SF* (1950–1960), which established the currency of the term "speculative fiction" as a broader (and more literary) umbrella than "science fiction." During the years in which those anthologies were published, she was perhaps the most influential arbiter of taste in the science-fiction world. And this is not to belittle the impact of her greatest single anthology, *England Swings SF* (1968), the book that introduced the British "new wave" to America.

At or near the height of her popularity and influence in the late 1960's, she "dropped out." She moved to Toronto and withdrew from activity in U.S. SF circles. Never a prolific writer, her output of SF nearly ceased as she moved on to another life, in broadcasting and in Canadian literary circles. The rest is chronicled in her distinguished afterword to the first major anthology of Canadian SF, *Tesseracts* (1985). This fine anthology hit Canadian SF with such force that it might be said to have been a major cause of the contemporary renaissance of Canadian SF. The writers were there. The fans were there. All that was missing was a publication to serve as a market for writers, a market that identified them as a group with unique characteristics and a unique history within the greater body of world SF. So Judy edited another anthology and gave Canadian SF a local habitation and the beginnings of an identity crisis.

Now, how could I have told you up front that what this book is about is critical alienation? I mean, and still have you read it?

Actually, I *couldn't* tell you, because I didn't know.

Had I but known—well, at the very least, I'd have tried to balance things out more.

And that would have been a mistake.

In any event, after all the readings and re-readings, separately and in sequence, I knew everything about this book except what its overall theme had turned out to be. I found out from someone who had never seen the book at all.

* * *

I was thinking about what I wanted to say back here, and I started asking people—everyone, anyone—to tell me why they thought SF (science fiction, speculative fabulation, sometimes surreal futures) is so popular now. What social value does the genre have, now, here?

I got a lot of familiar replies, about rehearsing future options, opening one's mind to alternative realities, using exotic sets and lights to focus on familiar problems, generally practising thinking the unthinkable.

True. It was science fiction, future fiction, SF, that taught us how to think about death and despoliation by radiation, chemical waste devastation, Big Brother, Star Wars and Nuclear Winter. So what's "unthinkable" now?

My daughter, appropriately, gave me the answer that curled my toes and shivered my neurons and made me see the *whole* book for the first time: *It's the only place you can do any useful thinking about the idea that there might not be a future:* the terminal fear that proliferates abortions and suicides, mass murders, mad leaders, terrorists and technical errors; the ultimate anxiety that makes people sorry they had children, and children not want to grow up.

And of course that's what most of this book is about: the children finding ways to grow up, the parents trying to help them. I didn't plan it that way; it's just that those were the stories that seemed to *work*.

You must understand that I am really a most improbable anthologist. I'm a poor scholar, not much of a collector or compiler, not at all a historian. (Call me a generalist, maybe, disseminator—someone once said *neophiliac*.) Nevertheless, this volume is my twentieth SF anthology, and the first nineteen brought me just enough dribs and drabs of fame and fortune so that I can now say brazenly (like in the Modern Art Joke): *I don't know anything about literary criticism, but I know what I like.*

What I like is getting my head turned around. I get off on fresh perceptions, widening horizons, new thoughts, and I like them best when they occur as a process in my own mind, rather than an exposition at which I am a passive spectator/receiver. What I look for in SF is the story (or verse—occasionally film—sometimes even essay) conceived and written in such a way as to suggest alternatives that will cause me to exercise my own imagination to broaden my own vision. To "ask the next question."

> A Martian with a mangled spear
> Is stuffing tarts in my left ear.
> If I turn off my hearing aid,
> Will I still taste the marmalade?

This synaesthetic gem was probably the beginning of this anthology. It was handed to me in December 1968 in an unhallowed hall of Rochdale College by an idealistic young academic already highly respected as poet, publisher and editor, but not yet famous for Alligator Pies, Garbage Delights and other tasty (*not* non-) sense. It turned my head around. I put it aside for my next anthology, which was some time coming.

Twenty is a nice round number.

The first SF anthology I edited, in 1951, was called *Shot in the Dark*, not so much for its interior surprises as to enable Bantam Books to pass it off on mystery readers if necessary. The saleability of SF was an unknown quantity at the time.

The time, as it turned out, was right. In the next eighteen years I did eighteen more collections. The last two, *SF 12* (Delacorte) and *England Swings SF* (Doubleday), were published almost back-to-back in 1968.

That was the same year I arrived in Toronto, a newly-landed immigrant with a U-Haul full of books, papers, plastic milk crates and foam pads. My new job as resource person at Rochdale would pay only room and board. I expected to have to do more anthologies for car-fares and cigarette money, and I figured Dennis Lee's verse to be my first Canadian inclusion for *SF 13*.

Thirteen was the lucky number: I never got around to doing it. (*SF 12* was the twelfth annual in the "Year's Best" series, and twelve years of claiming to present the *Best*—of anything—was more than enough. Better iconoclast than inconescent.) But by the time I realized I was not going to do another SF annual, I had learned a couple of things about Canadian SF.

In all the far reaches of Canada in 1968 there seemed to be only two people (well, make it 2¼) writing recognizable science fiction seriously: Phyllis Gotlieb and H. A. Hargreaves (and Chandler Davis *very* occasionally; adding my own output at the time, make it 2½). But in odd corners and coach houses (especially *the* Coach House Press) Canadians of rare talent and sensibility were writing truly-fabulous funny-serious social-commentary SF: Dave Godfrey, Ray Smith, D. M. Price, J. Michael Yates, Gwendolyn MacEwen, P. K. Page, Robert Zend, Christopher Dewdney and more, were stuffed in with the marmalade.

The seventies: I was becoming a Canadian and a broadcaster, and not thinking about anthologies at all. But (yes, Dennis, you'd still taste it) every switchoff was another switch on. I gave my SF collection to the Toronto Public Library to start the Spaced Out Library, and so became an occasional consultant. I was putting a lot of energy into The Writers' Union of Canada, so became involved with a schools-curriculum project outlining available Canadian science fiction. I wrote radio documentaries and magazine articles, and kept getting asked to do pieces on science fiction. No way I could miss out on what was happening in Canadian SF.

A lot was happening. Here, as elsewhere through the seventies, the most visible events were in book publishing (and selling). But we're talking

Canada: the busiest and healthiest area was of course academic. And to me, inquisitive immigrant, the most intriguing phenomenon was half-hidden under the surface of the literary mainstream.

As I read Canadian authors, and met them personally, I kept finding myself touching what I think of as "science fiction head space." Sometimes it was overt SF imagery, or a certain way of thinking about environment, a casual mixture of magic-and-realism, or an oddly familiar structural tension in the work. Then, one by one, leading Canadian authors began telling me about the impact of science fiction on their development: Berton, Laurence, MacEwen, Acorn, Purdy, Engel. Finally, I began to catch up on Canadian criticism. CanLit, I was told, is about *survival* and, characteristically, the environment may become almost a character in the story!

Of course! Just like SF. (Is this why Canadian mainstream authors, when they turn to SF, usually do a good job of it? U.S. and U.K. mainstreamers generally muck it up.)

Another (used-to-be) Canadian Fact I was learning was the prevalence of "secondary materials." You know—Canada was famous for documentaries, but never made feature films? That kind of thing.

In 1968, when the prestigious Modern Language Association officially declared the study of science fiction a suitable pursuit for scholars, Canadian critics and teachers were already doing it. Harry Campbell, then Chief Librarian in Toronto, must have followed a sure Canadian instinct when he offered to relieve me of my unwieldy collection and establish SOL (the Spaced Out Library) in 1970. By that time, Arthur Gibson and Peter Fitting were already organizing science fiction classes at the University of Toronto, Madge Aalto (the first SOL librarian) was teaching at York, Darko Suvin had a course at McGill and Tom Henighan was just about to start at Carleton.

SOL provided a focus, and increasingly, a resource. In '72, SOL and McGill co-sponsored *SeCon*, the Secondary Universe Conference which brought scholars, critics and teachers of SF together from all over Canada, along with their counterparts from other countries, and a scattering of SF writers. In 1973, a serious scholarly journal, *Science Fiction Studies*, began publishing in Montreal.

By the mid-seventies, most major Canadian universities had SF courses, and colleges and high schools were rushing to catch up. Some of the best teachers were encouraging students to write original stories for their term papers. And there were at least *five*-and-a-half working SF writers across the country, because Spider Robinson had moved up to Nova Scotia from the States, and Britishers Michael Coney and Andrew Weiner had settled in Victoria and Toronto.

(Actually, it was at least six-and-a-half, if you count the blessedly brief extrusion of Harlequin's kid brother, Laser Books, into the field. Laser published a whole series of a single cloned novel—same plot, same characters, different names, titles and bylines—before they discovered SF readers don't like predictable formulas. I won't count them.)

Other publishers were doing better, sometimes spectacularly so. True, most of them didn't *know* they were publishing SF, and most of the authors didn't know they were writing it, but at least twenty at-least-readable novels and one short-story collection of Canadian science fiction were published in Canada during the seventies, and some of them were very fine science fiction indeed: Ian Adams' *The Trudeau Papers,* Christie Harris' *Sky Man on a Totem Pole,* Blanche Howard's *The Immortal Soul of Edwin Carlysle,* Bruce Powe's *The Last Days of the American Empire,* and others of varying quality by John Ballem, Stephen Franklin, William Heine, Basil Jackson, Richard Rohmer, David Walker and Jim Willer. Monica Hughes, Suzanne Martell and Ruth Nichols, writing juveniles, were genre-identified; so was Marie Jacober, with a prize-winning adult novel in Alberta. H. A. Hargreaves' short-story collection, *North By 2000,* in 1975, must have been the first book labelled specifically as Canadian Science Fiction. Gotlieb, Coney and Robinson, of course, were publishing novels and short stories regularly under SF labels in the U.S. and U.K., and towards the end of the decade two new Canadian novelists were launched by U.S. genre publishers: Crawford Killian in 1978 and Edward Llewellyn in 1979. (Llewellyn's *The Douglas Convolution* was the first of only five novels completed before his untimely death in 1984.)

Actually in 1979, you might well have used up all your fingers and toes counting Canadian SF writers—if you could find them. One man did. No one, not even John Colombo, would seriously have tried to produce an anthology of contemporary Canadian science fiction at that point, but he did bring out a very different collection: *Other Canadas.*

John Robert Colombo is a good deal more than just another CanCult household name. I called myself an improbable anthologist; Colombo is the real thing: scholar, historian, careful compiler, indefatiguable researcher, voluminous reader, aggressive correspondent. The marvel is that an editor of these accomplishments should have had the imaginative flair to wish to use them in the service of a genre hardly anyone (except thee and me, John—and sometimes I wondered about *me*) believed existed—indigenous Canadian SF.

Other Canadas used the broadest possible definitions of source, form and content. It brought together a discriminating collection of science fiction and fantasy written by Canadians and/or about Canada over a time-span of more than two hundred years, including short stories, poetry, novel excerpts and critical essays. The selections, enriched with Colombo's informed and engaging notes, established once and for all the existence of the territory, and in effect proclaimed it open for exploration and settlement.

* * *

I am *not* a scholar. My files are famous for their gaps, and my notes for their irrelevance. It is time to apologize in passing to all the people unmentioned here (Susan Wood! How could I never have spoken of Susan Wood?) who were creating Canadian science fiction in the seventies, as I hasten to disclaim any ability to document the burgeoning productivity of the eighties.

(I was straying into television, returning to work on a novel. Still—)

Even the most casual reader had to be aware of the emergence of Eileen Kernaghan (choice science *fantasy*), William Gibson (all over *Omni*) and Donald Kingsbury (Hugo Award nominee for *Courtship Rite*). I knew that John Bell and Lesley Choyce brought out an anthology in 1981 similar in its premises to Colombo's book, but more modestly limited to the Atlantic provinces. I knew that an annual Canadian Science Fiction and Fantasy Award had been established. I was invited to *Boréal*, the Francophone SF conference, and realized that on the other side of the language barrier a positive ferment of activity was going on. And back in Anglophonia I kept hearing names I hadn't heard before.

So when Ellen Godfrey of Press Porcépic suggested a new anthology in 1984, I was only briefly surprised. Of course—the time was right (again). Canadian SF—a uniquely Canadian expression of perspectives on change and the future—had developed as inevitably as (say) Canadian feature films or Canadian Studies courses in foreign universities, from the same ongoing Canadian dynamic: a dialectic of international/immigrant influences and a growing awareness of a specifically Canadian cultural identity. Colombo did not *invent* the concept of *Other Canadas*; he located and described it.

The first *big* surprise then was realizing I really wanted to try to do the book.

Twenty *is* a nice round number. I guess I'd been away from it long enough. (Like sex and bicycles, it seems to come right back when you start again.)

The surprises kept coming. The next big one was not having to fight with my publishers (or educate them). Right from the beginning we were in agreement about the book we wanted to do: a sampling of some of the best contemporary Canadian SF—as described in the Foreword. ("We" were Godfrey, myself and Gerry Truscott, the Press Porcépic editor who did all the nitty-gritties: correspondence, contracts, copy-editing and consultation on selections.)

Another early surprise was the size of the mailing list compiled with help from John Colombo, John Bell (Ottawa-based editor/author/archivist), Rob Sawyer (young author with wide SF-fandom connections) and Doris Mehegan of SOL. Announcements of the project went out initially to more than seventy authors. Some were novelists who just *might* do a short story; many were mainstream writers who had occasionally done a bit of SF; but almost half of them were actually published science-fiction writers!

The numbers were great as growth-figures, but they were still small seen as a field to choose from; I think we were all astonished at how "contemporary" the book finally came to be. *I* certainly was.

We started out hoping—trusting—we wouldn't have to go back for material earlier than the seventies, but I was prepared to fall back on reprinting a few sixties classics from *Other Canadas*—Laurence's "A Queen in Thebes," Hood's "After the Sirens," Theriault's "Akua Nuten." And while we waited for the first submissions to come in, I speculated on the possibilities of excerpts from some of the novels (Adams, Howard, Kingsbury, Llewellyn, Powe . . .) and dug out the old marmalade file. There was Dennis Lee, Chandler Davis' "Hexamnion," and selections from Dave Godfrey's *Death Goes Better with Coca Cola*, Ray Smith's *Cape Breton Is the Thought Control Centre of Canada*, Gwendolyn MacEwen's *Noman*, P. K. Page's *The Sun, the Moon, and Other Stories*, J. Michael Yates' *The Man in the Glass Octopus*. . . .

We did not, as you know, use any of these; they kept getting bumped back into history because the really big, continuing surprise was the stuff that kept coming in the mail. Altogether, we received some 400 manuscripts from almost 140 authors, and (*talk* about surprises!) no more than half of them were first-reading rejects (for assorted reasons of literary inadequacy, banality, didacticism or because they fell outside the boundaries of our shared concept of "SF"). It's worth mentioning—happily, from where I stand (upon my prejudices)—that very little of what we read seemed to have been spawned by the proliferation of so-called Sci-Fi in the visual media. (We SF elite pronounce it *Skiffy* and never *never* use the term to describe *the right stuff*.) We had hardly any UFO-riders, cutesie ghosts, space battles, Wild West conquests of alien terrain, killer robots, virgin knights of the space orbits or born-again mythology.

We did have a handful of submissions—mostly fantasy—that fell outside our preconceptions, but persuasively enough to put them to the test: stories and poems from Mary Choo, Greg Hollingshead, Carlan LeGraff, Tom Marshall and Libby Scheier, and two dazzling, elegant pieces of writing from P. K. Page ("Birthday," a short story) and Gwen MacEwen (an excerpt from her new novel, *Noman's Land*). We agonized over these last two (which will both be in print elsewhere by the time this book is released; look for them), but in the end confirmed—*surprise* again!—that we were indeed in agreement on what did *not* fit within our otherwise amorphous definition. And of course we knew by then that we were getting more than enough quality work that fell well within our boundaries.

Of the thirty-two selections in this book, seventeen are published here for the first time (in the English language); only two were first published before 1980.

Talk about embarrassments of riches. . . .

By the time half the selections were fairly definite, I was still juggling about fifty more pieces of (very) roughly equivalent merits: a little flaw in logic here, a bit of battered syntax there. Toss a coin? Are some shortcomings more remediable than others? (We did, in fact, ask for and get two rewrites—but both were stories we had already decided to use.)

At this point in any anthology—well, anyhow, my anthologies—editorial decisions no longer rest solely on the excellence of the individual submission. The book is acquiring a *shape* that exercises its own influence. A story may be discarded because it is too close in theme and mood to one already chosen; or one piece might edge out another precisely because it *is* similar to something already included, but treats the topic very differently. At the same time, each reflective re-reading magnifies small flaws—and some flaws magnify more horrendously than others. The process is no longer *fair*.

That's when anthologizing stops being fun.

At this moment I can envision the pile of photocopies in my desk drawer organizing a protest march on my typewriter, demanding equal rights, while I snivel pathetically, "Hey, the book just wasn't *big* enough." Leading the march would be John Bell's "Centrifugal Force," Charles de Lint's "A Witch in Rhyme," Tom Henighan's "Tourists from Algol," Patrick Kernaghan's "Weekend Warrior" and Andrew Weiner's "Station Gehenna." Right behind them would be stories from David Beck, H. A. Hargreaves, B. C. Jensen, Christopher S. Lobban, J. M. Park, Ursula Pflug, Robert J. Sawyer, David Sharpe, Graeme Skinner and Ann Walsh. (Magazine editors and anthologists, please take note.)

It's not fair, I said. This is the time to talk about leaning over backwards, particularly addressed to those authors who received rejection letters from Gerry Truscott, the author of "Cee." This was one of the stories I juggled for weeks, and not until it landed inside the target did I know that the pseudonym "Pat Laurence" on the title page was Gerry's.

Did you ever try leaning over backwards *both ways at the same time*?

I owe some apologies and acknowledgements as well, in connection with French-language selections. We started out on a very high plane, determined to honour both official languages. I asked Élisabeth Vonarburg, the editor of *Solaris*, who presides over the effervescent francophone science fiction conference in Chicoutimi, to spread the word in French Canada. Sure, said I, submit in French; we'll get the things we want translated. I blush now for three of us, Canadian editors who read only one language. My thanks to Peter Fitting and Katie Cooke, and (much too late) to Marian Engel, who all read for me and advised me. (But somewhere deep inside I am wickedly grateful that I did not have *another* fifty stories to compare and match against each other.)

* * *

Leaning over backwards in two directions simultaneously, and assuming someone *else* on the team knows French—how Canadian can you get? I have written many pages, and discarded them, trying to dissect or describe why (beyond the authors' addresses) I feel this is truly a contemporary *Canadian* SF anthology. Now I wonder if pointing to Vonarburg and Truscott doesn't do it best? Not just the circumstances of their selections, but the statements of their stories as well.

We have met the Alien and it is us.

Maybe Pogo was a closet Canadian. Identifying the alien within is not an easy state of mind for Yanks or Brits. On the record, in this book, it seems a relatively confident assumption in the prevailing Canadian voice—even the immigrant voices.

Someone else can write the dissertation on those interactive dynamics of immigrant and native-born (and Native-born) Canadians/Canadiens. I am satisfied to sense, after months of immersion in Canadian futures, that there is something one just might call a Canadian consciousness, and that this unique sensibility of accepting-and-coping might just have something of value to offer to the uncertain future of a planet in perilous pain.

Toronto
July 1985

A Niche

Peter Watts

Peter Watts went to university in the 1970's ("it was supposed to be sort of a day job, until I broke through and became a best-selling author"). He did his doctorate on the physiological ecology of marine mammals and then sold his first story, "A Niche," which won the Aurora Award for best short-form in English for 1992 (in a tie with a Michael Skeet story). He has recently spent two years teaching in Ontario, and has written the narration for an award-winning documentary film. Currently he is working with a consortium of universities in the Pacific Northwest ("trying to figure out why Stellar sea lions are dropping like flies in the North Pacific. It's still a day job until I break through and become a best-selling author").

"A Niche" is Watts's only published fiction to date and is one hell of an impressive science fiction story. It manages to use many conventional hard SF ideas and tropes, and at the same time keep an ironic distance both from American hard SF and British "new wave" speculative fiction. The central characters are women, named Clarke and Ballard. We chose this story to begin an anthology of Canadian SF.

When the lights go out in Beebe Station, you can hear the metal groan.

Lenie Clarke lies on her bunk, listening. Overhead, past pipes and wires and eggshell plating, three kilometres of black ocean try to crush her. She feels the Rift underneath, tearing open the seabed with strength enough to move a continent. She lies there in that fragile refuge, and she hears Beebe's armour shifting by microns, hears its seams creak not quite below the threshold of human hearing. God is a sadist on the Juan de Fuca Rift, and His name is Physics.

How did they talk me into this? she wonders. *Why did I come down here?* But she already knows the answer.

She hears Ballard moving out in the corridor. Clarke envies Ballard. Ballard never screws up, always seems to have her life under control. She almost seems *happy* down here.

Clarke rolls off her bunk and fumbles for a switch. Her cubby floods with dismal light. Pipes and access panels crowd the wall beside her; aesthetics run a distant second to functionality when you're three thousand metres down. She turns and catches sight of a slick black amphibian in the bulkhead mirror.

It still happens, occasionally. She can sometimes forget what they've done to her.

It takes a conscious effort to feel the machines lurking where her left lung used to be. She is so acclimated to the chronic ache in her chest, to that subtle inertia of plastic and metal as she moves, that she is scarcely aware of them any more. So she can still feel the memory of what it was to be fully human, and mistake that ghost for honest sensation.

Such respites never last. There are mirrors everywhere in Beebe; they're supposed to increase the apparent size of one's personal space. Sometimes Clarke shuts her eyes to hide from the reflections forever being thrown back at her. It doesn't help. She clenches her lids and feels the corneal caps beneath them, covering her eyes like smooth white cataracts.

She climbs out of her cubby and moves along the corridor to the lounge. Ballard is waiting there, dressed in a diveskin and the usual air of confidence.

Ballard stands up. "Ready to go?"

"You're in charge," Clarke says.

"Only on paper." Ballard smiles. "As far as I'm concerned, Lenie, we're equals." After two days on the rift Clarke is still surprised by the frequency with which Ballard smiles. Ballard smiles at the slightest provocation. It doesn't always seem real.

Something hits Beebe from the outside.

Ballard's smile falters. They hear it again; a wet, muffled thud through the station's titanium skin.

"It takes a while to get used to," Ballard says, "doesn't it?"

And again.

"I mean, that sounds *big* . . ."

"Maybe we should turn the lights off," Clarke suggests. She knows they won't. Beebe's exterior floodlights burn around the clock, an electric campfire pushing back the darkness. They can't see it from inside—Beebe has no windows—but somehow they draw comfort from the knowledge of that unseen fire—

Thud!

—most of the time.

"Remember back in training?" Ballard says over the sound. "When they told us that abyssal fish were supposed to be so small . . ."

Her voice trails off. Beebe creaks slightly. They listen for a while. There is no other sound.

"It must've gotten tired," Ballard says. "You'd think they'd figure it out." She moves to the ladder and climbs downstairs.

Clarke follows her, a bit impatiently. There are sounds in Beebe that worry her far more than the futile attack of some misguided fish. Clarke can hear tired alloys negotiating surrender. She can feel the ocean looking for a way in. What if it finds one? The whole weight of the Pacific could drop down and turn her into jelly. Any time.

Better to face it outside, where she knows what's coming. All she can do in here is wait for it to happen.

Going outside is like drowning, once a day.

Clarke stands facing Ballard, diveskin sealed, in an airlock that barely holds both of them. She has learned to tolerate the forced proximity; the glassy armor on her eyes helps a bit. *Fuse seals, check headlamp, test injector;* the ritual takes her, step by reflexive step, to that horrible moment when she awakens the machines sleeping within her, and changes.

When she catches her breath, and loses it.

When a vacuum opens, somewhere in her chest, that swallows the air she holds. When her remaining lung shrivels in its cage, and her guts collapse; when myoelectric demons flood her sinuses and middle ears with isotonic saline. When every pocket of internal gas disappears in the time it takes to draw a breath.

It always feels the same. The sudden, overwhelming nausea; the narrow confines of the airlock holding her erect when she tries to fall; seawater churning on all sides. Her face goes under; vision blurs, then clears as her corneal caps adjust.

She collapses against the walls and wishes she could scream. The floor of the airlock drops away like a gallows. Lenie Clarke falls writhing into the abyss.

They come out of the freezing darkness, headlights blazing, into an oasis of sodium luminosity. Machines grow everywhere at the Throat, like metal weeds. Cables and conduits spiderweb across the seabed in a dozen directions. The main pumps stand over twenty metres high, a regiment of submarine monoliths fading from sight on either side. Overhead floodlights bathe the jumbled structures in perpetual twilight.

They stop for a moment, hands resting on the line that guided them here.

"I'll never get used to it," Ballard grates in a caricature of her usual voice.

Clarke glances at her wrist thermistor. "Thirty-four Centigrade." The words buzz, metallic, from her larynx. It feels so *wrong* to talk without breathing.

Ballard lets go of the rope and launches herself into the light. After a moment, breathless, Clarke follows.

There is so much power here, so much wasted strength. Here the continents themselves do ponderous battle. Magma freezes; icy seawater turns to steam; the very floor of the ocean is born by painful centimetres each year. Human machinery does not make energy, here at Dragon's Throat; it merely hangs on and steals some insignificant fraction of it back to the mainland.

Clarke flies through canyons of metal and rock, and knows what it is to be a parasite. She looks down. Shellfish the size of boulders, crimson worms three metres long crowd the seabed between the machines. Legions of bacteria, hungry for sulphur, lace the water with milky veils.

The water fills with a sudden terrible cry.

It doesn't sound like a scream. It sounds as though a great harp string is vibrating in slow motion. But Ballard is screaming, through some reluctant interface of flesh and metal:

"LENIE—"

Clarke turns in time to see her own arm disappear into a mouth that seems impossibly huge.

Teeth like scimitars clamp down on her shoulder. Clarke stares into a scaly black face half-a-metre across. Some tiny dispassionate part of her searches for eyes in that monstrous fusion of spines and teeth and gnarled flesh, and fails. *How can it see me?* she wonders.

Then the pain reaches her.

She feels her arm being wrenched from its socket. The creature thrashes, shaking its head back and forth, trying to tear her into chunks. Every tug sets her nerves screaming.

She goes limp. *Please get it over with if you're going to kill me just please God make it quick . . .* She feels the urge to vomit, but the 'skin over her mouth and her own collapsed insides won't let her.

She shuts out the pain. She's had plenty of practice. She pulls inside, abandoning her body to ravenous vivisection; and from far away she feels the twisting of her attacker grow suddenly erratic. There is another creature at her side, with arms and legs and a knife—*you know, a knife, like the one you've got strapped to your leg and completely forgot about*—and suddenly the monster is gone, its grip broken.

Clarke tells her neck muscles to work. It is like operating a marionette. Her head turns, and she sees Ballard locked in combat with something as big as she is. Only . . . Ballard is tearing it to pieces, with her bare hands. Its icicle teeth splinter and snap. Dark icewater courses from its wounds, tracing mortal convulsions with smoke-trails of suspended gore.

The creature spasms weakly. Ballard pushes it away. A dozen smaller fish dart into the light and begin tearing at the carcass. Photophores along their sides flash like frantic rainbows.

Clarke watches from the other side of the world. The pain in her side keeps its distance, a steady, pulsing ache. She looks; her arm is still there. She can even move her fingers without any trouble. *I've had worse,* she thinks.

But why am I still alive?

Ballard appears at her side; her lens-covered eyes shine like photophores themselves.

"Jesus Christ," Ballard says in a distorted whisper. "Lenie? Are you okay?"

Clarke dwells on the inanity of the question for a moment. But surprisingly, she feels intact. "Yeah."

And if not, she knows it's her own damn fault. She just lay there. She just waited to die. She was asking for it.

She's always asking for it.

Back in the airlock the water recedes around them. And within them; Clarke's stolen breath, released at last, races back along visceral channels, reinflating lung and gut and spirit.

Ballard splits the face seal on her 'skin and her words tumble into the wetroom. "Jesus. Jesus! I don't believe it! My God, did you see that thing! They get so huge around here!" She passes her hands across her face; her corneal caps come off, milky hemispheres dropping from enormous hazel eyes. "And to think they're normally just a few centimetres long . . ."

She starts to strip down, unzipping her 'skin along the forearms, talking the whole time. "And yet it was almost fragile, you know? Hit it hard enough and it just came apart! Jesus!" Ballard always takes off her uniform indoors. Clarke suspects that she'd rip the recycler out of her own thorax if she could, throw it in a corner with the 'skin and the eyecaps until the next time it was needed.

Maybe she's got her other lung in her cabin. Clarke muses. *Her arm is all pins and needles. Maybe she keeps it in a jar, and she stuffs it back into her chest at night . . .* She feels a bit dopey; probably just an after-effect of the neuroinhibitors the 'skin pumps her full of whenever she's outside. *Small price to keep my brain from shorting out—I really shouldn't mind . . .*

Ballard peels her 'skin down to the waist. Just under her left breast, an electrolyser intake pokes out through her ribcage.

Clarke stares vaguely at that perforated disk in Ballard's flesh. *The ocean goes into us there,* she thinks. *The old knowledge seems newly significant, somehow. We suck it into us and steal its oxygen and spit it out again.*

The prickly numbness is spreading, leaking through her shoulder into her chest and neck. Clarke shakes her head once, to clear it.

She sags suddenly, against the hatchway.

Am I in shock? Am I fainting?

"I mean—" Ballard stops, looks at Clarke with an expression of sudden concern. "Jesus, Lenie. You look terrible. You shouldn't have told me you were okay if you weren't."

The tingling reaches the base of Clarke's skull. She fights it. "I'm—okay," she says. "Nothing broke. I'm just bruised."

"Garbage. Take off your 'skin."

Clarke straightens, with effort. The numbness recedes a bit. "It's nothing I can't take care of myself."

Don't touch me. Please don't touch me.

Ballard steps forward without a word and unseals the 'skin around Clarke's forearm. She peels back the fabric and exposes an ugly purple bruise. She looks at Clarke with one raised eyebrow.

"Just a bruise," Clarke says. "I'll take care of it. Really. Thanks anyway." She pulls her hand away from Ballard's ministrations.

Ballard looks at her for a moment. She smiles ever so slightly.

"Lenie," she says, "there's no need to feel embarrassed."

"About what?"

"You know. Me having to rescue you. You going to pieces when that thing attacked. It was perfectly understandable. Most people have a rough time adjusting. I'm just one of the lucky ones."

Right. You've always been one of the lucky ones, haven't you? I know your kind, Ballard, you've never failed at anything . . .

"You don't have to feel ashamed about it," Ballard reassures her.

"I don't," Clarke says, honestly. She doesn't feel much of anything any more. Just the tingling. And the tension. And a vague sort of wonder that she's even alive.

The bulkhead is sweating.

The deep sea lays icy hands on the metal and, inside, Clarke watches the humid atmosphere bead and run down the wall. She sits rigid on her bunk under dim fluorescent light, every wall of the cubby within easy reach. The ceiling is too low. The room is too narrow. She feels as if the ocean is compressing the station around her.

And all I can do is wait . . .

The anabolic salve on her injuries is warm and soothing. Clarke probes the purple flesh of her arm with practised fingers. The diagnostic tools in the Med cubby have vindicated her. She is lucky, this time; bones intact, epidermis unbroken. She seals up her 'skin, hiding the damage.

Clarke shifts on the pallet, turns to face the inside wall. Her reflection stares back at her through eyes like frosted glass. She watches the image, admires its perfect mimicry of each movement. Flesh and phantom move together, bodies masked, faces neutral.

That's me, she thinks. *That's what I look like now.* She tries to read what lies behind that glacial facade. *Am I bored, horny, upset?* How to tell, with her eyes hidden behind those corneal opacities? She sees no trace of the tension she always feels. *I could be terrified. I could be pissing in my 'skin and nobody would know.*

She leans forward. The reflection comes to meet her. They stare at each other, white to white, ice to ice. For a moment, they almost forget Beebe's ongoing war against pressure. For a moment, they do not mind the claustrophobic solitude that grips them.

How many times, Clarke wonders, *have I wanted eyes as dead as these?*

* * *

Beebe's metal viscera crowd the corridor beyond her cubby. Clarke can barely stand erect. A few steps bring her into the lounge.

Ballard, back in shirtsleeves, is at one of the library terminals. "Rickets," she says.

"What?"

"Fish down here don't get enough trace elements. They're rotten with deficiency diseases. It doesn't matter how fierce they are. They bite too hard, they break their teeth on us."

Clarke stabs buttons on the food processor; the machine grumbles at her touch. "I thought there was all sorts of food at the rift. That's why things got so big."

"There's a lot of food. Just not very good quality."

A vaguely edible lozenge of sludge oozes from the processor onto Clarke's plate. She eyes it for a moment. *I can relate.*

"You're going to eat in your gear?" Ballard asks, as Clarke sits down at the lounge table.

Clarke blinks at her. "Yeah. Why?"

"Oh, nothing. It would just be nice to talk to someone with pupils in their eyes, you know?"

"Sorry. I'll take them off if you—"

"No, it's no big thing. I can live with it." Ballard shuts down the library and sits down across from Clarke. "So, how do you like the place so far?"

Clarke shrugs and keeps eating.

"I'm glad we're only down here for three months," Ballard says. "This place could get to you after a while."

"It could be worse."

"Oh, I'm not complaining. I was looking for a challenge, after all. What about you?"

"Me?"

"What brings you down here? What are you looking for?"

Clarke doesn't answer for a moment. "I don't know, really," she says at last. "Privacy, I guess."

Ballard looks up. Clarke stares back, her face neutral.

"Well, I'll leave you to it, then," Ballard says pleasantly.

Clarke watches her disappear down the corridor. She hears the sound of a cubby hatch swinging shut.

Give it up, Ballard, she thinks. *I'm not the sort of person you really want to know.*

Almost start of the morning shift. The food processor disgorges Clarke's breakfast with its usual reluctance. Ballard, in Communications, is just getting off the phone. A moment later she appears in the hatchway.

"Management says—" She stops. "You've got blue eyes."

Clarke smiles slightly. "You've seen them before."

"I know. It's just kind of surprising, it's been a while since I've seen you without your caps on."

Clarke sits down with her breakfast. "So, what does Management say?"

"We're on schedule. Rest of the crew comes down in three weeks, we go online in four." Ballard sits down across from Clarke. "I wonder sometimes why we're not online right now."

"I guess they just want to be sure everything works."

"Still, six months seems like a long time for a dry run. And you'd think that—well, they'd want to get the geothermal program up and running as fast as possible, after all that's happened."

After Lepreau and Winshire melted down, you mean.

"And there's something else," Ballard says. "I can't get through to Piccard."

Clarke looks up. Piccard Station is anchored on the Galapagos Rift; it is not a particularly stable mooring.

"Did you ever meet the couple there?" Ballard asks. "Ken Lubin, Lana Cheung?"

Clarke shakes her head. "They went through before me. I never met any of the other Rifters except you."

"Nice people. I thought I'd call them up, see how things were going at Piccard, but nobody can get through."

"Line down?"

"They say it's probably something like that. Nothing serious. They're sending a 'scaphe down to check it out."

Maybe the seabed opened up and swallowed them whole, Clarke thinks. *Maybe the hull had a weak plate—one's all it would take . . .*

Something creaks, deep in Beebe's superstructure. Clarke looks around. The walls seem to have moved closer while she wasn't looking.

"Sometimes," she says, "I wish we didn't keep Beebe at surface pressure. Sometimes I wish we were pumped up to ambient. To take the strain off the hull."

Ballard smiles. "Come on. Would you want to spend three months sitting in a decompression tank afterwards?"

In the Systems cubby, something bleats for attention.

"Seismic. Wonderful." Ballard disappears into Systems. Clarke follows.

An amber line is writhing across one of the displays. It looks like the EEG of someone caught in a nightmare.

"Get your eyes back in," Ballard says. "The Throat's acting up."

They can hear it all the way to Beebe; a malign, almost electrical hiss from the direction of the Throat. Clarke follows Ballard towards it, one hand running lightly along the guide rope. The distant smudge of light that marks their destination seems wrong, somehow. The colour is different. It ripples.

They swim into its glowing nimbus and see why. The Throat is on fire.

Sapphire auroras slide flickering across the generators. At the far end of the array, almost invisible with distance, a pillar of smoke swirls up into the darkness like a great tornado.

The sound it makes fills the abyss. Clarke closes her eyes for a moment, and hears rattlesnakes.

"Jesus!" Ballard shouts over the noise. "It's not supposed to do that!"

Clarke checks her thermistor. It won't settle; water temperature goes from four degrees to thirty-eight and back again, within seconds. A myriad ephemeral currents tug at them as they watch.

"Why the light show?" Clarke calls back.

"I don't know!" Ballard answers. "Bioluminescence, I guess! Heat-sensitive bacteria!"

Without warning, the tumult dies.

The ocean empties of sound. Phosphorescent spiderwebs wriggle dimly on the metal and vanish. In the distance, the tornado sighs and fragments into a few transient dust devils.

A gentle rain of black soot begins to fall in the copper light.

"Smoker," Ballard says into the sudden stillness. "A big one."

They swim to the place where the geyser erupted. There is a fresh wound in the seabed, a gash several metres long, between two of the generators.

"This wasn't supposed to happen," Ballard says. "That's why they built here, for crying out loud! It was supposed to be stable!"

"The rift is never stable," Clarke replies. *Not much point in being here if it was.*

Ballard swims up through the fallout and pops an access plate on one of the generators. "Well, according to this there's no damage," she calls down, after looking inside. "Hang on, let me switch channels here—"

Clarke touches one of the cylindrical sensors strapped to her waist, and stares into the fissure. *I should be able to fit through there,* she decides.

And does.

"We were lucky," Ballard is saying above her. "The other generators are okay too. Oh, wait a second; number two has a clogged cooling duct, but it's not serious. Backups can handle it until—get out of there!"

Clarke looks up, one hand on the sensor she's planting. Ballard stares down at her through a chimney of fresh rock.

"Are you crazy?" Ballard shouts. "That's an active smoker!"

Clarke looks down again, deeper into the shaft. It twists out of sight in the mineral haze. "We need temperature readings," she says, "from inside the mouth."

"Get out of there! It could go off again and fry you!"

I suppose it could at that, Clarke thinks. "It just finished erupting," she calls back. "It'll take a while to build up a fresh head." She twists a knob on the sensor; tiny explosive bolts blast into the rock, anchoring the device.

"Get out of there, now!"

"Just a second." Clarke turns the sensor on and kicks up out of the seabed. Ballard grabs her arm as she emerges, starts to drag her away from the smoker.

Clarke stiffens and pulls free. "Don't—" *touch me!* She catches herself. "I'm out, okay, you don't have to . . ."

"Further." Ballard keeps swimming. "Over here."

They are near the edge of the light now, the floodlit Throat on one side, blackness on the other. Ballard faces Clarke. "Are you out of your mind? We could have gone back to Beebe for a drone! We could have planted it on remote!"

Clarke does not answer. She sees something moving in the distance behind Ballard. "Watch your back," she says.

Ballard turns, and sees the gulper sliding toward them. It undulates through the water like brown smoke, silent and endless; Clarke cannot see the creature's tail, although several metres of serpentine flesh have come out of the darkness.

Ballard goes for her knife. After a moment, Clarke does too.

The gulper's jaw drops open like a great jagged scoop.

Ballard begins to launch herself at the thing, knife upraised.

Clarke puts her hand out. "Wait a minute. It's not coming at us."

The front end of the gulper is about ten metres distant now. Its tail pulls free of the murk.

"Are you crazy?" Ballard moves clear of Clarke's hand, still watching the monster.

"Maybe it isn't hungry," Clarke says. She can see its eyes, two tiny unwinking spots glaring at them from the tip of the snout.

"They're always hungry. Did you sleep through the briefings?"

The gulper closes its mouth and passes. It extends around them now, in a great meandering arc. The head turns back to look at them. It opens its mouth.

"Fuck this," Ballard says, and charges.

Her first stroke opens a metre-long gash in the creature's side. The gulper stares at Ballard for a moment, as if astonished. Then, ponderously, it thrashes.

Clarke watches without moving. *Why can't she just let it go? Why does she always have to prove she's better than everything?*

Ballard strikes again; this time she slashes into a great tumorous swelling that has to be the stomach.

She frees the things inside.

They spill out through the wound; two huge viperfish and some misshapen creature Clarke doesn't recognize. One of the viperfish is still alive, and in a foul mood. It locks its teeth around the first thing it encounters.

Ballard. From behind.

"Lenie!" Ballard's knife hand is swinging in staccato arcs. The viperfish begins to come apart. Its jaws remain locked. The convulsing gulper crashes into Ballard and sends her spinning to the bottom.

Finally, Clarke begins to move.

The gulper collides with Ballard again. Clarke moves in low, hugging the bottom, and pulls the other woman clear of those thrashing coils.

Ballard's knife continues to dip and twist. The viperfish is a mutilated wreck behind the gills, but its grip remains unbroken. Ballard cannot twist around far enough to reach the skull. Clarke comes in from behind and takes the creature's head in her hands.

It stares at her, malevolent and unthinking.

"Kill it!" Ballard shouts. "Jesus, what are you waiting for?"

Clarke closes her eyes, and clenches. The skull in her hand splinters like cheap plastic.

There is a silence.

After a while, she opens her eyes. The gulper is gone, fled back into darkness to heal or die. But Ballard is still there, and Ballard is angry.

"What's wrong with you?" she says.

Clarke unclenches her fists. Bits of bone and jellied flesh float about her fingers.

"You're supposed to back me up! Why are you so damned passive all the time?"

"Sorry." *Sometimes it works.*

Ballard reaches behind her back. "I'm cold. I think it punctured my diveskin—"

Clarke swims behind her and looks. "A couple of holes. How are you otherwise? Anything feel broken?"

"It broke through the diveskin," Ballard says, as if to herself. "And when that gulper hit me, it could have . . ." She turns to Clarke and her voice, even distorted, carries a shocked uncertainty. ". . . I could have been killed. I could have been killed!"

For an instant, it is as though Ballard's 'skin and eyes and self-assurance have all been stripped away. For the first time Clarke can see through to the weakness beneath, growing like a delicate tracery of hairline cracks.

You can screw up too, Ballard. It isn't all fun and games. You know that now.

It hurts, doesn't it.

Somewhere inside, the slightest touch of sympathy. "It's okay," Clarke says. "Jeanette, it's—"

"You idiot!" Ballard hisses. She stares at Clarke like some malign and sightless old woman. "You just floated there! You just let it happen to me!"

Clarke feels her guard snap up again, just in time. *This isn't just anger,* she realizes. *This isn't just the heat of the moment. She doesn't like me. She doesn't like me at all.*

She never did.

Beebe Station floats tethered above the seabed, a gunmetal-grey planet ringed by a belt of equatorial floodlights. There is an airlock for divers at the south pole, and a docking hatch for 'scaphes at the north. In between there are girders and anchor lines, conduits and cables, metal armour and Lenie Clarke.

She is doing a routine visual check on the hull; standard procedure, once a week. Ballard is inside, testing some equipment in the Communications cubby. This is not entirely within the spirit of the buddy system. Clarke prefers it this way. Relations have been civil over the past couple of days—Ballard even resurrects her patented chumminess on occasion—but the more time they spend together, the more forced things get. Eventually, Clarke knows, something is going to break.

Besides, out here in the void it seems only natural to be alone.

She is examining a cable clamp when an angler charges into the light. It is about two metres long, and hungry. It rams directly into the nearest of Beebe's floodlamps, mouth agape. Several teeth shatter against the crystal lens. The angler twists to one side, knocking the hull with her tail, and swims off until barely visible against the dark.

Clarke watches, fascinated. The angler swims back and forth, back and forth, then charges again.

The flood weathers the impact easily, doing more damage to its attacker. The angler lashes its dorsal spine. The lure at its end, a glowing worm-shaped thing, luminesces furiously.

Over and over again the fish batters itself against the light. Finally, exhausted, it sinks twitching down to the muddy bottom.

"Lenie? Are you okay?"

Clarke feels the words buzzing in her lower jaw. She trips the sender in her diveskin: "I'm okay."

"I heard something out there," Ballard says. "I just wanted to make sure you were . . ."

"I'm fine," Clarke says. "It was just a fish, trying to eat one of the lights."

"They never learn, do they?"

"No. I guess not. See you later."

"See—"

Clarke switches off her receiver.

Poor stupid fish. How many millennia did it take for them to learn that bioluminescence equals food? How long will Beebe have to sit here before they learn that electric light doesn't?

We could keep our headlights off. Maybe they'd leave us alone . . .

She stares out past Beebe's electric halo. There is so much blackness there. It almost hurts to look at it. Without lights, without sonar, how far could she go into that viscous shroud and still return?

Clarke kills her headlight. Night edges a bit closer, but Beebe's lights keep it at bay. Clarke turns until she is face to face with the darkness. She crouches like a spider against Beebe's hull.

She pushes off.

The darkness embraces her. She swims, not looking back, until her legs grow tired. She does not know how far she has come.

But it must be light-years. The ocean is full of stars.

Behind her, the station shines brightest, with coarse yellow rays. In the opposite direction, she can barely make out the Throat, an insignificant sunrise on the horizon.

Everywhere else, living constellations punctuate the dark. Here, a string of pearls blink sexual advertisements at two-second intervals. Here, a sudden flash leaves diversionary afterimages swarming across Clarke's field of view; something flees under cover of her momentary blindness. There, a counterfeit worm twists lazily in the current, invisibly tied to the roof of some predatory mouth.

There are so many of them.

She feels a sudden surge in the water, as if something big has just passed very close. A delicious thrill dances through her body.

It nearly touched me, she thinks. *I wonder what it was.* The rift is full of monsters who don't know when to quit. It doesn't matter how much they eat. Their voracity is as much a part of them as their elastic bellies, their unhinging jaws. Ravenous dwarfs attack giants twice their own size, and sometimes win. The abyss is a desert; no one can afford the luxury of waiting for better odds.

But even a desert has oases, and sometimes the deep hunters find them. They come upon the malnourishing abundance of the rift and gorge themselves; their descendants grow huge and bloated over such delicate bones . . .

My light was off, and it left me alone. I wonder . . .

She turns it back on. Her vision clouds in the sudden glare, then clears. The ocean reverts to unrelieved black. No nightmares accost her. The beam lights empty water wherever she points it.

She switches it off. There is a moment of absolute darkness while her eyecaps adjust to the reduced light. Then the stars come out again.

They are so beautiful. Lenie Clarke rests on the bottom of the ocean and watches the abyss sparkle around her. And she almost laughs as she realizes, three thousand metres from the nearest sunlight, that it's only dark when the lights are on.

* * *

"What the hell is wrong with you? You've been gone for over three hours, did you know that? Why didn't you answer me?"

Clarke bends over and removes her fins. "I guess I turned my receiver off," she says. "I was—wait a second, did you say—"

"You guess? Have you forgotten every safety reg they drilled into us? You're supposed to have your receiver on from the moment you leave Beebe until you get back!"

"Did you say *three hours*?"

"I couldn't even come out after you, I couldn't find you on sonar! I just had to sit here and hope you'd show up!"

It only seems a few minutes since she pushed off into the darkness. Clarke climbs up into the lounge, suddenly chilled.

"Where were you, Lenie?" Ballard demands, coming up behind her. Clarke hears the slightest plaintive tone in her voice.

"I—I must've been on the bottom," Clarke says. "That's why sonar didn't get me. I didn't go far."

Was I asleep? What was I doing for three hours?

"I was just . . . wandering around. I lost track of the time. I'm sorry."

"Not good enough. Don't do it again."

There is a brief silence. They hear the sudden, familiar impact of flesh on metal.

"Christ!" Ballard snaps. "I'm turning the externals off right now!"

Whatever it is gets in two more hits by the time Ballard reaches the Systems cubby. Clarke hears her punch a couple of buttons.

Ballard comes out of Systems. "There. Now we're invisible."

Something hits them again. And again.

"I guess not," Clarke says.

Ballard stands in the lounge, listening to the rhythm of the assault. "They don't show up on sonar," she says, almost whispering. "Sometimes, when I hear them coming at us, I tune it down to extreme close range. But it looks right through them."

"No gas bladders. Nothing to bounce an echo off of."

"We show up just fine out there, most of the time. But not those things. You can't find them, no matter how high you turn the gain. They're like ghosts."

"They're not ghosts." Almost unconsciously, Clarke has been counting the beats: *eight . . . nine . . .*

Ballard turns to face her. "They've shut down Piccard," she says, and her voice is small and tight.

"What?"

"The grid office says it's just some technical problem. But I've got a friend in Personnel. I phoned him when you were outside. He says Lana's in the hospital. And I get the feeling . . ." Ballard shakes her head. "It sounded like Ken Lubin did something down there. I think maybe he attacked her."

Three thumps from outside, in rapid succession. Clarke can feel Ballard's eyes on her. The silence stretches.

"Or maybe not," Ballard says. "We got all those personality tests. If he was violent, they would have picked it up before they sent him down."

Clarke watches her, and listens to the pounding of an intermittent fist.

"Or maybe . . . maybe the rift changed him somehow. Maybe they misjudged the pressure we'd all be under. So to speak." Ballard musters a feeble smile. "Not the physical danger so much as the emotional stress, you know? Everyday things. Just being outside could get to you after a while. Seawater sluicing through your chest. Not breathing for hours at a time. It's like— living without a heartbeat . . ."

She looks up at the ceiling; the sounds from outside are a bit more erratic now.

"Outside's not so bad," Clarke says. *At least you're incompressible. At least you don't have to worry about the plates giving in.*

"I don't think you'd change suddenly. It would just sort of sneak up on you, little by little. And then one day you'd just wake up changed, you'd be different somehow, only you'd never have noticed the transition. Like Ken Lubin."

She looks at Clarke, and her voice drops a bit.

"And like you."

"Me." Clarke turns Ballard's words over in her mind, waits for the onset of some reaction. She feels nothing but her own indifference. "I don't think you have much to worry about. I'm not a violent person."

"I know. I'm not worried about my own safety, Lenie. I'm worried about yours."

Clarke looks at her from behind the impervious safety of her lenses, and doesn't answer.

"You've changed since you came down here," Ballard says. "You're withdrawing from me, you're exposing yourself to unnecessary risks. I don't know exactly what's happening to you. It's almost like you're trying to kill yourself."

"I'm not," Clarke says. She tries to change the subject. "Is Lana Cheung all right?"

Ballard studies her for a moment. She takes the hint. "I don't know. I couldn't get any details."

Clarke feels something knotting up inside her.

"I wonder what she did," she murmurs, "to set him off like that?"

Ballard stares at her, openmouthed. "What she did? I can't believe you said that!"

"I only meant—"

"I know what you meant."

The outside pounding has stopped. Ballard does not relax. She stands hunched over in those strange, loose-fitting clothes that Drybacks wear, and stares at the ceiling as though she doesn't believe in the silence. She looks back at Clarke.

"Lenie, you know I don't like to pull rank, but your attitude is putting both of us at risk. I think this place is really getting to you. I hope you can get back online here, I really do. Otherwise I may have to recommend you for a transfer."

Clarke watches Ballard leave the lounge. *You're lying,* she realizes. *You're scared to death, and it's not just because I'm changing.*

It's because you are.

Clarke finds out five hours after the fact: something has changed on the ocean floor.

We sleep and the earth moves, she thinks, studying the topographic display. *And next time, or the time after, maybe it'll move right out from under us.*

I wonder if I'll have time to feel anything.

She turns at a sound behind her. Ballard is standing in the lounge, swaying slightly. Her face seems somehow disfigured by the concentric rings in her eyes, by the dark hollows around them. Naked eyes are beginning to look alien to Clarke.

"The seabed shifted," Clarke says. "There's a new outcropping about two hundred metres west of us."

"That's odd. I didn't feel anything."

"It happened about five hours ago. You were asleep."

Ballard glances up sharply. Clarke studies the haggard lines of her face. *On second thought, I guess you weren't.*

"I . . . would've woken up," Ballard says. She squeezes past Clarke into the cubby and checks the topographic display.

"Two metres high, twelve long," Clarke recites.

Ballard doesn't answer. She punches some commands into a keyboard; the topographic image dissolves, re-forms into a column of numbers.

"Just as I thought," she says. "No heavy seismic activity for over forty-two hours."

"Sonar doesn't lie," Clarke says calmly.

"Neither does seismo," Ballard answers.

There is a brief silence. There is a standard procedure for such things, and they both know what it is.

"We have to check it out," Clarke says.

But Ballard only nods. "Give me a moment to change."

They call it a squid; a jet-propelled cylinder about half a metre long, with a headlight at the front end and a towbar at the back. Clarke, floating between Beebe and the seabed, checks it over with one hand. Her other hand grips a sonar pistol. She points the pistol into blackness; ultrasonic clicks sweep the night, give her a bearing.

"That way," she says, pointing.

Ballard squeezes down on her own squid's towbar. The machine pulls her away. After a moment Clarke follows. Bringing up the rear, a third squid carries an assortment of sensors in a nylon bag.

Ballard is travelling at nearly full throttle. The lamps on her helmet and squid stab the water like two lighthouse beacons. Clarke, her own lights doused, catches up with Ballard about half-way to their destination. They cruise along a couple of metres over the muddy substrate.

"Your lights," Ballard says.

"We don't need them. Sonar works in the dark."

"Are you just breaking the regs for the sheer thrill of it, now?"

"The fish down here, they key on things that glow—"

"Turn your lights on. That's an order."

Clarke does not answer. She watches the twin beams beside her, Ballard's squid shining steady and unwavering, Ballard's headlamp slicing the water in erratic arcs as she moves her head . . .

"I told you," Ballard says, "turn your—Christ!"

It was just a glimpse, caught for a moment in the sweep of Ballard's headlight. She jerks her head around and it slides back out of sight. Then it looms up in the squid's beam, huge and terrible.

The abyss is grinning at them, teeth bared.

A mouth stretches across the width of the beam, and extends into darkness on either side. It is crammed with conical teeth the size of human hands, and they do not look the least bit fragile.

Ballard makes a strangled sound and dives into the mud. The benthic ooze boils up around her in a seething cloud; she disappears in a torrent of planktonic corpses.

Lenie Clarke stops and waits, unmoving. She stares transfixed at that threatening smile. Her whole body feels electrified, she has never been so explicitly aware of herself. Every nerve fires and freezes at the same time. She is terrified.

But she is also, somehow, completely in control of herself. She reflects on this paradox as Ballard's abandoned squid slows and stops itself, scant metres from that endless row of teeth. She wonders at her own analytical clarity as the third squid, with its burden of sensors, decelerates past and takes up position beside Ballard's.

There in the light, the grin does not change.

After a few moments, Clarke raises her sonar pistol and fires. We're here, she realizes, checking the readout. *That's the outcropping.*

She swims closer. The smile hangs there, enigmatic and enticing. Now she can see bits of bone at the roots of the teeth, and tatters of decomposed flesh trailing from the gums.

She turns and backtracks. The cloud on the seabed has nearly settled. "Ballard," she says in her synthetic voice.

Nobody answers.

Clarke reaches down through the mud, feeling blind, until she touches something warm and trembling.

The seabed explodes in her face.

Ballard erupts from the substrate, trailing a muddy comet's tail. Her hand rises from that sudden cloud, clasped around something glinting in the transient light. Clarke sees the knife, twists almost too late; the blade glances off her 'skin, igniting nerves along her ribcage. Ballard lashes out again. This time Clarke catches the knife-hand as it shoots past, twists it, pushes. Ballard tumbles away.

"It's me!" Clarke shouts; the 'skin turns her voice into a tinny vibrato.

Ballard rises up again, white eyes unseeing, knife still in hand.

Clarke holds up her hands. "It's okay! There's nothing here! It's dead!"

Ballard stops. She stares at Clarke. She looks over to the squids, to the smile they illuminate. She stiffens.

"It's some kind of whale," Clarke says. "It's been dead a long time."

"A . . . a whale?" Ballard rasps. She begins to shake.

There's no need to feel embarrassed, Clarke almost says, but doesn't. Instead, she reaches out and touches Ballard lightly on the arm. *Is this how you do it?* she wonders.

Ballard jerks back as if scalded.

I guess not . . .

"Um, Jeanette . . ." Clarke begins.

Ballard raises a trembling hand, cutting Clarke off. "I'm okay. I want to g . . . I think we should get back now, don't you?"

"Okay," Clarke says. But she doesn't really mean it.

She could stay out here all day.

Ballard is at the library again. She turns, passing a casual hand over the brightness control as Clarke comes up behind her; the display darkens before Clarke can see what it is.

"It was a Ziphiid," Ballard says. "A beaked whale. Very rare. They don't dive this deep."

Clarke listens, not really interested.

"It must have died and rotted further up, and sank." Ballard's voice is slightly raised. She looks almost furtively at something on the other side of the lounge. "I wonder what the chances are of that happening."

"What?"

"I mean, in all the ocean, something that big just happening to drop out of the sky a few hundred metres away. The odds of that must be pretty low."

"Yeah. I guess so." Clarke reaches over and brightens the display. One half of the screen glows softly with luminous text. The other holds the rotating image of some complex molecule.

"What's this?" Clarke asks.

Ballard steals another glance across the lounge. "Just an old biopsyche text the library had on file. I was browsing through it. Used to be an interest of mine."

Clarke looks at her. "Uh-huh." She bends over and studies the display. Some sort of technical chemistry. The only thing she really understands is the caption beneath the graphic.

She reads it aloud: "True Happiness."

"Yeah. A tricyclic with four side chains." Ballard points at the screen. "Whenever you're happy, really happy, that's what does it to you."

"When did they find that out?"

"I don't know. It's an old book."

Clarke stares at the revolving simulacrum. It disturbs her, somehow. It floats there over that smug stupid caption, and it says something she doesn't want to hear.

You've been solved, it tells her. *You're mechanical. Chemicals and electricity. Everything you are, every dream, every action, it all comes down to a change of voltage somewhere, or a—what did she say—a tricyclic with four side chains . . .*

"It's wrong," Clarke murmurs. *Or they'd be able to fix us, when we broke down . . .*

"Sorry?" Ballard says.

"It's saying we're just these . . . soft computers. With faces."

Ballard shuts off the terminal.

"That's right," she says. "And some of us may even be losing those."

The jibe registers, but it doesn't hurt. Clarke straightens and moves towards the ladder.

"Where are you going? You going outside again?" Ballard asks.

"The shift isn't over. I thought I'd clean out the duct on number two."

"It's a bit late to start on that, Lenie. The day will be over before we're even half done." Ballard's eyes dart away again. This time Clarke follows the glance to the full-length mirror on the far wall.

She sees nothing of particular interest there.

"I'll work late." Clarke grabs the railing, swings her foot onto the top rung.

"Lenie," Ballard says, and Clarke swears she hears a tremor in that voice. She looks back, but the other woman is moving to Communications. "Well, I'm afraid I can't go with you," she's saying. "I'm in the middle of debugging one of the telemetry routines."

"That's fine," Clarke says. She feels the tension starting to rise. Beebe is shrinking again. She starts down the ladder.

"Are you sure you're okay going out alone? Maybe you should wait until tomorrow."

"No. I'm okay."

"Well, remember to keep your receiver open. I don't want you getting lost on me again . . ."

Clarke is in the wetroom. She climbs into the airlock and runs through the ritual. It no longer feels like drowning. It feels like being born again.

She awakens into darkness, and the sound of weeping.

She lies there for a few minutes, confused and uncertain. The sobs come from all sides, soft but omnipresent in Beebe's resonant shell. She hears nothing else except her own heartbeat.

She is afraid. She isn't sure why. She wishes the sounds would go away.

Clarke rolls off her bunk and fumbles at the hatch. It opens into a semi-darkened corridor; meager light escapes from the lounge at one end. The sounds come from the other direction, from deepening darkness. She follows them through an infestation of pipes and conduits.

Ballard's quarters. The hatch is open. An emerald readout sparkles in the darkness, bestowing no detail upon the hunched figure on the pallet.

"Ballard," Clarke says softly. She does not want to go in.

The shadow moves, seems to look up at her. "Why won't you show it?" it says, its voice pleading.

Clarke frowns in the darkness. "Show what?"

"You know what! How . . . afraid you are!"

"Afraid?"

"Of being here, of being stuck at the bottom of this horrible dark ocean . . ."

"I don't understand," Clarke whispers. The claustrophobia in her, restless again, begins to stir.

Ballard snorts, but the derision seems forced. "Oh, you understand all right. You think this is some sort of competition, you think if you can just keep it all inside you'll win somehow . . . but it isn't like that at all, Lenie, it isn't helping to keep it hidden like this, we've got to be able to trust each other down here or we're lost . . ."

She shifts slightly on the bunk. Clarke's eyes, enhanced by the caps, can pick out a few details now; rough edges embroider Ballard's silhouette, the folds and creases of normal clothing, unbuttoned to the waist. She thinks of a cadaver, half-dissected, rising on the table to mourn its own mutilation.

"I don't know what you mean," Clarke says.

"I've tried to be friendly," Ballard says. "I've tried to get along with you, but you're so cold, you won't even admit . . . I mean, you couldn't like it down here, nobody could, why can't you just admit—"

"But I don't, I . . . I hate it in here. It's like Beebe's going to . . . to clench around me. And all I can do is wait for it to happen."

Ballard nods in the darkness. "Yes, yes, I know what you mean." She seems somehow encouraged by Clarke's admission. "And no matter how much you tell yourself—" She stops. "You hate it in here?"

Did I say something wrong? Clarke wonders.

"Out there is hardly any better, you know," Ballard says. "Outside is even worse! There's mudslides and steam vents and giant fish trying to eat you all the time, you can't possibly . . . but . . . you don't mind all that, do you?"

Somehow, her tone has turned accusing. Clarke shrugs.

"No, you don't." Ballard is speaking slowly now. Her voice drops to a whisper: "You actually like it out there. Don't you?"

Reluctantly, Clarke nods. "Yeah. I guess so."

"But it's so . . . the rift can kill you, Lenie. It can kill *us*. A hundred different ways. Doesn't that scare you?"

"I don't know. I don't think about it much. I guess it does, sort of."

"Then why are you so happy out there?" Ballard cries. "It doesn't make any sense . . ."

I'm not exactly "happy," Clarke thinks. Aloud, she only says, "I don't know. It's not that weird, lots of people do dangerous things. What about free-fallers? What about mountain climbers?"

But Ballard doesn't answer. Her silhouette has grown rigid on the bed. Suddenly, she reaches over and turns on the cubby light.

Lenie Clarke blinks against the sudden brightness. Then the room dims as her eyecaps darken.

"Jesus Christ!" Ballard shouts at her. "You sleep in that fucking costume now?"

It is something else Clarke hasn't thought about. It just seems easier.

"All this time I've been pouring my heart out to you and you've been wearing that machine's face! You don't even have the decency to show me your goddamned eyes!"

Clarke steps back, startled. Ballard rises from the bed and takes a single step forward. "To think you could actually pass for human before they gave you that suit! Why don't you go find something to play with out in your fucking ocean!"

And slams the hatch in Clarke's face.

Lenie Clarke stares at the sealed bulkhead for a few moments. Her face, she knows, is calm. Her face is usually calm. But she stands there, unmoving, until the cringing thing inside of her unfolds a little.

"Yes," she says at last, very softly. "I think I will."

Ballard is waiting for her as she emerges from the airlock. "Lenie," she says quietly, "we have to talk. It's important."

Clarke bends over and removes her fins. "Go ahead."

"Not here. In my cubby."

Clarke looks at her.

"Please."

Clarke starts up the ladder.

"Aren't you going to take—" Ballard stops as Clarke looks down. "Never mind. It's okay."

They ascend into the lounge. Ballard takes the lead. Clarke follows her down the corridor and into her cabin. Ballard dogs the hatch and sits on her bunk, leaving room for Clarke.

Clarke looks around the cramped space. Ballard has curtained over the mirrored bulkhead with a spare sheet.

Ballard pats the bed beside her. "Come on, Lenie. Sit down."

Reluctantly, Clarke sits. Ballard's sudden kindness confuses her. Ballard hasn't acted this way since . . .

. . . Since she had the upper hand.

"—might not be easy for you to hear," Ballard is saying, "but we have to get you off the rift. They shouldn't have put you down here in the first place."

Clarke does not reply. She waits.

"Remember the tests they gave us?" Ballard continues. "They measured our tolerance to stress; confinement, prolonged isolation, chronic physical danger, that sort of thing."

Clarke nods slightly. "So?"

"So," says Ballard, "did you think for a moment they'd test for those qualities without knowing what sort of person would have them? Or how they got to be that way?"

Inside, Clarke goes very still. Outside, nothing changes.

Ballard leans forward a bit. "Remember what you said? About mountain climbers, and free-fallers, and why people deliberately do dangerous things? I've been reading up, Lenie. Ever since I got to know you I've been reading up—"

Got to know me?

"—and do you know what thrillseekers have in common? They all say that you haven't lived until you've nearly died. They need the danger. It gives them a rush."

You don't know me at all . . .

"Some of them are combat veterans, some were hostages for long periods, some just spent a lot of time in dead zones for one reason or another. And a lot of the really compulsive ones—"

Nobody knows me.

"—the ones who can't be happy unless they're on the edge, all the time—a lot of them got started early, Lenie. When they were just children. And you, I bet . . . you don't even like being touched . . ."

Go away. Go away.

Ballard puts her hand on Clarke's shoulder. "How long were you abused, Lenie?" she asks gently. "How many years?"

Clarke shrugs off the hand and does not answer. *He didn't mean any harm.* She shifts on the bunk, turning away slightly.

"That's it, isn't it? You don't just have a tolerance to trauma, Lenie. You've got an addiction to it. Don't you?"

It only takes Clarke a moment to recover. The 'skin, the eyecaps make it easier. She turns calmly back to Ballard. She even smiles a little.

"No," she says. "I don't."

"There's a mechanism," Ballard tells her. "I've been reading about it. Do you know how the brain handles stress, Lenie? It dumps all sorts of addictive stimulants into the bloodstream. Beta-endorphins, opioids. If it happens often enough, for long enough, you get hooked. You can't help it."

Clarke feels a sound in her throat, a jagged coughing noise a bit like tearing metal. After a moment, she recognises it as laughter.

"I'm not making it up!" Ballard insists. "You can look it up yourself if you don't believe me! Don't you know how many abused children spend their whole lives hooked on wife beaters or self-mutilation or free-fall—"

"And it makes them happy, is that it?" Clarke asks with cold disdain. "They enjoy getting raped, or punched out, or—"

"No, of course you're not happy!" Ballard cuts in. "But what you feel, that's probably the closest you've ever come. So you confuse the two, you look for stress anywhere you can find it. It's physiological addiction, Lenie. You ask for it. You always asked for it."

I ask for it. Ballard has been reading, and Ballard knows: Life is pure electrochemistry. No use explaining how it feels. No use explaining that there are far worse things than being beaten up. There are even worse things than being held down and raped by your own father. There are the times between, when nothing happens at all. When he leaves you alone, and you don't know for how long. You sit across the table from him, forcing yourself to eat while your bruised insides try to knit themselves back together; and he pats you on the head and smiles at you, and you know the reprieve has already lasted too long, he's going to come for you tonight, or tomorrow, or maybe the next day.

Of course I asked for it. How else could I get it over with?

"Listen," Clarke says. Her voice is shaking. She takes a deep breath, tries again. "You're completely wrong. Completely. You don't have a clue what you're talking about."

But Ballard shakes her head. "Sure I do, Lenie. Believe it. You're hooked on your own pain, and so you go out there and keep daring the rift to kill you, and eventually it will, don't you see? That's why you shouldn't be here. That's why we have to get you back."

Clarke stands up. "I'm not going back." She turns to the hatch.

Ballard reaches out toward her. "Listen, you've got to stay and hear me out. There's more."

Clarke looks down at her with complete indifference. "Thanks for your concern. But I can go any time I want to."

"You go out there now and you'll give everything away, they're watching us! Can't you figure it out yet?" Ballard's voice is rising. "Listen, they knew about you! They were looking for someone like you! They've been testing us, they don't know yet what kind of person works out better down here, so they're watching and waiting to see who cracks first! This whole program is still experimental, can't you see that? Everyone they've sent down—you, me, Ken Lubin and Lana Cheung, it's all part of some cold-blooded test . . ."

"And you're failing it," Clarke says softly. "I see."

"They're using us, Lenie—don't go out there!"

Ballard's fingers grasp at Clarke like the suckers of an octopus. Clarke pushes them away. She undogs the hatch and pushes it open. She hears Ballard rising behind her.

"You're sick!" Ballard screams. Something smashes into the back of Clarke's head. She goes sprawling out into the corridor. One arm smacks painfully against a cluster of pipes as she falls.

She rolls to one side and raises her arms to protect herself. But Ballard just steps over her and stalks into the lounge.

I'm not afraid, Clarke notes, getting to her feet. *She hit me, and I'm not afraid. Isn't that odd . . .*

From somewhere nearby, the sound of shattering glass.

Ballard is shouting in the lounge. "The experiment's over! Come on out, you fucking ghouls!"

Clarke follows the corridor, steps out of it. Pieces of the lounge mirror hang like great jagged stalactites in their frame. Splashes of glass litter the floor.

On the wall, behind the broken mirror, a fisheye lens takes in every corner of the room.

Ballard is staring into it. "Did you hear me? I'm not playing your stupid games any more! I'm through performing!"

The quartzite lens stares back impassively.

So you were right, Clarke muses. She remembers the sheet in Ballard's cubby. *You figured it out, you found the pickups in your own cubby, and Ballard, my dear friend, you didn't tell me.*

How long have you known?

Ballard looks around, sees Clarke. "You've got her fooled, all right," she snarls at the fisheye, "but she's a goddamned basket case! She's not even sane! Your little tests don't impress me one fucking bit!"

Clarke steps toward her.

"Don't call me a basket case," she says, her voice absolutely level.

"That's what you are!" Ballard shouts. "You're sick! That's why you're down here! They need you sick, they depend on it, and you're so far gone you can't see it! You hide everything behind that—that mask of yours, and you sit there like some masochistic jellyfish and just take anything anyone dishes out—you ask for it . . ."

That used to be true, Clarke realizes as her hands ball into fists. *That's the strange thing.* Ballard begins to back away; Clarke advances, step by step. *It wasn't until I came down here that I learned that I could fight back. That I could win. The rift taught me that, and now Ballard has too . . .*

"Thank you," Clarke whispers, and hits Ballard hard in the face.

Ballard goes over backwards, collides with a table. Clarke calmly steps forward. She catches a glimpse of herself in a glass icicle; her capped eyes seem almost luminous.

"Oh Jesus," Ballard whimpers. "Lenie, I'm sorry."

Clarke stands over her. "Don't be," she says. She sees herself as some sort of exploding schematic, each piece neatly labelled. *So much anger in here*, she thinks. *So much hate. So much to take out on someone.*

She looks at Ballard, cowering on the floor.

"I think," Clarke says, "I'll start with you."

But her therapy ends before she can even get properly warmed up. A sudden noise fills the lounge, shrill, periodic, vaguely familiar. It takes a moment for Clarke to remember what it is. She lowers her foot.

Over in the Communications cubby, the telephone is ringing.

Jeanette Ballard is going home today.

For over an hour the 'scaphe has been dropping deeper into midnight. Now the Systems monitor shows it settling like a great bloated tadpole onto Beebe's docking assembly. Sounds of mechanical copulation reverberate and die. The overhead hatch drops open.

Ballard's replacement climbs down, already mostly 'skinned, staring impenetrably from eyes without pupils. His gloves are off; his 'skin is open up to the forearms. Clarke sees the faint scars running along his wrists, and smiles a bit inside.

Was there another Ballard up there, waiting, she wonders, *in case I had been the one who didn't work out?*

Out of sight down the corridor, a hatch creaks open. Ballard appears in shirtsleeves, one eye swollen shut, carrying a single suitcase. She seems about to say something, but stops when she sees the newcomer. She looks at him for a moment. She nods briefly. She climbs into the belly of the 'scaphe without a word.

Nobody calls down to them. There are no salutations, no morale-boosting small talk. Perhaps the crew have been briefed. Perhaps they've simply figured it out. The docking hatch swings shut. With a final clank, the 'scaphe disengages.

Clarke walks across the lounge and looks into the camera. She reaches between mirror fragments and rips its power line from the wall.

We don't need this any more, she thinks, and she knows that somewhere far away, someone agrees.

She and the newcomer appraise each other with dead white eyes.

"I'm Lubin," he says at last.

Ballard was right again, she realizes. *Untwisted, we'd be of no use at all.* But she doesn't mind. She won't be going back.

Mother Lode

Phyllis Gotlieb

In his chapter on "The Establishment of Canadian Science Fiction (1958–83)" in his scholarly history, *Canadian Science Fiction and Fantasy,* David Ketterer begins: "Unquestionably, Phyllis Gotlieb was the key figure during this 'establishment' period of Canadian SF, in spite of the fact that she is better known as a poet. . . . The quantity and quality of her SF output were unrivaled. Indeed, such was the paucity of real competition, it might be argued that from the sixties to the early eighties Phyllis Gotlieb *was* Canadian SF. From a purist point of view, she may still be." Not until the work of William Gibson and Donald Kingsbury in the 1980's did another SF writer in Canada have anywhere near the impact on the world SF community of Phyllis Gotlieb (and not until the 1980's was there any real consciousness in the world community that Spider Robinson, living on a commune in Canada, had become a Canadian SF writer). She has published five books of poetry, written five radio plays, and a mainstream novel, *Why Should I Have All the Grief?* (Toronto, 1969). But the majority of her writing has been SF.

Gotlieb's first SF story was published in 1959 and her first novel, still her most famous, *Sunburst,* in 1964 by Fawcett Books in the U.S. Many other excellent stories appeared over the next thirty years, including her Nebula Award nominee novella, "Son of the Morning," which became the title story of her only short story collection in 1983. Only one of her stories was originally published in Canada; all the rest first appeared in the U.S. SF magazines and original anthologies, until the late 1980's and the advent of *Tesseracts,* the second volume of which Gotlieb coedited. She also published five more SF novels between 1976 and 1989. She is unquestionably the dean of Canadian SF writers.

It is extraordinarily appropriate, given the evolution of Canadian SF in the 1980's and beyond, that the leading writer was a woman and a poet, especially given that the other leading figure to whom Canadian SF writers could look in the eighties as a role model was Judith Merril. Each of them in her own way stood for an intimate connection of SF to contemporary literature. And for a distinctly political commitment. Both had grown and flourished in the American SF publishing field (still the leader in SF publishing) and could lend authority to a nascent SF movement in the mid-eighties.

We have chosen "Mother Lode" for this book as a representative of Gotlieb's finely crafted SF and as an example of her mastery of the conventional forms of standard science fiction in the early 1970's. It is notable that the central character is a competent, intelligent woman, the one unconventional element in this quietly subversive story.

The Amsu spend their lifetime foraging in a zigzag course between the ice rings and the asteroid moons of Epictetus VI, called Apikiki by most of its inhabitants. The local name provokes laughter among some visitors, but the Amsu do not. They are a kilometer in length, and occasionally the young and ignorant ones try to engulf a ship; since they are protected by GalFed, these incidents lead to embarrassing complications.

Amsuwlle was old and wise: she ate ore, drank ice and kept on course. When the Surveyor *Limbo*, a fast cruiser, docked with her on short notice, she extruded her siphon, planted it smartly over the lock door with a solid *flump*, paced the ship without wobble or quiver till the door opened, and flooded the lock with cold water.

:Good luck.: Threyha was Sector Co-ordinator and ESP on the *Limbo*. She sent a last picture of herself from her tank, waving a languid scaly hand.

:Thank you.: For nothing. Elena Cortez was waiting in a wetsuit with oxygen tanks; the current whirled her like a top and pulled her into the tube. It sealed behind her and retracted, pleating as it went, to the vast phosphorescent chamber of Amsuwlle's gorge.

She spun in the dim turbulence, fighting ore chunks and luminous gas bubbles and trying to muffle an explosion of awful panic. *Out! Out! Out!*

:What a pity to cause you such inconvenience.:

A valve opened close by and decanted her into a spherical cavity; the rocks and liquids sucked out, the wet walls squeezed her gently, *:Never fear, Zaf is here!:* the sinus filled with gas, and she hung in its center, then spiraled toward the wall and landed in a puddle of silt. Amsuwlle had begun to spin.

:The air is quite good, my dear. Welcome aboard!:

She pulled off the mask. There was air all right, cold and damp; it smelled of stale water and wet metal, with an overtone of tart cool flesh like a melon's and no hint of decay. She unbuckled the tanks, shivering, scrubbing at her face with cold crinkled hands to wipe away the sweat of fear and embarrassment. She watched the faint ripples of light on the walls, listened to the whish and slap of water, the suck and blubber of valves, and seven or eight hearts going boom, whicker, thack, flub, tickatick with no ascertainable co-ordination, as if a clockmaker had set all his timepieces going at once and the grandfathers, alarms, turnips, electrics, chronometers went on telling their own time.

A round red glow of light grew on the dark wall before her, and something like a black arm came through, tipped with two horns instead of fingers, one of them hung with a penlight.

"Well, Zaf, I am a terrible coward. Anyway, it is good to see you again."

Zaf pulled his length through the valve. He was about the size and thickness of a python, and except for his gleaming blackness and his horns, looked much like an annelid worm. He smelt faintly of sulfur compounds.

"A great pleasure," he said, and dipped his anterior end. It had a mouth and behind that a silver light-sensitive band. The air was not good for him:

he was strapped with a tank, and tubes ran into several of his gill slits; with the free ones he manipulated air into speech. He was an ESP but also the soul of tact; he used his strange warble to communicate with all speaking creatures. A Solthree pushed his way through, a tall heavy man with red hair and beard. "I'm Roberts," he said. "I suppose Zaf's told you who we are. Jones is spraying and Takashima's sleeping. God, it's cold in here." He rubbed his hands, twitched his eyes in every direction except hers. "You'll want a change and a hot drink. No alcohol on board, I'm afraid."

"I know," Elena said. Nothing inflammable was carried on an Amsu, and foreign bodies stored and recycled their own wastes. :*What is worrying him, Zaf?*:

:*Dear lady, I never pry. That is your business.*: Mild ESP chuckle. :*But I think he must have some idea why you are here.*:

Elena Cortez, an enthusiastic student of interterrestrial relationships, had the unhappy task of telling people where to get off. When a new colony was seriously disturbing the ecology or the native civilization of a planet, no matter how perfect it might be from the point of view of its settlers, she had GalFed authority to ask it to shift, remove, or disperse itself. She had no power to shift or remove it herself, nor to threaten to do so. Otherwise she would not have lived through many tacky situations. She was a distant early warning. She warned gently, listened to impassioned arguments calmly, and almost always succeeded at the unpleasant work. When she did not succeed, she accepted refusals gently. The colony, if endangered, was left to itself; if it was a danger, it was left to legal, political or military authorities. Those who rebuffed Elena always lived, or did not live, to learn better.

Amsuwlle spun gently against the flow of planetary debris. Unlike her hearts, the grooved excurrents on her sides worked in co-ordination jetting silvery threads of vapor to keep her on course. She was shaped like a vegetable marrow, and from a distance seemed just as smooth. Closer she was dappled with pale light-sensors and huge opalescent patches; closer yet her skin was ridged and grooved in a brain-fold pattern; it was flexible but firm. At her mouthless front end she had a sensory network fine enough to taste a single microgram, at the rear end an ovipositor, midway two intake siphons and an excretory tube. She excreted compacted nuggets of titanium, tungsten, vanadium, selenium and other useful metals. Because of that she was protected by GalFed and men rode her along her jagged path, spraying her eggs to keep down fungus and scraping calcareous deposits off her arteries.

Since she did not expect to stay long, Elena carried one coverall in her waterproof bag. It was of the good grey stuff GalFed fitted its surveyor teams with, and she had painted a pattern of leaves and flowers all over it; it was sufficiently incongruous in the tiny dayroom, lined in polythene, where one lamp hung overhead and every once in a while the amoeboid shape of a cell or parasite, swimming free in tissue fluid, flattened itself against the translucent wall.

There was room for only one more at the table; the men's heads almost knocked against hers: Roberts, the research geologist, whose beard bristled an inch away; Zaf hanging in coils from some kind of rack and looking like a caduceus; Dai Jones, a little dark wiry man, the only miner of the lot; and round-faced Takashima, the heir to an electronics firm who was taking a look at one of the sources of his components. Hearts beat around them in endless pulses of disharmony.

:*You have all been happy here, Zaf?*:

:*Oh indeed all Solthrees love the Amsu. For myself of course it is east, west, home is best. That is an apothegm of our philosopher-king Nyf.*:

:*It's well-known; his fame travels far.*:

:*Now you are laughing at me, Elena.*:

:*Never, Zaf. You know I don't behave that way. I am always happy to learn how closely distant peoples think.*:

She said aloud, "Perhaps you know why I am here. You can see I have never boarded an Amsu before, but I am taking over liaison in this sector because your regular, Par Singri, is ill with fungous bronchitis and I am subbing."

"I thought Zaf was our liaison," Jones said.

"Between you and Amsuwlle, yes. Here I am liaison between the Amsu and Zaf at this end and GalFed at the other." She squeezed the last drop from her bulb of tea and refilled it.

"What's the emergency?"

"There have been delays in rendezvous with ore carriers. Amsunli was four standard days late on her last trip and Amsusdag two days."

"What's that supposed to mean? Hell, you get delays in all kinds of space shipping, and the Amsu aren't machines, they're animals."

"They have been charted for fifty years . . . in the last three years more than half the deliveries have been delayed. And there is more. Twelve days ago Amsutru was going to meet with the ore carrier *Raghavendra*. Then nine days late she is found squashed in a mess against Asteroid 6337 with her crew dead, every one, and also a prematurely hatched larva burrowing through her siphon."

A small silence. Jones clasped his hands tightly. "Amsutru? My God, Jack Tanner was on her. I knew him."

"No man has ever died on one before . . . and, you know, there are not that many Amsu—never more than twenty-five at once."

"A freak accident," Roberts said.

"Yes, maybe."

"But you're here. You expect something to happen here."

"Oh, I hope not. But . . . you are thirteen days out and twelve to go . . . you are eighteen hours behind schedule. You have been aware of that, haven't you?"

"Sure we're aware of it! We get course checks on radio from the space-light transmitters."

"What do you expect to do about it, Dr. Cortez," Jones asked. "We can't give the old lady a kick in the shins."

"Has anything odd happened?"

"Not that we know. We figured everything was going all right."

"That's likely true. But still, Amsutru is gone, and you can understand why GalFed is concerned."

"But what do you intend to do?" Roberts asked.

"Well, no one has ever turned an Amsu around, have they? Maybe we will not have any more delay, and I will just look around and have a nice ride."

Takashima laughed. "I think you will end up doing jobs like us, Dr. Cortez. Amsuwlle has no room for tourists."

"But if there is trouble?" Roberts persisted.

"I would hope, gentlemen, that we would all be able to get the hell off."

"Well, Zaf . . ." They were alone, and Elena did not feel she had done very well. She was a small dark woman from Venezuela, very delicately boned, with thick black hair falling to her shoulders. Her ancestry was a mixture of all the local peoples, and her skin color balanced light brown with terracotta. Happily mongrelized, she had the knack of making herself at home among very disparate peoples, but she did not normally handle the complaints of ore shippers, especially ones who shipped on Leviathans. "I am a fish out of water," she said.

"I think you have another image in mind," said Zaf, as Amsuwlle's liquid pulses thudded.

"Well, I am very . . . no, I am not discouraged. This is odd. I feel quite calm."

"Good."

"But I should not be. I heartily dislike this assignment—"

"Since I asked for help, I am afraid I am to blame."

"Oh no! It is Par Singri who was stupid enough to get sick. He would have done better here. I enoy being with you, and I have nothing against Amsuwlle, but I do not like to be in places where things are always throbbing and bubbling . . . yet I am calm." She clasped her wrist and studied her watch. "My pulse is normal."

"Then I suppose that is not so good."

"Now you are laughing at me . . . but I admit I am being irrational." She looked around till her eye lit on the waste container with its empty bulbs. "Some kind of drug? I don't know which one of those is mine."

"There are no drugs on board—oh, Roberts brought some Banaquil for his nerves, but he stopped using it after the first few days, and no one has touched it. It is a prescription drug. He considers it a weakness to take pills and had only enough to last the trip."

"I have no drugs except a little painkiller for an ear infection because I was afraid being underwater would start it again . . . but I feel a little sleepy . . . and a little dull. Have the men behaved strangely? Have they changed at all since they came on board?"

"They don't quarrel at all and that is strange for Solthrees—but on the Amsu they are never together long enough."

"Do you feel different since you have been here?"

He shifted his tanks. "Let me damn well tell you I miss my mud, and this synthetic stuff is wishy-washy to a disgusting degree."

Elena laughed, but when he had gone, she collected four of the discarded bulbs and took them to her cabin.

She sat on her bunk and looked at them. There was a drop or two in each. *Elena, you are just being stupid.* She turned the faucet set into the living wall, drew a little water into a cup and tasted it. It was deliciously cold and good, otherwise not unusual in any way. Yet, she did not feel quite herself. *Of course you should feel tired from what you have been through, and any other effects are probably from spinning on this creature. Even your old friend Zaf thinks you are an idiot.*

:*I do not.*:

:*Now you are prying!*:

:*Elena dear, however stupid you may think you feel, it is a fact that Amsutru got lost and we are behind schedule. You were chosen to come here on very good ground and even the wildest suspicion you have must be checked out.*:

:*Good, Zaf. Now I may let my fantasy run wild . . . you know the* Limbo *is pacing us?*:

:*I am aware of it. How long is Threyha giving us her kind attention?*:

:*Until I can find her an answer, querido.*:

:*I hope she will not be bored on such a long slow trip.*:

:*Ask her how to modify our equipment to test the water for Banaquil and also three or four of the main tranquilizer groups. Try out the liquid in these bulbs and also the main water supply . . . and, oh yes, we do have distilled water for emergencies?*:

:*Indeed, but a canister will take quite a lot of your cabin space.*:

:*I am traveling light, and I am not expecting company.*:

There was nothing else to do but try to sleep. Even with the drowsiness it was not so easy with all the distractions in the very walls.

Then think about water.

What the Amsu produced was regularly tested—between trips. On board it was Zaf's task to make sure it was maintained to GalFed specs, but he checked for substances poisonous to Solthrees and his own Yefni, not psychotropic drugs that wouldn't have any effect on him.

Roberts' Banaquil had not been touched. Outside source. She threw out politics, plots and pirates. The arrangements with the Amsu were the results of agreements among many peoples; the profits were parceled out equitably. She knew the sector very well; it was thoroughly patrolled, and local rivalries kept to a minimum. No one had ever stolen ore. The Amsu were happy to be well cared for; they were not particularly intelligent, but they had some ESP and knew ways of containing and rejecting substances—and persons—they thought might do them harm.

She went to sleep, finally, among the bubblings and thuddings, the pale wash of phosphorescence over the walls, the huge living engine of a sentient being.

A call to the unconscious woke her, and she opened her airlock. It was a tiny chamber almost fully occupied by Zaf, coiled around a canister of distilled water.

"There is Banaquil in the water supply, five milligrams per liter, and in all of the bulbs too. Nothing else, you may be thankful."

"I may, but I think I am not. Who is putting it in?"

"Elena, this is hard to explain, Amsuwlle is synthesizing it. Who could put it in when Roberts' supply has not been touched? The others don't even know of it."

"But . . . why? And how did she get it? All the wastes are recycled. From sweat?"

"I can show you, I think. Will you let me squeeze into your cabin for a moment?"

Inside, he bent his head low and with the sharp tip of a horn drew a gash between two of his black rings.

"Zaf!"

"Don't be frightened. I heal fast." He pulled the cut apart with a sinuous movement, and a globule of viscous yellow blood dropped slowly to the floor. It lay there a moment, spread slightly, and in a few moments sank without leaving a mark, absorbed. "Roberts cut himself on one of his instruments. Oh, nine or ten days ago . . . she knew of his drugs, and his nervousness, through me, probably . . ."

"And picked it up from that tiny specimen?"

"Very simply. She tracks ore fields by traces as small as one microgram. She is just as sensitive within."

"But why?"

"Oh dear . . . can you not guess? Because of the quality on which all of our mining operations depend." He gathered his coils together and began to move backward out of the cabin. "Amsuwlle loves to please."

"Wait!" She gave him a hard look, very difficult because the eye band ran around his head, and there was no place to bring a focus to bear. "You know of such things that have happened before."

"That's true, I don't deny it."

"And you have reported them?"

"Of course, Elena! They proved of great interest to anatomists and psychologists . . . administration did not find them worrisome."

"What kind?"

"One of the first Amsu we used grew an extra heart to deliver more heat and oxygen to this part of her body for our sake—and incorporated the change in her genetic material . . . would you find that worrisome?"

"I think . . . one day, perhaps, it might be."

"Possibly. Now I will let you finish your sleep. I must work."

"Wait. What about the Banaquil?"

"It can be gotten rid of—with tact—and do you think it wise? Of course it cannot have been in the water longer than ten days, and there is no worry about withdrawal symptoms with such small amounts . . . and the men are disturbed enough now. Whatever you choose."

Elena paused. "You must help me decide. If things are left as they are, we may fall farther behind."

"Something must change. We have introduced a new element—yourself, my dear. And I doubt—I do not know what an opium den is, but you have a thought about men lying around asleep—I doubt that is what happened with all the other delays. The drug is only one factor in this unhappy situation." The lock door closed behind him.

And beyond it came a furious thrashing and thumping.

:Zaf, what is it? What's wrong?:

:She refuses to open up. I cannot get through the valve.:

:Come back in here.:

:I am required to take accounting of the stores, and believe me, you and I will not be comfortable together in one cabin for any length of time.:

:I am not very comfortable myself right now. I will come out.:

:If you wish, though I doubt it will help. Bring your oxygen.:

The crew quarters were in a storage area off the posterior intestinal canal, a blind sac divided mainly by natural walls partly fortified by inert plastics. A little airlock with an artificial opening had been built into each cabin. Elena's lock had two other openings: one to the neighboring lock and a natural one to the great water conduit Zaf was trying to get out to.

:Go through to the other lock,: Elena said.

:That would be difficult. It opens outward and it is full of water.: He hunched up a coil and slammed it against the rubbery valve into Amsuwlle's belly. Elena ran her fingers over the puckered surface trying to find give in it. There was none.

:Why is she doing this?: She was not afraid of enclosed spaces, and for the moment was too curious to be frightened.

:I am trying to find out, if I can be allowed to think.:

:Think good, Zaf. Think mud.:

:I am going to make mud if I don't get out of here pretty damn fast.:

For all that he looked like a cross between a worm and a python Zaf was vastly different from either. He could wind but not slither: his integument was a single helix of cartilage, a powerful and fairly rigid casing with not much give between its whorls. His two horns curved one to the front and one to the rear, and on his home planet he wound through the mud like a corkscrew or a post hole digger; the muscular black spring of his body was strong enough to pierce shale and sandstone as well. He could rip Amsuwlle's internal tissues more easily than he had slit his own.

Perhaps that consideration reached some important ganglion in Amsuwlle's constitution, for after a moment the valve opened with an elastic *blap* and a rush of water and debris slammed against them. Zaf whirled away to his tasks. *:Not very polite,:* was his only comment.

:But you haven't told me why!:

:Oh Elena! Can you not understand? She needs us!:

Elena wrung out her leotard and wrapped herself in a blanket.

She needs us. Us = Jones, Roberts, Takashima—and Zaf. They serve, she provides. She does not need me. I am the interloper (and keep it down and far back now ((who may take them away))). And Zaf? He is disturbed. Can I trust him, my friend of so many years? Yet he called for help, he brought me here—and who else is there?

"There is nothing in the men's psych reports to suggest abnormal bonding with the Amsu."

She and Zaf were alone in the dayroom. Since there was no real night or morning, everyone chose his own schedule. Elena drank coffee sparingly and ate something that seemed to be moistened chicken feed. She had no intention of living solely on distilled water derived from recycled wastes.

"Of course not. They are all within normal range. Roberts is thirty-eight years old, a bachelor, helps support old parents, lady friend nine years no immediate plan to marry, takes pleasure in playing music on some kind of blowpipe with group of people, mild frustration and resentment common to age and situation—among Solthrees.

"Takashima is twenty-seven, married with two children, overindulges in food, generally content, only complaint he has no one to play Japanese chess with.

"Dai Jones, forty-one, comes from large family now scattered, impoverished background, hard worker, divorced no children, unfortunate experiences with women, feels or is unattractive to them.

"Make of that what you will, *I* don't know what it means. I have no time to lie around in loops and chatter. I must work."

"I will come with you."

She followed, bubbling and gasping in the cold vaults, while he zapped suspicious-looking amoebae with antibiotic bullets and used a strigil like a giant squeegee to scrape and collect calcium fibers from the walls of the pale blood vessels that Amsuwlle obligingly emptied for him one by one.

:*Zaf, there are no psych reports on the Amsu.*:

:*There was no need for them as long as there was no danger.*:

:*Did you never try to find out?*:

:*Oh, I ask always, but she has not much to say. No language! In feeling it is always: nice, good, or: pain, heaviness. They reproduce slowly, very slowly, and of the two eggs Amsuwlle is carrying, one is malformed and will abort. Sometimes . . . there is almost something like "thank you." They are not very strong for the terrible conditions they live in . . . look, here is a softness in the wall . . . I think she is developing an aneurysm. It may burst.*:

:*Could that kill her?*:

:*In the artery from the heart that feeds her principal ganglion, yes. This is not a serious one. We can have it fixed.*:

:*But Zaf, don't you realize—*:

:*In a moment, Elena. Come with me.*: He squeezed through a tiny opening and pulled her after.

Of the great and marvelous chambers Amsuwlle contained there was no end.

For all the freakish richness of her nervous system, she was only the elaboration of a very simple animal found in small on many worlds. She was essentially a skin on the outside and an alimentary canal within; she had no limbs to move and her musculature was all visceral: it served mainly her hearts, intestines, blood vessels and reproductive organs. Between her gut and her horny epithelium were tremendous sinuses of almost liquid protoplasm, broadly netted with cables of nerve and vein and swimming with strange arrow-shaped creatures of pale mauve, a meter long and with luminous nuclei. :*Mesenchyme,*: Zaf said. :*They do odd jobs and turn into specialized cells when Amsuwlle needs them.*:

To Elena the diaphanous swimmers seemed like choirboys serving an altar, and the vast cavity with its glimmering lights and pumping organ hearts trembled in the atmosphere of an ancient cathedral.

:*This is beautiful.*:

:*Yes, even a Yefni may admire it.*:

:*I wonder if it was an aneurysm that killed Amsutru.*:

:*Oh, Elena, how you must spoil things! That kind of serious malfunction never occurs except in very old animals, and we never ride them beyond a certain age. A minor one such as she has now she could heal herself.*:

:*Still—*:

Something grabbed her hard round the middle and squeezed.

Zaf swung his lantern round. A girdle of mauve iridescence, its nucleus elongated and writhing, was doing its best to divide her in two. Zaf bent his head and hooked it off with one horn, snicked a bladed claw from his tail and sheared it neatly in half. The halves, forgetting their errand, dashed off in opposite directions.

Elena's mask had slipped, she was doubled and choking. Zaf slapped it on true, and she howled inward a lungful of air. Then he dumped his light and scraper and looped a coil around her. A flock of devilish choirboys dove at them with solid thumps. Zaf twitched his blade, the arrows retreated a space and swiftly coalesced into an enveloping mantle to engulf foreign bodies. Zaf freed Elena and butted her away; she drifted outward through the light jelly till she found a handhold on a minutely pulsing capillary. Her own pulses were roaring, and she watched the battle through sparkles in her eyes, in the light of the mesenchyme itself. Protoplasm, no matter how ill-intentioned, was no worthy adversary for any Yefni. He ripped and slashed with horns and tail till they exploded in quivering spheres and expanded, a liquid nebula, outward to darkness.

Still in a fury, he found Elena, coiled her, and spun her toward the valve. It did not open at his touch; he wrenched it viciously with his horns, and it shrank bleeding milky essence.

He watched in silence as she lay twisted on the cabin floor, vomiting.

After a little while she pulled herself up and said, "I am better now. Get out and let me change."

"Change now. I am all modesty." He shoved his head among his coils.

She coughed and then sighed. "Oh, Zaf."

When she was dressed, she said, "I have started something and now it is too much, you know. I should not have come."

"Perhaps."

"But I am come, I am here. Now I better finish."

"Yes," he said sadly.

Jones slaps his hand on the cool melon-wall, no favors asked and none given, old lady . . .

finning his way through nave and apse while the hearts boom like organs, Roberts does not ask whether the whale loves Jonah, or consciously wish to write a poem or hymn rather than a paper on the alchemy of its digestive processes, but he does not hurry . . .

Takashima, adored only son of the magnate, is free for the moment of that grim warlord of the assembly line, cheerfully navigates a monster of ancient myth and finds her curiously gentle . . .

Gentle.

Elena sighed.

"I must tell the men . . . something. They should leave, and I have no authority to force them off. Listen—I think the hearts are changing rhythm. I must be mistaken; I could not have gotten to know them that well."

"Oh, but you did. Everyone does. I told Amsuwlle to reroute the blood away from her weakened artery."

"That was kind of you, under the circumstances," Elena said.

"Under the circumstances we need all the safety we can get."

"Lady, you must think we're fools. We can't leave the ore here for anybody to take." Jones was working at keeping his voice down.

"The *Limbo* is pacing us. She'll make sure nobody takes the ore. Nobody has even tried for forty years."

"The *Limbo*? Spying?"

"No. Only making sure we are safe. We are not safe. Amsuwlle has become a hostile environment. Zaf has told you."

"There was no hostility till you came," Roberts said.

"Then let us say she does not care for me. I am the wrong person for the job, and it was a mistake to send me. I cannot help that, but it seems to be true. I came in peace, but she seems to consider me a threat because I must ask you to leave if there is any danger here. She cannot bear that because she depends on you, perhaps too strongly. If that has made her hostile, then she is a threat, and I must ask you to leave even if it is my fault. I cannot force you. All I can do is ask, even beg. We must get off!"

"Even at the cost of everything we'd have to leave?"

She held out her hands. "I tell you, there is no other choice!"

Roberts gave the table a hard slap. "Get off if you like, and take anyone you want with you. I waited three years for this chance, and I'm not giving it up now." He got up and left. Jones followed with a dark angry face.

Takashima shrugged in confusion. "I don't know what is happening, but I like life. I help anyway I can."

"You can," Zaf said. "Contact the *Limbo* by radio, tell them to alert the ESP and stand by. I will instruct you, but I think it best that I don't try to do it myself right now."

"This is stupid." Elena wiped her forehead. "Threyha's one of the strongest ESPs in the Galaxy. She should be alert."

"You know how Khagodi are. She is far too busy to send her friend Zaf little messages of love. I am lucky if she gives me a tenth of her mind for a moment once in a while." He did not have enough power to reach the ship by himself and was sensitive about it.

"I am foolish and ungrateful. I did not thank you for saving my life."

"Disregard it. Just arrange your mind for me, please. It is confusion."

"I would like to arrange it for myself."

"If you wish to finish the work, my dear, and give Threyha a pro tem report, you had better do it before all hell explodes."

"Yes . . . I know." The pulses and their cells were butting against the walls.

Elena rapped her head with her knuckles. "When I came on board, the men realized they might have to leave, and they became quite upset . . . in the case of Roberts the journey was a great privilege, for Takashima a holiday he longed to have, for Jones his main livelihood. That is reasonable. But then also, I believe, they suffered from the last twinges of an old Solthree superstition that a woman brought bad luck to a men's working ship . . . and now, in a way, they have made it come true . . .

"Amsuwlle has just enough sense to absorb this . . . and she dearly loves, as you say, to please them. You became the unconscious channel and reinforcement of their uneasiness—of course you cannot help that—and she became disturbed. She finds all of this feeling an irritant and wants to eject the cause of it, me, and the instrument, you. That is simple emotional mechanics."

"They are the ones whose emotions began this cycle, and she is not attacking them."

"I think you have a different relationship with her. Theirs is a more primitive male-female relationship, based on a psychodynamic concept of Solthrees and a few other races, they call it Edipo—oh, I am so tired I can't remember what they call it in *lingua*—yes, Oedipus complex."

Zaf absorbed that for a moment and chuckled with a burble of gills. "How amusing." He was an egg-laying hermaphrodite.

"Yes, very." She rubbed her eyes. "Has Takashima reached them?"

"He is broadcasting. Go on."

"That is all there is to say about the situation here right now. It will clear up when we leave. But it is the future I am worried about. Men tend and use machines and think of them as if they are female; they ride and tend the Amsu as if they are machines—but Amsuwlle is no machine, she is living matter, she *adapts* for them, grows extra hearts, redirects her blood supply, her musculature, her liquids . . . not in normal evolutionary patterns, nor by the eugenic principles men use to breed cattle, but only because their attentions give her a feeling of well-being . . . she does not adapt for her survival, but for theirs. Will a redistributed circulatory pattern improve the quality of her offspring? If she synthesizes drugs, what will that do to her heart actions? . . . On Solthree they breed an animal called a dog for household pet, and sometimes a dog will attach itself so strongly to its owner that when he dies it will not eat or sleep but simply pine and languish until it dies as well. Then men write tearful songs about the faithfulness of the poor creature, but it has simply been destructive of itself and disturbed the evolutionary pattern of its species . . .

"Fifty years ago there were between eighteen and twenty-two Amsu circling Apikiki. Every few years the breeding cycle slows down, and they conjugate to interchange genetic material—but fifty years in the progress of even such a big, slow animal should give you more than your present population of twenty-five with all the scraping of arteries and egg spraying and patching of aneurysms . . . only two eggs in this huge beast, and one is malformed. What does she care? Men are caring for her, and they are satisfied with what they get. Eggs can be placed anywhere, and if necessary men will lead her to the ice and the ores . . ."

Before she could say another word they floated gently to the center of the room.

What—

And slammed against the side wall. Elena cried out at the bruising of her shoulder; Zaf had been driven into a knot and was struggling to untangle himself. Vibration pushed them jaggedly to the opposite wall, then sliding into the ceiling.

:She has stopped spinning.:

Zaf untwined himself; Elena wiped blood off her mouth from her bitten tongue, droplets hovered in a cloud round her face. "What?"

Zaf grabbed at his tank, floating a meter away. *:Breaking radio contact . . . shooting her jets in irregular vapor pattern.:* He snorted an air bubble out of the tube. "White noise field."

"Do something, Zaf!"

"Like what?"

The hearts went boom, whicker, thack-thack; the mesenchyme cells butted their snouts on the walls; the waters roared all about them.

"Takashima?"

"He has air, but the radio is under a heap of wet gravel. The others are knocking about in the jelly near the egg chamber."

"Those things will get at them."

"She has no time to bother with that." Zaf hooked himself onto a handhold, yanked open a locker door, and got out the cauterizer he would have used to repair the weakened artery. He slipped a new power cell into it.

"What are you doing?"

"Taking a precaution." He ran the white-hot beam around the frame of the plastic cabin door.

"But, Zaf, you're sealing us—"

"I am sealing her out." The valve beyond opened, and water struck like a fist. The door buckled, shuddered, and held. "Just in time."

The lights went out. "Ventilation will go next," Zaf said. "You will want oxygen." He found tanks in the locker. The luminous arrows, colors of lightning, swarmed and swarmed outside the cabin.

Elena sucked on the dead air of the tank. :*It is a good thing you know what to do in emergencies, Zaf.*:

He said nothing to that, and perhaps it was not the time to ask how many such emergencies there had been. Amsuwlle's entire orchestration of living matter, hearts, waters, cells, rock and ice fragments, was breaking against the frail plastic shell.

Another lurch and the sealed door became their floor.

:*She is changing course.*:

:*Can the* Limbo *follow?*:

:*If Takashima made contact*—oh, *Great Heavens, she is expelling the faulty egg to lead them off course!*:

A wrenching shudder filled the whole body—

:—*and oh, the Heavenly Shell, the other has gone with it, it has gone . . .*:

The light came on, the air freshened, the internal tempest died down into the endless beating of hearts. Floor became floor, and Amsuwlle spun to her own unknown destination. She had made a choice and had chosen her crew.

Zaf, in a rage, jittered up and down, bouncing on the spring of his body. "She has lost them both! She is shattered and wrenched, and I am done!"

"Zaf, please!"

"Everything is ruined, and I am lost! Oh, why could you not have stopped this?" He sprang toward her and ripped off her mask. "Why?"

"Zaf!"

"The eggs are gone, we are lost, going somewhere out into space where we will all starve before she lets us go—no *Limbo*, no radio, no base—all my responsibility—and no help! All you can do is say please, please!"

Elena, completely disoriented, could only stare at him.

His tail rose, the blade snicked and touched her shin. "Look at me. Have you ever read my psych report? You did not think it necessary? It says I am a man of great courage, intelligence and resourcefulness, very sympathetic to and fitted for work on Amsu. On Amsu. You understand? Do you see me sitting in an office at GalFed Central with my coils in knots and my sulfur mud dripping all over? Or hopping about city roads like—like your toy, a pogo stick? or flying an airship or starship—without hands? Do you?"

She said nothing, and Zaf, her friend of twelve years, drew a light line with his blade under her chin toward the windpipe. "You do not understand."

She found a voice. "Do all those other ESP liaisons feel so lonely and unfitted on all those other Amsu, and patch them up and play down the reports, and ride them for their pride?"

"I am the only man of my world to become a GalFed official."

"And my family worked half their lives to send one of them to the stars." She put her hand on his head between the horns and pushed the sharp slicer out of her mind. "Oh, Zaf, you asked me to come."

"I asked you . . ." the blade did not waver, "and Par Singri is not sick; he is only a little man who thinks little square thoughts and feels he has done something brilliant when he fits them into a big square. I convinced Threyha to send you . . . because I saw how things were going . . . you were my friend . . . and I thought you would be able to stop it before everything got ruined."

She tried not to think of her husband at GalFed Central or her family who had worked so hard in a hard land; her hand rested lightly on his head. "I am sorry I have failed you. And I am sorry for Amsuwlle."

"I am not. She would not have cared if she had killed me, and I have thought only of myself." The blade withdrew and he bowed his head. "That is what is so terrible." He flung his head from side to side. "The eggs are lost and we are going nowhere! And—oh, Elena, the men! They are still in the egg chamber!"

Both of them were clinging to the tattered rim of the chamber wall; their oxygen tanks were nearly empty, and they were shivering almost hysterically with chill. They would not have been there, or anywhere else, if part of Amsuwlle's intestinal tract had not given way when the eggs were so violently ejected and filled the egg chamber and blocked the now flaccid ovipositor with rock, silt and coagulating protoplasm. The stuff had not quite stopped and was still pushing outward with slow but glacial force.

Zaf wound his length about Jones and Roberts and hooked his way by head and tail like a climber of ice, in slow steps backward; his mind, wide open, broadcast his misery and despair.

Back in the dayroom they stared at each other with haggard faces.

"I suppose you were right," Roberts said. "We should have tried to get off earlier."

"It doesn't matter," Elena said dully. She sighed. "We'd better see if we can't get Takashima."

The room was a mess; Zaf had used his blade to reopen the door, and no one worried about locks and valves any more. Locker doors had broken open with the violence of Amsuwlle's writhings; tanks and canisters were dented or burst. "We don't have much food," Jones said. Packages had spilled, their contents fouled with splatters of mud. "It won't matter for very long, will it?"

:Oh, don't give up hope quite so soon, my dears.:

Jones yelped. "Ohmigawd, what's that?"

"Be at ease, gentlemen," Zaf said without much relief. "That is Threyha."

Once again the spin stopped, and they floated; once again the siphon extruded dutifully and thumped on something hard, and down through it went the rush of waters. Amsuwlle was being obedient again.

It was not easy to be anything but obedient to Threyha. In a few minutes she gave them her image in the sinus leading from the siphon. The floor sagged from her weight, upward of six hundred kilos, and there was no room for her height of three meters. She simply nudged the ceiling with her scaly pointed jaw and it shrank away, thumped the floor with her heavy tail and it firmed and flattened under her. *:I am not coming any further or the poor thing will have another rupture.:* She smoothed down her opalescent scales and stood properly erect. *:And I must get back to my tank.:* She was amphibian, but preferred water. *:Collect Takashima and come to me.:*

"How—"

:Very easily. When she let go that second egg and all that loose protoplasm, she left a beautiful trail . . . and when a Khagodi cannot outthink an Amsu, it will be a wet day in the desert. Now hurry please.:

While they were gathering themselves together as best they could, she got a good hard hold on Amsuwlle's ganglia and nerve networks and sent her slowly back on course. Then she flashed a few orders, and the mesenchyme slavishly arranged themselves in neat layers to replace valves and membranes. *:What a mess. She is not going to be the same.:*

"Neither will we," said Zaf.

:That can be discussed later. You are going to ride her to rendezvous.:

They left Zaf in the dayroom. "I suppose I will not see you again for a long time, Elena," he said sorrowfully.

:You will see each other in fifteen days at debriefing,: Threyha said from the entrance. *:Sentimental farewells are not in order.:*

There were no sentimental farewells for Amsuwlle. Elena and the men dragged themselves aboard the *Limbo* without a word.

Threyha did not have or need a voice. Her telepathy was a stentorian bellow, but always under perfect control. While she was still in the lock of her tank, waiting for it to fill with her own world's mixture of waters, she directed a beam of thought. *:Elena.:*

:Leave me alone. You deceived me. Par Singri is not sick.: She was scrubbing herself with a cloth, trying to get off the layers of silt, sweat, dried protoplasm and other accretions of her term on Amsuwlle.

:Zaf was too proud to ask you personally when he was so frightened, and I wanted him on egalitarian terms with you.:

:Now you will have him punished.:

:Of course not. But I cannot allow him to make himself any sicker. I have a good

Psychman, a methane breather with eighteen legs and blue eyes in his knees, who will cure him of the notion that his shape is too peculiar to be of use to GalFed . . . : She waved her arms through the water to freshen it. *:This stuff is always stale slop no matter how they aerate it . . . spare me from people with feelings of inferiority! Only man of his planet in GalFed! We have invited fifteen of his cousins to join us; likely they will accept, and then he will boss them unmercifully.:*

:What of me? I have not done very well.: She thought of the great wounded creature, half killed with kindness, wrenched out of shape and aching with bewilderment.

:You spoke when necessary and shut up otherwise. It's what you are paid for. I will put forward your recommendation that we implant the Amsu with robot monitors and except for emergencies service them at rendezvous. Otherwise let them take care of themselves. Now you deserve a good sleep, because in twelve hours you are going to board Amsumar: we have a low-priority emergency—:

"Oh, no!"

:—from the ESP, who happens to be my nephew; he is a bright sensible boy but a bit frantic. It will take you a day or two to cool that, and we will be back in good time to meet with Zaf and Amsuwlle. You would say there is nothing like getting into the water again to cure a fear of drowning.:

:Threyha, why do you not simply take over the universe?:

:I hate authority. And of course no other Khagodi would obey me. One last thing: aside from my nephew the crew on Amsumar are all female beetle types from Procyon-something, and you will not have to worry about being considered a— what do you call it? Jinx or Jonah?:

"One is as good as another," said Elena, and fell asleep.

HOME BY THE SEA

Élisabeth Vonarburg

Translated from the French by Jane Brierley

Élisabeth Vonarburg, teacher, SF writer, and critic, was born in France and moved to Canada in 1973. She began to write SF stories in the 1970's and her first novel, *Le Silence de la cité* (1981—*The Silent City*, 1988) won two prizes in France—she was the first writer outside of France and the first woman to win the Grand Prix de la SF française. She was the fiction editor of *Solaris* for eleven years, and has been an indefatigable advocate of French Canadian SF. David Ketterer calls her "the leading figure in Quebec SF today." *Twentieth Century Science Fiction Writers* calls her "a prime mover in the establishment of a French Canadian school of science fiction and its blossoming into a unique Québécois independent current of culture."

Vonarburg learned to speak English from listening to Joan Baez records in the 1960's, and writes articulate criticism in English. But she writes fiction in French. Her recent essay "So You Want to Be a Science Fiction Writer?" gives an extensive autobiographical and critical look at writing SF in a language other than English: " . . . when I began writing SF, at eighteen, I felt energized, not crushed, by the American tradition(s), I felt buoyed, not embarrassed, by the French one(s), and I never thought that literature and SF were two distinct categories."

Her first story in English translation was published in the first *Tesseracts* volume; then the publisher asked her for a novel and she had one, previously published in France, to translate *(The Silent City)*. She makes the point that outside the U.S. and perhaps the U.K., there is no such thing as a career in SF for writers. "What if you are a young Québécois SF writer, descendent of French conquerors who have been conquered, living an uncertain francophone life in a predominantly English-speaking continent, and reading almost nothing but American SF? (And what if you are a young Québécois allophone?) Well, you write stories about Captain John McSmith, born in New York, commanding the Starship Counterprize and conquering the universe. Not one European aboard the ship, never mind a Québécois. And you don't do this by choice, with a neat historical-or-something explanation for this absence, but by sheer (hysterical) blindness, simply because you *cannot see* Québécois in the stars: you're not even sure what it is to be Québécois now, then what could it be in the *future*! Of course, you can always write about Aliens who are underdogs, or living in the cracks of a not so future dominating culture which is not yours—and you do, and if you are a woman, why, that sort of makes sense too."

Her SF is feminist but not polemical, and deeply concerned with psychology. As is, for example, "Home by the Sea."

Images of sorrow, pictures of delight
Things that go to make up a life . . .
Let us relive our lives in what we tell you
(Home by the Sea, Genesis)

"Is it a lady, Mommy?"

The small girl looks at me with the innocent insolence of children who say out loud what adults are thinking to themselves. A skinny, pale, fair-haired child of five or six, she already looks so like her mother that I feel sorry for her. The mother gives an embarrassed laugh and lifts the child onto her lap. "Of course it's a lady, Rita." She smiles excuse-her-please, I smile back oh-it's-nothing. Will she take advantage of it to launch into one of those meaningless, ritual conversations whereby neighbors assure each other of their mutual inoffensiveness? To cut her off, I turn toward the window of the compartment and look purposefully at the scenery. Heading to the north the train follows the system of old dykes as far as the huge gap breached four years ago by the Eschatoï in their final madness. The scars left by the explosions have nearly disappeared, and it almost seems as though the dyke were meant to stop here and that the waters had been allowed to invade the lowlands as part of some official scheme. We cross the narrows by ferry, and are once more in the train, an ordinary electric train this time, suspended between the two wide sheets of water, to the west rippled by waves, to the east broken by dead trees, old transmission towers, church spires, and caved-in roofs. There is a mist, a whitish breath rising from the waters like a second tide ready to engulf what is left of the man-made landscape.

Is it a lady? You obviously don't see ladies like me very often in your part of the world, little girl. Cropped hair, boots, army fatigues, a heavy jacket of worn leather; and the way I was sitting, grudgingly corrected when you and your mousy mother came in—a real lady doesn't sprawl like that, does she, even when she's by herself. The *lady* actually likes to be comfortable, believe it or not, and in her usual surroundings she doesn't have to worry much about what people think. The lady, little girl, is a recuperator.

But she couldn't tell you this; she didn't want to see your big, stupid eyes fill with terror. All the same, you don't get to see a real live bogeywoman every day. I could've told you a few things. Yes, I know, *If you're not good the Recuperator will get you, and he'll say you're not a real person and put you in his big sack.* As a matter of fact, we don't put human specimens in our big sacks right away, you know; only plants and small animals. Big animals are injected with tracers once they've been put to sleep for preliminary tests. If the Institute researchers discover something especially interesting, they send us back for it. I could've told you all this, little girl, you and your mother, who would probably have looked at me with superstitious fear. But who cares what recuperators really do, anyway? They go into the contaminated Zones to bring back horrible things that in other times might have been plants, animals, humans. So the recuperators must be contaminated too, mentally if nothing else. No, no one apart from the Recuperation Agency cares what the recuperators really do. And no one, especially not the Institute, wonders who they really are, which suits me just fine.

"Why did they break the dyke, Mommy?" asks the small girl. She's sensed that it would be a good idea to change the subject.

"They were crazy," says the mother curtly. Not a bad summing up. Fanatics, they were—but it comes to the same thing. You see, they thought the waters would keep rising, and they wanted to help the process along: The End of the Damned Human Race. But the waters stopped. So did the Eschatoï, by the way; it was one of their great collective suicides. But this time there weren't enough of them left to start the sect afresh—nor enough energy in the new generations to be fanatic. The prolife people have simmered down too. Even the Institute doesn't believe in its own slogans any more. The Rehabilitation of the Marvelous Human Race. But that's just it: the human race isn't reproducing itself well or adequately. It probably wore itself out with its frenetic activity during the Great Tides and seismic catastrophes at the end of the last century. Now it's going downhill, although no one dares say so straight out to the Institute and its people. True, there are fewer earthquakes, fewer volcanic eruptions, the sun breaks through the clouds more often, and the waters have stopped rising, but that's nothing to get excited about; it's not a human victory. Just a blind, natural phenomenon that peaked by pure chance before destroying what was left of the human race. And I, little girl, I who am not human, I collect what the Institute calls specimens in the contaminated Zones—specimens that are also, in their way, what is left of the human race.

I who am not human. Come on, now, didn't I get over that long ago? But it's a habit, a lapse, a relapse. I could've answered you just now, little girl, by saying, "The lady is an artifact, and she's going to see her mother."

But that very word requires so much explaining: *Mother.* At least I have a navel. A neat little navel, according to the medic who checked me out before my abortive departure for Australia and the Institute. The current artifacts have large, clumsily made navels that the scanner immediately picks up as not being the real thing. But you, now, it's almost invisible, extraordinary, what technical skill your . . . And there he stumbled: *mother, creator, manufacturer?* He came out of his scientific ecstasy, suddenly conscious that after all someone was listening who hadn't known the truth. None of the other tests had ever revealed anything! But this Medical Center is connected to the Institute, and new detection methods have been developed that didn't exist when you were, er . . . (he cleared his throat—he was very embarrassed, poor man) *made.*

Yes, she made me like this so I could pass for a human being. Almost. In spite of everything I thought then, she surely didn't foresee that I'd learn about it this way. I probably wasn't meant to know until the end, with its unmistakable signs. Why? Am I really going to ask her? Is this why I came? But I'm not really going to see her. I'm passing by, that's all. I'm on my way to the Hamburg Zone.

Oh, come on! I know damn well I'll stop at Mahlerzee. I will? I won't? Am I still afraid, then? That cowardice that made me burn all my bridges, swear never to ask her anything, when I found out. But it wasn't only cowardice (you see, little girl, the lady always tends to exaggerate, to be too hard on herself). It was a question of survival. It wasn't because I was afraid or desperate that I ran away after the medic's revelations. I didn't want to see the others waiting for me outside. Not Rick, especially not Rick . . . No, if I remember rightly, that lady of fifteen years ago was in a fury—still is—in spite of everything. A huge fury, a wild, redeeming fury. Surely this was why, on coming out of the Medical Center, she found herself heading for Colibri Park. It was there that she'd first seen the Walker.

Colibri Park. The first time you go there you wonder why it's not called Statue Park. Of course, there is the transparent dome in the middle of the main lawn, enclosing its miniature jungle with hummingbirds that flit about on vibrating wings, but what one really sees are the statues. Everywhere, along the alleys, on the lawns, even in the trees, believe it or not. The young lady first came there with Rick, her lover, and Yevgheny, the typical streetwise city boy who teaches small-town greenhorns the score. The lady was sixteen. She'd barely been a month in Baïblanca. One of the youngest scholarship students at Kerens University. A future ornament of the Institute. The fledgling that had fled the nest, slamming the door as she went, so to speak. And all around her and her lover, there were the wonders of Baïblanca, the capital of Eurafrica. I could say it was El Dorado for us, but you probably wouldn't know what El Dorado is.

Yevgheny had pointed out, among the people strolling by, the Walker— a man moving slowly, very slowly. He was tall and could have been handsome, had something in his bearing been as imposing as his height. But he walked listlessly, you couldn't even call it sauntering. And then, as he passed them by, that blank face, those eyes that seemed to be looking far off, perhaps sad, perhaps merely empty . . . He'd been walking like this every day for almost ten years, Yevgheny had said. The sort of thing old men do . . . That was it, he walked like an old man. But he didn't seem all that old, barely in his thirties.

"He was never young, either," Yevgheny said. "He's an artifact."

And I'd never heard the word. How had my *mother* managed to keep me from ever hearing it? At least Rick seemed as stupid as I was. Yevgheny was delighted. "An artifact—an organic work of art. Artificial! Obviously you don't see them running around the streets of Mahlerzee or Broninghe."

This one wasn't doing much running either, Rick remarked. Yevgheny smiled condescendingly: this artifact was at the end of the road, used up, almost finished.

He made us go past the Walker and sit on one of the long benches facing the central lawn. Then he launched into a detailed explanation. Not many of these artifacts were made nowadays; they'd gone out of fashion, and there had been incidents. During their fully active period, they were far more lively than the Walker (who moved slowly, so slowly, toward the bench). Very lively, in fact. And not everyone knew they were artifacts, not even the artifacts themselves. Thirty years earlier, the great diversion in the smart circles of Baïblanca was to bet on who among the new favorites in the salon of this or that well-known personality was an artifact, whether or not the artifact knew, whether or not the artifact's "client" knew, whether or not either would find out, and how either would react. Particularly the artifact.

There were *Sheep* and there were *Tigers*. The *Tigers* tended to self-destruct deliberately before their program terminated, sometimes with spectacular violence. A biosculptor had made a fortune this way. One of his artifacts had reacted at knowing what it was by setting out to kill him; there was always some doubt about the precise moment when an artifact stopped working completely, and the biosculptor gambled that his would self-destruct before getting him. He almost lost his bet. Instead, he merely lost both arms and half his face. It wasn't serious: the medics made them grow back. After several premature deaths among the elite of Baïblanca in those inopportune explosions, the government put a stop to it. This didn't keep the biosculptors from continuing for a while. Artifacts popped up now and then, but no more *Tigers* were made; the penalty was too stiff.

Yevgheny rattled all this off with a relish that disgusted the young lovers. They didn't know much about Baïblanca yet; they had heard the Judgementalists fulminating against the "New Sodom," and now they understood why. This decadent society wasn't much better than that of the Eschatoï, the dyke-destroyers whom it had survived . . . Rick and Manou understood each other so well, little girl. They were so pure, the brave new generation. (Oh, what high-flown debates we used to have, late into the night, about what we'd do for this poor, ailing world once we were in the Institute!)

With Yevgheny, they watched the Walker reach the bench and sit down beside the blue-clad sleeper. Yevgheny began to laugh as he felt the lovers stiffen: the Walker wouldn't do anything to them even if he heard them, which wasn't likely! It was an artifact, an *object*! But didn't he say they sometimes self-destructed? "I told you, they aren't making any more *Tigers*!"

The final moments of the *Sheep* weren't nearly as spectacular. They became less and less mobile, and finally their artorganic material became unstable. Then the artifacts vaporized, or else . . . Yevgheny rose as he spoke, and went over to the sleeper in blue. Bending his index finger, he tapped her on the forehead. "Or else they turn to stone."

The young woman in blue hadn't moved; neither had the Walker. He seemed to have seen and heard nothing. He was contemplating the Sleeper. When Yevgheny, all out of breath, caught up with Rick and Manou, he finished what he was saying: "... and you know what they call those two? Tristan and Isolde!"

He nearly died laughing. He probably never understood why we systematically avoided him afterward. We had some moral fiber, Rick and I. Small-town greenhorns are better brought up than Baïblancans.

You know, when you come right down to it, little girl, probably nothing would have happened, or not in the same way, if I hadn't been so much like her, like my *mother*. But of course I was. Oh, not physically. But in character. Typically pigheaded. Our reconciliations were as tempestuous as our rows. We had a marvelous time, we two. She told me the most extraordinary stories; she knew everything, could do everything, I was convinced of it. And it was true—almost. A man—what for? (Because one day, you must realize that too, the matter of fathers always comes up.) And at this point I distinctly sensed a wound somewhere in her, deep down, a bitterness, despite her efforts to be honest. ("They have their uses," she had said, laughing.) But really the two of us needed no one else; we were happy in the big house by the beach. She took care of everything: lessons, cooking, fixing things; and the toys when I was little, made of cloth, wood, anything! Taïko Orogatsu, you see, was a sculptress. I still picture her now, smudges up to her elbows and even on her face, circling her lump of clay like a panther, talking to herself in Japanese. Of course, I didn't understand any of it. I thought it was magic. She was determined to hold on to her language, but she never taught it to me. It was all she kept of Japan, where she had never set foot. Her ancestors had emigrated long before the Great Tides and the final submersion. She didn't even have slanted eyes.

But I'm not going to tell you about my memories of that time, little girl. Perhaps they're lies. Real memories? Implanted memories? I don't know. But even if they are implants, she wanted them that way. They must reveal something about her, after all, because I can also remember her faults, her brutal practicality, her impatience, our interminable, logical arguments that would cave in beneath her sudden arbitrary decision: that's-the-way-it-is-and-you'll-understand-later. My adolescent whining also was typical. Another series of implanted memories? Impossible to find out, unless I asked her. Did I really go through the adolescent crisis, I-want-to-live-my-own-life-and-not-yours, or do I merely *think* I walked out slamming the door? Looking back now, however, isn't it really the same thing? That old-fashioned career as a space pilot, did I want it for myself, or to thwart her? So as not to go into biotronics as she wanted me to? Did I really mean it? In the end, when I fled the Medical Center after the medic's revelation, what really hurt wasn't the loss of a future career destroyed before it even began; I didn't shed any tears about it later either.

I didn't cry at all, in fact. For years. It almost killed me. The young lady who'd just found out she was an artifact was furious. Can you understand that, little girl? Beside herself with fury and hate. The Taïko who had done this, who had done this to me, who had *made* me, she couldn't be the Taïko of my memories! Yes, she was. But I couldn't have lived with a monster all those years without realizing it? Yes, I could. She had done this to me so that I would find out like this, go crazy, do dreadful things, kill myself, kill her, anything? It was not possible! Yes, it was. A monster, underneath the Taïko that I thought I remembered. Two contradictory images met in my head, matter/antimatter, with myself in the middle of the disintegrating fire. Infinite emptiness, as the pillars of a whole life crumble.

Well, the lady was so gutted that she scarcely remembers the weeks that followed, you see. She dropped deep beneath the civilized surface of Baïblanca, into the submarine current of nonpersons. Threw her credentity card into an incinerator! Disappeared, as far as Kerens University was concerned—and the Institute, and the universal data banks. And you know what? It's extraordinarily easy to live underwater once you've given up breathing. The current wasn't fast or cold; the creatures who lived there were so indifferent that it was almost like a kindness. I haven't any really coherent memory of it. The shop where no questions were asked. The mechanical work, day in, day out. An empty shell. Automaton. I was never so much an artifact as then. And of course, the nightmares. I was a time bomb ready to explode, I had to become an automaton to protect myself. So as not to begin thinking, mainly, and especially not to begin feeling.

But one day, quite by chance, the lady encountered the Walker. For weeks after that she followed him around in horrible fascination. He walked slower and slower, and people turned to look at him—those who didn't realize what he was. And then it happened, in broad daylight. I saw him on the Promenade, walking so, so slowly, as though he were floating in a time bubble. It wasn't his usual hour at all. And there was something about his face, as though he were . . . in a hurry. I followed him to Colibri Park where the Sleeper slept, uncaring, in full sunlight. The Walker halted by the bench, and with impossible slowness he began to seat himself beside the motionless woman; but this time he did not simply sit: he curled up against her, placing his head in the crook of the arm on which the Sleeper was resting her head. He closed his eyes and stopped moving.

And the lady follower sat down beside the Walker now at his final destination, and watched his flesh become stone. It was a slow and ultimate tremor rising from his innermost being, rising to the surface of his skin and then imperceptibly stiffening, while the cells emptied out of their sublimated substance and their walls became mineral. The extinction of life, as lightly as the passing shadow of a cloud.

And I . . . I felt as though I were awakening. I stayed there a long time, beginning to think, to feel again. Through the fury, I sensed . . . no, not peace, but a resolve, a certainty, the glimmer of an *emotion* . . . I didn't know what end had been planned for me—explosion or petrification—but I found that I could bear it after all. It wasn't so terrible in the long run. (I was absolutely amazed to find myself thinking this way, but that was all right: astonishment also was an emotion.) It was like one of those incurable diseases of which the outcome is at once certain, quick, and curiously problematical. You know it will happen, but not when or how. There were lots of humans who lived like this. So why not me?

Yes, astonishment was the initial emotion. The idea of revenge only came later. *I would not give her the satisfaction of seeing me die before my time.* I would not put on such a performance for her. I would not make a spectacle of myself.

But I still had enough sense of showmanship to sign on as a recuperator. No. There were two ways of completely covering one's tracks. Either go and live in a Zone, or go and hunt in a Zone. The really theatrical thing to do would have been to go and live in a Zone: "I'm a monster, and I'm joining the monsters." Whereas becoming a recuperator . . .

Well, the lady still had a perverse streak, in spite of everything. She was meant to be caught in the net, and instead found herself doing the catching, ready to spring the traps in which she would capture these quasi-humans, these para-animals . . . these *specimens.* She could have become very cruel. She could have. But she saw too many sadistic recuperators, fanatics, sick people. And then she inevitably recognized herself in her prey. She was teetering on the razor's edge between disgust and compassion. But she came down on the side of compassion; this recuperator was not a bogeywoman, after all. On the side of compassion. "By accident," or "because of adequate programming," or "because I had been properly brought up." It comes to the same thing as far as results are concerned, and that's all that counts.

That's what Brutus thought. The only result that counted for him was that I opened the cage and let him go. Brutus. He called himself this because the neoleprosy had only affected his face then, giving him a lion's muzzle. Quite handsome, as a matter of fact. One finds everything in the recuperators' cage, little girl, and this *specimen* was terribly well educated. There are still lots of operational infolibraries in the Zones.

"The complete programming of artifacts is a myth maintained by the Institute. Actually, it's not as simple as that. Implant memories? Yes, perhaps. But mainly, biosculptors who are into humanoïd artifacts insert the faculty of learning, plus a certain number of predispositions that won't necessarily develop, depending on the circumstances—exactly as it is for human beings." How strange to be discussing the nature of conscience and free will with a half-man crouching in the moonlight. Because yes, Brutus often came back to see me, little girl, but that's another story.

The lady went on being a recuperator . . . after Brutus, however. Not for the sake of delivering specimens to the far-off Institute, but to help them escape. If absolutely necessary, I bring back plants and animals. But not the quasi-, pseudo-, para-, semi-*people*. How long will I be able to go on like this? I suppose that will be another story too. Perhaps it won't be much of a story, after all. The people at the Institute don't really care. In Australia they're so far away from our old, sick Europe. They work at their research programs like sleepwalkers, and probably don't even know why any more. They merely keep on with what they're doing; it's a lot simpler.

And as you can see, little girl, the lady has also kept on with what she was already doing. She's been at it for quite some time. Thirty-two years old and no teeth missing, when most known artifacts only last a maximum of twenty years in the active phase. So one day, having seen how her fellow recuperators thinned around her—radiations, viruses, accidents, or "burn-outs" as the Agency refers to the madness that overtakes most of them—she began to doubt whether she really was an artifact. And she had the tests run again. Not at the Kerens Medical Center, naturally. But one of the axioms of Baïblanca is that everything legitimate has its underground counterpart. In any case, my artifacticity was confirmed! The only reasonable hypothesis was that I wasn't really thirty-two years old and had only fifteen years of actual existence behind me. My birth certificate was false. And all my memories until the time I left home were implants.

And it bothers me. Not only because I must be nearing my "limit of obso-lescence," as the second examining medic so elegantly put it while admir-ing the performance of my biosculptress, just as the first had. But because I wonder why she made me like this, with *these* memories. So detailed, so exact! I've got a right to be a little curious, after all, since I've made my peace with the inevitable, up to a point. It doesn't matter so much now about not asking her anything. I'll be very calm when I see her. I'm not going there to demand an explanation. It's past history. Fifteen years ago, I might have. But now . . .

You want to know what the lady's going to do? So do I. See Taïko before she dies, is that all? Because she's old, Taïko is. Fifty-seven is very old now; you may not live that long, little girl. The average lifespan for you humans is barely sixty, and getting shorter all the time.

See Taïko. Let her see me. No need to say anything, in fact. Just to satisfy my conscience, liberate it, prove that I've really made my peace with myself. (With her? Despite her?) See her. And show her, to be honest. Show her that I've survived, that she's failed if she built me merely to self-destruct. But she can't have wanted that. The more I think about it the less it fits with what I remember about her—even if the memories are implants. No. She must have wanted a "daughter" of her own making, a creature who'd adore her, not foreseeing the innate unpredictability of any creation, the rebellion, the escape . . . *If* I really did escape. But if this is also a pseudomemory, what on earth can it *mean?*

Usually, little girl, the lady takes some reading material or music with her when she's travelling; otherwise she thinks too much. Why didn't I bring along anything to keep me occupied this time? Because I didn't want to be distracted on the way north, to the past? Because I'm trying to work up nostalgia for memories that were probably implanted? Come on, Manou, be serious. I might as well go and have something to drink in the dining car. There's no point keeping on like this, speculating. I'll ask, she'll explain. People don't do what she's done without wanting to explain, surely. Even after all this time.

Perhaps you wonder, little girl, how the lady knows that Taïko Orogatsu is still alive? Well, she took the precaution of checking it out. Without calling the house, of course.

Really, is there any point going? It's perhaps another kind of cowardice, an admission of something missing somewhere inside me. Do I really need to know why she made me this way? I've made myself since. And anyway, I'm going into the Hamburg Zone. I'm not *obliged* to stop.

There, the train has finally ground to a halt. Mahlerzee. You see, little girl, the lady's getting off here.

Try to work up nostalgia? Artificial memory or no, it's impossible to avoid clichés: flood-of-memories, changed-yet-unaltered scenery. The wharf completely submerged by the high tide, the avenue of statues almost buried in the sand. The terrace with its old wooden furniture, the varnish peeled off by the salt air. An unfamiliar black and white cat on the mat in front of the double doors, slightly ajar to show the living room beyond. Not a sound. The porcelain vase with its blue dragon, full of freshly cut flowering broom. I should call out, but I can't, the silence oppresses me. Perhaps she won't recognize me. I'll say anything, that I am a census-taker, that it's the wrong house. Or simply go . . . But, "Hello, Manou," I didn't hear her coming, she's behind me.

Small, so small, diminutive, like a bird. Was she like this? I don't remember her being so frail. The hair is quite white, tousled, she must have been having an afternoon nap. The wrinkles, the flabby cheeks, chin, eyelids. And yet her features seem clearer, as though purified. And the eyes, the eyes haven't changed, big and black, liquid, lively. Try to think: she recognized me, how? Make out her expression . . . I can't, it's been so long that I've lost the habit of reading her face—and it's not the same face. Or it's the same but different. It's her. She's old, she's tired. I look at her, she looks at me, her head thrown back, and I feel huge, a giant, but hollow, fragile.

She speaks first: "So, you recuperated yourself." Sarcasm or satisfaction? And I say, "I'm going into the Hamburg Zone, I'm catching the six o'clock train," and it's a *retort*, I'm on the defensive. I thought we'd chat about trivialities, embarrassed perhaps, before speaking about . . . But it's true she never liked beating about the bush, and then when you're old there's no time to lose, right? Well, I haven't any time to lose either! No, I'm not going to get angry in order to stand up to her; I've learned to control that reflex. It kept me alive, but it's not what I need here. I don't, absolutely don't, want to get angry.

She doesn't make it easy for me: "Not married, then, no children?" And while I suffocate in silence she goes on: "You left to live your own life, you should have been consistent, lived to the full. With your gifts, to become a recuperator! You stopped halfway! Really, I didn't bring you up like that."

I can't mistake her tone. She's *reproaching* me, she's *resentful*!

"You didn't make me like that, you mean! But perhaps you didn't make as much of me as you think!" There we go, fighting. It can't be true, I'm dreaming; fifteen years, and it's as though I left last week!

"So you actually took the trouble to find out? If you'd taken a little more trouble, you'd have learned that artifacts are not necessarily sterile. True, the Institute buried the really pertinent data, but with a little effort. . . . But you didn't even try, eh? So sure you were sterile! When I think of the pains I took to make you completely normal!"

I cool down. Suddenly, somewhere, I cross a threshold, and once over it I'm incredulously calm. That's Taïko. Not a goddess, not a monster. Just a woman set in her ways, with her limitations, her goodwill, her unawareness. I hear myself saying almost politely, "Still, I failed their tests."

Apparently she's crossed a threshold of her own at the same time, in the same direction. She sighs. "I should have told you sooner. When you were little. But I kept putting it off. And then it was too late, you were right in the middle of the terrible teens, and I lost my temper. I couldn't tell you just then, you can understand that! Well, yes, I should have; perhaps it would have calmed you down. I was so furious after you left. I expected a phone call, a letter. I said to myself, at least the Institute can't find out about her. And in fact they know nothing. The Kerens medic called me first. A nice person, actually. He never told. You were a brilliant student that disappeared without a trace. They offered me their sympathy, you know, Kerens and the Institute. Afterward, I tried to have you found. Why didn't you call me, you stubborn mule?"

I'm the one being accused, can you beat that? I stare hard at her. And all of a sudden it's too much. I burst out laughing. So does she.

We're still the same, after all this time.

"But you came, anyway. None too soon either."

After that, a long silence. Embarrassed, pensive? *She* is pensive. "You ought to try. Having children. There's no guarantee you'll succeed, but it's highly probable. Have you really never tried?"

Does she realize what she's *saying*?

"What, there's never been anyone?"

Rick, the first, yes. And a few others, initially as a challenge, just to see, and after that because it didn't really matter what I was, thanks to Brutus. But still! I retort that knowing you're an artifact doesn't exactly make for harmonious relations with normal humans.

"*Normal humans!* I can't believe my ears! You were born, the fact that it was in the lab down there doesn't change anything. You grew up, you made mistakes, and you'll make more. You think, you feel, you choose. What more do you want? You're a normal human being, like all the other so-called artifacts."

Oh yes. Like the Walker and the Sleeper, I suppose? I grit my teeth. She looks me in the eye, impatient: "Well, what's the matter?" Doesn't even let me try to speak. "There may have been biosculptors who were stupid or crazy, but that's another matter. Of course some artifacts were very limited. The Institute made sure of it by suppressing the necessary data, all Permahlion's research. They made him practically an outlaw, fifty years ago, and after that they did everything to discourage artorganics. But it didn't keep us from carrying on."

I can't understand what she is saying. She must see it, and it gives her fresh cause for annoyance. "Well, what do you think, that you're the only one in the world? There are hundreds of you, silly! Just because the original human race is doomed to disappear sooner or later doesn't mean that all life must end. It was all right for the Eschatoï to think that way, not for you!"

And suddenly, quietly, sadly, "You really thought I was a monster, didn't you?"

What can I say? I subside onto the sofa and she sits down as well, not too near, slowly, sparing her knees. Yes, she's old, really old. When she becomes animated, the expression in her eyes, her way of talking, her leap-frog sentences are there; but when she's quiet it all flickers out. I look away. After the silence, all I can find to say is, "You made others? Like me?"

The answer is straightforward, almost absentminded: "No. I could have made others, probably, but for me, one baby was already a lot."

"You made me . . . a baby?"

"I wanted you to be as normal as possible. There's nothing to prevent artorganic matter growing as slowly as organic matter. Actually, it's the best way. The personality develops along with it. I wasn't in a hurry."

"But you never made others . . . in the usual way?"

A sad-amused smile: "Come on, Manou. I was sterile, of course. Or rather, my karyotype was so damaged that it was unthinkable to try to have children in the usual way, as you put it. But you're a lot more resistant than we are. The beauty of artorganics is that one can improve on nature. That's the danger as well. But in the long run, it means I was able to give you a chance to adapt better than we could to the world you'd be dealing with. Do you remember? You were never sick when you were little."

And I still heal very quickly. Oh yes, the medic in the Kerens Center pointed that out. That was a constant factor in artifacts. Not a proof, however; there had been a fairly widespread mutation of this kind about a hundred years earlier. "It is from studying this phenomenon, among others, that artorganic matter ended up being created. There are still instances of it among normal humans." It was a parallelism, he emphasized, not a proof. But an indication that, combined with others, added to the certainty of my being an artifact.

"I'm telling you"—she's still adamant—"you should try to have children."

She's really determined to know whether or not her experiment has worked, is that it?

"Thirty-two is a bit late, don't you think?"

"A bit late? You're in your prime!"

"For how long?"

I'm standing up, fists clenched. I wasn't aware of getting up, wasn't aware of shaking. If she notices it, she gives no sign. She shrugs: "I don't know." And before I can react she smiles the old sarcastic smile: "At least as long as I, in any case. Longer, if I've been successful. But for exactly how long I don't know."

She looks straight at me, screwing up her eyes a little. Suddenly no longer old and tired, she's ageless; so very gently sad, so very wise. "You thought I could tell you. That's why you came."

"You made me, you should know!"

"Someone made me, too. Not in the same way, but someone made me. And I don't know when I'm going to die either." The small, ironic smile comes back. "I'm beginning to get some idea, mind you." The smile disappears. "But I'm not certain, I don't know the date. That's what being human is like, too. Haven't you learned anything in fifteen years? The only way to be sure is to kill yourself, which you didn't. So keep on. You'll still live long enough to forget lots of things and learn them all over again."

And she looks at the old watch that slides around her birdlike wrist. "Two hours before your train. Would you like something to eat?"

"Are you in a hurry for me to leave?"

"For our first time it would be better not to try our luck too far."

"You really think I'll come back?"

Gently, she says, "I *hope* you'll come back." Again the sarcastic smile. "With a belly this big."

I shake my head; I can't take any more. She's right. I rise to get my bag near the door. "I think I'll walk back to the station."

Still, she goes with me onto the terrace and we walk down to the beach together. As we pass one of the statues, she puts a hand on the grey, shapeless stone. "It was his house, Permahlion's. He brought the statues here himself. He liked to scuba-dive when he was young. I was his very last pupil, you know. He made the first artorganic humans, but he didn't call them artifacts. It killed him, what was done to them after him."

As always when the sun finally breaks through the clouds, it gets hot quickly. As I shrug off my jacket, I see her looking at me; she barely reaches my shoulder. It must be a long time since she was in the sun; she's so pale.

I scan the distance for something else to look at. A few hundred yards from the beach there seem to be shapes jumping in the waves. Dolphins? Swimmers? An arm above the water, like a sign . . .

She shades her eyes. "No, they're Permahlion's mermaids. I call them mermaids, anyway. I don't know why, but they've been coming here for several seasons. They don't talk and they're very shy." At my stupefied silence, she remarks acidly: "Don't tell me you have something against humanoïds?"

No, of course not, but . . .

She brushes off my questions, her hands spread in front of her: "I'll look for everything there is about them in the lab. You'll be able to see it. If you ever come back." A cloud seems to pass over her rapidly, and she fades again. "I'm tired, my daughter. The sun isn't good for me these days. I'm going to lie down for a bit."

And she goes, just like that, without another word or gesture, a tiny figure stumbling a little in the sand. I want to watch her go, and I can't watch her go, as though it were the last time, perhaps because it is the last time, and "my daughter" has lodged itself in my chest somewhere; it grows, pushing my ribs, and the pressure becomes so strong that I shed my clothes and dive into the green, warm water to swim toward the sea creatures. My first burst of energy exhausted, I turn on my back and look toward the house. The tiny silhouette has stopped on the terrace. I wave an arm, I shout, "I'll come back, Mother!" I laugh, and my tears mingle with the sea.

UNDER ANOTHER MOON

Dave Duncan

Dave Duncan was born and educated in Scotland, but has lived in Canada since 1955. Duncan writes that "after a long career as a petroleum geologist, he discovered it was easier to invent his own worlds and switched to writing." He has published seventeen novels in the past eight years, about evenly divided between fantasy and science fiction, two short stories, and one poem. His SF novels, beginning with *A Rose-Red City* and *Shadow* (both 1987), have all appeared from Del Rey Books in the U.S. with notable commercial success. His best-known fantasy is the *Seventh Sword* sequence; he is currently completing the four-volume "Man of His Word" fantasy series. His SF novel *West of January*, perhaps his best work to date, won the 1990 Aurora Award for best long-form work in English.

The *Science Fiction Encyclopedia* comments: "Dave Duncan's work has all the flamboyance of tales written strictly for escape, but (as has been noted by critics) never for long allows his readers to forget what kind of problems he is inviting them to dodge. His most virtuoso passages seem almost brazenly to dance with despair." "Under Another Moon" is a tale of love and death that blurs distinctions between fantasy and SF. It seems, hauntingly, to echo Le Guin's *The Left Hand of Darkness* and to cast a penumbral glow over its world. It is a dance of death and a dance of triumph.

Was this what being a man was? Was this what being an earl was? Jauro stood in his own hall, before his own assembled household, and listened in furious silence as his honour was trampled in the dirt, his courage mocked, his ancestry insulted.

Did they think he was a milksop woman who would endure such abuse?

Blood roared in his ears and his fists trembled with a yearning to draw and smite the upstart envoy who came in the name of the king, this bearer of the royal scorn. Lackey! Coward! Were he not wrapped in the king's office, he would not dare speak such words before the earl of Rathmuir; not in his own hall, not anywhere. Or, if he tried it, he would die.

Yet in truth he was more like to slay Jauro instead, for he was larger and older, a man in his prime. No grey showed in his beard, and his eyes were quick. The sword arm left uncovered by his furs was a conspicuously thicker and hairier arm than Jauro's was, and his powerful fingers were already crooked for the draw. His stance was that of a man poised to provoke violence and then meet it, a man enjoying his mission, reveling in the rage he was rousing, a rage that would not be hidden by the earl's fair beard. Behind him stood six stalwarts of the royal fyrd—greyer, capable veterans, smirking in silence as the young victim squirmed under their burly leader's scorn.

And all around the walls, the earl's own people listened also, in shock and dismay: the white-haired elders on their stools, the children standing behind them, the women in turn at their backs, holding their babies, or clasping their daughters' shoulders. Back of them all stood the men, teeth glinting within their beards, and their hands clenched on their sword hilts. It was the custom that the men stood at the rear for such a reception, and the reason was obvious, although Jauro had never realized it before—if he were to draw against the visitors, he would be dead before his own fyrd could struggle through the others to aid him. Blood would muddy the rushes on the clay floor, and the earl's blood would flow first.

Acrid smoke roiled from the fireplaces. Beyond the open door at the far end of the hall, misty tendrils of rain swept over the royal horses and the two men left out there to hold them. The early dusk of winter was closing in, and the hall was growing dim—and cold also, unless it was only rage that darkened Jauro's sight and moved on his arms like an icy breath, raising the hairs on them and chilling the sweat below his fur cloak and cloth leggings. Nothing was clear to him but the face of the envoy, the hateful close-bearded young man whose eyes were laughing even as he spouted this hateful royal insolence. This vomit of lies, this pig piss!

And the envoy looked far smaller than he had done only minutes earlier; he was shrinking as Jauro's fury choked off discretion. Was this what being a man was? Young the earl might be, but he was no virgin in mortal combat; he had seen the colour of men's lifeblood and he could feel a rising lust to see it again. Soon, very soon, he would decide that dying was better than hearing more of this *horsefarting*.

Just before he lost control, it ended: "Thus spake His Majesty, King Reggalo, the Merciful, the Just." Silence, and the envoy's eyes shone with cruel pleasure as he waited for the response.

The fires crackled, and even the hiss of the rain seemed audible in the hush. How could so many be so quiet? Water dripping through the thatch played a faint staccato rhythm in corners. A child whimpered and its mother put a hand over its mouth.

Jauro took a deep breath, then another, as he fought for calm, as he planned his words lest they tremor and betray him.

Be a man!

"We thank you for His Majesty's message." His voice came out deep and strange to him, but it was gratifyingly steady. He heard a small sigh at his back. He had been meant to hear it—Fromto was relieved that the words were no more warlike than that. But they were defiance nonetheless.

"His Majesty's command!" Mockery twisting the tight-coiled blackness of the envoy's beard.

"I shall send my reply before the end of the least-month."

The envoy put his head on one side, while his companions shifted and glanced around. "Reply? You misheard, Earl Jauro."

"I heard. But we have barely buried our dead. We must tend our wounded, our widows and our orphans. Bands of rebels still roam the moors. His Majesty will comprehend that my duty to the safety of my people is also my duty to His Majesty."

"His command was specific—you will accompany us, and your daughter also."

To argue would seem like weakness, but his people were listening, and it was their blood Jauro's defiance was risking—his own blood was already as good as spent. They deserved a reason.

"Evildoers have spoken untruths to His Majesty. My loyalty is unswerving."

"You will be given a hearing," the envoy promised, and his smile made the promise a threat.

"Also, my child is not yet old enough to consider marriage."

The envoy's eyes seemed to dance with merriment. "His Majesty understood that your family matured young—or was Your Lordship deprived of comfort?"

Insult! Fromto growled softly in the background, and Jauro's hand twitched towards his sword hilt. At once the envoy's hand was on his own, in a move too fast to see. Deadly fast! So Reggalo had sent his best brawler, who would either slay Jauro out of hand or parry his thrusts to impotence—and to draw against the king's envoy would be treason. It was a trap within a trap.

With a mighty effort, Jauro spread his fingers and moved them away from danger. "His Majesty has been misinformed on many matters."

The envoy sneered and released his sword in a flamboyant gesture. "The child will benefit by completing its childhood in the civilized surroundings of His Majesty's palace."

Some of the men by the walls muttered angrily—Jauro silenced them with a glare. "But this is my heir we are discussing. I must consider the child's welfare. His Majesty's daughter, this Princess Uncoata . . . I understand her first marriage proved sterile. She has a crooked back and her wits are the laughingstock of the markets?"

"Your Lordship is the one misinformed," said the envoy, his companions' open amusement belying his words. "We speak of Prince Uncoato, a man of undoubted strength and virility who yearns to know his bride. A larger, heavier man than Your Lordship."

Little Thorti given to an idiot cripple? Tiny, delicate Thorti with her trilling song and her smoke-gray eyes? Jauro's throat knotted at the images that came to his mind—he had seen that shambling Uncoato once, and shuddered to think what such a monster might have become since. Sweat was trickling down his face; he could stand no more of this. "I repeat that His Majesty has been misinformed on many matters. I shall gather my witnesses and send my reply within three days."

"His Majesty's command—"

Jauro roared. "You have far to ride before dark, Your Grace!"

Satisfaction twisted the envoy's lips. He had sought to provoke violence, but this response would do: royal edict rejected, hospitality refused, treason, defiance, open revolt. The king's command had been crafted to produce nothing less.

"Then in sorrow I bid Your Lordship farewell." The man bowed, but the move barely reached his shoulders. In contempt he turned his back, and his supporters moved aside to let him through. They clutched their sword hilts and glanced warily around as they followed him to the door. Wet leather squeaked in their boots.

Jauro stood and watched the departure, his whole body trembling with suppressed fury.

Fromto was speaking at his back. "Loothio! Follow and see which way they ride. Ambloto—gather your band and saddle up, lest they do mischief on their way."

Sensible, practical Fromto! Jauro was still too tense to have thought of those things. He started to turn, and was suddenly encircled by rope-thin arms. It was Thorti, the smoke-gray eyes filled with tears, peering up at him in horror.

"Mother! You must not flaunt the king!"

Jauro tried to break free, and the child clung fiercely—tiny and yet made strong by desperation; far smaller than he had been at that age, and he was not a large man, as the envoy had so greatly enjoyed mentioning.

"Be still!" he barked. He glanced over Thorti's head to the elders, who were on their feet now, gathering into a group and starting to jabber shrilly. Their bald heads and wispy white beards shone in the gloom. "Venerable ones—prepare your counsel, and we shall hear you shortly."

"Mother!" Thorti cried, louder now. "You must not defy the king just for my sake. I shall marry the prince, if that is his royal will."

"Never!" Jauro untwined himself and, laughing, swung his child up at arms' length so their eyes were level. It was no strain—he could have held the stance for hours—but then he saw the hurt and humiliation flower in those smoky eyes. *Idiot!* Children of this age scorned such baby games. He changed his hold to a hug, clasping Thorti tight to his furs.

"You also have grown, my beloved," he said. "You are so heavy now!"

Thorti's voice came softly, privately into his ear. "It is almost time! The prince or another!"

"What!" Thorta?

He lowered her gently to the floor, as though she were suddenly fragile. He sank down on one knee and stared at the eager blush now spreading over the tiny bird-like face.

"Already? Oh, my sweet! When?"

Her words quavered with the conflict of joy and fear: "Yesterday! It came yesterday."

His child a woman! His heart overflowed with sudden memory of his own youth, and of the fearsome transition to adulthood—long wanted, yet unexpectedly sudden, welcome and yet terrifying. He struggled for words, and could not find them, as he so often could not find words for his child now. Thorti . . . Thorta . . . was tense under his gaze, not responding to his smile, frightened of the muscular, hairy warrior he had become. For almost two years now, he had felt a growing sense of loss and guilt whenever he spoke with his child; in the three days since his return it had been worse than before, an unbearable pain in his throat. Clumsy and tongue-tied, he could do nothing but hug the tiny form, and pat the thin shoulders. *Thorta, Thorta, my beloved!* When had they lost each other? Why could he not put his feelings into words?

Was that also part of being a man?

Blinking, he glanced up to see if Fromto had heard the news, but he was still snapping orders as the men fought their way to him through the crowd—sending out patrols and setting guards, ensuring that no band of hotheads took off after the envoy on some crazy mission of misplaced honour.

Jauro kissed his daughter's forehead. "I congratulate you, my dearest Thorta. I am sorry that such good tidings are marred by coming at so evil a time." How cold that sounded, how dismally inadequate! "But it is not only your welfare I have in mind. Were I to obey the king's command and go with his messengers, then my life would not be worth a pail of chicken droppings."

She gasped. "But why? What have you done to deserve the king's frown?"

What indeed? "Nothing at all! Others have lied about me. Once I have prepared my case, I can go to His Majesty and clear my name." He smiled gently—if a bearded face ever could smile gently. Thorta seemed unconvinced, and he knew there were sharp wits in that little head. "To clear the honour of our house!" he insisted. "I shall not bequeath you a blemished scutcheon. But now I must speak with your father. Stay with Lallia."

With a sharp stare that tore at his heart, Thorta stepped back, biting her knuckles. Feeling again that he had betrayed her, Jauro rose and slapped a hand on Fromto's shoulder. "Come!" he said, and headed for the doorway that led to the private apartments. Lallia moved forward to speak, but he strode by her without a glance. He feared what bitter gloating he might read in his wife's face.

He marched down the black corridor and memory guided him to the heavy plank door of his chamber, which creaked on its rusty hinges as it always did. The room was dark, and felt dank yet stuffy, the familiar sour odor of the furs on the bed magnified by the winter dampness. It faced west, and the window was a blurred red glow of sunset shining through the panes of cowgut, although other specks of brightness showed white, where rain had washed the chinking from the logs.

Outside the cattle were bellowing at the lateness of their milking, and distant shouts and whinnyings told of the patrols saddling up. A muddy job that would be . . .

For a moment Jauro stared uneasily at the bloody glow of the casement—was it perhaps an omen, a warning from the gods? Rain drummed on it when the wind moved, and the wind itself breathed softly through the gaps. He had made such windowpanes himself, when he was young and his fingers more suited to a needle than a sword. He remembered his mother thanking him and praising his workmanship, and he had been proud-to-bursting of that praise. Hagthra, his mother . . . And Hagthro was barely three years in his grave now, and already the earldom as good as lost, if the king wanted it lost. Three years of blood and battle.

He jumped at a sound behind him. Fromto had entered unheard and was striking a flint. A tiny flame flickered on tinder, seeming impossibly bright. Then a rush blazed up with a hiss, and the cramped cell was filled with golden light, making shadows leap on plank and log, on the bed high-piled with marten pelts, on hanging shields, on pikes and swords leaning in a corner, on an iron-bound chest.

There was gray in Fromto's beard, and worry had creased his face like a rutted track. He kicked backward, and the door creaked and slammed.

For a moment the two gazed at each other, then the older man hung the rushlight on a sconce and struck his favorite pose, with left hand on sword hilt and the other on his hip. "Trouble comes with three moons, they say."

"And I should have been born under another," Jauro said sadly. "Why? What has provoked this?"

Fromto regarded him steadily for a moment. "For counsel you must speak to the elders. I am a warrior yet, My Lord."

Silver in his beard, grizzled locks fringing a barren scalp, and yet he was undoubtedly a warrior: big-shouldered, solid. He was still taller and broader than Jauro. And he was deeply troubled if he did not trust himself to use a more affectionate form of address—but more likely it was Jauro's self-control he distrusted.

"You are still the best warrior I have, but you are also my best advisor. We both know what the elders will say. I can feel the iron in my heart already—or do you think he will chop off my head?"

"Reggalo hates making decisions. He may just throw you in jail to rot."

"He has made this one fast enough." Jauro thought sourly of the latest battle—three score men lost, many more wounded. The toll could easily have been much greater, but good fortune had saved his earldom yet again, and now it was to be stolen from him by the overlord in whose name he had fought.

Fromto was shaking his big head. "The plan may have been made long since. Had you lost, he would have moved against the rebels. Since you won, he moves against you. He may not even have heard the outcome himself yet. The orders could have been drawn a middle-month ago, or more."

"But why?" Jauro demanded again, fighting to keep his voice steady. "Why should he doubt my loyalty? Is he afraid I will raise arms against him? That's crazy! I can't field one man to his ten."

The old swordsman turned and sat on the bed, making the thongs creak, and he slumped there in silence, as though weary of battles. Remembering that there could always be ears at knotholes, Jauro settled at Fromto's side, and the bed swayed alarmingly. "Well?" he said quietly.

"You are the victim of your own success, My Lord. You have astonished them all. When Hagthro died and a woman inherited, it seemed inevitable that the ravens would take Rathmuir. And now Rathmuir stands triumphant, and the ravens are scattered. A wild border upland is become a safe and loyal province. And the king has three daughters and four sons he acknowledges."

"Little has been my doing. It was you who made Rathmuir a land fit for a prince."

Fromto glanced around with something like his usual wiry humor. "If I did, then I served you ill, my dearest lord. But you are too modest. It was always for you we fought, and now it is your cunning that lets our little band rout hordes so great. Had the men not trusted you at the bridge . . ."

Was it a sign of age that Fromto liked to fight old battles, or a sign of youth that Jauro had no patience for them? There had been too many battles in the past three years. Hagthro had been barely cold before the earl of Lawnshor and the sheriff of Highcastle had decided to divide his fief between them. It had been Fromto who had raised the fyrd, who had out-marched, and out-maneuvered, and in the final reckoning out-fought the aggressors. Today that hairy ox of an envoy had brazenly accused Jauro of personal atrocities, but Jauro had been home with the women the whole time.

No sooner had Lawnshor and Highcastle been settled, than Earl Sando of Sandmuir had tried to gather up the pieces. That time Jauro had been there to watch his churls die for him, tending horses, aiding the wounded.

And when the Trinians had come over the border, he had been a full combatant. He had served his own cause as a pikeman in his own fyrd through that whole long, brutal summer. He had scars to prove it.

But he had taken his rightful place in the campaign against the rebels; he had commanded. He had become a man. Or had he? He felt desperately unsure of himself now. Would any true man have stood silent under that brutal tirade from the envoy? It was easy enough to wave a sword and lead a charge when bloodlust ran hot in the veins and three hundred men roared along behind. Any man or woman or child could do that, any fool. What man—real man—would have submitted to what he had endured this evening? He had stood there tongue-tied like a craven woman.

"I should have listened to the elders," he said harshly.

The elders had advised him to join the rebels, not fight them.

Fromto chuckled. "The old forget honour and courage as they forget so many other important things. You were loyal to your liege, and that is no small jewel in your coronet."

"A shame that my liege were not more loyal to me," Jauro said bitterly.

Muscle tensed in the big man's sword arm, flexing the puckered lines of old scars. "Truly! But had you marched with the rebels, you would have died with them. The cause is hopeless while Reggalo holds the south. Here or farther down the road . . . they would never have reached the plains."

Possibly, but the rebels had made many mistakes, which Jauro had been able to exploit, mistakes they would not have made had he been at their head. The campaign had revealed that he had a talent for tactics—but evidently no skill in politics, for his loyalty had been repaid in treachery. The elders had been correct.

There was no more resistance left, no one to trouble Rathmuir, so the royal spider hoped to gift it to his ogre daughter. A marriage of Thorta to Uncoato would wrap Jauro's earldom in a legal shroud that the other nobles could see buried without much scruple.

What man would submit to such injustice?

He sat in glum silence, not even objecting when Fromto put his arm around him. Indeed, that felt seductively good, a memory of times past. The rushlight hissed and sparked; rain drummed against the casement, but the fading bellows of the cattle reminded him of the slow move of summer sun on dairy walls, and the warm smell of cows. Milking and sewing and rearing babies . . . they seemed very pleasant occupations in retrospect.

"Remind me," he said. "I wanted this, didn't I?"

Fromto chuckled. "I did warn you. You were only thirty-two—"

"Thirty-three! Well, almost."

"And you are still not yet thirty-five! Few complete menopause by then. Many do not even start until they are forty. And your change was swift."

"Completed?" Jauro blurted the word, then added in a whisper, "I do not feel very complete. I feel stuck halfway."

"You do not behave so! Shall I go back to calling you 'Jaura'? Or even 'Jauri'? What would you do if I did?"

"I would start by cutting out your lights and throttling you with them."

"You see? But I can still be a friend. Friends give comfort, and you have just been dealt a sorry blow, a most foul blow. Oh, love! Did you think men never had doubts, or fears, or regrets?"

"No, of course not."

"And surely Lallia has now no cause to—No, do not rage, man! I am merely teasing."

The earl forced himself to relax again. A real man should be able to stand teasing, if it were kindly meant, as this was. He no longer had the option of feminine tears. But he was too tense tonight for humor, and he wondered why Fromto was wandering so far from the point.

Then a hard jab of shame brought understanding. "The men are calling me 'Jaura,' you think? After what I did tonight . . . what I didn't do?"

Fromto laughed. "No! No! They may have been puzzled, for they are simple souls, but they trust you—there is not a man in the fyrd who would not trade his backbone for yours, love. Few men anywhere could have resisted the urge to draw under such abuse." The hug tightened. "I was proud of you! Strife is not always the path of true manhood, but new men rarely know that; it needs be learned. The road is hard, but we all must travel it. I have helped all I can, my love."

Jauro smiled, hiding his uneasiness. Was the big man being so unusually sentimental because he was feeling vulnerable himself? "I could have done nothing without you, husband! I need you still, and never more than now. Counsel me! Why does the king bring these false charges?" Again he tasted injustice like gall in his mouth.

But his query failed to call back the man of action, the decisive Fromto of tiltyard and battlefield. The old warrior sighed. "If one of your thralls had a nubile daughter and you wanted to have pleasure of her . . . I know you don't, but suppose in this case you were determined to do so. What would happen?"

Jauro squirmed. He had been tempted many times in the last two years. Since the flames of manhood had blazed up within him, he could hardly see a tallish child without secretly wondering how close it was to menarche and womanhood. Women's desire was slower and deeper and more purposeful. Man's lust was fire and instant madness, and some earls had no scruples in the matter. The odd one would even claim the maidenhead of every adolescent in his fief.

"Then I would have my pleasure of her, I suppose."

"Exactly. No one could stop the earl, or would dare try. Why do you think your people love you? Your mother was the same—he did not steal the virgins either. But Reggalo has decided to steal your fief, and no one can stop the king. We are too remote for you to have friends at court, and your neighbors were your foes. Their neighbors are now frightened of you, or jealous. No one will take your part, no one who matters."

Then the great shoulders straightened at last, the comforting arm was withdrawn, and the voice hardened in purpose. "Had you drawn against the envoy, then the lords must have all condemned you. This way a few may yet waver, and blunt the edge of the enemy's purpose. And certainly your forbearance has won us time to restore our arms, My Lord! Even if they dare a winter advance, they will need at least a great-month to assemble the fyrd—"

Jauro sighed. Was this the man who had taught him strategy? He had aged visibly during the last campaign, but he should not be so blind as this. "We do not resist!"

"What?"

"Even if we wanted to, there is no time. You said yourself that Reggalo's plans were made several least-months ago. He would have brought up his fyrd to . . . to the Azburn valley, probably. Or closer. We stopped the rebels, but he was ready had we failed. The envoy will be there by dawn. And by dawn I must be gone."

"My Lord!" The wrinkles in Fromto's shadowed face seemed to writhe in dismay. He was still shocked. "Rathmuir will stand by you! After so much blood, we shall never—"

"Too much blood!" This time, strangely, it was Jauro who put his arm around Fromto. "The fyrd has bled too often to uphold my house! This time is different. The others came to loot and drive off, so the men of Rathmuir fought for their own livings as well as mine. But the king wants the fief intact. I am the only obstacle. I must go."

He watched the outward signs of struggle in the warrior's face. Finally Fromto said coldly, "Whither can you flee?"

Good question! The Trinians would be happy to use Earl Jauro for archery practice. West lay the sea. "To Andlain, I suppose."

"Cross the ranges in winter?"

"Why not? Others have." He was strong, and young for a man; in the last campaign he had endured hardship as well as any.

Fromto shook his head sadly. "You do not know what storms can do in the passes. Even large parties may vanish. And what of Thorti?"

What indeed? Jauro had forgotten the danger to his child.

His daughter!

"Thorta!" he said, smiling at his former husband.

A gasp. "No! When?"

"It just . . . She just told me, before we came here. Yesterday, she said." Jauro smiled at the astonishment on the older man's face. "Our child is become a woman. Now you have a son, and I a daughter."

The old warrior blinked eyes that had become suddenly shiny in the wavering torchlight. "You must . . . or I, I suppose . . . must counsel her. Yet she is fourteen, so it was due! She will find a woman to counsel her . . ."

Jauro's sense of loss came stabbing back. "You think I have forgotten so soon?"

"Of course not, love! I doubt if any man or woman has ever forgotten the terrors of menarche. I just meant that talk about such things comes better from women, somehow." After a moment, he added, "It was not your fault, you know! Our bodies do these things without asking our permission."

Jauro made a vague chuckling noise to dismiss the subject and ease the pain. "You will miss her, I know, but she must come with me, and you must stay. Enjoy your well-earned retirement!" Feeling his eyelids prickle, he forced a smile and gently tweaked the grey-streaked beard. "And you must take a new wife now, Fromto, my husband. You have waited too long."

He had lost this argument before, and hated it because of the absurd jealousy it always aroused in him, but this would be the last time. And this sad severance was also a part of his entry to manhood, a step that Fromto had delayed far too long. "I command you, as your earl! It is your duty. We have many widows who will rejoice to marry so great a warrior, so fine a man. I will happily testify to your skills."

Fromto did not respond to the joking, and Jauro was astonished to see tears flood those weary eyes. He had seen them burn with the joy of battle; he had seen them wild with passion, but he could not recall ever seeing tears in them before. Not even when the twins died.

"Husband?"

Fromto hesitated, then blurted out: "Jauro, do you love me no more?"

"How can you ask? After all we were to each other . . . how could I not?" He thought of the nervous virgin he had been, so awed when the virile Fromto had proposed to her. He thought of seventeen years of marriage, of passion and suffering shared, of the gentle strength and comfort so freely given. He thought that all in all he had been a good wife, but Fromto had been the sort of husband every child dreamed of winning. "Of course I . . . I love you, husband, and always will. But—"

The old man clapped a hand on his knee. "Sweet words come hard to men's lips, do they not? But if you love me, then why will you have me put to death? Do you think I have no enemies? Do you think Prince Uncoato will ask me to lead his fyrd for him?"

"By the gods and moons!" How could Jauro have overlooked that? A king who would so betray a loyal vassal would be capable of taking vengeance on his relatives and underlings. "Of course you will have to come with us!" His heart skipped with joy as he realized that he would not be parted from Fromto. He could have found no more stalwart companion for the trek—nor for the lonely future beyond.

Fromto sighed with relief. "My lord is gracious! And also an optimist, if he thought he could stop me. I trust you as I trust no other man, but you are taking my son over the passes in winter!"

Again Thorta! But Jauro dare not leave her, and he would not gamble his daughter's life as heedlessly as he would his own. He must have companions, and who better or more obvious than Fromto?

"And Lallia," the old man said, "and—"

"Not Lallia!"

Fromto frowned. "My Lord . . ."

"No. She stays—I shall find another to replace her." Lallia had been a terrible mistake. In the three days since he returned from the last battle, Jauro had barely spoken with his wife, and he had not summoned her to his bed—but the problem was now obviously solved. "The king will find her a husband more to her taste. As Thorta comes with us, we shall need some stalwart companions, and she should have female company. You must mount a whirlwind courtship! Is there any mature widow who comes to mind, who would agree to depart with us?"

The frost-fringed lips smiled cryptically. "Most like."

Jauro laughed with relief, "That is good! I do not need a yattering elder to advise me, I need a strong sword at my side—a wife will keep you young, husband."

"Young? I am sixty-two!"

"And virile as any hot-blooded forty-year-old!"

Fromto smiled bashfully, then nodded. "As my lord commands."

How strange that felt! The positions of a lifetime were shifting and it was Jauro who must guide and comfort Fromto, as though the plow must pull the ox. Life was a constant drizzle of little surprises like that, reminding him that he was a man now.

"Go and congratulate your son on her womanhood, and then see to your wooing! We have a least-month's work to do before dawn!"

The big man nodded, and rose. Jauro stood also, and for an awkward moment the two men hesitated. Then they embraced—briefly, and without words.

The door creaked twice and closed behind the old warrior. The rushlight flared and then dimmed. The room stank of its greasy smoke.

Exile! What future for a dispossessed earl, fleeing from his overlord? Jauro put the thought out of his mind, deciding he would deal with the future when it arrived. Lately he seemed to spend much less time worrying— was that another sign of manhood, or something purely personal, perhaps stemming from his rank?

Now to dispose of his finery . . . He winced at a twinge of stiffness in his leg, where a Trinian sword had drawn his first blood. Wet weather always found that wound. He threw open the lid of the chest, and pulled off the skimpy gold chain that he had donned to impress the envoy. He unwrapped his sable robe and tossed it on the bed, unbuckled his sword and threw that after. He was reaching down to find his favorite old shabby bearskin kirtle, when the door creaked again and the room brightened. Shivering in the cool dampness of the evening, he straightened.

Lallia closed the door and leaned against it, studying him. She had brought a lantern, and in its steady glow he was at once aware of his nudity, for his leggings hid nothing of importance. Trust the wretched woman to catch him at such a moment!

Desire flared up in him instantly. This was what it was to be a man— slaved by passion, perpetually vulnerable to lightning strokes of lust.

"You are leaving," she said.

"You have your revenge at last."

She smiled grimly.

"You came to gloat, I suppose?" he growled. His body was reacting shamelessly to her calculating inspection.

"Despite all the blood you have shed, your earldom is taken from you and you must flee?"

"I should have been born under another moon."

She smiled again, but more cryptically.

She had been Sando's only son, and the wife of his chief thane, Chilo. Sando had died in battle, and his two daughters also. Fromto had put Chilo to death and had wanted to slay Lallia. That had been the first time Jauro had exercised his authority to overrule his former husband, the leader of his fyrd. Goaded by unfamiliar male impulses, he had fallen instantly and hopelessly in love with this gorgeous woman. He had called out to save her, proclaiming that he would take her as his wife—and his voice had cracked into an absurd soprano as he did so. He could still remember the titters of his men.

And he could not forget his shame and her derision when he had first tried to consummate that enforced marriage. Since then he had matured, and things had been different—but never easy. And his desire had never faded. Even now it was making him giddy, after two great-months of lonely sleep in wet heather.

Her braids hung dark as a raven's wing, her eyes shone black like a moonless night.

"Gloat, then!" he snapped. "Enjoy your victory. I hope Reggalo finds you a more satisfactory husband."

"That could not be," she said softly. She hung the lantern on the other sconce and then raised her hands to the ties of her robe.

Unbelieving, he watched as she shed the garment, letting it fall to the packed clay of the floor.

"What trickery is this?" he demanded hoarsely. Was she trying to delay his departure to make time for some foul treachery?

Lallia dropped the linen from her loins and stood naked before him, shivering. "I must attend my lord, as is my duty."

He opened his mouth to send her away, and could not do it. His heart beat ever faster as he stared at the pale perfection of her skin, of a body even lovelier than he had remembered. He had never borne breasts like those, save when suckling Thorti. Now his were shrunk to useless flat pads of muscle, hidden beneath a thickening yellow thatch. Other organs had sprouted from his groin to compensate for the loss, and a painful throbbing there betrayed his desperate need.

She came close, peering up at him. "Husband?"

He took her in his arms distrustfully. "Why?"

"For love."

"Love? After all those kind words? The mockery? The hate?"

She blinked sudden tears. "Could you not see? Must a man forget so soon how a woman thinks?"

"I never thought as you do." The room was cold, and he pulled her tight against him. He had grown taller since he first embraced her.

"Act now," she whispered, "and talk later."

He lifted her onto the bed and pulled a fur over them both. She came alive in his arms like a wildcat, and they coupled madly, frantically, gloriously. They cried aloud in the sharing of rapture.

It was like nothing he had ever experienced, certainly not with her, nor even in his first youthful passion with Fromto. The joy of giving joy was familiar, the physical ecstasy more intense, but he also discovered echoes of every other gratification he had ever known—rage of battle, thrill of hunting, joy of conquest . . . the contentment of being needed as a babe needs its mother, of being wanted as his child had wanted him, the satisfaction of possession and the strength of a protector, of being gentle when he could be strong, and of might prevailing. It was everything to him, as love had never been before, at once a simpler, easier act and a more consuming response, a totality of many wants that had been separate for him in the past. And as his excitement crested beyond containment, he thought that this more than anything must be what made men what men were, what he was. Fromto had been right, his state was no longer in doubt. And finally thought ended as he gloried in the culminating proof of manhood.

And in the long limp silence that followed, the damp astonishment, he realized that he was still wearing his leggings and boots.

"Oh, my love!" he panted in the musty darkness under the furs. "My love, my love! Why now?"

For a while he got no reply, then she sniffed, as though ready to weep. "I said unkind things, My Lord."

"Unkind? I never met a woman with such a tongue."

She sniffled more, then chuckled. "Thank you, My Lord! You did not see? And it did not work. I could never make you force me."

"Force you? *Force you?*" He threw back the hem of the rug so he could see her face in the lantern glow. The rushlight had gone out. "Force a woman?"

"Chilo did," she whispered. "When he was drunk. When the time was wrong. Often."

"Moons preserve me! Lady, I swear . . . I was taught loving by Fromto, and in fifteen years he never tried to force me once." He shuddered. Fromto was as strong as man could be, and as gentle as feathers with a woman. "You *wanted* that?"

"Oh, my love!" She cuddled closer. "I did want you, even at the first. But you had slain my husband, my father, my brothers. To confess to love seemed like betrayal—yes, I wanted you to force me. To save my shame. Desperately I wanted that."

He was too stunned to speak.

"And you never would," she said. "No matter how I taunted you. So I had to yield, sacrificing my pride to my need for you."

"Oh, Lallia!"

Was this what it was to be a man—hopelessly confused by women? He recalled arguments with Fromto on this very bed, with the big man being strangely obtuse and closed to reason. Lately his thinking had seemed much clearer.

So Jauro had won his love at last, and must leave her. How cruel the gods!

"When?" he whispered. "I loved you when I first set eyes on you. When did you first feel . . . feel that you did not hate me?"

"I do not know. Perhaps when the women told me how gentle you had been as a woman, with Thorti, and then when I saw how your men worshipped you."

"And as a kid I could steal cookies better than any. Now the truth?"

She sighed. "The first time you tried to bed me, my love."

He groaned as the embers of his shame blazed up anew.

"You were so enraged," she said, "and yet you did not blame me, you blamed yourself. That was when I knew I had found a far better man than Chilo. A better man than I have ever known, I think."

He snorted disbelievingly. "I was too young, too impatient."

"The change is easier when one is older, they say. The blood runs cooler. You will help me when my turn comes . . ." They kissed. After a moment, though, she whispered, "Is it true what they say?"

"What do they say?" he asked angrily.

"That you changed so young because you refused Fromto after you inherited the earldom? Celibacy is said to hasten the change."

"No, it is not true!"

It had been Fromto who had refused Jaura. He had been away a long time on the first campaign, and when he had returned they had sadly agreed to try, so that the earl might sooner become a man, as was fitting. But Jaura had not been able to sustain their pledge. She had begged and entreated and tried all her feminine wiles. Fromto had been the steadfast one, sleeping night after night on the floor in lonely agony. Oh, what he owed to that man!

"It is not true," Jauro lied. "It just happened—perhaps the strain of Hagthro's death . . ." He fell silent, thinking that she did not believe him.

"When the king gives you to another," he began, and she stopped him by putting her lips on his.

"I will come with you."

"No! I will not allow it! I shall be an outlaw, a wandering fighter seeking to serve others for charity. You must—"

"What of your son?" she whispered.

"Son?"

"I carry your child, My Lord, the child that will one day become your son, when it reaches menarche."

"Are you sure?" he demanded, thinking that every husband in the history of the world must have greeted that news with the same question.

She chuckled happily. "Either that or I have reached menopause, and I never heard of anyone becoming a man at twenty-two."

Take a pregnant woman over the passes in winter?

Or leave an unborn child behind to die by the king's spite?

Jauro ran strangely callused fingers over the smoothness of her belly and, speechless, turned his face away. Today he had lost a child to womanhood, and now was promised another to replace it. He would be a father as well as a mother, and this time teach archery and horsemanship instead of weaving and housewifery and . . .

But today he had also lost his earldom.

He was dallying in bed with a woman when he should be attending to his duties. In one sweep of motion he leaped to the floor, and the bed creaked mightily.

"I must go!" he snapped to Lallia's cry of protest. "What will they think of me out there?" They would think he was hiding under the furs, weeping! He rummaged to find his sword and belt it on him. The sword came first now, always.

Then he heard voices raised, and his scalp prickled in sudden apprehension. He had been negligent. There had been too much noise outside, men and horses both, and he had not heeded. Dogs were barking. He draped his sables loosely about him and threw open the door, ignoring a whine of complaint from his wife—women! He stormed along the corridor, heading for the brightness of the hall and the shouting, yet remembering that he had been mightily annoyed with Fromto a few times when he had cut short lovemaking for business. Was being a boor a necessary part of being a man? Oh, well, he would certainly take Lallia with him now, and they had years ahead to indulge in that sort of thing.

The hall was in disarray, a crowded, noisy confusion of torchlight and shadows. The meal had been interrupted, and there were tables and benches everywhere, half the men of the household stamping around flashing swords, and there were women and children mixed in with it all.

Jauro headed for the apparent center of the confusion, while glancing vainly around for Fromto. His husband must be outside, organizing the fugitives' departure, or possibly attending to his wooing.

He bellowed, and the swords were sheathed. Big, shambling men moved hastily out of the way as their young earl bore down on them and arrived at the cause of the tumult, strangers.

There were three of them, unarmed, white-bearded and frail, almost elders. They all looked shaky, red-eyed, exhausted by their journey. Their boots and leggings were thickly mudded, their furs dripped rain on the rushes.

Jauro recognized the leader at once, and with a considerable shock. He bowed, wishing he had taken the time to make himself more presentable. "Our house is honoured to receive Your Holiness."

The old man shook his head sadly, appraising Jauro with eyes still bright, yet hooded. "I fear not, My Lord." He raised a mittened hand as his host began to speak of chairs and warmth and wine. "I can not accept your hospitality, young man."

Only enemies refused hospitality. What new evil had inspired Reggalo to send his high priest? He had not brought the arrogance of the first envoy, although he was still regarding Jauro with priestly hauteur. "You spurned the king's summons, obviously."

"Obviously. Did you not meet the envoy upon the trail?"

"We must have missed him down by the marshes. We have followed him for many hours hoping to catch him before he arrived. We had more horses, but he drove his mounts hard." The priest paused, glancing around, and then reached within his furs. "The summons he delivered is withdrawn."

That ought to be good news, but Jauro was sure it wasn't, as he accepted the packet now offered him. "Your Grace—a seat by the fire, at least?"

Even that small hospitality was refused.

The hall had fallen silent now, men and women clustering in separate knots among the shadows. The fires crackled and some of the torches hissed. Children were sobbing, unnerved by the tension.

Jauro broke the seal and read the warrant in the shaky light, holding it at arm's length. Once upon a time he had stitched the finest hem in the household. Now his eyes were warriors' eyes, which could see a hawk blink but fared poorly on a scribe's crabbed hand.

Still, the message was clear enough, and the meaning drifted in around his heart like snow. He looked up to the venerable messengers who had brought it, and the priest read the question on his lips.

"Yes, I think you can trust that," he said bitterly. "As much as anything can be trusted. It was the best we could do, My Lord."

Jauro nodded, not wanting to speak yet. Certainly the list of witnesses was impressive enough, men known for honour. As far as a king's word went it was . . . well, it would be less treacherous than the mountains in winter, if not by much.

His furs were being tugged by the gnarled hand of Mindooru, one of the elders—shrunken and bent, leaning on a cane and constantly mumbling and drooling, shaking a head that was quite hairless except for a white fringe at the back. Of course the elders would have sent Mindooru. It was Jauro's father.

"Tell me, son?"

Jauro glanced around again for Fromto, and could not see him anywhere. Then he started to read the warrant again.

"Out with it!" Mindooru mumbled. "What's he say this time? It's bad, but not as bad, right? Crab apple tastes sweet after wild cherry, mm?"

Jauro nodded, repelled by the convoluted thinking. "The offer of marriage is withdrawn. Fromto can be regent and choose Thorta's husband. No proscriptions. That's about it."

The elder nodded, as though it had expected nothing else.

Oh gods, but it hurt, it hurt!

The high priest flinched before Jauro's accusing stare. "I said it was the best we could do! He'll not go for anything less, I'm certain."

"But why?" What had he done to deserve this?

"Why?" Mindooru shrilled. "I'll tell you why, son. Because he's frightened of you!" It began to weep.

The priest bit his lip, and then nodded agreement.

Jauro felt stunned. For a moment he clutched at a crazy hope that this was all some sort of elaborate joke, the kind of hazing new men got from the fyrd—but he was long past his first whiskers, and they would not treat their earl so.

No, it was real. Yet did his achievements really seem so impressive, so threatening? An unbeatable earl who might one day decide to move against tyranny? He had never dreamed that others might see him as such a man.

"Where's Fromto?" he demanded, looking around again.

"He can't help you," croaked the elder. "I can't. This one you do alone, son." The hands on its cane trembled. Tears streamed down its wrinkles. Even the end of its nose held a drop, and its thin, bent shoulders were heaving with sobs. Children wept. Women wept. Elders wept. Men did not.

For the first time in almost twenty years, Jauro would make a decision without consulting Fromto. But Mindooru was right—this one was his alone. This, too, was part of manhood—it felt like his first boar hunt.

He straightened his shoulders, and peered around until his eyes found

Thorta's face—a tiny patch of horrified whiteness among the women. He sent her a smile, but shook his head when she began to come forward. He knew that words would lodge in his throat like fishbones. *May you rule this land for many years, my darling, as woman and man, and raise daughters and sons to our line.* He could never say that aloud. *I love you no less than I ever did, even if I haven't said so lately!* Nor that. Once, maybe. Not now.

He thought of Lallia and the unborn child he would never see; and he thought of the snow-locked ranges, of the storms, of frost and starvation.

He looked down at the sniveling wreck of his father. At least he would be spared *that!*

Fromto would do his duty.

All around the hall stood the angry knots of men, muttering angrily— the grizzled survivors, the best warriors, companions who had shared wet ditches with him, shared triumph and terror. They had bled together, these men and he. They wanted to bleed more.

Go home now, he wanted to tell them. *Go home to your flocks and fields, to your plows and nets. Go home; live in peace; grow in wisdom.*

But they would be shamed if he said that. And what of the younger adults, the women who would be warriors for his daughter? They were huddled in other groups with the children who would be their wives. The widows would change first, of course; that was the gods' way of restocking the fyrd. *I hope you all live out your lives in peace,* he thought, *but I don't expect it.*

He unbuckled his sword and thrust it at Mindooru, which almost dropped it. "Here, father!" Jauro raised his voice, remembering the elder was deaf. "You taught me to use this, remember? Long ago. You taught me too well!"

He turned back to the priestly envoy and the searching eyes, and he forced out the lying words: "I confess my treason."

He saw relief then, and something else he could not place. It was not a return of arrogance. Not contempt. Not pleasure. Surely not admiration?

As he strode out to die for his loved ones, Jauro reflected sadly that this also was sometimes part of being a man.

REMEMBER, THE DEAD SAY

Jean-Louis Trudel

Jean-Louis Trudel has degrees in physics and astronomy, and is presently studying for a second M.A. in philosophy and history of science at the University of Toronto. He writes SF both in French and in English. He has also written cultural commentary and SF criticism for several publications, in French and in English, in Canada and the U.S., including *The Ottawa Citizen, Solaris, The New York Review of Science Fiction*, and *Locus*.

His fiction in English has appeared in *Tesseracts*, volumes 3 and 4, *Ark of Ice*, and *On Spec*. He is also the author of more than a dozen stories in French, published in *imagine . . ., Solaris*, and in Canadian and Belgian anthologies. He has also collaborated with Yves Meynard on several stories, and they are presently at work on a novel. Trudel's three novels in French include *Le Ressuscite de L'Atlantide*, serialized in *imagine . . .* from 1985–87; his recent young adult novel, *Aller simple pour Saguenal* (1994); and *Pour des soleils froids*, (Paris: Fleuve Noir Anticipation, 1994).

Trudel's contribution to the organizing of conventions, and the editing and publication of SF newsletters in Canada, as well as his frequent reports and reviews in English of francophone SF for U.S. publications, have made him an important figure in the interactions of the French and English Canadian SF communities. The story included here, "Remember, the Dead Say," is a Quebec Separatist story in English, a common topic for satire or violent partisan fantasies (David Ketterer devotes a few pages to this subgenre of Canadian literature). It is too obvious, and yet too delicate and complex a topic for many Canadian SF writers (see Vonarburg's comments). Trudel is up to the task in this unique and thought-provoking—and perhaps elegaic—piece.

The child is blond, a boy with golden hair and eyes of an indefinite grey-blue which have no more tears to shed since Daddy was killed by a sniper's bullet. He is called Brendan, Devin . . . maybe Gerald? He is running. In fact, he's been running towards the river and safety for two days, ever since he left his family's cottage in the northern hills, among the pines. He has run across the city streets strewn with shattered bricks, in the midst of the smoking ruins of wooden bungalows and the blasted shells of low-rises, and the river was always in front of him, getting closer and closer.

But no, now he is running across the cold terrazzo tiles of a shopping center, from floor to floor, running down to the dirty concrete of the parking levels. No shoppers there, no cars here. Only people huddled in small groups, sprawled on mattresses or sleeping bags, jealously standing guard over small hoards of boxes and cans. As he runs, he shouts:

"Les avions! Les avions s'en viennent!" The Canadian jets, the F-18 S1 fighter-bombers; where S stands for "smart...."

The boy has run alongside the stony trench of the boulevard linking the main bridges, where the last defenders are encamped with mortars, a few remaining APCs, and howitzers. The boy knows that the pilots won't distinguish between the desperate troops and the neighbouring buildings where Hull's former citizens have found shelter from the shelling and the small arms fire. Even though the office towers are festooned with red crosses.

And the bombs that will glide down laser paths, finding the sky-lights over the shopping center's atrium or the stairway shafts of the parking, will not pick and choose among their victims. The boy runs in the last shadows of the federal buildings. On the other side of the deserted stretch of pavement, if he jumps over the fallen poles of the streetlights and somehow scrambles down the grassy slope, there is an arm of the Ottawa river. On the other side, OttawaOntarioCanada. ...

The planes shriek across the sky and the boy leaps from the shadows.

She combed the snow out of her beard.

The driving snow was definitely freakish for December in Lowell, O.T. It might not have seemed so out of place in January, when flurries harried the town for two or three days a year, outlining the scaly bark of the palm trees with filigrees of dirty white and then melting in a few hours, leaving a puddle in every pothole. She was much too recent a newcomer to remember when Massachusetts winters had entailed more snow than sleet.

The old comb had lost teeth and its black plastic was scarred, but she stowed it carefully in a back pocket after wiping it. She dared not lose it. She avoided stores where the monitors might see past the beard or the mikes might catch the hint of accent in her roughened voice. Besides, she rather liked its battered condition; it reflected her own predicament.

She forced herself to walk on, plowing into the cold wind. Overhead, azure bunting decorated with golden fleurs-de-lis fluttered in the gusts, faded black letters proclaiming in French the fiftieth anniversary of Québec's war of independence. The sidewalk was broken in places, covered with icy patches elsewhere, and she concentrated on her footing. A broken leg would mean a visit to the hospital, and unavoidable discovery.

Beards had been a fad before the latest series of wars, like breasts for men, furred tails, cat's eyes or werewolf teeth. She'd chosen a beard to match her mousy brown hair, back then, and this unadventurous choice had proven wise in unforeseen ways. Alterations could not be reversed without elaborate genosurgery—though she had contemplated permanent depilation—and most genochemists had died during the years of destruction. The genochemists had not relied on anything as gross as massive testosterone injections. Growing a beard on a woman had not been the point, that was old hat, but rather doing it without affecting the body's delicate biochemical balance.

Now though, the beard allowed her to masquerade as a man and to walk the streets unchallenged. The law of the Franco-Maghrebi Coalition was the Sharia and it imposed the veil on all women past a certain age, as well as seclusion except for absolutely necessary errands—not that either was really unwise with the Sun blasting ultraviolet at an ozone-poor Earth. Only the women among the troops of Québec, the Coalition's sole North American ally, enjoyed a special dispensation.

The old thoroughfare that paralleled the river came to an end at another waterway. The nineteenth-century town center of Lowell was now behind her and so she bore left, recalling the directions whispered to her aboard the rickety Amtrak train she had taken to Omaha, capital of the Free States, an oasis amid an encroaching desert. She'd spent two days in Omaha, waiting for the eastbound train, doing the things expected of any Canadian tourist. A quick videocamming of the Whiter House, a brief tour of the Senate in session, and a peek from afar, *sans* camera, at the rebuilt Pentagon.

That had been but a few weeks before the war: the quick Franco-Maghrebi thrust from the occupied Maritime Confederacy, the nuking of the Albany staging point of the F.S.A. First Army, the overrunning of the defenses along the Hudson wasteland, the indecisive battle around Syracuse, and, two months later, the signature of the ceasefire in forlorn Ottawa by delegates from Marseilles and Omaha, witnessed by Canadian officials from Winnipeg.

By then, she'd arrived in Lowell. She'd lived the war through the Net, as she accessed the last screams of the dying, the encrypted communications of the military, the grainy battlefield pics, the verbal confrontations of supporters of both sides, and even sometimes the streams of biomonitor data, each packet crowded with the life of a man or woman, and each packet practically meaningless for an eavesdropper like her, safe in the basement of an aging clapboard house. She'd been astonished to discover a few last pacifists, and gripped by the unfolding battles, and pained by the suffering of the wounded keying in to reaffirm they still existed: whatever it was, if it were modulated electronically, it eventually left a residue on the Net, like the sediment of the centuries descending upon the ocean floor.

In those days, she'd craved the Net and its raw emotions to help her forget that she was afraid. The empty streets outside had seemed to expect, to *want* soldiers to come walking through the wind-blown leaves of early autumn, and yet everyone was afraid of spotting the first green uniform that would change all their lives forever. However, Lowell was too small and too close to radioactive Boston, smitten in an earlier war fought with deadlier weapons and with other enemies, avenged by smouldering towns called

Kazan and Smolensk. The Franco-Maghrebi columns had by-passed unimportant Lowell and, in the end, the first forces to enter it had come from Québec after the ceasefire had fixed the zones of influence for a time. Since then, most voices on the local Net had died away.

"Do you speak French, mister?"

"*Excusez-moi, mais parlez-vous français?*"

"*Assalaamu aleikoum, tifnam arabi?*"

"Please, please, do you speak Arabic?"

She almost broke her stride, memories fragmenting and whirling away. The supplicants lined the street in front of the Québec military headquarters. They waved sheets of plastic inscribed in the Roman or Arabic alphabets. She looked straight ahead and walked on, tried not to betray her knowledge of French, steeled herself against flinching.

She knew what the documents were. The same had been sent to everybody with a surname which seemed either French or Arabic in origin. Notices of retroactive recognition of citizenship, as they were called by the occupiers. Draft notices, she called them, since military service went with citizenship for Québec or the Franco-Maghrebis. Anyway, such was their real purpose and they were couched in such ornate French or flowery Arabic that the recipients, sons of long-ago immigrants who'd only learned a few words of their ancestral languages in childhood, if at all, could hardly decipher their meaning.

She walked faster. If her name had not been Pat Doyle, she might have received one. In Kapuskasing, her family had spoken French for over a century. At times, her mind reeled from the welter of her identities, which burdened her with a dozen masks. Francophone in English-speaking Canada, Métis in a land owned by others, and now a Canadian in Lowell, formerly a city of the F.S.A., but now an "Occupied Territory" of the Franco-Maghrebi Coalition.

As a Canadian, she could be shot as a spy; as a francophone, drafted; as a Métis, who could claim kinship with the rich farmers of Denendeh, interned as an illegal alien. . . .

And she didn't even know for sure what the Sharia dictated for women using men's clothing. On the whole, she preferred to be an American, even in an occupied city.

A Québécois patrol came towards her and she bobbed her head up and down in submission as she changed sidewalks. The long coat in which she shivered hid well the curves still left in spite of a starvation diet, but there was no percentage in taking chances.

The soldiers did not spare a glance. Thin scraggly men were the norm in Lowell.

Québec! She mastered an urge to spit on the pavement they had walked on. She'd come to Lowell to find the mass grave of distant relatives, the Marcottes, on behalf of La Nouvelle Patente, the one organization that had linked francophones in Canada, Denendeh, the Maritime Confederacy, and the F.S.A. During the previous war, the Marcottes and others like them had been shot as Québec spies, for a country they'd never even visited. Only babies had been spared, put up for adoption, and lost in the records. They were safe somewhere, she hoped: Louis, Richard, Julie. . . . Only a small atrocity begotten by others begotten by hatreds born of a long twisting history, which only the victors could afford to forget: if she found the grave, she was to send back for money with which to build a memorial.

And then she'd met the stranger aboard the train who'd whispered to her of coming wars and defeats.

Defeat, she knew. You lived, you cried, and then you got used to it.

Pat had flung her teen-age years at the burning forests of northern Ontario, like so many others in Kapuskasing, refusing to let the futility of it erode her youthful determination. The fires had become more and more frequent as the greenhouse effect worsened. She remembered the smell of smoke that stayed in the clothes, the black grit getting in the eyes, the resin scent that would not wash off her hands after mere hours of work. A few days were enough for a fire fighter to merge with the fire she was fighting, growing into a creature of wood and sooty air, of water and black earth, arms an extension of axe-handles or shovels.

They'd saved villages like Val-Rita and towns like Longlac, but she'd quit after shooting the last *buck*—she'd been with a younger cousin, David McCaughey, scouting the woods downwind of a late-summer fire. The overworked planes were supposed to come, but such pledges were written on the wind, and a fire-break had to be planned. She had a gun, in case the fire chased something dangerous out of the woods and into their path. The afternoon had been hot, the air heavy, and they'd tried for a short-cut, scrambling down a wooded slope to the edge of a small lake. And then they'd seen the *buck*. It bellowed in pain. The animal's pelt hung in blackened tatters and its antlers seemed to smoke still. They'd never seen a moose this far south.

It stood there for what seemed like forever, its cries of anguish echoing back from the hills. David had pulled at her arm, wanting to go on and detour around the wounded beast. She hadn't budged, moved in spite of herself and struggling with an obscure feeling of recognition. Then, in one swift motion, she had shouldered the gun and shot.

The next day, she had handed in her resignation from the fire-fighting squads. The moose had stayed behind, maybe, when others had moved north away from sweltering summers and the increasing human presence. Maybe it had come back. But there was no going back, and the forests could not be saved as long as the climate continued to get hotter.

That was the first time she had tasted bittersweet defeat, the bitterness of losing mingled with the relief that came with no longer having to fight.

"À quoi tu penses?"

"Kawkwy!"

She reddened as she realized she'd answered in Michif, which had been the language of her Métis grandfather, and then paled as she realized the question had been put to her in French. Lost in the past, she'd stopped to shelter in a doorway of the Archambault funeral home. She glanced up at the man who had spoken:

"Who are you?"

At the same time, she withdrew her hands, numbed by the cold, into the arms of her coat. The lining held a dozen *fléchettes*, tipped with Tabun-filled capsules.

"Je sais qui tu es, Patline," he said.

She almost gasped. He'd used her full name.

"What do you mean?" she replied.

"Tu es Patline Doyle, tu as grandi à Moonbeam et tu as été envoyée par la Nouvelle Patente pour arranger la construction d'un monument commémoratif à la mémoire des victimes des massacres de mars."

"What are you saying? I was born and raised in Manchester, up north, in New Hampshire," she said, unwilling to admit defeat too quickly. Only a *provocateur* would speak French so openly. The man threw back the hood of his coat: a tiara of metal and glass imprisoned his skull. Greying hair showed through in places, but the device seemed to be a melded part of the head. The face was lined with furrows born of worry or fear, but the deep-set eyes burned into hers.

"I'm Marc Gendreau, a gatekeeper of the Net," he laughed tiredly, "and we cracked the secret access codes of the Nouvelle Patente a long time ago. I probably know more about the organization than you. I even know about that Arab draft dodger you hid in your basement for a week. . . . Je suis recherché par la Sûreté militaire."

She sighed, at once impressed and alarmed. If Québec's counter-intelligence police were truly hunting for him. . . .

"How did you find me?"

"You used your pocket comp to check the weather forecast when you were in front of the church. I traced your call to the nearest relay and I guessed where you were going."

"Very well, but let's not stay here." If he was a *provocateur*, he was toying with her. She preferred the alternative. "And hide your hardware." He started at that, but obediently pulled the hood over his head.

She launched into a brisk walk, head lowered against the wind. He half-ran to catch up and he asked:

"Going to the Marcotte house?"

She did not answer and she continued to lead the way till she turned into the empty lot. She was suddenly reassured by his ignorance of her true destination.

The mob had burned down the house of the Marcottes. The snow was resurrecting it, outlining the concrete foundation and the broken stumps of walls, piling up around the heaps of rubble. The living-room had been there, she guessed, at the back of the house; she could picture the parents watching their kids at play in that wide backyard which extended down to the water's edge. One of the parents would have yelled out from time to time to warn the children away from the water. . . .

She followed the winding path of flagstones which ended on the threshold of the ruined house, but she did not continue. Stepping on the concrete flooring always made her feel as if she were desecrating a tomb. Instead, she led the way around the side.

Strangely enough, she had no such compunction about treading the ground where they had buried the bodies. It was a backyard as wide as a playing field, extending down to the water. The snow was driving down with a renewed fierceness and she could not even see to the edges of the field as she peered into the whirling snowflakes.

It had been during the last war but one, when the Franco-Maghrebis had overwhelmed the Maritime Confederacy—after Québec had unexpectedly joined in the fighting, capturing Edmonston and pushing down to Fredericton, breaking the back of Maritime resistance. As the combined armies had moved down to Saint John, closer and closer to the F.S.A. border, the war scare had spread to the whole of New England. Several Lowell families— Bédards, Merciers, Royers—guilty of being too ostentatiously francophone, had been rounded up as spies, had seen their houses burned, and had been shot later that night. Nothing more was known. The leaders of the mob had never been identified. The dead do not testify.

Pat had even had trouble finding the spot where the Marcottes and the others were buried. Nobody knew, or was willing to tell a stranger. The remaining francophones around town were afraid to talk. She'd plugged into the Net for unending days and nights in the hope of catching a hint. Finally, she'd used her Net expertise to assemble a slightly illegal interception program; it scanned every private and public electronic conversation for a month before coming up with the slightest of allusions. It had been enough, though.

She stopped in the middle of the field and turned towards Marc. The snow curtained them off from prying eyes.

"Well, Marc, who are you? You don't have a Québec accent."

"I *was* born and raised in Pelham, in what was New Hampshire, but I trained as a roving trouble-shooter, a specialist of Net patch-up jobs. I was in Amherst when the invasion started. Since then, I've been moving, struggling to keep a Net channel open, but I'm running out of luck, and time, and money."

"Alors? Que veux-tu?" she asked, eyes narrowing. She did not need more complications to interfere with what had seemed to be such a simple mission.

"Que tu viennes avec moi, Patline. Come with me: I said I was a gatekeeper, but that's only part of the truth. This last war was just another installment in the conflict between North America and Europe, but the fighting, the bombings, the troop movements are merely the overt war. Another war has begun, Pat, and this one is invisible. It's a war for control of the Net."

He brushed some snow off the rim of his hood and added: "I'm a soldier now in this underground war. On one side, there are the Franco-Maghrebis, who want to shut down all access to the continental Net where debate is free, information is cheap, and gems are stirred in along with the manure. On the Net, you can debate the Koran, the Sharia, and whether Mohammed was forewarned of the ozone layer's weakening or not. Without the Net, the Franco-Maghrebis can feed you all the news they want you to have. On the other side, a group is forming, rather undefined—it includes all Netters, à la limite. We take action against the disruptor viruses of the Franco-Maghrebis; we try to locate their taps on the lines; we buy new hardware when the Franco-Maghrebis confiscate what's already there; sometimes we simply play the role of reporters or researchers—what is on the Net is as important as having the Net. . . ."

"So, why me?" she asked. "And isn't there a section of the F.S.A. army that deals with electronic skirmishing?"

"The military experts have enough to do with defending the access to their own files. As for you, we saw what you did to find the burial spot—an ingenious little program—and we'd like to have you. Especially since you speak French—French-speaking programmers are as rare as vacuum tubes nowadays on our side, and we expect to face a lot of datastream in French from now on. Would that affect your loyalties? Having to work against Québec programmers, I mean?"

"I didn't notice the F.S.A. having any qualms about old loyalties when they nuked the British Fleet to keep the Franco-Maghrebis from getting it intact," she answered drily. And any loyalty she felt for Québec was very old indeed.

"Good, good. But there is another reason. My reserve funds are practically worthless now that the area is occupied, and I know that you will be getting some hard currency soon."

She almost smiled. It was true; she'd sent for the memorial money from the Nouvelle Patente as soon as she'd found the killing field.

"Yes, Marc, but there's still that old question: why should I trust you?"

"We were both caught behind the lines. I think we have to trust each other."

"I don't know about that. I don't even know what side of the line I was on originally. . . ."

"We need that money!" he pronounced. "The Franco-Maghrebis will be selling the hardware they took from the F.S.A. army. It'll be a bit battered, but with universal compatibility, we can use it to replace the hardware the Franco-Maghrebis have been confiscating left and right since the beginning of the occupation. I've got to be in Springfield in three days for the auction, impersonating a Montréal resaler."

"So, you want me to start by committing larceny. . . . The money is being entrusted to me to build a memorial."

"A memorial to the dead. What I'm offering you is a memorial to the living. Pat, I believe that the Net is vital if we are to have any hope for the future."

"Come to my place tomorrow, Marc," she said, as she strode away. She had to think.

"Et cette nuit? I just arrived in town and I have nowhere to sleep."

"Va voir Laura Daigle, 46 rue Merrimack."

Surprise was in his eyes for a twinkling, and Patline realized that she'd spoken in her natural tone of voice instead of her usual rough whisper. She stroked her beard in contemplation as she turned her back and walked down to the waterside, where there was a path.

A few houses further, behind the decaying hulk which had been some kind of school decades ago, she found the small Catholic shrine—a grotto of concrete where glowed candles the last of the faithful came to light. The Way of the Cross, with its faded inscriptions in French, ended at the top of the concrete mound. She climbed the steps to check the surroundings. Nobody in sight.

However, when she walked back down to the mouth of the grotto, a shape appeared in the greyness. She stopped and then looked around for more, but the man was alone. He did not acknowledge her presence as he stepped up to the altar. In his threadbare windbreaker, he had the look of a refugee from the Mexican state of Alta California—blond, bronzed, and breathtakingly thin.

Aware of the man's scrutiny, she knelt in front of the crucifix and barely remembered how to cross herself. The Doyle family had been Catholic once, but she had always scorned keeping up appearances when the heart did not believe.

She turned after a suitable pause to the small table with a Holy Bible and a ledger, both plastic-wrapped. She opened the latter, flipping past the pious scrawlings in Spanish, Greek, or Polish, went to the back page, and blinked at finding a sealed envelope stuck to the inner cover. The agent aboard the Omaha train had instructed her to look for messages there. Even back then, the inner councils of the F.S.A. had expected a war with the Franco-Maghrebis before Christmas and had expected to lose. They had already been preparing resistance, and she'd let herself be persuaded to take part in order not to jeopardize her cover as a Canadian Net programmer hired for a small job in Lowell. She had checked the mail drop a hundred times, and this was the first there was anything.

"Don't you know your own name?" The voice boomed into her ear.

"I'm sorry. I was thinking." She grasped the old pen, and wrote down her name with a flourish. As she put back the pen, she smoothly detached the envelope and pocketed it.

"What's in the envelope?" Was there the slightest hint of a Québec accent in the blond man's voice. She smiled faintly:

"It's a greeting card I got today for my birthday. Didn't you see me take it out of my pocket to let it dry?"

"No, I guess not." He did not pursue the matter. "Did you spot a strange man on your way here? Medium height, grey hair, in a brownish parka?"

"Couldn't see much, with the wind." She was suddenly sure that he was an agent of the *Sûreté militaire.*

"Of course. . . . Can you speak French?"

"Oh, juste un peu," she forced out with a quaver. The man's eyes seemed to weigh for a moment the build of a potential recruit. He probably judged her too scrawny to be worth his time, and he dismissed her:

"You should come to Québec; it's impossible to learn to speak French right elsewhere, and French can't survive outside it. Good jobs for bilinguals, too."

She assented mutely, and he moved off into the snow-filled gloom. She hesitated, filled with renewed mistrust of everybody and everything. Were Marc and this man part of some subtle ploy by the *Sûreté?* Who could she trust? Even if Marc was for real, didn't her commitment to the Nouvelle Patente or the F.S.A. resistance come first? She glanced at the Bible, and, on a whim, as she mocked herself inside, she opened it to a random page and bent down to read.

"5. And the sons of Rimmon the Beerothite, Rechab and Baanah, went, and came about the heat of the day to the house of Ishbosheth, who lay on a bed at noon. 6. And they came thither into the midst of the house, *as though* they would have fetched wheat; and they smote him under the fifth *rib*: and Rechab and Baanah his brother escaped. 7. For when they came into the house, he lay on his bed in his bedchamber, and they smote him, and slew him, and beheaded him, and took his head, and gat them away through the plain all night."

From the Second Book of Samuel. . . . She felt the words indict her for impudence in seeking advice she didn't believe in, anyway, and yet she had to grin at the ironies. Advice about backstabbing, as if she needed it! The dilemma was in choosing which back to stab! She remembered some of her grandfather's Michif and shouted it suddenly to the unseen sky:

"*Kishay Menitou! Weechihin!*"

There was no answer, and in fact her grandfather's prayers had rarely been answered. She left.

When she got home, a man in uniform was waiting on her doorstep, and she almost shrank from him. Her grandfather had drummed into her an instinctive abhorrence of police; Zachary Allard had relished telling how his crooked nose had been broken by police officers unfriendly to Métis. The beating had prompted his move from the Prairies to northern Ontario.

However, even if the *Sûreté militaire* was on her tail, the man was older than the average security officer, and he started by handing her a package. She went inside, locking the door behind her—the courier could wait a bit before being paid—and pulling down the blinds, and then opened the package to find a roll of silver *écus*. Enough to build a fitting memorial to the Marcottes and the other victims of the March massacres. . . .

She invited the courier inside and served him some of her quickly vanishing stock of maple brandy. Whatever happened, she would be able to leave Lowell, quit living in disguise, and return to a freer land. What would she look like without a beard? She found she'd forgotten. . . .

"À la vôtre!" They clinked glasses. He reminisced about the first Independence Battalions of Québec. He claimed he had been in one of them when it marched down St-Denis street in Montréal, in disordered ranks of paunchy volunteers who brandished antiquated Glock light machine guns and sang *Gens du pays* with a terrified fervour, cheered on by the throng packed on the sidewalks and in the cafés. They had felt like heroes, surely doomed, but tears of joy streamed down their faces as they realized that the age-old dream of a nation was coming true. Québec was standing up after four centuries of colonization.

Pat muttered something under her breath about betraying part of their past, but she knew Québec had been given little choice. Its people had dreamed of a peaceful country, that would never aspire to play the game of weltpolitik, but they had been compelled to arm and to defend themselves, till the logic of history led them to do unto others what had been done to them.

He did not hear her. They had been hoarse with shouting and singing, and they all thought they would be sent up the Outaouais to liberate Hull from the Canadian Army. However, his battalion had been ordered to stay and wipe out the Westmount pockets of resistance. The house to house fighting had been ugly, against older men and women who refused to be third-class citizens and sang an anthem composed by a French-Canadian as their houses burned around them. . . . He came back from the past as if burnt by it, and asked suddenly what happened when dreams two hundred years old came true? She did not answer. Precious few dreams had come true for her.

She sang old songs with him, careless for once. Let the neighbours hear them singing in French! They danced a bit, to old tunes from the twentieth century that he remembered hearing when they were nearly new. He was the first to fall asleep.

That left her to contemplate alternatives. Going back to Canada. Staying in Lowell to help the F.S.A. resistance—the traditional work of spying, sabotage, and guerilla warfare, glamourous but deadly. Leaving with Marc.

Past, present, future. It was too neat. She had lain on her cot to reflect, and she fell asleep in the middle of remembering the moose she had killed.

When she woke up the next morning, she found an old razor and shaved. The epicene ambiguity of the new face she discovered as she cleared the last of the stubble startled her. She stared at herself for a moment without being able to decide who she recognized, and then went to the door to watch the street. Refugees were coming in from the war zone.

The snow had changed into a cold, pattering rain. Standing on her doorstep, she watched the little groups of men and women shuffle down the street, towards the town center. A man dressed in the same rags, arms empty, came towards her door.

"Are you ready to go?" he asked.

"I know I cannot go back, but what hope do you offer me?" She wanted more than the lonely glory of joining the F.S.A. resistance, clinging to a sense of separateness and tight-knit camaraderie as she had done all her life. Yes, she wanted more, she wanted a change.

"The name of the game is survival, Patline. Look at us! You come from Canada, I from the good old U. S. of A., and a hundred years ago nobody would have bet that we would still speak French to each other. Why? Because we were the pioneers of the electronic community. No ghettoes for us, no Little Italys, no Chinatowns. We can be found across the continent, but we are invisible. Our grandparents used to come home from a day at work in English or Japanese, and light up the television, turn on the radio, plug in the modem. . . . Et ils pouvaient alors se parler en français. No borders. One community from sea to sea to sea. Something France only allowed briefly over there—remember the Minitel crackdown? But even if the Franco-Maghrebi tanks roll to the Pacific, we have a chance, I say, as long as the Net survives and continues to carry more information than a thousand AIs could filter."

"Do you really think they'll invade the F.S.A.?"

"Why not? For us, America is a broken-down dream. Both sides lost when the old United States decided to tackle the new Russia. But for Europeans, America is still the next best thing to a second chance."

She smiled, and pushed the door open. Her travel bag, with the roll of écus secured in a hidden pocket, was on the other side. She shouldered it, and heard reproving ghosts wail. You need to be alive to remember, she almost said, but she simply turned towards Marc. "Let's go."

"What do you want me to call you?"

It was a new life, after all. They would look for Pat Doyle if *he* disappeared . . . they would find a courier asleep in her flat. She remembered an old book:

"Call me Maria. . . ."

The boy's hair is black and curly, and his skin remembers the Mediterranean sun he was born under. He is called Esmail, Tahar . . . maybe Ahmed. He has grown up in the narrow alleys of the new housing built within the walls of the old fort on the hill, once surrounded by houses, now isolated by the rising sea at each high tide. His father is a colonel in the garrison of this place called Halifax.

When he's sent to bed, he clutches a pocket comp and later burrows under the blankets before turning it on and accessing the children's Net. The first time he innocently logged on, he was caught by his parents and only kept the comp because it was indispensable for his studies.

The lure of the forbidden is strong. He's learned to be careful. There is a hierarchy of Nets, accessed through gates requiring ever more intricate passwords. He has followed fierce electronic debates, which have made him blush at times and introduced him to heresies he had never heard of. Yet, his greatest shock was the revelation that one of the more articulate and thoughtful of the Netters, only identified by a nom de guerre, was in fact his own younger sister, whom he had always ignored.

The debates have made him question quietly, looking up quotes in the Koran and wondering about the pre-eminence of the Sharia. His old beliefs have slowly dropped away, half-dissolved by the acid of critical analysis. Tonight, he thinks he can join the real underground Net, the one with the hottest, darkest shareware and the most heterodox opinions on the most forbidden topics. He runs through the gamut of the lower levels, thankful that the occult hierarchy is accessible. Sometimes, no entrance can be found; a connection has been shut down by the Sûreté informatique, a brief victory in the incessant fight against the clandestine Net. Finally, he types in the ultimate codeword:

"Liberté."

ONE

Heather Spears

Heather Spears, writer and artist, has published nine collections of poetry and three books of drawings since 1958. Her poetry books, *How to Read Faces* (1986) and *The Word for Sand* (1988), both won the Pat Lowther Award. The latter also won the Governor General's Award for poetry. Her art has been in six juried and sixty-seven solo exhibitions in Europe, the U.S., and Canada. She lives presently in Copenhagen, where she is a freelance artist, drawing instructor, and is pursuing graduate studies at the University of Copenhagen in Arabic and in English Studies.

In 1989 she began to write science fiction as well, both stories and novels. Her SF trilogy, *Moonfall* (1991), *The Children of Atwar* (1993), and *The Taming* (1994), is set in the same future world as "One." "She is able to sidestep many of the givens of genre SF while never losing sight of its prime directive: to create a sense of wonder," says Douglas Barbour. "I have no hesitation about placing Spears next to Le Guin—one of the most literate and intelligent SF writers. . . ."

Tasman's earliest memories were not good ones. A brightness not escapable—she is lying in a transparent box and being watched. Also touched. She is also crawling about in it—the memories were not really that early, for her life up to the age of four was punctuated by these periods in the box—and the faces of the watchers, large and oval, behind the transparent walls that are rather moist, slippery, and warm. Two faces prevail: these are the faces of her mothers, they carry over to the times at home, which seemed to her to have always been in the Darkening of the year, shadowy. Mamel's face, the large oval swimming on the right, gentle, the eyes not always ready to meet hers, looking askance, up and away as if asking for help. Mamar's on the left, a mirror likeness but something firmer, the set of the mouth a little tighter, the look more steady. Tasman is lifted out of the box and suckled on their breasts. Otherwise watched, touched by fingers, instruments. Other faces watch her. Always twinned.

She suffered, as one "suffers" an illness—and hers was an inexplicable congenital deformity—surely long before she was aware of her ordinary physical boundaries, though she explored her motor powers—her hands were not the box or the sheets, her will extended her fingers or clasped them, her voice uttered noises that were not the clicks and bleeps of the machines, she learned by ordinary effort to grasp her feet, roll over, sit up. Her handicap became evident to her not so much from her own sense of her body as from the looks and touches—the anxiety and commiseration in her mothers' (in Mamar's, resignation like a continuous exhalation of breath, in Mamel's something still complex and unfinished, as if at war with itself). And this look or something like it but distanced, in the other faces, a curiosity that saw her as an object, and, in some who cared for her from time to time, fear. Even avoidance of touch (which is the severest of punishments), or a touch that was superficial and diffident, with no meeting of eyes.

So there was no particular moment when Tasman, growing, learning to walk and speak, became aware of what she was. In one sense she had always been aware: she saw that human communication is not always worried, or fearful, or diffident, or impossible to establish; she knew this by the way the adults around her communicated with each other; so that the deep twin-bond that was everywhere was learned by her through observation and in exile.

> *Stronger than father, stronger than mother,*
> *Sister to sister, brother to brother.*

An innocent nursery-rhyme now, that had once been a battle-cry, in the far-off times of the Barbarians. Mamar and Mamel, leaning into each other's smiles.

Her weaning was formal, but private. Knowing no better, she accepted her gifts and made the short speeches and felt in part what she ought to have felt. She was four years old, the ceremony rather early, but there was no reason to extend infancy in her case. ("She can only suck her fingers, after all.") Perhaps here, standing before her mothers, with the decorative blue wax still tingling and cooling on her lips, for the first time she really understood what it meant to have no twin to turn to. The ceremony was performed at home. The final lines were not said, or their responses. She was used to being bereft, but not this frightened.

They lived in Lofot on the Barents Sea in a small, level house, the roof of which formed most of the yard. The city was modern. She remembers it mostly in Darkening, its lights that swelled and changed colour, gradual and ordinary, through the hours. The colours through the verdant leaves, and shimmering in long vertical pathways on the canals. She had no fathers. They had gone away, they were dead in the Savannahs, stories of them were muddled in her mind with the Great Tales. She thought they were Travellers, because she wanted to believe this, tellers of letters, though in actuality they had gone away in the aftermath of her birth, escaping. Mamel told stories to her, so early that they became confused with the little she knew of her fathers, and she let it remain like this. The hero Saduth Twel, whose twin was bitten in the ear by a venomous snake as he slept.

"But wasn't the Twel waking?"

"It happened so fast, Twel was looking the other way. Nothing could save the Twar and he commanded his brother, using the strong oath, to garotte him before the poison reached their lungs, and he did, with an arm belt, and the Twar died looking into his eyes, and did not loosen the belt, even as he was dying.

> *He struggled not / against his brother:*
> *He died and wished him life."*

"Then what happened?"

"Twel felt very sick, he knew he must leave Twar and bury his mind in the desert, but he had no tools except the short knife. But he threaded the wire out of the other arm belt, and with this he did the act."

Tasman's hands moved involuntarily to her neck. "How could he live?"

"He stanched the blood, he buried the Twar mind in a basket of long grass. Twel was very sick. For two days he mourned.

> *'It would be better for me*
> *To go with you into death.*
> *Why have you wished me life?*
> *You are content, but I am alone.' "*

"Alone," whispered Tasman. The word was archaic, almost taboo. She shivered.

"Why do you tell her these tales?" asked Mamar in the rote speech and received the rote answer, "Because she asks, and because they are part of our heritage."

"Did Saduth Twel live?" asked Tasman.

"He came to Whalsay, and he was crawling. They saw him from the city, moving across the valley between Whalsay and Hoy Mountain, in the open marshes. His face was black. He lived, because it was the wish of his twin. That is a long time ago."

"Who was the hero?"

"They were both heroes, but it is called the Tale of the hero Saduth Twel."

The story absorbed Tasman; she speculated about heroes, and her fathers. A snake had killed them surely, and in the real story, the Twar would not be so unkind as to wish life on his Twel, he would drag the belt loose at the last minute "with both hands," his need for air stronger than his will. They would wrestle on the ground like the unweaned, yelling and biting at each other's ears and noses, the sharp crack of their skulls would resound in the desert:

Bad sound / worst of all,
The moon will fall, the moon will fall.

She had seen children chided with this verse, and going untouched for punishment. And she had heard this sound in the street, unmistakable, as she lay on the bushy roof and watched them playing. And once, at night—shouts outside and that awful whiplash crack, and the sound of feet running.

And she'd seen the moon past the lights, or cool and seemingly smaller in the daylight sky; they said it would fall one day, it was nearing the earth. But not in these generations. Wise men not yet born would prevent this, said her mothers. There is a great Book in Manchu, an entire city, dedicated to this learning. The moon and the earth would be friendly, there would be conversation between them in those unimaginable days, they would turn their faces to each other in kindness. There would be two worlds.

Tasman, at her weaning, was given garments that Mamel made specially for her. They were the usual sleeved tunics, but only one sleeve was open to pull over her head, the other was closed with seams and stuffed. Though Tasman had many of these tunics as she grew, she came to call them by one name, Pillowmarie. At four, she resisted wearing Pillowmarie furiously, but her mothers kept it on her with intricate ribbons tied behind her shoulders ("She might as well get used to it.") and gradually she realized that her freedom outside the house was greater, going with her mothers to receive food or walking with them along the dykes was now possible, even when people were about—though there were stares, the adult looks were at least subdued and apologetic, not frightened or hostile.

Her mothers were overprotective, making her wear Pillowmarie in the house. She knew they had conversations about this and arguments, tears also, when she was supposed to be asleep. Mamel saying, "It will train her to tilt her head."

And Mamar: "Nothing will make her normal. We believed she was a Twel mind, heart heavy, but she has not revealed it. I can't feel it."

"She's both and the Twel's strongest."

Tears. "Have her, then. Twel—you were the one who couldn't bear it."

Tasman did not understand much of this. The Pillowmarie was placed on her right one day, on her left another. It was as if they were waiting for her to show a preference. The cloth flopped against her ear, interfered with her peripheral vision. She sensed her mothers watching. She sat by them and ate, now out of her own bowl. The bowl, a weaning gift, was double, and she ate with both hands. Pillowmarie bobbed against her temple. If Mamel painted a face on Pillowmarie, would it breathe or eat? Hardly.

* * *

Sometimes, at night, Tasman talked to herself, but she could not pretend she had a twin. Her hands talked, or perhaps the location of her two play personalities was in her shoulders. She chose to become the voice of one side or the other—such play was listened to and remembered by Mamar for medical Book. Tasman lying on the sleeping pallet and talking softly:

"I am going to Book soon." (Pause.) *"And-you-come-too"* (a courtesy speech). "Then I am going to World *and-you-come-too*. In the Lightening of the year. There is a big story in Book and I'll read it to you. Thank you. I'll draw you pictures, it will have a desert in it, a Savannah. They give you colours in Book, and you can have lights. You can colour with lights. *Fire in my mind, water in your mind.* I want to light real fires, big ones. Aren't you afraid? I'm not afraid, I'm going to Book soon and you aren't even there."

This last was said with some satisfaction. Tasman did want to learn and had really no problem in choosing Book instead of World. World children did not have an institution, but wandered. That they could play with fire was an enormous enticement. They played with fire and on the beaches and touched real things. At Book, nothing was real. The excitement was that it was seemingly endless, doors opening doors as if forever. The children might ask anything at all and the answers prepared them for more asking. Most children went to Book, eagerly, when they were weaned, which could be at five or nine or even later if they were male. They had played enough with the world by then, though some would choose to return to it. Weaned twins had to work out where they most wanted to go. *Real fire burns Book. Book is a fire that burns forever.* It was a lesson in co-operation. Sometimes a Twel at Book never learned to read, but drew endlessly while his brother read or played with numbers; the screens were all double. There were laboratories as well as libraries. The teachers were there to show them how to use Book, to find the answer to anything they wanted.

Tasman had to wait longer than her fifth year before there was a Book that could or would take her. And that single attempt proved disastrous.

Even with Pillowmarie her appearance at Book frightened the smaller children, and the older ones were interrupted. Questions were suddenly not about subjects that had interested them before, but about Tasman; scared twins her own age clung to the teachers: "What happened to her twin?" But the older children wanted to know about the oldest Tales. Tasman, meanwhile, miserable at a double screen she had so looked forward to manipulating, drew aimlessly while big boys passed behind her and whispered to each other. "Let us ask to read this, this is about the Barbarians." By the end of the morning, no one was interested in anything else. Teachers stroked her but she felt anxiousness in their touch. She wanted to go home.

"Will you choose World, then?"

"I want Book, not World, I want Book."

And now Tasman, too, wanted to know about the Barbarians, to learn to read the oldest Tales. But no Book would take her.

Her mothers had received a letter she did not hear, but they spoke of it. They stopped taking her past the yard, even with Pillowmarie. It was approaching the Darkening of the year. She lay on the roof, in the heat, watching the low sun beyond the fronds, the bit of glistening sea past the dykes to the northwest.

> *"In the night of the afternoon / we will come*
> *calling. In Darkening, we will touch you /*
> *where no one has touched you since your weaning."*

An old love song, voices intertwining, from a roof farther down the street. Soon the blue lights of afternoon would cover the city and the leaves, and the white jasmine, would all be turned blue. She leaned forward, tucking Pillowmarie under her chin. When I learn to read, she thought, I will read the oldest Tales first of all.

"Mam, tell me about the Barbarians."

Mamar spoke sharply. "You will learn that at Book, we know so little."

"I want to go to Book now. Tell me what you know."

Mamel sighed. "I will tell you something—Mar can sleep if she likes." They stroked Tasman; she sensed Mamar's touch, resigned and now gentle.

"Once upon a time, there were more Barbarians than people on the earth. Although they were human, they were fierce and cruel. They lived in great cities that are now ruins in the Sheath, and it is difficult or impossible to explore those places because of the heat. But some people say that when the moon comes near, it will be cool there and we will again traverse the earth."

"How could the Barbarians live there, when it is so hot?"

"It was not so hot then, Tasman. They lived there very well."

"Did they come and kill us?"

"No, our race lived there too. At first, there were very few of us—and when we were born, they killed us if they found us. But parents also killed their own children. Every bicephalic child was killed, it was a decree, but some were saved—in the cities in their medical Book; they say the fathers of our race, Janus, lived to maturity because they were in Book. But there is another Tale about Janus."

"Tell me."

"It was in the place called Lond, which is a great fiery ruin now on the far edge of the Savannah in the Peninsula. Janus was born. Their mother was a Barbarian among Barbarians, and she looked at them and said,

'This was a hard birth, and I knew / Who you
would be, Janus my sons. / I knew my thighs
/ Would nearly break bearing you. / My face
is black. / I cannot walk, or I would hide you.'

So she gave them to her husband and begged him to kill them, because she could not hide them and there were by then too many in the medical Book; and some said, they also killed them there. Her husband, however, took pity on them, and wrapped them up and took them into the east part of that country, and no one stopped him."

"Was it Darkening?"

Mamar spoke. "In Book, you will learn that it becomes dark and light very swiftly in the Sheath of the world."

"So he ran in the dark," went on Mamel, "and in the light he rested and hid. He gave them the milk of animals. I do not know how they survived. Janus's grown body fathered twins, their mothers were much younger, that was Effe, some say they were only eleven years old but perhaps they were thirteen or fourteen."

"Were Effe hid in Book?"

"Surely, Tasman, but they were considered too young to be watched. Effe and Janus had many children while they lived. *Effe Twel and Effe Twar, / First Mothers, help me to bear.*"

"Were their children killed?"

"Not all. Janus had a kind of fortress city by then in the eastern Peninsula. It was the time of the terrible slaughterings and mutilations. But no more Barbarians were being born. I do not know why the old Barbarians did not learn love, or surrender, but it is said that their loneliness was eating into them and they were crazed. Remember that they had powerful cities and enormous wealth. They lived long into our age but they died. They preached and practised genocide against our race. It is said, they refused to look at their own children, but had them killed. Wherever they found us, they killed us."

Tasman looked from one to the other of her mothers' faces. Mamar's gaze was steady and sad. Mamel's difficult, the eyes not yet finished with crying, the mouth stretched a little into a smile. She said, "At Book the other children asked about the Barbarians when they saw you. That does not mean you have anything to do with that ancient race. You are good and kind, and no one knows why you were born untwinned. You asked us about the Saduth because of this, and we told you, because it is good for you to know that being alone is possible on the earth."

They told Tasman the other Tale of Janus also, and no one knows which one is true, or whether they really lived. But not of the mutilations (and he may have been one), most of whom did not live, because it is said that in

Lond and Camp David and some of the other cities, there were two and three generations who were unilaterally garotted, and who garotted their infant children, and held the power like kings; but they were overthrown. There were many old Tales, some more terrible than these.

One morning when Tasman was nearly six, she was told that there was a Book that would take her. "It is very small," her mothers said, as they dressed her and combed her hair. "It is on the outskirts of the city and we will take you there every day in the cars."

"You knew about it yesterday. You heard a letter when I was sleeping."

"Stay still. Where do you want Pillowmarie?"

"I don't care. Twell: I'm going to Book."

They did not tell her that it was an institution connected to the medical Book, and fortunately it was in a separate building, and going in the closed cars Tasman would not even see the place she disliked so much. With Pillowmarie hooded on her left shoulder, she sat upright all the way.

When her mothers left her, and she was taken in and shown around, Tasman saw that it was indeed small. The few children in evidence were strange and silent, most clinging to teachers. The screens looked primitive, like the ones at the markets. There were more teachers than screens. The teachers with her sat down with her and stroked her. They told her they were called Var Fadel and Fadar.

"You are not my Fa," said Tasman angrily. She did not like them, their touch reminded her of medical Book and they were light-skinned.

"We are going to introduce you to some little friends," they said, and took her over to a corner where, with feet pulled up close to their chest, towheaded twins about five years old were eating out of a double bowl. The teachers half-stroked, half-pushed Tasman to persuade her to sit down in front of them, and gave her a bowl with the same food in it—sliced star fruit and bananas. Then they left her.

Tasman observed the little boy-heads closely. The Twel was eating, and their right hand was "pretending to be Twar," she could see that, and pretending to feed the Twar. But the Twar was not eating. His head looked too small. Not by much, but to glance from one to the other was enough to confirm it. His jaw was small and slack. Though his eyes moved, they did not fix. The right hand pushed food into the slack mouth and it remained there. Tasman's eye caught the Twel's in a reciprocative sharp, scared glance. For once she saw someone who did not see or judge her, he was too much on the defensive, too absorbed to be repelled or amazed. He went on trying to feed the Twar, not looking at him, pretending the Twar was doing it. Both wore protective muffs on their adjacent ears; Tasman had seen this on babies. When the Twar moved his head, in a clumsy jerk, away from the Twel, their right hand smeared the banana on his cheek.

Tasman said, "You were doing that *with both hands,* I saw you."

The Twel stared at her, furious. His own mouth full of banana, he had to swallow hastily before he could splutter, "Go away. *Leave us.*" The formal sounded funny. Tasman backed up a little. He did not look at her again, and pulled their feet in closer. *With both hands* and *with both feet,* thought Tasman. If she said it, what would he do?

It might have been possible to be friends with the tow-headed Twel, who after all had looked at her with clear human dislike, without fear, as an equal and not as a curiosity. He was angry at her not because of her malformity, but because of her interference. It was obvious he was going to be loyal to his brother, find in him what comfort and what communication—it was a choice encouraged by his parents, and by Book also; the teachers did not try to intercede for Tasman. She later saw the Twel, whose name was Semer, playing at building a city with other children, and talking with them, and animatedly bringing his Twar into the game, using their right hand: "Now my Twar is raising the dyke"—and the others, though fully aware of the deception, did not deride it.

Tasman liked Semer Twel, but her liking couldn't allow him that silly pretense. "*Leave us,*" that pretentious adult command, was all he ever said to her, and it was a phrase she could not even answer back with, as it had no singular.

She explored the screens and found them too simple, and when she asked for the pictures for the Old Tales she was told there were none "just here" or "just now." Fadel said, "You may ask for whatever you want, this is Book," but it was a strange Book if the pictures you wanted to learn to read from were not there. What words shall I learn, she wondered, and did not know what else to ask. Finally she recalled the Tale of Saduth Twel, and asked for that, but again her teachers denied her. Perhaps tomorrow, they said, indeed ashamed. "We will try to locate it."

"It must be in all Book," insisted Tasman. If they were denying it, they were just too stupid to find it.

In the afternoon, more children arrived. There were lively twins in a chair on wheels, because they could not walk. They were pretty, with a mass of thick, lustreless black hair that was forever entangled. Though they looked only about eight years old, their teeth were already blackened. Tasman wanted to ask them about that, but they stared at her like street children, fascinated and repelled, and then talked softly to each other. Their glances in her direction were deceptive, devious; they were no longer pretty then, and Tasman sensed they'd soon wheel their chair over to the screens and smile with their mouths only, and ask her cruel questions for their own reasons. She ran to the Fa and stayed at their feet, lifting her arms to be stroked.

"I don't want those blackteeth to talk to me," she said.

Fadar Var said, "Come, then, and talk to other little friends." They took her this time across to a second room which had no screens, but a lot of sleeping ledges and long shallow steps covered with rugs. Teachers were sitting with twins there, but stood up and went out when the Fa nodded to them.

Left sitting on the steps was a very small figure. Tasman, led closer, was startled by the great difference in the twins' faces, but then realized that the Twar was bald, or almost so; he had some tufty baby-hair but his bluish-gray scalp showed clearly. The Twel's hair was cropped short, but thick as fur.

Close up, Tasman knew that the Twar mind was dead. She had heard of this, but it had seemed to her like the Tales, and nothing you would encounter in real life. She stood open-mouthed, staring this time the way she herself was stared at, and the Twel's look, downcast, did not prevent her. Somehow the Twar head had been braced, its very stiffness making it more lifeless. Its eyes, half open, were blue around the lids as if bruised. There was a piece of brown transparent tape on its jawline. There were strange, short marks on its scalp, like drawn lines or cuts healed.

"Twel Kistat, this is Tasman," said the Fa gently, almost in unison. They stooped and stroked his arms and chest but he did not look up. He turned his furry head, still downcast, towards his twin, and began in a slow, dreamy motion to clean the corners of its eyes, and smooth the hairless brows. The dark fingers were small, thin, delicate as a girl's. Tasman knew, with a sudden conviction, that this Twel would not live.

> *Sickness did not kill him,*
> *But he did not wish life.*

The Fa were as good as their word and produced the Saduth Tale, and so she learned to read, and demanded the Brother-murder, in which the notorious Twar Yvar twisted and heat-sealed a wire garotte on his Twel, out of jealousy, doing it so swiftly that the Twel could not break free; yet the Twel in a final act of almost superhuman strength broke his murderer's neck— revenge even in death is sweet.

"Where did you hear this Tale?"

"My mothers tell many tales to each other, it is an amusement. Sometimes when they think I am asleep."

The Fa compromised, and produced the ballad, as if rhymes made it more acceptable. But it was not really a Tale, it was modern, it had happened in this generation.

Because she was ignored or repelled by the other children, Tasman read voraciously. She demanded tales of love and jealousy, the old Romances. She only half-wanted to read the oldest Tales, about the Barbarians; what

Mamar had told her was enough for now, and the Tales were there, she would read them when she was ready.

She heard no sounds from the second room, and, if she had had her way, she would have stayed clear of it. But the Fa took her in every day for a time. The Twel never acknowledged her, and she never heard him speak. She went against her will. Once, after the Fa had spoken to his teachers and together quietly for a long time, they persuaded her to go in alone; they said, "Just tell him, Tasman, tell him it is possible to live." She wanted to refuse, but they looked really unhappy—"beautiful in sadness"—so she walked in stiffly, and stood in front of him on the soft floor.

"Twel Kistat, it is possible to live," she said, as if repeating a letter.

He did not look up. She squatted in front of him, where he sat on a higher step. She could see up into his face, and he looked toward her, but whether he saw her or not she could not tell. She whispered, "Look at me."

The blind, dead head, fixed on its stalk like a burnt lamp, was raised while his hung forward. Yet it was the Twel cheeks that were ruddy, it was he who was breathing. Suddenly furious, she jumped up and began to tear at the binding tape behind her shoulders, but she could not find the ties. She burst into tears. Something gave, and she pulled the sleeve over her head, and flung Pillowmarie on the floor in a heap.

"Look at me! It is possible!" she shouted, stamping with rage and the futility of it. Could she have torn that Twar head away so easily, she'd have done so. The Twel looked up. His eyes could not cry any more but he saw her. Perhaps his look said only, "I do not want to live like that," or perhaps he had said this already, once and for all. Her own life, which felt at that moment like a vigorous, crackling fire in her body, persisted for its own reasons. They could not understand each other. The Twel turned away, laying his silent face against his brother's grey temple.

Tasman ran back to the door where the Fa and some others waited. Then she ran back across the room again, grabbed up her tunic. They came to meet her. She was embarrassed now and ashamed. "Put this on me!" Did the Twel hear her, as she went out with the adults murmuring around her?

One day she received a visit at Book. These tall, earnest but smiling twins stayed only a short time, but she would have liked them as her teachers, and for a while she believed they would be. They did not approach her, or stroke her or speak to her, but listened and watched while the Fa talked with her about what she had read and was reading. Did she draw? Sometimes she drew while she was listening to Book. Could she show the strangers how she did this?

Tasman drew her version of a Savannah, something like the Saduth pictures, but with many more snakes in it, made of different coloured lights, while a rather boring Book told her the way numbers multiplied. It was a demonstration, neither subject interested her particularly then, but she wanted to please the strangers.

"Tell us what this is," said Fadel, pointing to Pillowmarie.

"It is not anything. I used to call it Pillowmarie when I was small. It is so I do not get stared at, so I can live." Anticipating their next question, she added, "I wear it either side, I am not really Twel."

Then she was ashamed, because what she was saying was private, the way she talked to her mothers; it did not make sense, and she could tell how the Fa were upset by it, their faces made ugly by her saying it. But the strange Twar spoke, just once, whether to her or to the Fa she was not sure.

"There are many people who are not really Twar mind or Twel mind, it is only an appellation. It is all right to have said this."

The words comforted her. But the strangers did not touch her, and the Fa said they would not come back again. She was so disappointed that she put them out of her mind. She did not tell her mothers of the visit, and did not remember it, when she saw them again. Other events overtook her, the outside world of other people. Though she was unable to make friends at the little Book, she was learning, and she went at it with a greediness that filled her days. The stares of the black-teethed twins made her miserable, but she was quicker than they could be, and stayed away from them. Had she been able to choose, she would have continued at Book despite the bad parts. But the cars were withdrawn. Mamel and Mamar found other drivers who agreed to take them, but often they were late, or would not take her mothers back again.

"You do not need to *accompany-us*," she offered, but they refused to let her go alone. They remained in that part of the city all day. Once, the cars were so late in fetching her from Book, that they almost decided to walk. "We must find a house in this quarter." Then that was what her mothers were doing all day, looking for a new place to live. No one would have them. Mamel cried at night.

Then they were stoned. The cars jerked and stopped. It was on the way to Book. "Go on, go on," urged her mothers. Stones banged on the lid. The cars went on suddenly and fast. At Book, Tasman ran in, she did not wait to hear her mothers arguing with the drivers. Her mothers appeared early in the afternoon. "We cannot get cars," she heard them say to the Fa. "We will have to walk, and we are not sure whether we can protect her."

All the teachers were standing with them inside the entrance. The Fa was saying, "It is all right. She can stay here till you arrange something. Medical Book must agree to it."

What was wrong? If medical Book agreed to keep her, would she have to live in the box again? Silent, Tasman waited while they talked and talked. Perhaps the Fa liked her mothers, and would let them stay too, and sleep with them. She did not like the Fa, but, seeing their hands on her mothers' breasts as they talked, she knew there was sympathy and felt a little hopeful.

She ended up staying in medical Book, somewhere in the large, main building, going to her Book with the Fa in the morning by an interior path, and seeing her mothers settled in rooms she was unable to reach on her own. She slept with other children on a long pallet. There were no boxes but the room had that same constant white brightness, the lights did not change colour with the hours, and this reminded her of her times in the box. The other children were always drowsy or asleep when she left them, and when she returned to bed. She supposed they were sick. Sometimes she cried at night, missing her mothers' nearness.

> *Mamar, Mamel,*
> *Never apart,*
> *Two hands, two breasts,*
> *Two smiles, one heart.*

The Fa had arranged it and it was all that could be done. Each day they took her to eat with her mothers. They ate there also. It was a windowless place, perhaps underground. Mamar and Mamel looked thinner, and tired. After supper, Tasman lay down on the pallet in the adjoining room. She heard their low voices.

"Is it possible?" Mamar said, "Are we to be driven out?"

"It is Moonfall hysteria. We can't suggest anything better than making her a Ward of this Book. No one's happy about it, but it has been offered." That was Fa Twar speaking: he had a squeaky voice.

She heard Mamel stand up suddenly *with both feet* as was her way: "No, no no" (the imperative speech). "That is what the Barbarians did to our race, do you realize that? She would be . . ." Her voice lowered. Someone pulled the curtain up across the opening. Their voices went on for a long time.

"Tasman. Tasman, come, we are going away." She woke roughly, not sure where she was. She was still in her mothers' rooms. They pulled on her leggings and wrapped hoods over her head and Pillowmarie. The Fa were there. They walked, Tasman half running, a long way by interior paths. No one spoke. At a street, cars were waiting. It was short Darkening and the city's lights were a dim orange. The outside air was hot and humid, full of the smell of orchids and gardenias and fire smoke off the dykes. In the cars, she lay across the laps of her mothers and the Fa. She did not ask where they were going. No stones struck the cars, yet it was as if the adults' bodies were stiffened in anticipation of it, of something bad.

The Fa helped them out, and they walked a very long way among bushes, while the world's light grew stronger and clearer. They came, finally, to a low-roof house that seemed quite overgrown with fronded trees. Tasman could hear water running or breathing, as on a long beach, but almost no city sounds.

The Fa went away.

*   *   *

Tasman did not return to Book, or to the city for five years. Her mothers told her that medical Book knew where they were and would provide for them. But no one came to see them except the Fa, and these visits were infrequent.

Tasman got used to the Fa, even to her mothers' whispering "Var" in the night, but she never liked them. Sometimes she told herself stories like the old Romances, and in these stories, the Fa were even younger, like big clumsy-spoken boys, and her mothers were not really her mothers, but more beautiful and self-assured. Some predicament had landed them on an island, and their rescue (which included the dismissal or death by accident of the Fa) was by Travellers arriving on a raft, with beautiful black faces and huge warm hands. Was Tasman there? Not really. But in other stories, she tried to imagine herself loved, the way young girls do, crossing hands, but it did not work, her lovers were faceless. Perhaps, remembering the tow-head Semer Twel and his half-minded twin, she could imagine them well-grown, Twel's look still defiant, and she told herself stories that ended, after long, complex trials, with kisses. But she was fastidious; the retarded twin had to be replaced by one who was blind and recovered his sight by some heroic, intuitive deed on her part. Certainly she wanted to court and be courted by the tow-head Twel first, yet he had to be twinned, as a matter of course, and handsomely. These were stories she created word for word, but never told.

She was in World now, literally, her days spent at the overgrown tidal stream behind the house, and on the great beach that lengthened, running out to the horizon and in again, fast and shallow, swiftly becoming water, becoming sand, like a great breathing. It was dangerous to walk on the flats and it was forbidden, but sometimes at Lightening she did this, late, when the moon hung pocked and bloated overhead and really did look closer, and the warm water swilled past her ankles outward, with a hurrying, whispering sound. When it was gone, and everything was steady and silent, she would run back, imagining it turning and chasing her, a long translucent wave like a skin or a curtain blowing. Two pools near the house filled and emptied too, twice a day, and they bathed there; it was simple and refreshing.

Soon after she was eleven, in Darkening, two events came almost upon one another: her mothers got sick and the Fa took them back to the city. These events were not connected, yet seemed so. For days her mothers had lain slow and feverish in the house. Mamar told her how to care for their body, which seemed to be leaking, diminishing. "Are you trying to become pregnant?" she asked, wondering. She has an idea, suddenly, of another like her, another deformity—

"No, we cannot."

"You could, the Fa have been with you. You said what happened to me would not happen again anywhere—"

"We are sure that it would not. But we are unable to bear more children. No, this is just a sadness in our body, an infection—"

"Did the Fa make you sick?"

"No, Tasman—"

By the time the Fa came with their news, her mothers were well enough to receive it happily, though they had become very thin and weak—they looked old now, Tasman thought, seeing them with the eyes of the Fa, who were still young and whose faces were less beautiful today in complexity— perhaps the Fa wanted them closer, but not their sickness, and perhaps they would desert them, as her real fathers had done. But she misinterpreted this.

"It is a dispensation and amnesty," said Fadel, after they had embraced and lain down. "We have a letter to say to you, and you can hear this for yourselves. It is for you, and there is a temporary one for Tasman. Medical Book has arranged it. Do not be worried that Tasman's is temporary. It is a victory."

"She is too old for your Book now, surely," said Mamar. Tears shone on her cheekbones.

"We do not know what will happen. There are changes in medical Book. They may want to test her again."

Tasman knelt between them where they lay talking, and placed her hands adult-fashion one on the Fa's chest and one on her mothers' breasts.

"I do not want to go to medical Book for tests, or live in the city unless I can go to a real Book. I will wear a new Pillowmarie if I have to, Mamel will make them again, but I need to go to Book."

"We do not know what is going to happen to you. We do not believe you have any choice." The Fa Twar placed his hand over hers. "Your mothers need to go home."

Whoever had lived in their house had taken good care of it. Much of it had been renewed. The streets looked smaller. The dykes had been raised again and the sea was no longer visible from the roof. Tasman realized how happy her mothers were to be back: they touched everything welcome, as she had touched the leaves and sand and stream and low, fronded doorway in the north farewell. Here, though larger, the rooms seemed cramped and dull. The lights of the city seemed less magical than she remembered them, and far less lovely than the stars she had watched from the beach. Worse, it was not possible to go about freely. She wore the new Pillowmarie and tried, but the looks she got shrivelled her courage. And her mothers did not encourage her, they were uneasy unless she was at home. It was best to be indoors or on the roof, and she put Pillowmarie aside. The Fa came very often to see her mothers but they looked restless; it was as if they came with rumours rather than news. "There is no news," she was told, and this was to reassure her, she felt. It was obviously out of the question to think about going to Book, and she no longer asked. She became apprehensive whenever she saw them:

would she be forced to go into medical Book, and be tested? What did that mean? Past the roof, the city shone and changed colour and sounded. She waited.

One day she came in off the roof when the Fa had been and gone and had not called her. Her mothers were on the pallet. Mamar was caressing Mamel's face, which was streaked with tired tears. Mamel's eyes were closed.

"Is she asleep?" asked Tasman, but it was Mamel who answered, "Almost," and the hand gently pushed itself away. Mamar lay back, and gestured for Tasman to sit down. She turned her face from Mamel.

"It has been worked out. You are going away, to live in a city called Uppsal, and do Book," she said in a level voice.

Tasman stared. "Is this decided?"

"Yes" (the emphatic).

Mamar went on: "It is in the Savannahs. Good men have told us in a letter brought by a Traveller, that you can live there. It is a great Book, and a very old one."

"It is their Book then, and will not be mine," said Tasman, and burst into tears.

"Tasman, it is true it will be their Book, but it is not medical, the Fa have also assured us of this. Medical Book is not happy that you are going, but they have been overruled. It is a place where you can learn much and be protected. Do you understand this?"

Tasman was silent.

"If you stay here, you cannot remain with us and you cannot perhaps live. This is how it is for you."

"I would wish to be treated as an adult, even if my teeth are white as milk. I would wish to hear the letters."

"We have not yet learned them. The Fa will tell you them, surely, word for word. We will give a good farewell. We will finish with it, I promise you."

They sat up suddenly and Mamel, jerked awake, stared at Tasman with wide, frightened eyes that suddenly swam with tears. "It is not finished but it will be finished," said Mamar. They pulled Tasman in against their breasts. She shut her eyes against their warmth but she could still see the incompleteness in Mamel's face.

"The old will be finished before the new is allowed to begin," quoted Mamar, her voice breaking. "Good men will come for you.

"It will be within the year, quite soon," she went on more calmly. "Before it is too hot to travel."

They came at Lightening, the Sorud, standing very tall in the doorway, and she thought this was how her fathers must have looked—so distant and courteous and upright, with their blackened teeth and long, widely-spaced eyes. Their hair was long and thick and loosely twined, hanging down their chest between their heads in a single braid whose end-strands were bleached almost white, as she had heard the hair of Savannah-dwellers can be. Sorud Twel had a much broader face, the muscles masseter and orbicularis mundi were thick and mobile, and it was he who spoke and laughed and smiled. Sorud Twar was silent, his face rather gaunt and inward, yet she felt him inviting her to come to him, and sat on the floor close to his hand. But it did not move, only the Twel's caresses of courtesy acknowledged her as he spoke with her mothers, and touched her almost absentmindedly in the way of men caressing female children, light strokes, up and down her back and arms and sides.

The private leave-taking and the formal one were both over. Tasman had no more crying left to do, nor did her mothers; they saw each other expressionlessly, grief had wrung them well. And she had said good-bye to the Fa as well, forgiving them in tears of rage; no longer jealous, she could see clearly their love-bond to her mothers as she put it behind her. And she had touched the house intimately in all its particulars, so that now as she passed the rooms for the last time she sensed them as familiar but withdrawn. She was ready.

The trip to the south terminus took most of the day. She lay against the Sorud in the cars in a kind of exhaustion of spirit, but did not sleep. The Twel again caressed her, his hand moving slowly the length of her gloved foot, the arch and ankle, then up and down her legs, sides, arms.

Then she felt the Twar hand move very gently to her shoulder and across her throat to the meeting of her clavicles, the "salt cellars" there, his narrow adult fingers very gently pressing and touching. "Are you of medical Book?" she asked, but not afraid, because there was a difference in his touch.

"No," he said, using the emphatic, that broached no argument. "Historical, it is called." She had never heard that word.

"It was I who named you, Tasman," he said. "I sent that name in a letter eleven years ago, in answer to a request from the Namers in your city. I saw you once again, when you were six. I have never forgotten you."

Later, he was to tell her, "I believe you are a true Barbarian. And I do not believe they were terrible savages, even though they did their best to destroy us, and nearly succeeded. They were also people, their race walked, and you will learn this. We have archives that tell good Tales about them, they lived and did Book under this very place where we live. When we become less afraid of our past, we will be able to remember these things. And sometimes, Tasman, when I have had my head in Book for many days, and thought only of these things, and I look up and see you, I see what you really are."

He did not say these things now, but they were contained in the strange word he had used, and in his touch, which was curious but not like the medical Book which had touched her there and measured her and made her feel even more deformed under their proddings and stares.

His fingers moved around her naked neck, her throat so small in the far too loose single sleeve Mamel had sewn her, frail and exposed like a stem without leaves, a stripped branch. They slid behind her ears, and reaching down seemed to draw and gather her narrow shoulders upward, joining her sad, simple head to her body by their large and gentle stroke—a completion and together-sensing. Her nape tingled, and the surface muscles of her face; she felt them changing at the edges of her eyes, like sadness acknowledged. He is making me beautiful, she thought; his touch was different than anyone else's had ever been, even her mothers'.

The Uppsal terminal lay far across the northern Savannah. The Sorud stretched, and lifted her out of the cars, and then the provisions, strapping them across their upper arms and thighs. They stepped out of their cumbersome footgloves, and Tasman did the same, and felt on the soles of her feet the heat of the world. She stared about her. There was not even scrub forest here, only low bushes, and sand that in places was freshly blown across the path. They began to walk southeastward. Tasman saw and saw again the place where surely her fathers had fallen. The dry earth reached between her toes, and smelled sweet, some herb she seemed to recall, but could not name. The sun was low over the long smooth slopes to the northwest.

Sorud Twar was silent, but the Twel told her about Uppsal, and where she would live, just as he had told her mothers—with them, eating out of their bowls and drinking from their cups. He told her about Book, but she could not imagine it; it was deep, he said, and cool, there were real things in it, as well as screens and copies, it was like the Tales of the ruins, but it was not ruins, it was a modern city.

She did not ask, but she did not think there were children at the Uppsal Book, certainly not where she would be with the Sorud, and this was good, because she had never felt like children, and did not now. She walked taller at the Sorud's side.

The Twel told her also about the Savannahs, and Tasman knew it was he who loved to go there, away from the city, it was because of him that their hair was bleached white.

"There is a great plain to the east, and they say it is an old sea bed, at least, Twar says so, and he is called a Great Authority." He laughed softly. "There are wells there, and yeast farms, it is not all wild. But farther east it is wild. We have gone farther, making fires and paths, it is not so dark at Darkening, we can see by the stars and moon, and it is cooler then. Twar sleeps, but there is a ruin we will go to soon, and he dreams of this place, because it was a great Barbarian city, and it is accessible, we have been told. It is farther than the ruin Len."

"I have never been to World," said Tasman, "but I have played on the shore all the time we lived north of the city."

"Then you will go to World with me." His voice was warm and joyous.

She walked until Darkening, holding the Twel's large hand and listening to him, and then they lifted her up and carried her, baby-fashion, her legs straddling their hip-bundles on either side, and what she guessed was not the bundles but their own, darker burden, alive and comfortable between her thighs as they strode forward. She remembered part of an old song: *When our teeth are made black / When we are touched in the new / old places.* Her bare feet hung free.

Weary, she pressed her face into their braided hair, that smelled stale and good, like wood smoke. The air was cooling. The Twel's hand caressed her back and shoulder blades, up and down, but she kept herself awake, until at last it stayed, supporting her; and she felt the Twar hand, harmonious, release its support and move to her vestigial seventh cervical, and cover her nape and rest there. Then, she allowed herself to fall asleep.

THE LONELINESS OF THE LONG-DISTANCE WRITER

Lesley Choyce

Lesley Choyce is an energetic force in Canadian SF. He teaches part-time at Dalhousie University in Halifax and runs Pottersfield Press in Lawrencetown Beach, Nova Scotia (which published, among other titles, Terence M. Green's *The Woman Who Is the Midnight Wind*). He coedited, with John Bell, *Visions from the Edge* (1981), a (mostly?) reprint anthology of SF stories from Atlantic Canada. His own collection of SF stories, *The Dream Auditor*, ("science fiction short stories that accurately describe alternate worlds not at all unlike the one we live in") was published in 1986. Perhaps his most significant recent achievement is in editing the anthology *Ark of Ice* (Pottersfield Press, 1992) a mixture of reprint and original fiction that includes both a majority of the best contemporary Canadian SF writers and a carefully chosen selection of work by fine Canadian writers not normally associated with the genre, such as Timothy Findlay, W. P. Kinsella, Tom Marshall, and Geoffrey Ursell, on the theme of the future of Canada.

"The Loneliness of the Long-Distance Writer" is reprinted from his collection. It is perhaps reminiscent of nothing so much as Ray Bradbury's fiction, which uses the tropes and figures of science fiction to acute moral purpose.

Even now I sometimes have my doubts about being a writer. I mean, it's not like I have a big audience.

There is a grand total of four readers in this solar system who see my work. Dolph Tonkins for one—but then he was the devil that planted the seed in me to begin with. Sister Theresa McCullough in her home for aging nuns in Dunvegan is the second. And then there's Tess, also cloistered away, but under different circumstances. And, of course, she's much younger. Without her I would have given up long ago.

As far as I know, no one else in the solar system can read. Reading is such an ancient custom that no one (including me sometimes) can see for what conceivable purpose it stands. The university keeps me alive here out of some sort of respect for the prehistorics, I suppose. I think old farts like Mellaghy and Bustrom teaching in the Ancient Cultures Department still feel that there was something more to writing than just whimsical foppery. That it might have had something to do with communication. But certainly not in any way related to the way it is known today.

"How can you communicate, if you can't *be* there?" they all argue. "You'd be missing all the bloody parts." Meaning of course arms, legs, facial expression. "No one could possibly take it seriously. It was just a fashionable mclune, a form of stand-up comedy."

So that makes me a sort of court jester, and way the hell out of my century at that. Thanks a lot, Dolph.

But then it was Dolph who saved my life. When I was a kid, you see, my old man had us living in a condovillage just east of Darkday City. Unlike other lucky families we were stuck on the moon instead of somewhere more interesting farther out. The only thing appealing about the place was that I could take a dustbike out for a spin as often as I wanted once I had passed the driving test. My father, however, was always warning me: "Dammit, Rick, don't go spookin' around on the dark side or I swear, I won't let you ride that friggin' thing for the rest of your life."

Of course, the dark side, only about twenty kilometres away, was what interested me most. So off I went. Ten miles in I burned out a light. The auxiliary package was weak, no doubt because I hadn't recharged it since I bought the thing. I tried to navigate my way back to the line with about two and a half watts against eternal night. Just my luck, I wiped out in an overly ambitious dust pit, flipped over the rig and landed on a sharp piece of pure nickel which put a tiny crescent rip in my suit. I started to get dizzy and kept trying to focus on the light line, way the hell off and just before I passed out I had the good sense to flip on the SOS blaster.

Dolph was the guy who found me. He was probably the only living creature within five kilometres. He had himself a comfy little geocell tucked under a ledge at the bottom of a crater. A true recluse. And talk about your weird ideas. He showed me piles of paper with stuff written all over. Words.

"So?" I asked.

"So, I want you to learn how to do it," he told me, as I lay there still recovering.

"What the Murphy for?" I said, beginning to worry if this was all part of some weirdo religion like the Cosmic Church of Carnal Knowledge or something.

"Because you owe it to me, bud. I saved your life."

"Oh." I was beginning to see his point. Besides, I was getting used to learning totally useless skills. It seemed to be what civilization was all about.

I sat through the first of many lessons concerning writing, certain that the old turkey was whacked out of his gourd, but nonetheless I owed it to him.

Dolph was totally opposed to holovision and refused to ever allow a single holoversion of himself made. "It saps your soul, Rick, I'm sure of it. A fake light image of you that looks exactly like you in every respect travelling off somewhere and doing your talking for you."

"Well, it can do more than talk, it can do . . . well, almost anything. That's communication, buster!" I was a rotten student, and so defensive of the society that I had come from.

Later I could see the problems with holos. Take the university for example. Most of the kids don't ever show up for class, but send their holos instead. Shimmering light visions sit in the seats, answer questions, make passes at each other behind the teacher's back. A lot of weirdness goes on. The profs are so adept at holos and have such sophisticated transmitters that very few people can tell if it is a holo or an original who's up front lecturing on astrophysics and neuro-palaeontology.

We've become a very leisurely society. It causes a lot of hardship. I'd hate to tell you about how many cases the shrinks have to deal with where the originals get themselves confused with their own holos or where somebody makes so many improvements over himself through a holoversion that they call it quits altogether. I mean, once you've perfected yourself and it's not you, then what? I don't think Mellaghy or Bustrom ever use holos, at least not for teaching. But even they don't know how to read. Mellaghy argues that he doesn't really think most of us are even *physically* capable of it. He says it's more or less something we've evolved out of, like the primitive way that men and women used to have sex.

According to Dolph, that's a lot of bull. Dolph claims to have fathered his own kid. I mean physically. She lives alone in a tiny geocell on Ganymede, where she writes poetry. I don't know how Tess became a poet. Or why. Dolph was a confessional novelist. He was happy that I wanted to stick with novels and short fiction.

"One poet in the family is enough," he said.

"What do you mean, *family*?" I said.

"I just mean figuratively," he said as he brought down the heavy blade of the self-fashioned paper cutter. Dolph had to manufacture all of his own paper. "As far as I know, I'm the only paper manufacturer in the solar system," he'd brag. Which is probably true since he does supply Tess and Sister T. and, of course, me.

Without a doubt, I have more paper in my possession than anyone on Earth. Sister Theresa, of course, has a small stock. She's neither a novelist nor a poet, but has taken on the dubious role of literary critic. She uses words and paper more sparingly. And every other writer alive depends on her judgment—all three of us.

Sister T. has angered me more than once with her criticism. "Put more oomph in it," she'd say. "More life. Develop characters, not just stereotypes." Or "a sensitive mind and spirit, but your work lacks the necessary grace and cohesiveness," would be another one of her comments to a piece I had laboured on for months.

Theresa's claim to fame is that she has read real "books." Not too many scholars hold credence to the fact that there ever was such a thing as widespread use of books. Could you imagine a writer writing for more than a handful of readers? I think the old girl has a good imagination, but what the hell, that's what it's all about, eh? (She's also requested that I "clean up the language." However, I learned from Big Dolph himself and he's responsible for my vocabulary.)

In the end, I always forgive her for all her insults, which are always well-meaning. And I can't afford to alienate the reading audience that I have. Bustrom has offered to try to help me turn my first novel, *Two and a Half Watts Against Eternal Night*, into a holovision performance creating composite characters and all. Imagine the audience I'd have! But alas, Dolph would kill me and Tess might never forgive me. That I couldn't afford.

Tess does have a few of her mother's traits. She can be critical. She reduced me to tears when she commented on my recent book, *The Nocturnal Mission*. She called it "sophomoric and shallow." I had tried to write a humorous book about nickel mining on an asteroid, but I don't think I could quite pull it off. And like Theresa, Tess doesn't use much paper. You know how long it takes the old-style cargo ships to get from the moon to Ganymede. And Dolph's complaining that it's getting harder to locate the right supplies.

In case I haven't mentioned it, I'm in love with Tess. Love, that is, as I understand it. None of this bullshit about priming up a perfect holoversion of yourself and transmitting it over to a chick's house where she has to quickly get out the tape of herself at her best. You might as well be watching DV. I'm not even sure these college kids bother with romance anymore at all. Not with holos or anything. It's one more thing that might as well be called irrelevant.

But I picture Tess tucked away in her little geocell on the outskirts of nowhere on Ganymede writing out her short heart-wrung poetry on tiny portions of paper. She writes about love and rocks and stars; if you ask me, it is a little corny and she suffers from all those faults that she accuses me of. But it takes me a lot more words to accomplish the faults. And I've never read what Sister Theresa has to say about her daughter's poetry.

Someday, I was sure, Tess and I would get our lives woven together somehow and settle down, maybe right there on Ganymede and do nothing but write and make love in the primitive style, which must have been the way that Dolph and Sister T. did it if Tess is their composite daughter. It all still baffles me, I assure you.

It also occurs to me that we're all getting rather old and could be producing much more if we were taking advantage of the technology at hand. I'm pushing ninety and probably halfway through life, and, let's face it, most of society thinks that I'm a good-for-nothing. It's productivity that counts. New devices, new fuels, new methods for bouncing around the universe. Everyone is always trying to get somewhere. And it all involves spending money. Success, as you know, means not how much money you've made, but how much you can spend.

That's why I almost got my writer-in-res post at the university taken away from me. Lord knows, I wouldn't have been replaced. They were pissed at me for sitting on my butt and doing nothing but scratching ink spots on paper. I tried to explain that this was my fifth and perhaps greatest novel, *Vindictive Destinies*. Ninety-four per cent of the faculty said it was a lot of crapola. And good old Mellaghy and Bustrom, loyal to the word and to me to the end, finally came up with something. They had been sniffing around in some ancient computer tapes. "Half the friggin' things turned to dust when we tried to run them through the IBM replica," Mel complained. They always came across old stuff that was valueless and irrelevant, and nobody paid them much attention anyway. But this tape concerned a research vessel sent off towards Epsilanti 5 in what most scholars call prehistory—thousands of years before holos. Well, according to the dynamic duo, this ship was going so slowly that they (or their descendents) were probably still at it.

The response from the faculty senate was unanimous: "So?"

"So," Bustrom responded, "people in those days read. They read books. If they're still out there, their descendents that is, why not overtake them with a little care package. Mellaghy's got the co-ordinates. We can send a micro-warp cargo most of the way there, freeze it down to sub light and pull up alongside. They're sure to pick it up."

The faculty thought it was absurd, of course. But it was expensive and they could get a gumment grant for any project that was new and costly, so it was passed by a majority. We got quite a lot of publicity and we were all thought to be crackpots which seemed to cheer up the whole school in a way. Sister T. and Tess had their doubts about it and thought that I was being corrupted by "crass commercialism." But I have to admit I was tempted by the thought of having an audience larger than three. You can imagine how absurd it appeared to most; trying to communicate with the descendents of the ancients rambling around in space for who knows how long in a decrepit old space tub. And I stewed for weeks over which one to send. I only had one manuscript of each and I had sworn never to let anyone read them in a form other than in the actual print. Tess, Theresa and Dolph had all read all my work and there wasn't really anyone else to read here, so I figured I had little to lose. I sent off *Two and a Half Watts*. The micro-warp was equipped with a homer on it so it was just a matter of sitting back and waiting for the reviews. In the meantime I began a romantic novel called *The Girl Within the Cloud* which I intended to woo dear Tess with. If the university wanted to keep me on, they'd have to let me work out of the auxiliary campus network in the University of the Outer Planets. I wasn't about to sit around Earth for much longer. Tess was out there writing sonnets somewhere and I intended to be with her.

"Very quaint," Dolph had said, "but I'm proud of you."

Tess wrote back that she wasn't opposed to the idea but that for her, love could only be real if it was physical. So I promised her that it would be physical. I hoped I would figure out something when I got there.

Sister T. asked me if I was sure I knew what I was getting into and reminded me that Tess had been conceived "the primitive way" and that I might find her different.

Well, I had some doubts, I admit. But when word came back from the Epsilanti 5 crew concerning *Two and a Half Watts* I felt like I could do anything. There were apparently a hundred descendents on the ship and they understood the language, they were in fact, *readers*. A Captain J. T. Morganthal wrote back, ". . . a moving masterpiece, had me crying and laughing, the best thing read on this vessel in generations. . . . Send more!"

So we sent off *Mission* and *Destinies* and even one that I had kept hidden in a drawer for years. Mellaghy and Bostrum went on locating more and more derelict ships and I was commissioned to produce at least one novel a year for each. What bliss!

They talked Dolph into sending off a dozen manuscripts to a supposed ancient colony of Earthlings in the Horsehead Nebula along with introductions by Sister T. concerning the state of the literary art on Earth. (In her view, we were achieving an unprecedented peak of interest in the novel.) But I was having a hard time convincing them of the validity of "publishing" poetry. (That's what we called the new wave of manuscript exports.) Particularly, they had their doubts about Tess, who had been, of course, conceived by the primitive method; whatever that exactly was, few people had any idea. But in the end, Mellaghy and Bustrom came through again. It was always possible to convince Earthlings to dump money into space since the potential still seemed to exist, whereas another dollar spent on Earth was like throwing good money after bad. After all, a worn out planet is a worn out planet.

And I have been assigned my long-sought-after writer-in-res post on Ganymede. I've decided not to send a holoversion ahead first to get things settled there and make artificial acquaintance with Tess. Instead, I will arrive with nearly half a ton of paper and a century's supply of pens and ink.

Tess has recently sent me a poem about the view of Jupiter from her back door, something that speaks of eternity and vigilance. Something called an ode.

Bustrom arrived the other day almost in tears. He thought he was the messenger of bad news, but I already knew. When I leave the university, I'll be able to take my paper and my ink, but there's no way to take along the circuits from my cubicle that keep me going. I have to leave behind my longevity. I've been unplugged before. Not that I've wandered around outside on this planet like the freaks. I just write better when I'm unplugged. Without all the hormone stabilizers, you go up and down better. A writer shouldn't be up all the time. It makes for lousy prose.

So I'll move to Ganymede and lop off a hundred years. Living that far off the beaten path of the neural networks, I could never depend on good reception. Besides, Tess has never been plugged in. Dolph and Sister T. planned it that way. Like Dolph explained it: "Sometimes you get more out of a short life."

I've got fifteen—maybe twenty—years tops. Tess is only thirty. She'll outlive me to go on writing ballads, elegies, epics even. That doesn't bother me a bit. I'll have had my shot at literature. My novels will be out there skidding through space in those faster-than-light bookmobiles, seeking out generations of lost readers sent wandering through darkness in the primitive years. They are waiting to be illuminated by my manuscripts. "Immortality by any other name. . . ."

USER FRIENDLY

Spider Robinson

Spider Robinson began publishing SF stories in 1973, the year he moved to Canada, and was cowinner of the John W. Campbell Award for best new writer in SF in 1974. By the early 1980's, he had won the Hugo Award three times, the Nebula once, and become one of the leading reviewers of the SF field. He has written seven novels (the best known is *Stardance*, written in collaboration with his wife, Jeanne Robinson) and published five collections of short fiction (three of which comprise his humorous series set in Callahan's saloon).

Robinson is a writer of wit and energy, given to puns and allusions. *Twentieth Century Science Fiction Writers* refers to his use of dialogue and internal monologue as a style more lyric than narrative, and goes on to claim that "the lyric quality of Robinson's SF is his means of fusing social critique with technological optimism, two themes that do not easily join in the hard SF universe. . . ." "User Friendly" is a fine example of Robinson's fiction, and is perhaps his most specifically Canadian piece.

When he saw the small, weatherbeaten sign which read, "Welcome to Calais, Maine," Sam Waterford smiled. It hurt his mouth, so he stopped.

He was tired and wired and as stiff as IRS penalties; he had been driving for . . . how long? He did not really know. There had been at least one entire night; he vividly remembered a succession of headlight beams coring his eyeballs at some time in the distant past. Another night was near, the sun low in the sky. It did not matter. In a few more minutes he would have reached an important point in his journey: the longest undefended border in the world. Once past it, he would start being safe again. . . .

He retained enough of the man he had once been to stop when he saw the Duty-Free Store. Reflex politeness: a guest, especially an unexpected one, brings a gift. But the store was closed. It occurred to him distantly that in his half-dozen trips through these parts, no matter what time he arrived, that store had always been closed. The one on the Canadian side, on the other hand, was almost always open. Too weary to wonder why, he got back into his Imperial and drove on.

He had vaguely expected to find a long line-up at the border crossing, but there was none. The guards on the American side ignored him as he drove across the short bridge, and the guards on the Canadian side waved him through. He was too weary to wonder at that, too—and distracted by the mild surge of elation that came from leaving American soil, leaving the danger zone.

It was purely subjective, of course. As he drove slowly through the streets of St. Stephen, New Brunswick, the only external reminders that he was in Canada were the speed limit signs marked in metric and the very occasional bilingual sign (French, rather than the Spanish he was used to in New York). Nonetheless, he felt as though the invisible band around his skull had been loosened a few notches. He found a Liquor Commission outlet and bought a bottle of Old Bushmill's for Greg and Alice. A Burger King next door reminded him that he had not eaten for . . . however long the trip had lasted so far, so he bought something squishy and ate it and threw most of it up again a few miles later.

He drove all the rest of that evening, and long into the night, through endless miles of tree-lined highway interrupted only seldom by a village speed-trap, and once by the purely nominal border between the provinces of New Brunswick and Nova Scotia, and he reached the city of Halifax as the sun was coming up on his left. Dimly he realized that he would shortly be drinking Old Bushmill's and talking, and he expected both to be equally devastating to his system, so he took the trouble to find the only all-night restaurant in Halifax and tried eating again, and this time it worked. He'd had no chance to change his money, but of course the waitress was more than happy to accept Yankee currency: even allowing him a 130% exchange rate, she was making thirty-seven cents profit on each dollar. The food lifted his spirits just enough that he was able to idly admire Halifax as he drove through it, straining to remember his way. It had been many years since any city in America had looked this pleasant—the smog was barely noticeable, and the worst wino he noticed had bathed this year. As he drove past Citadel Hill he could see the Harbour, saw pleasure craft dancing on the water (along with a couple of toothless Canadian Forces destroyers and a sleek black American nuclear sub), saw birds riding the morning updrafts and heard their raucous calls. He was not, of course, in a good mood as he parked in front of Greg and Alice's house, but he was willing to concede, in theory, that the trick was possible.

He was still quite groggy; for some reason it seemed tremendously important to knock on the precise geometrical center of Greg's door, and maddeningly difficult to do so. When the door opened anyway it startled him. His plans stopped here; he had no idea what to do or say next.

"Sammy!" His old college buddy grinned and frowned simultaneously. "Jesus, man, it's good to see you—or it would be if you didn't look like death on a soda cracker! What the hell are you doing here, why didn't you—"

"They got her, Greg. They took *Marian*. There's nothing I—"

Suddenly Greg and the front of his house were gone, replaced by a ceiling, and Sam discovered that he was indoors and horizontal. "—can do," he finished reflexively, and then realized that he must have fainted. He reached for his head, probed for soft places.

"It's okay, Sam: I caught you as you went down. Relax."

Sam had forgotten what the last word meant; it came through as noise. He sat up, worked his arms and legs as if by remote control. The arms hurt worse than the legs. "Got a cigarette? I ran out—" He thought for a moment. "—yesterday, I think."

Greg handed him a twenty-five-pack of Export A. "Fill your boots. Have you eaten more recently than that?"

"Yeah. Funny—I actually forgot I smoked. Now, that's weird." He fumbled the pack open and lit a cigarette; his first puff turned half an inch to ash and stained the filter. "Did I drop the bottle?"

"You left it in the car." Greg left the room, returned with two glasses of Irish whiskey. "You don't have to talk until you're ready."

Sam restrained the urge to gulp. If you got too drunk, you had *less* control of your thoughts sometimes. "They took her. The aliens—you must have read about them up here. They *appropriated* her, like losing your home to municipal construction. Sorry, railroad's coming through, we need your universe. No, not even that polite—I didn't even get the usual ten percent of market value and a token apology."

"Christ, Sam, I'm sorrier than I know how to say. Is she . . . I mean, how is she taking it?"

"Better than I would. She's still alive."

Greg's face took on the expression of a man who is not sure he should be saying what he is saying, but feels compelled to anyway. "Knowing you, the way you feel about such things, I'm surprised you didn't kill her yourself."

"I tried. I couldn't. You know, that may just be the worst part."

"Ah, Sam, Sam—"

"She begged me to. *And I couldn't!*"

They waited together until he could speak again. "Damn," he said finally, "it's good to see you." And it would be even better to see Alice. She must be at work, designing new software to deadline.

Greg looked like he'd been missing some sleep himself. Novelists often did. "You might as well get it all out," he said. "How did it happen?"

Sam nodded slowly, reluctantly. "Get it over with. Not a lot to tell. We were laying in bed together, watching TV. We'd . . . we'd just finished making love. Funny, it was better than usual. I was feeling blessed. Maybe that should have warned me or something. All of a sudden, in the middle of David Letterman's show—do you get him up here?"

"We get all the American shows; these days, it's about all we get. Go on."

"Right in the middle of Stupid Pet Tricks, she just got up and left the room. I asked her to bring me back some ice water. She didn't say anything.

A few moments later I heard the front door open and close. I didn't attach any significance to it. After five or ten minutes I called to her. I assumed she was peeing or something. When she didn't answer I got up and went to make sure she was all right. I couldn't find her.

"I could *not* figure it out. You know how it is when something just does not make sense? She wasn't anywhere in the apartment. I'd heard the door, but she couldn't have gone out—she was naked, barefoot, her coat and boots were still in the hall closet. I couldn't imagine her unlocking the door for anyone we didn't know, certainly not for someone who could snatch her out the door in two seconds without the slightest sound or struggle. I actually found myself looking under chairs for her.

"So eventually I phoned the police, and got all the satisfaction you'd expect, and called everyone we knew with no success at all, and finally I fell asleep at four A.M. hoping to God it was some kind of monstrous joke she was playing on me.

"Two government guys in suits came that night. They told me what had happened to her. Sir, your wife has been requisitioned by aliens. Quite a few people's husbands and wives have been. And we wouldn't do anything about it if we could, which we can't. They were good; I never laid a hand on them. When I calmed down enough they took me to the hospital to see her. She was in pretty good shape, all things considered. Her feet were a mess, of course, from walking the streets barefoot. Exposure, fatigue. After the aliens turned her loose, she was raped by four or five people before the police found her. You remember New York at night. But they didn't cut her up or anything, just raped her. She told me she almost didn't mind that. She said it was a relief to be only physically raped. To be able to struggle if she wanted, even if it didn't help. To at least have the power to protest." He stubbed his cigarette out and finished his drink. "Strange. She was just as naked while she was possessed, but no human tried to touch her until afterward. Like, *occupado*, you know?"

Greg gave him his own, untouched drink. "Go on."

"Well, God, we talked. You know, tried to talk. Mostly we cried. And then in the middle of a snuffle she chopped off short and got up out of the hospital bed and left the room. I was so mixed up it took me a good five seconds to catch on. When I did I went nuts. I tried to chase after her and catch her, and the two government guys stopped me. I broke the nose of one of them, and they wrestled me into somebody's room and gave me a shot. As it was taking hold I turned and looked sideways out the window, just in time to catch a glimpse of her, three flights down, walking through the parking lot. Silly little hospital gown, open at the back, paper slippers. Nobody got in her way. A doctor was walking in the same direction; he was a zombie too. Masked and gloved, blood on his gloves; I hope he finished his operation first . . .

"She came home the next day, and we had about six hours. Long enough to say everything there was to say five times, and a bunch of other things that maybe should never have been said. This time when she left, she left dressed, with an empty bladder and money to get home with when they let her go. We had accepted it, taken the first step in starting to plan around it. Only practical, right?" He shook his head, hearing his neck crack, and finished off the second drink. It had no more effect than had the first.

"What happened then?"

"I got in the car and drove here."

For the first time, Greg looked deeply shocked. "You left her there, to deal with it *alone*?"

Someone grasped Sam's heart in impersonal hands and wrung it out. Greg must have seen the pain, and some of the accusatory tone left his voice. "Jesus wept, Sam! Look, I know you. You've written three entire books on brainwashing and mind-control, 'the ultimate obscenity,' you call it: I know how uniquely horrible the whole thing must be to you, and for you. But you've been married to Marian for *ten years,* as long as I've been married to Alice—how could you possibly have left her?"

The words came out like projectile vomit. "I *had* to, God damn it: I was *scared*!"

"Scared? Of what?"

"Of *them,* for Christ's sake, what's the matter with you? Scared that the thing would look out of her eyes and notice me—and decide that I looked . . . *Useable.*" He began to shudder, and found it extremely hard to stop. He lit another cigarette with shaking hands.

"Sam, it doesn't work that way."

"I know, I know, they told me. Who said fear has to be logical?"

Greg sat back and sighed deeply, a mournful sound. There was a silence, then, which lasted for ten seconds or more. The worst was said, and there was nothing else to say.

Finally Sam tried to distract himself with mundane trivia. "Listen, I saw the 'No Parking' sign where I parked, I just didn't give a damn. If I give you my keys, will you move it for me? I don't think I can."

"Can't do it," Greg said absently. "I don't dare. They could fine me four hundred bucks if I get caught behind the wheel of an American-registered car, you know that."

The subject had come up on Sam's last visit, back in 1982. Marian had been with him, then. "Sorry. I forgot."

"Sam, what made you decide to come *here*?"

He discovered that he did not know. He tried to analyze it. "Well, part of it is that I needed to tell somebody the whole thing, and you and Alice are the only people on earth that love me enough. But there wasn't even that much logic to it. I was just terrified, and I needed to get to someplace safe, and Canada was the nearest place."

Greg burst out laughing.

Sam stared at him, scandalized. "What's so funny?"

It took Greg quite a while to stop laughing, but when he did—despite the smile that remained on his face—Sam could see that he was very angry.

"Americans, no shit. You're amazing. I should be used to it by now, I guess."

"What are you talking about?"

"About you, you smug, arrogant bastard. There are nasty old aliens in the States, taking people over and using them to walk around and talk with, for mysterious purposes of their own—so what do you do? Take off for Canada, where it'll be safe. You just *assume*, totally unconsciously, that the aliens will think like you. That they'd never bother with a quaint, backward, jerkwater country like Canada, The Retarded Giant On Your Doorstep! Don't you read the papers?"

"I don't—"

"Excuse me. Stupid of me: it probably wouldn't make the Stateside papers, would it? You simple jackass, there are *three times* more Canadians hagridden than Americans! Even though you've got ten times the population. They came here *first*."

"First? No, that can't be, I'd have heard—"

"Why? We barely heard about it ourselves, with two out of the sixteen channels Canadian-originated. It ain't news unless and until it happens in the friggin' United Snakes of America!" He had more to say, but suddenly he tilted his head as if he heard something. "Hell. Stay there." He got up and left the room hastily, muttering to himself.

Sam sat there, stunned by his old friend's inexplicable anger. He finished his cigarette and lit another while he tried to understand it. He heard a murmur of voices elsewhere in the house, and recognized the one that wasn't Greg's. Alice was home from work. Perhaps she would be more sympathetic. He got up and followed the sound of the voices, and it wasn't until he actually saw her that he remembered. Alice hadn't worked night shift in over a year—and she had a home terminal now anyway . . .

She was in pretty fair shape. Face drawn with fatigue, of course, and her hair in rats. She was fully dressed except for pants and panties; there was an oil or grease stain on the side of her blouse. She tried to smile when she saw Sam.

"He caught me sitting on the john," she said. "Hi, Sam." She burst into tears, still trying to smile.

He thought for a crazy second that she meant her husband. But no, of course, the "he" she referred to was not Greg, but her—

—her *rider*. Her User . . .

"Oh, my dear God," he said softly, still not quite believing. He had been so sure, so unthinkingly convinced that it would be safe here.

"Naturally the Users came here first," Greg said with cold, bitter anger, handing his wife the slacks she had kicked off on her way out the door some hours before. "We were meant for each other, them and Canadians. Strong, superior parasites from the sky? Who just move right in and take over without asking or apologizing?" His voice began to rise in pitch and volume. "Arrogant puppetmasters who show up and start pulling your strings for you, dump you like a stolen car when they're done with you, too powerful to fight and indifferent to your rage and shame? And your own government breaks its neck to help 'em do whatever they want, sells out without even stopping to ask the price in case it might offend 'em?" He was shouting at the top of his lungs. "Hell, man, we almost didn't even notice the Users. *We took 'em for Americans.*"

Alice was dressed again now. Her voice was soft and hoarse; someone had been doing a lot of talking with her vocal cords recently. "Greg, shut up."

"Well, dammit all, he—"

She put a hand over his mouth. "Please, my very beloved, shut your face. I can't talk louder than you this time, my throat hurts."

He shut up at once, put his own hand over hers and held it tightly against his face, screwing his eyes shut. She leaned against him and they put their free arms around each other; the sight made Sam want to weep like a child.

"Greg," she said huskily, "I love you; part of me wants to cheer what you just said; many Canadians would. But you're wrong to say it."

"I know, baby, I know *exactly* the pain Sam's going through, don't I? That's why I got mad at him, thinking his pain was bigger 'cause it was American. I'm sorry, Sam—"

"That's only part of why you're wrong. This is more important than our friendship with Sam and Marian, my love. Pay attention: *you would never have said what you said if there'd been an Inuit in the room.* Or a Micmac, or a French Canadian, or a Pakistani. You'd never have said it if we were standing in North Preston, talking to someone who used to live in Africville 'til they moved all the darkies out to build a bridge approach. Don't you see, darling, everybody is a Canadian now. Everybody on Earth is now a Native People; a Frog; a Wog; a Paki; a Nigger—gradations of Niggerhood just don't seem all that important any more.

"Gregory, some of the Users wear a human body as though it ought to have flippers, or extra legs, or wings—I saw one try to make an arm work like a tentacle, and break it. There are a lot of different races and species and genuses of User—one of the things they seem to be using Earth for is a conference table at which to work out their own hierarchy of power and intelligence and wealth. I've heard a lot of the palaver; they don't bother to turn my ears off because they don't care if I hear or not. Most of it I don't understand even though they do use English a lot, but a few things I've noticed.

"If two neighboring races discover that one is vastly superior to the other in resources or wisdom or aggressiveness, they don't spend a lot of time whining about the inequity of it all. They figure out where it looks like the water is going to wind up when it's finished flowing downhill, and then they start looking for ways to live with that.

"I've never heard a User say the words, 'It's not fair.' Apparently, if you can form that thought, you don't reach the stars. The whole universe is a hierarchy of Users and Used, from the race that developed the long-distance telepathy that brought them all here, down to the cute little microorganisms that are ruthlessly butchered every day by a baby seal. We're part of that chain, and if we can't live with that, we'll die."

The three were silent for a time. Finally Sam cleared his throat. "If you two will excuse me," he said softly, "I have to be getting back home to my wife now."

Alice turned to him, and gave him a smile so sad and so brave that he thought his heart might break. "Sam," she said, "that's a storybook ending. I hope it works out that way for you. But don't blow your brains out if it doesn't, okay? Or hers. You write about mind-control and the institution of slavery because subversion of the human free will, loss of control, holds a special horror for you. You're the kind that dies fighting instead. Marian isn't. I'm not. Most humans aren't, even though they like to feel they would be if it came to it. Maybe that's why the Users came here.

"It may be that you and Marian can't live together any more; I don't know. I do know that you need twelve hours sleep and a couple of good meals before it's safe to let you back on the highway—and Greg and I badly need someone to talk to. My User won't be back for another ten hours or so. What would you say to some eggs and back bacon?"

Sam closed his eyes and took a deep breath. "I guess I'd say, 'Hello there—do you mind if I use you for twelve hours or so?' " *And turn you into shit in the process,* he thought, but he found that he was ashamed of the thought, and that was something, at least. "Can I use your phone?"

"Only if you reverse the charges, you cheap Yankee son of a bitch," Greg said at once, and came and hugged him hard.

DISTANT SIGNALS

Andrew Weiner

Andrew Weiner lives in Toronto. He came to Canada in 1974, with an M.Sc. in social psychology from the London School of Economics, already a published SF writer. His first story appeared in 1972 in the innovative original anthology *Again, Dangerous Visions*. He did not, however, achieve publication regularly until the end of the 1970's and has published forty stories since 1979 in SF magazines and anthologies worldwide. His stories have been translated into many languages, been nominated for both the British Science Fiction Award and the Aurora. Two of his stories were filmed in the U.S. for the television show *Tales from the Darkside*. His nonfiction pieces have appeared everywhere from *New Musical Express* to *Reader's Digest* and *Macleans*. *Distant Signals and Other Stories* is the title of his short story collection, which appeared in 1989 from the publishers of the *Tesseracts* books. He has published one novel, *Station Gehenna* (U.S., 1987). Yet he recently announced his disenchantment with science fiction, its garish art, and defensive attitudes in an article entitled "SF—Not!", concluding with the following cry of frustration: "But I do wonder whether some people might prefer at least a quiet and dignified obscurity to one involving publication with spaceships on the cover. And I wonder whether those people might include me."

There was something not quite right about the young man.

His suit appeared brand new. Indeed, it glistened with an almost unnatural freshness and sharpness of definition. Yet it was made in a style that had not been fashionable since the late 1950s. The lapels were too wide, the trousers too baggy; the trouser legs terminated in one-inch cuffs. The young man's hair was short—too short. It was parted neatly on the left-hand side and plastered down with some sort of grease. And his smile was too wide. Too wide, at least, for nine o'clock on a Monday morning at the Parkdale Public Library.

Out for the day, was the librarian's first and last thought on the matter. Out, that is, from the state-run mental health centre just three blocks away.

"I would like," said the young man, "to be directed to the TV and film section."

His voice, too, had an unnatural definition, as if he were speaking through some hidden microphone. It projected right across the library. Several patrons turned their heads to peer at him.

"Over there," said the librarian, in a very pointed whisper. "Just over there."

STRANGER IN TOWN. Series, 1960. Northstar Studios for NBC-TV. Produced by KEN ODELL. From an original idea by BILL HURN. Directors included JASON ALTBERG, NICK BALL, and JIM SPEI-GEL. 26 b/w episodes. Running time: 50 minutes.

Horse opera following the exploits of Cooper aka The Stranger (VANCE MACCOBY), an amnesiacal gunslinger who wanders from town to town in search of his lost identity, stalked always by the mysterious limping loner Loomis (TERRY WHITE) who may or may not know his real name. Despite this promisingly mythic premise, the series quickly degenerated into a formulaic pattern, with Cooper as a Shane-style savior of widows and orphans. The show won mediocre ratings, and NBC declined to pick up its option for a second season. The identity of Cooper was never revealed.
See also: GUNSLINGERS; HOLLYWOOD EXISTENTIALISM; LAW AND ORDER; WESTERNS.

MACCOBY, VANCE (1938?–). Actor. Born Henry Mulvin in Salt Lake City, Utah. Frequent guest spots in WAGON TRAIN, RIVERBOAT, CAPTAIN CHRONOS, THE ZONE BEYOND, etc. 1957–59. Lead in the 1960 oater STRANGER IN TOWN and the short-lived 1961 private eye show MAX PARADISE, canceled after 6 episodes. Subsequent activities unknown. One of dozens of nearly interchangeable identikit male stars of the first period of episodic TV drama, Maccoby had a certain brooding quality, particularly in b/w, that carried him far, but apparently lacked the resources for the long haul. See also STARS AND STARDOM.

> —From *The Complete TV Encyclopedia*,
> Chuck Gingle, editor.

There was something distinctly odd about the young man in the white loafers and pompadour hair-style, the young man who had been haunting the ante-room of his office all day.

Had the Kookie look come back? Feldman wondered.

"Look, kid," he said, not unkindly, "as my secretary told you. I'm not taking on any more clients. I have a full roster right now. You'd really be much better off going to Talentmart, or one of those places. They specialize in, you know, unknowns."

"And as I told your secretary," the young man said, "I don't want to be an actor, I want to hire one. One of your clients. This is strictly a business proposition."

Business proposition my ass, Feldman thought. *Autograph hunter, more like.* But he said wearily, "Which one would that be? Lola Banks? Dirk Raymond?"

"Vance Maccoby."

"Vance Maccoby?" For a moment he had to struggle to place the name. "Vance Maccoby?" he said again. "That bum? What the hell do you want with Vance Maccoby?"

"Mr. Feldman, I represent a group of overseas investors interested in independently producing a TV series for syndicated sale. We want Mr. Maccoby to star. However, we have so far been unable to locate him."

"I haven't represented him in years. No one has. He hasn't *worked* in years. Not since . . . what was that piece of crap called? *Max Paradise?* I don't like to speak ill of former clients, but the man was impossible, you know. A drunk. Quite impossible. No one could work with him."

"We're aware of that," the young man said. "We've taken all that into consideration, and we are still interested in talking to Mr. Maccoby. We think he is the only man for the part. And we believe that if anyone can find him, you can."

The young man opened his briefcase and fumbled inside it. "We would like," he continued, "to retain your services toward that end. And we are prepared to make suitable remuneration whether or not a contract should be signed with Mr. Maccoby and whether or not you choose to represent him as agent of record in that transaction."

"Kid," Feldman began, "what you need is a private detective—" He stopped and stared at the bar-shaped object in the young man's hand. "Is that gold?"

"It certainly is, Mr. Feldman. It certainly is."

The young man laid the bar on the desk between them.

"An ounce of gold?"

"One point three four ounces," said the young man. "We apologize for the unusual denomination."

He held open the briefcase. "I have twenty-four more such bars here. At the New York spot price this morning, this represents a value of approximately fifteen thousand dollars."

"Fifteen thousand dollars to find Vance Maccoby?" Feldman said.

He got up and paced around the desk.

"Is this stuff hot?" he asked, pointing to the briefcase, feeling like a character in one of the more banal TV shows into which he booked his clients.

"Hot?" echoed the young man. He reached out and touched the gold bar on the desk. "A few degrees below room temperature, I would say."

"Cute," Feldman said. "Don't be cute. Just tell me, is this on the level?"

"Oh, I see," said the young man. "Yes, absolutely. We have a property which we wish to develop, to which we have recently purchased the rights from the estate of the late Mr. Kenneth Odell. There is only one man who can star in this show, and that is Vance Maccoby."

"What property?"

"*Stranger in Town,*" said the young man.

"I KNEW IT," SHE SAID. "I KNEW YOU WOULD COME BACK."

"YOU KNEW MORE THAN I DID," COOPER SAID. "I WAS FIVE MILES OUT OF TOWN AND HEADING WEST. BUT SOMETHING . . . SOMETHING MADE ME TURN AROUND AND COME BACK HERE AND FACE THE KERRAWAY BROTHERS."

"YOU'RE A GOOD MAN," SHE SAID. "YOU COULDN'T HELP YOURSELF."

"I DON'T KNOW IF I'M A GOOD MAN," COOPER SAID. "I DON'T KNOW WHAT KIND OF MAN I AM." HE STARED MOROSELY AT THE CORPSES STREWN OUT ON THE GROUND AROUND THE RANCH HOUSE. "I JUST COULDN'T LET THE KERRAWAYS TAKE YOUR LAND."

HE MOUNTED HIS HORSE. "TIME TO BE MOVING ON," HE SAID. "YOU TAKE GOOD CARE OF YOURSELF AND LITTLE BILLY NOW."

"WILL YOU EVER COME BACK?"

"MAYBE," HE SAID. "MAYBE AFTER I FIND WHAT I'M LOOKING FOR."

"I THINK YOU FOUND IT ALREADY," SHE SAID. "YOU JUST DON'T KNOW IT YET. YOU FOUND YOURSELF."

"THAT MAY BE SO," COOPER SAID. "BUT I STILL GOTTA PUT A NAME TO IT."

HE RODE OFF INTO A RAPIDLY SETTING SUN.

The video picture flickered, then resolved itself into an antique Tide commercial. Hurn cut the controls. He turned to the strange young man in the too-tweedy jacket and the heavy horn-rimmed glasses.

"That?" he said, gesturing at the screen. "You want to remake that . . . *garbage?*"

"Not remake," the young man said. "Revive. Continue. Conclude. Tell the remainder of the story of the stranger Cooper, and the re-acquisition of his memory and identity."

"Who cares?" Hurn asked. "Who the hell cares who Cooper is or what he did? Certainly not the viewers. Do you know how many letters we got after we cancelled the series? Sixteen. Sixteen letters. That's how many people cared."

"That is our concern, Mr. Hurn. We believe that we do have a market for this property. That is why we are making this proposition. We are prepared to go ahead with or without you. But certainly we would much rather have you with us. As the main creative force behind the original series—"

"Creative?" Hurn said. "Frankly, that whole show to me was nothing but an embarrassment. And I was glad when they cancelled it, actually. I wrote those scripts for one reason and one reason alone. Money."

"We can offer you a great deal of money, Mr. Hurn."

Hurn gestured, as though to indicate the oriental rugs on the floor, the rare books in the shelves on the wall, the sculptures and the paintings, the several-million-dollar Beverly Hills home that contained all this.

"I don't need money, Mr.—what did you say your name was?"

"Smith."

"Mr. Smith, I have all the money I could ever want. I have done well in this business, Mr. Smith. Quite well. I am no longer the struggling writer who conceived *Stranger in Town*. These days I choose my projects on the basis of quality."

"You disparage yourself unnecessarily, Mr. Hurn. We believe that *Stranger in Town* was a series of the highest quality. In some ways, in fact, it represented the very peak of televisual art. The existential dilemma of the protagonist, the picaresque nature of his journeyings, the obsessive fascination with the nature of memory . . . That scene . . ." The young man's eyes came alive. "That scene when Cooper bites into a watermelon and says, *"I remember a watermelon like this. I remember summer days, summer nights, a cool breeze on the porch, the river rushing by. I remember a woman's lips, her eyes, her deep blue eyes. But where, damn it? Where?"*

Hurn stared, open-mouthed. "You remember *that*? Word for word? Oh, my God."

"Art, Mr. Hurn. Unabashed art."

"Adolescent pretension. Fakery. Bullshit," Hurn said. "Embarrassing. Oh, my God, how embarrassing."

"In some ways trite," the young man conceded. "Brash. Even clumsy sometimes. But burning with an inner conviction. Mr. Hurn, you must help us. You must help us bring back *Stranger in Town*."

"You can't," Hurn said. "You can't bring it back. Even if I agreed it was worth bringing back—and I'll admit to you that I've thought about it on occasion, though not in many years. I've always had a sense of it as a piece of unfinished business. . . . But even if I wanted to help you, it couldn't be done. Not now. It's too late, much too late. You can't repeat the past, Smith. You can't bring it back. It's over, finished, a dead mackerel."

"Of course you can," Smith said. "Of course you can repeat the past. We have absolutely no doubt on that question."

"Boats against the current," Hurn said. "But no, no, I can't agree. It's like when those promoters wanted to reunite the Beatles."

"Beetles?" Smith asked. "What beetles?"

"The Beatles," Hurn said, astonished. " 'She Loves You.' 'I Want to Hold Your Hand.' Like that."

"Oh, yes," Smith said vaguely.

Where is this guy from? Hurn wondered. *Mongolia?*

"What exactly is your proposition, Mr. Smith?"

The young man became business-like. He pulled a sheaf of notes from his briefcase. "One episode of *Stranger* was completed but not edited when the cancellation notice came from the network. We have acquired that footage, and it would be a simple matter to put it together. We have also acquired five scripts for the second season, commissioned prior to the cancellation. And we have an outline of your proposal for subsequent episodes, including a concluding episode in which the identity of Cooper is finally revealed. We would like you to supervise the preparation of these unwritten scripts and to write the final episode yourself. We are looking at a season of twenty-six fifty-minute episodes. For these services we are prepared to pay you the equivalent of two million dollars."

"The equivalent, Mr. Smith?"

"In gold, Mr. Hurn." The young man picked up the large suitcase he had brought with him into the writer's house. He opened it up. It was packed with yellowish metallic bars.

"My God," Hurn said. "That suitcase must weigh a hundred pounds."

"About one hundred and twenty-five pounds," said Mr. Smith. "Or the equivalent of about one million dollars at this morning's London gold fixing."

The young man, Hurn recalled, had carried in this suitcase without the slightest sign of exertion. He hefted it now as though it were full of feathers. Obviously he was not as frail as he looked.

"Tell me, Mr. Smith. Who is going to star in this show?"

"Oh. Vance Maccoby. Of course."

"Vance Maccoby, if he is even still alive, is a hopeless alcoholic, Mr. Smith. He hasn't worked in this town in twenty years. I don't even know where he is. Have you signed up Vance Maccoby, Mr. Smith?"

"Not yet," the young man said. "But we will. We will."

"My name's Loomis," said the tall man with the limp, as he stood beside Cooper at the bar. He picked up the shot glass and stared into it thoughtfully.

"First or last?" Cooper asked.

"Just Loomis," said the man.

"I'm Cooper," said the other. "Or at least that's what I call myself. One name's as good as another. There was a book in my saddle-bag by a man named Cooper. . . ."

"You forgot your name?"

"I forgot everything," he said. "Except how to speak and ride and shoot."

Loomis drained his drink. "Some things a man don't forget," he said.

Cooper stared at him intently. "Have I seen you in here before? There's something familiar. . . ."

"I don't think so," Loomis said. "I'm a stranger here myself."

The edges of the TV screen grew misty, then blurred. The picture dissolved. Another took shape. A bright, almost hallucinatorily bright summer day. A farm house. Chickens in a coop. The door of the house open, banging in the wind.

The camera moved through the door, into a parlour. Signs of struggle, furniture up-ended, a broken dish on the floor. A man stooped to pick up the fragments.

"Aimee?" he called. "Aimee?"

The camera moved on, into a bedroom. A woman's body sprawled brokenly across the bed. The window open, the curtain blowing. And then a face, a man's face, staring into the room. His arm, holding a gun. A gunshot.

Darkness closed in. Outside, the shadow of a man running away. A shadow with a kind of limp.

And back, suddenly, to the bar.

"You all right, Cooper?"

"I'm all right," he said, gripping the bar tightly. "I'm all right."

"Yehh," said the fat bald man in the armchair. "Let's hear it for the strong silent ones."

He picked up his glass from the TV table in front of him, made a mocking toast to the blank screen, then winked to his old agent, Feldman, sitting on the couch next to the young man. There was something a little odd about the young man, but the fat man was too drunk to put his finger on it. Maybe it was the Desi Arnaz hair cut. . . .

"Vance," Feldman said. "Vance I—I hate to see you like this."

"Like what?" said the fat man who had once been Vance Maccoby. "And the name is Henry. Henry Mulvin."

He raised his bulk from the armchair and waddled into the tiny kitchen of the trailer to refreshen his drink.

Feldman looked helplessly at the young man.

"I told you, Smith. I told you this was pointless. You're going to have to find yourself another boy. Jesus, there must be hundreds in this town."

"There's only one Vance Maccoby," the young man said firmly. "Mr. Feldman, would you leave us together for a while? I promise you that I'll be in touch in the morning with regard to contractual arrangements."

"Contractual arrangements? You're whistling in the wind."

"I can be quite persuasive, Mr. Feldman. Believe me."

I believe you, Feldman thought. *Or what would I be doing in this stinking trailer?*

When the sound of Feldman's Mercedes had disappeared into the distance, the young man turned to Vance Maccoby.

"Mr. Maccoby," he said almost apologetically, "we have to have a serious talk. And in order to do that you will have to be sober."

"Sober?" The fat man laughed. "Never heard of it."

"This won't hurt," the young man said, producing a flat, box-like device from his pocket and pointing it at the fat man. "It will merely accelerate the metabolization of the alcohol in your bloodstream." He pushed a button.

"But I don't *want* to be sober," the fat man said. He began to cry.

"When this is all over, Mr. Maccoby," the young man said soothingly, "you need never be sober nor unhappy ever again."

*   *   *

"Guess I should ride on," Cooper said. "You got a nice little town here and I could easily settle in it. Easily. But a man can't settle anyplace until he knows who he is."

"You think he knows?" the girl asked. "You think that limping man knows who you are?"

"Yes, he does," Cooper said. "He knows, and he's going to tell me. Fact is, he's itching to tell me. He thinks he just wants to kill me, but first of all he wants to tell me. Otherwise he would have just finished me off back at Oscar's barn. Him and me, reckon we got ourselves a piece of unfinished business. But he's got the better of me, because he knows what it is."

"He may kill you yet," the girl said, dabbing at the tears that had begun to well up in her eyes.

"I can take care of myself."

"Will you come back?" she asked. "Afterward?"

"Maybe so," he said. "Maybe so."

He rode off into the distance.

"Print it," said the director. "And see you all tomorrow."

Carefully, Vance Maccoby dismounted from his horse and began to walk back to his dressing room. Bill Hurn fell in step with him.

"That was good stuff, Vance," he said.

Maccoby smiled, although it was more like a tic. The skin of his face had been stretched tight by the face-lift operations, so that his usual expression was even blanker than it had been in his heyday. He took off his hat and ran his hand through his recently transplanted hair. Under the supervision of the strange young man called Smith, he had lost close to a hundred pounds in the three months prior to shooting.

For all of these changes, Maccoby close up looked every one of his forty-six years. The doctors could do little about the lines around his eyes, and nothing at all about the weariness in them. And yet the camera was still good to him, particularly in black and white. Hurn had argued fiercely on the subject of film stock, but Smith had been adamant. "It must be black and white. Just like the original. Cost is not the question. This is a matter of aesthetics."

Black and white helped hide the ravages of time. It just made Maccoby look more intense, more haunted. Perhaps that was why Smith had been so insistent. But Hurn doubted that. In many ways Smith was astonishingly ignorant of the mechanics of filmmaking.

"I didn't know," Maccoby said, "that *he* was still in here." He pointed to his chest.

"Cooper?"

"Maccoby," he said. "Vance Maccoby. Inside me, Henry Mulvin. Still there, after all these years. I thought I'd finished him off for good. But he was still in there."

Maccoby had not, to Hurn's knowledge, touched a drop of alcohol in six months. He was functioning well on the set, with none of the moodiness or tantrums that had marked his final days in Hollywood. But the stripping away of that alcoholic haze had only revealed the deeper sickness beneath: his unbearable discomfort with himself, or rather with the fictional person he had become—Vance Maccoby, TV star. Isolated, cut off, torn away from his roots, existing only on a million TV screens and in the pages of mass-circulation magazines.

Was that, Hurn wondered—and not for the first time—why he had made such a great Cooper? Despite his mediocrity as an actor, there had never been anyone else to play the role.

"Vance," he said. "Henry. . . ."

"Call me Vance. You always did. That's who I am here. For this little command performance."

"Vance, why did you agree to do this?"

"Why did you agree, Bill? And don't tell me it was the money. You don't care about the money any more than I do. You have all you want. I had all I needed to stay drunk."

"I don't know," Hurn said. "Smith . . . He just made it seem so *important*. Like there were millions of people just sitting around waiting for a new season of *Stranger in Town*. He flattered me. And he tempted me. This was my baby, remember, and the network killed it. And I suppose there was a part of me that always wanted to do this. Finish it properly, tie up all those loose ends . . . And yet I know the whole thing is crazy. This show will never run on a U.S. network. Not in black and white. Unless we put it straight into reruns." He snickered. "Maybe that's the plan. I mean, who would even know the difference? This whole thing is so—1960."

They had reached Maccoby's dressing room.

"Well," Maccoby said, "Smith is telling the truth, in a way. There *are* millions of people waiting for this."

"In Hong Kong? North Korea? I mean, where does he expect to sell this stuff? Who are these overseas investors of his? How can he piss so much money away like water, and how does he expect to ever recoup it? The whole thing is bizarre."

"Oh, it's bizarre all right," Maccoby said. "It sure is bizarre." He glanced up briefly into the hard blue sky. Then he said, "Well, I better get cleaned up."

"You killed her," Cooper said. "You killed her and you tried to kill me. But some-how I survived. And I crawled out of there, halfway out of my mind. And I crawled into the desert. And a wagon train found me. And they carried me along with them, and nursed me. And when I woke up I didn't even know my name. You took it. You took away my name."

"Stevens," Loomis said. "Brad Stevens." His hand did not waver on the gun.

"Oh, I remember that now," he said. "I remember it all. I remember Aimee . . . I remember it all."

"I'm glad about that," Loomis said. "I truly am. I've been waiting for you to remember for the most wearisome time. Not much sense in killing a person when he doesn't even know why."

He tightened his grip on the trigger. "But there's something more," he said. "More than that. Something you couldn't remember, because you never knew. Something I have been meaning to tell you for a long time. Longer than you could imagine."

"Make sense," said the man who called himself Cooper. "Make some kind of sense."

"Your name," Loomis said. "It ain't really Stevens. Not really. The name you've been trying so hard to remember isn't even your real name. Isn't that a hoot? Isn't that the funniest thing you ever heard?" He laughed.

"Make sense," said the man on the ground. "You're still not making any."

"Stevens," Loomis said. "That's just a name they gave you. The folks who picked you out at the orphanage. Picked out the pretty little baby. That was their name. Good God-fearing folks. But they only wanted the one, and they wanted a baby, not a full-grown child. And for sure they didn't want a gimp."

"I was adopted? You're saying I was adopted? How could you know that?"

"I was there, little brother. I was there. I was the gimp they passed over for the pretty little baby. I was only four years old at the time. But some things you really don't forget."

"Brother?"

"Right," Loomis said. "You and me, we're children of the very same flesh. Arnold and Mary Jane Loomis. Nobody ever changed my name. Nobody wanted the poor little cripple boy."

"Our parents . . ."

"Dead," Loomis said. "Indians. They killed Pa. Killed Ma, too, after they were through with her. Would have killed us, too, except they got interrupted."

Slowly, deliberately, the man who had been called Cooper climbed to his feet. "We were separated?" he said.

"For nearly thirty years. You eating your good home cooking and me eating the poor-house gruel. You growing into a solid citizen and marrying and farming. And me drifting from town to town like a piece of dried-up horse dung blown around by the wind. Never finding a place I could call home. And looking, looking for my little brother. And finally I found you. . . ."

"Why?" he asked. "Why did you do it?"

"I didn't mean to . . ." Loomis faltered. "It was like a kind of madness came over me. Seeing your house and your farm and your wife, everything you had and I didn't, everything I hated you for having . . . But I don't know. Maybe that was what I was intending all along, intending to make you suffer just a little of what I *had to suffer. I don't know. I don't think I meant to kill Aimee, but when I did I knew I would have to kill you, too. And I thought I did. And then I saw you alive. And I realized that you didn't remember, didn't remember a single thing. So I just waited, watched and waited, until you did start to remember. So you would know why I had to kill you. And now it's time. It's time."*

"You can't stand yourself, brother, can you?" said the man who had been called Cooper. "You and you, they don't get along at all. I can understand that. I been through a little of that myself. Not knowing who the hell I was or what I might have done or what I should be doing. But you find out. Maybe not your name, but how you should be living. If you're any good at all, you find that out."

He took a step toward Loomis. "But you're not any good, brother, and you never were. Sure, you had some lousy breaks, sure you did. But that isn't any kind of excuse for what you did. You're just no good to anyone, not even yourself. And if you kill me, you'll have nothing to live for. Nothing. Because nobody will know your name and nobody will care."

Another step.

"But I care, brother. I care in the worst way. You made me care. Buzzing around me like some house-fly waiting to be swatted. Waiting for me to remember. Trying to make me remember. Remember you."

Another step. He was only a few paces from Loomis now. He glanced down to his own gun on the floor of the stable. It was nearly within reach.

"Stay there," Loomis said. "Stay right where you are."

He took another step.

"I remember you, brother. For what you did to me. No one else will. Kill me and you'll be alone again, alone with yourself, the way you always were. Run away now and you'll have something to keep you going. Fear, brother. Fear. That's a kind of something. Something to make you feel alive. And me, too. I'll have something to keep me going, too."

Loomis took a step backward. "Don't move," he said. "Don't move or I'll kill you now."

"What are you waiting for?" his brother asked him.

The gun wavered in his hand.

The man who had called himself Cooper stooped swiftly and scooped up his own gun from the floor.

Two guns blared.

Loomis stood straight for a moment. A strange smile spread over his face. And then, slowly, he crumpled to the floor of the stable.

The other continued to stand, in the clearing smoke, holding his wounded left arm.

"Damn," he said softly. "Damn."

The lights in the screening room came up. One man was applauding vigorously. Smith. All heads turned toward him.

"Bit of an anticlimax," Hurn said, "don't you think? We were afraid it might be. I think, in a way, we were afraid of having to finish it."

"On the contrary, Mr. Hurn," Smith said. "On the contrary. It's absolutely perfect. Perfect. Real mythic power. A glimpse into the human condition. Into a world in which brother must slay brother, even as Cain slew Abel. *Archetypal*, Mr. Hurn. Archetypal."

He stood up and addressed the small crowd.

"I want to thank all of you," he said, "for making this possible. In particular I want to thank Mr. Hurn and the one and only Vance Maccoby, without whom none of this would have been possible."

Maccoby grinned in a spaced-out way. Hurn could smell the drink on his breath from two rows away.

The cure didn't take, he thought. *Well, it took for long enough.*

"I will be leaving town tomorrow," Smith said, "and I will not be returning in the near future. So let me just say what a wonderful group of people you have been to work with, and what a great, great privilege this has been for me."

There was still, Hurn reflected, something rather odd about the young man. He was dressed now in what could pass as the uniform of the young Hollywood executive—safari jacket, open-collar sports shirt, gold medallion, aviator shades—and yet there was still something not quite *right* about it. He looked as if he had just stepped out of central casting.

"The show," Hurn said, as Smith headed toward the door. "When is the show going to run?"

"Oh, soon," Smith said. "Not in this country, at the present time, but we have plenty of interest overseas."

A Canadian tax shelter? Hurn wondered. *One of those productions that never actually play anywhere? But surely they would not have gone to so much trouble.*

"Where?" he persisted. "Where will it run?"

"Oh, faraway places," Smith said, fingering his aviator shades. "Far, far away." He disappeared through the door. Hurn would not see him again.

"Far away," Hurn repeated to himself.

"Very far," Maccoby said, staggering a little as he rose from his seat in the back row. He was quite drunk.

"You know something I don't know?" Hurn asked, following him from the screening room.

"Very far," Maccoby repeated, as they stepped into the parking lot. The smog was thin that night. Stars twinkled faintly in the sky. "About twenty light-years," he said, looking up.

"What?"

"Twenty light-years," he repeated. "Twenty years for the signals to reach them. Distant, distant signals. And then they stop. The signals stop. Before the story ends. And they don't like that."

"They?"

"Smith's people. Our overseas investors. Our faraway fans."

"Wait a minute," Hurn said. "You're telling me that our show was picked up . . . out there?"

Now he, too, craned his head to look up into the night sky. He shivered.

"I don't believe it," he said.

"Sure you do," Maccoby said.

"But it's crazy," Hurn said. "The whole thing is incredible. Up to and including the fact that they picked on our show."

"I wondered about that myself," Maccoby said. "But you've got to figure that their tastes are going to be, well . . . *different.*"

"Then he really meant it," Hurn said. "When he said that our show was—what did he call it? The peak of televisual art."

Maccoby nodded. "He really meant it."

"Art." Hurn tested the word on his tongue. "Life is short but art is long. Isn't that what they say? Something like that, at any rate."

"Right," Maccoby said absently. "Art. Or something like that."

He was staring now at the great mast of the TV antenna on the hill above the studio.

"Signals," he said again. "Distant, distant signals."

THE WOMAN WHO IS THE MIDNIGHT WIND

Terence M. Green

Terence M. Green was born in 1947, the year the World SF Convention was held in Toronto for the first time, and teaches secondary school in Toronto. He has been publishing SF since the late 1970's and his early stories are collected in *The Woman Who Is the Midnight Wind* (1987). He has also published two SF novels (*Barking Dogs*, 1988; *Children of the Rainbow*, 1992), as well as articles, interviews, reviews, poetry, and stories in many U.S. and Canadian magazines, journals, and newspapers. Both novels were marketed out of category, as contemporary fiction. The *Science Fiction Encyclopedia* calls his stories "lean and subtle."

He is profiled in Canadian *Who's Who* and is the recipient of a Canada Council Project Grant for fiction writing and four Ontario Arts Council Writer's Reserve Grants. Although a majority of his works fit comfortably into the category of SF, he has managed his literary career so as to emphasize his fiction as contemporary literature. He is therefore thus far not well-known in the SF community outside of Canada. This is a shame, because his best stories are generally finely crafted SF that deserve to be considered beside the best work in the field worldwide.

Juturna, 20–4–3

I really should have started a journal seasons ago. Probably when I first arrived on Juturna. Or at least when Jacques died.

But I did not.

I am starting one now.

I am hoping, I guess, that this may shape my life, however weakly. This is, of course, a mild delusion of grandeur. Just mild though. Nevertheless, if I choose to delude myself, very well, then I choose to delude myself. In this, I feel akin to the rest of my species.

20–4–7

Knowledge that a woman who has injured you is aging is, indeed, a constant vengeance.

Since I am no longer a young woman, this observation strikes me pointedly. Being one of Juturna's original colonists, I have been here twenty J-years. I have forgotten the formula that I knew when we immigrated, but I think that I am now about fifty Terran years old. I stopped worrying about it—mostly after Jacques died.

Note the irony that I am the woman who has injured me—many times, in many ways. I am not sure that reflecting upon my aging can ever be adequate vengeance for my various follies.

Am I a woman more sinned against than sinning?

Most often I think not.

20–4–9

I think of Jacques often.

He was too good for me. No politician, Jacques. No language but the language of the heart.

Who would have guessed that I would outlive him?

I, who connived to marry him, to have a mate to light out to the stars with. . . . In his innocence, he wedded me, took me unto him, as they might say classically, and together we leapt the stars to Juturna.

This journal turns increasingly inward. I had no idea of what it might evolve into, but I think I'm surprising myself. Perhaps I am no longer young enough for the guile needed merely to catalogue the events of each day. Indeed, my days are seldom different from one another any more. Three days a week I do volunteer work at the hospital. Such work is desperately needed.

I am the one who needs it.

20–4–10

Juturna—why here?

Jacques' work, of course. He loved the idea of being one of the top engineers on a Colony World; he was also idealistic and romantic enough to want the challenge.

Challenge. The word seems alien to me now.

As a Class-A World, we are fully equipped with high-tech via the Lightships that come down on the Big Continent weekly.

I am no scientist, but I know the basics about my world. I know that Juturna is about 420 light-years from Earth in the direction of Ursa Major. I know that Juturna is the only habitable planet in our system of eight planets. I know that our sun is a K2 star, slightly cooler and redder than Sol, that Juturna is similar in size to Earth (a bit larger, actually), that the seasons are longer, that we rotate rapidly enough to stimulate a cyclone-breeding Coriolis force, so that our weather is usually quite awful. And wet.

What else do I remember? Let me see. That our sun is not up to Sol in mass or luminosity, that we are quite close to our sun (the closest planet, in fact), that it's a good ol' star, about five billion years old and counting. . . .

I am cataloguing at last. Is this what my journal will be?

Somehow, I do not think that it is enough.

20-4-12

I am endeavouring to treat the subject of myself best. But many questions arise.

Should I treat the days objectively? Or should I subjectively treat my emotional reactions to the days as they pass?

Can I indulge in a stream-of-consciousness style? Can I be all things to myself? Will I be fully honest? Or is that last the stance of a fool?

In truth, I know that I am writing this because I am no longer young (such an understatement!). Perhaps I see this as my testament to posterity, my feeble attempt to live beyond my physical years. In my more idealistic moments, I see it as a chance to record and comment on the atomic particles of truth that I have stumbled across in my voyage through both the chronological and the light-years. In my more cynical moments, I see it as a form of therapy. It is probably, in small measure, both.

My hands are arthritic as I write this; the dampness of the day seizes my right knee with pain. I cannot totally escape my physical self as I sit here, but perhaps I can peer further inward, down the funnel of my ego.

Perhaps.

Today at the hospital, for instance, I spent time with a woman who was suffering horribly from a blood disorder that is causing epidermal purpura, and swelling of the joints. She is a young woman, recently arrived with her husband. The doctors say that it is an allergic reaction to something, but they cannot pin it down.

And how could they pin it down? Man has known Juturna for such a brief span. Adaptation of a species to an environment, as we know it, swallows aeons. Yet the Juturnans adapt to their environment daily, and prior to our arrival there was no such thing as "species"—just "Juturnans."

The Juturnans themselves are products of specific evolution, are they not? In this great, damp world, they are awesome in their alienness, profound in their similarity to us. The closest Terran composite would be a reptile-human, though of course they are neither reptile nor human, but merely Juturnan (can I use this word to describe a complexity?). The rain, the wetness, the vast seas—all have contributed to the evolution of these solemn creatures.

Jacques had found them—the Juturnans—fascinating.

And what had he known of anthropology? An engineer, supervising road-building, bridge-building. . . . He had often sat on one of his river projects and watched a lone, grey-skinned shape emerge from the undergrowth, study him and his crew with curious and perplexing eyes, then fade unassumingly back into the omnipresent greenery. There was an undefined concept of *laissez-faire* that permeated relations between us and them.

Jacques had said many times that he should make notes of their behaviour patterns—for those who could better interpret them.

But that was before the mudslide.

That was before I was left here alone.

20–4–14

Today I stayed at home all morning, venturing out only in the afternoon for exercise and some shopping.

I am tired.

I ache.

Tomorrow I will go to the hospital to try to forget my own pains. Such irony.

Tonight, as I sit in bed, I will read a story or two from the works of the Irish writer Liam O'Flaherty. I have worked my way through Hemingway, Faulkner, Poe, Lawrence, Joyce in the last five seasons. O'Flaherty is a concise *évocateur* of landscapes and emotions. His descriptions of the awesomely desolate Aran Islands of his birthplace remind me in many ways of our settlement on Juturna. There is the same mixture of beauty and ugliness.

Juturna has yet to produce a Literature. How long does it take, I wonder? Who will capture this place for future generations?

Perhaps we are too busy surviving as yet to afford the luxury of creating our own art. We must import it still.

My hands are cold. I fold them one in the other as I sit here in the evening.

20–4–15

I must catalogue an event.

Today, at the hospital, a Silent Child was born.

It has never happened before in Egerton—although such creatures have been born in two of the larger cities on the Big Continent. The entire community is unsettled; word-of-mouth has spread the news like cell-division.

I, myself, am unable to comprehend the bizarre nature of the incident. I focus on the mother. Why would she do it?

I would have aborted.

But then, I would never have had intercourse with a Juturnan in the first place.

Why would she?

Why would *anybody*?

We are strange creatures, we humans. We are often as alien to one another as we are to an "alien" species.

With whom are we to relate?

I once read, while browsing through some old books on rhetoric at the library, something that Winston Churchill observed in a radio broadcast early in the twentieth century: "... we learn that we are spirits, not animals, and that something is going on in space and time, which, whether we like it or not, spells duty."

If I could only be certain of what this duty is. Churchill seemed so sure. But then, it was the strength of his convictions, the strength of his personality, that forged for him his place in history.

Something is definitely "going on in space and time."

But what duty does it describe?

20–4–17

The first sign, they say, occurs when the doctor pulls the child from its mother's womb, anticipating the cry of life that should ensue. But the Silent Child does not cry out. Nor does it breathe, speak, laugh or cry as it grows.

Yet it lives.

It is half human, half Juturnan.

And just as we fail to understand what it is to be human most of the time, we definitely fail to grasp what it must be to be Juturnan.

Juturnans, as we know from rare autopsies performed upon cadavers stumbled upon through accident (or fortuitous circumstances, if you wish), are silent; they have no larynges. More importantly, they are changing rapidly, converging with *Homo sapiens* almost before our eyes. They have adapted fully to their wet world, surely evolving from their seas as we did from ours, but with this new evolutionary wrinkle. The only constant from generation to generation seems to be the ability to survive for long periods of time without breathing. The popular theory is that they extract oxygen through the mucous membranes of their pharynges and cloaca, and probably through their skin as well. In this, they are not unlike Terran turtles. There is another school of thought that believes Juturnans can dispense with respiration completely, deriving energy from an oxygenless breakdown of glycogen.

Whatever. They are one of the universe's magnificent complexities, and there is much for us to learn yet . . . as indicated by the fact that cross-breeding is indeed a reality, if not a pleasant one.

But what drove this woman to such a demeaning act?

Why would she bring such a creature into the world?

All my reservations convince me that it would be best for all if the doctors did not allow them to live after birth. Perhaps simply tell the mother that it had been still-born.

My curiosity is scudding along like the night-clouds. To have this happen right here in Egerton! It is astounding.

This is a rupture in the colonial fabric which represents the casting aside of the ultimate taboo. This miscegenation has no context, other than mythology. But this is no myth—no minotaur or Pan. This is a reality. And therein lies its horror, its fascination.

What will the mother do?

Others, apparently, gave their Silent Children up for adoption, in all cases, and all re-emigrated, with full governmental co-operation.

And the Children?

Well, strange as they are, they do live and thrive; and they do breathe, but in the manner of Juturnans—that is, almost intermittently, and without concern for the process.

They learn, and seem to understand much. Yet we do not understand them.

20–4–19

Today I visited the mother. My curiosity was overpowering, and I do have access as a "charitable volunteer." The doctors thought that I might do some good.

She is young—so young. A mere girl. Not more than fifteen or sixteen J-years old. I know now why she did not abort. She had not the sense nor the knowledge.

She was propped in bed watching video, eating candy and combing her hair—which is dark and stringy. She is not attractive. The poor child has an acne problem and is slightly overweight. Her eyes are hazel, quick, darting and shallow. She said to call her Marie—a lovely name.

I came prepared—for what? For disgust? For morbid voyeurism? Whatever it was that I had anticipated melted away during the course of my stay with Marie. She does not have full comprehension of either her act or its consequences. In truth, kindly put, she is not very bright.

We chatted for a while about how she felt, and all her responses were concerned solely with her physical pains, her bodily functions. The Child, she told me quietly, and with a faraway look in her eyes, would be given up for adoption. She and her family could either re-emigrate or re-locate on the Big Continent. Her father, a farmer, apparently favoured the latter, feeling there would be sufficient anonymity for them all there.

For their sakes, I hope that he is right.

I asked her if she had seen it. The Child.

She said "no," adding that she did not want to see it either. Her eyes became distant again, then hardened like marbles. Her mouth compressed tightly.

I dropped the subject.

She returned to her juggling of pastimes: watching video, combing her hair, and selecting another sugar-coated pacifier.

I said that I would visit her again, if she wished. She smiled, but did not indicate "yes" or "no."

"I don't want to move away," she said, finally. "All my friends are here. But I guess I'll have to."

She was chewing nonchalantly as I left.

20-4-22

I went to see it today. The Child. It is a male. To my surprise, bewilderment even, he looked no different from other infants in the nursery, except for a dark, grey-green pigmentation, and his stillness.

He was awake but silent.

I was prepared to be repelled, frightened, sickened. I was none of these. He is just a baby. As I looked upon him, I confounded myself by feeling slightly moved. *This* I was not prepared for.

His gaze suddenly locked onto my own. Can he see me? I wondered. What does he know, if anything?

For five minutes or more I let him play upon the scale of my emotions.

Then, scarcely aware that I was doing it, I lifted him gently, held him as one would any infant, while we stared into, and perhaps through one another.

I am a woman, and today, despite his strangeness, the Child comforted me.

I have learned something here. Not about aliens. About myself.

I must sort it out. Carefully.

20-4-24

Women: wiser than men?

A woman understands the importance of her femininity; a man never seems to grasp his masculinity. The explosiveness of the male life-force has always struck me as so frenzied, that it must preclude any true self-evaluation. I have always entertained the wonderful conceit that my woman's slower rhythms keep me more truly in touch with the more harmonious elements of the universe.

Even here on Juturna, where the soil is powder-grey when dry, more often mud when wet; where the daytime skies are wildly crimson, and the nights are haunted by a midnight wind . . . even here, I try to place myself, however roughly, in space and time. . . .

Since Jacques died, there have been others. And as much as they felt any seduction was theirs, I knew that it was mine.

I see them, and I see myself, swirling in gaseous clouds, and I sense the tides of my planet; I become a part of it. They are always separate.

It is true.

I do not know why the wind blows at night here on Juturna, but I know this: the wind is a woman.

I tended my garden today, pulling a few weeds from among the blueyes. But the more I separated the weeds from the delicate domestics, the less certain I became as to which was the intruder. My decision to groom the totality appeared suddenly presumptuous.

I am lying in bed tonight, writing this, aware of the arbitrariness of casual living.

Outside, it is black, and the wind is singing.

20–4–26

I cannot keep myself from the Child. When I should be visiting the bed-ridden, as I have promised to do, I go instead to him. I sit beside him, and allow his hand to squeeze my index finger. The contact is becoming more important than I could ever have dreamed.

Louisa, the nurse whose hours coincide with mine, watched curiously at first; but today she could contain herself no longer.

"You know," she began, with no little hostility, "what that thing is—what it means."

We were sorting and folding linens—the white for the third floor, blue for the second.

"I don't know what you mean," I said.

"They say that those things have been modifying and transmogrifying for ages—that they are the only species here because they consume everything else."

"You're talking about the Silent Child?" I knew what she was talking about.

"I'm talking about that thing in there—that thing that's taken your fancy." Her tone was just shy of scorn now.

"It's only a baby, Louisa."

"From what I've read," she continued, "the Juturnan sperm—or whatever it is—consumes the ovum and extracts all the genetic information from it. It's just the opposite of human conception."

She straightened, folded a blue pillowcase, looked at me sternly. "It's as if *they* are devouring *us*." She set the pillowcase aside to add emphasis, sighed, then added: "I'm at a total loss as to how you can be at ease with that thing the way you are. I think the whole thing is creepy."

I did not respond. Louisa said no more, perhaps out of embarrassment. She had said what she felt needed saying.

I am having strange thoughts of late. I am having even more trouble recording them here, since they do not flow smoothly or logically. They spring from a deep well, bubble forth for brief instants, then seep back quietly, as if into soft loam.

Words will not carry them forth.

They will not catalogue.

20-4-28

I wonder where my daughter is, what she is doing now? Is she still on Earth, or has she too, like so many others her age, lighted to the stars to seek a grail?

I was a terrible mother to Genevieve. But then my first marriage was terrible—terrible in its brevity and futility. Pierre took Genevieve after the divorce, and I did nothing to contest it.

Jacques . . . he was the ship that was leaving port, and I set sail on him. He was holed on a reef, sank rapidly, ungracefully, beneath the mud of Juturna. I am marooned.

I did not count on this.

On Juturna, the clouds move more swiftly than on Earth. When I sit in the afternoon and watch them race across the crimson skies, I feel a part of some frantic movement. I must breathe deeply to relax.

My thoughts, of late, excite me as the clouds do.

One can gaze directly at the sun here, and then contemplate the blurry outline of shadows that it casts so feebly.

The shadows are my thoughts.

20-4-29

When I taught Earth history to children here on Juturna, before my arthritis demanded that I cease, my life was busy enough to prevent me from reflecting on it too deeply. These days that I have free now, and my sojourns at the hospital, have altered this. My life passes through the sieve of my mind, and that which remains is insufficient.

The tide in my affairs is at the flood. I can ride it out, or I can remain marooned.

The Child.

I see him again tomorrow.

20-4-30

I have spoken to Dr. Van Huizen. We had a lengthy discussion. I feel that he understands.

I will not write more today. I cannot. I must feel it first. I am on the edge.

I think I have decided. Finally, I have something of sufficient import about which to make a decision. Perhaps I understand my Churchillian "duty" better.

20-4-31

At any rate, it is done.

More tomorrow.

I cannot write. My thoughts are swollen, like my heart.

20–5–6

The recent days have left me unable to either journalize or speculate articulately. I can take time now, to try. There was no problem really. In fact, they were quite happy to have the matter resolved so neatly.

There are few who will take a Silent Child. Although I am not well, I will manage, since he will require so much less care than a normal child. The Council cannot afford to be overly fussy; we have, after all, Colony conditions of population and parochialism.

Are the Silent Children the first generation of new Juturnans—the adaptation of *Homo sapiens* to the environment? Perhaps they can communicate in ways that we cannot yet grasp. The universe is, after all, large, and there is much more silence than noise, much more void than matter. Perhaps we are the aberration, not the Juturnans. These Children, in many senses, belong here; they will blend perfectly.

As Jacques has blended. Into the powder-grey soil. Into silence.

As I will blend.

Even as Genevieve, my flesh, exists, tacitly, among the stars, a memory.

The gaps exist.

The silence drowns the wawling of birth.

Jacques spoke of Challenge. I think I finally understand.

I feel at peace with myself tonight as I sit here with Yves, the child, his tiny fingers clenched on my thumb. The woman who is the midnight wind is singing, and, for me alone, the planet is rotating fiercely.

THE WINTER MARKET

William Gibson

William Gibson moved to Toronto in 1968 from the U.S. and in 1972 settled in Vancouver, B.C. In the late 1970's he began to publish fiction and in such short stories as "Johnny Mnemonic" in the early 1980's invented "cyberspace" (the concept of a space created by the worldwide network of linked computers, which humans can "jack into"). This idea was incorporated into his first novel, *Neuromancer* (1984), which took the SF world by storm, winning the Philip K. Dick Award, the Nebula Award, and the Hugo Award, among others, for best SF novel of the year, and made Gibson internationally famous as the avatar of "cyberpunk." He published two sequels to *Neuromancer, Count Zero* and *Mona Lisa Overdrive*; a short-story collection, *Burning Chrome*; a novel in collaboration with Bruce Sterling, *The Difference Engine*; and has become a writer of the first rank in SF and widely read outside the field. His most recent novel is *Virtual Light.*

Gibson's hip, noir atmosphere and his clear, sharp style have particularly strong associations with postmodern fiction. His models include William S. Burroughs and J. G. Ballard, and he writes to a large extent consciously in reaction against traditional SF. That he has chosen Canada as his home is a point of pride to many younger Canadian SF writers, who see his work as a potential model. One need only look to the stories by, say, John Park, Claude-Michel Prévost, Jean-Louis Trudel, and certain others in this book, to find traces of Gibson's influence on younger Canadian writers in the last decade.

"The Winter Market" is not only one of his finest short works, but also the most "Canadian" of his stories to date.

It rains a lot, up here; there are winter days when it doesn't really get light at all, only a bright, indeterminate grey. But then there are days when it's like they whip aside a curtain to flash you three minutes of sunlit, suspended mountain, the trademark at the start of God's own movie. It was like that the day her agents phoned, from deep in the heart of their mirrored pyramid on Beverly Boulevard, to tell me she'd merged with the net, crossed over for good, that *Kings of Sleep* was going triple-platinum. I'd edited most of *Kings*, done the brain-map work and gone over it all with the fast-wipe module, so I was in line for a share of royalties.

No, I said, no. Then yes, yes, and hung up on them. Got my jacket and took the stairs three at a time, straight out to the nearest bar and an eight-hour blackout that ended on a concrete ledge two metres above midnight.

False Creek water. City lights, that same grey bowl of sky smaller now, il-luminated by neon and mercury-vapour arcs. And it was snowing, big flakes, but not many, and when they touched black water, they were gone, no trace at all. I looked down at my feet and saw my toes clear of the edge of concrete, the water between them. I was wearing Japanese shoes, new and expensive, glove-leather Ginza monkey boots with rubber-capped toes. I stood there for a long time before I took that first step back.

Because she was dead, and I'd let her go. Because, now, she was immor-tal, and I'd helped her get that way. And because I knew she'd phone me, in the morning.

My father was an audio engineer, a mastering engineer. He went way back, in the business, even before digital. The processes he was concerned with were partly mechanical, with that clunky quasi-Victorian quality you see in twentieth-century technology. He was a lathe operator, basically. People brought him audio recordings and he burned their sounds into grooves on a disk of lacquer. Then the disk was electroplated and used in the construction of a press that would stamp out records, the black things you see in antique stores. And I remember him telling me, once, a few months before he died, that certain frequencies—transients, I think he called them—could easily burn out the head, the cutting head, on a master lathe. These heads were incredibly expensive, so you prevented burnouts with something called an accelerometer. And that was what I was thinking of, as I stood there, my toes out over the water: that head, burning out.

Because that was what they did to her.

And that was what she wanted.

No accelerometer for Lise.

I disconnected my phone on my way to bed. I did it with the business end of a West German studio tripod that was going to cost a week's wages to re-pair.

Woke some strange time later and took a cab back to Granville Island and Rubin's place.

Rubin, in some way that no one quite understands, is a master, a teacher, what the Japanese call a *sensei*. What he's the master of, really, is garbage, kipple, refuse, the sea of cast-off goods our century floats on. *Gomi no sensei*. Master of junk.

I found him, this time, squatting between two vicious-looking drum ma-chines I hadn't seen before, rusty spider arms folded at the hearts of dented constellations of steel cans fished out of Richmond dumpsters. He never calls the place a studio, never refers to himself as an artist. "Messing around," he calls what he does there, and seems to view it as some extension of boyhood's perfectly bored backyard afternoons. He wanders through his jammed, littered space, a kind of minihangar cobbled to the water side of the

Market, followed by the smarter and more agile of his creations, like some vaguely benign Satan bent on the elaboration of still stranger processes in his ongoing Inferno of *gomi*. I've seen Rubin program his constructions to identify and verbally abuse pedestrians wearing garments by a given season's hot designer; others attend to more obscure missions, and a few seem constructed solely to deconstruct themselves with as much attendant noise as possible. He's like a child, Rubin; he's also worth a lot of money in galleries in Tokyo and Paris.

So I told him about Lise. He let me do it, get it out, then nodded. "I know," he said. "Some CBC creep phoned eight times." He sipped something out of a dented cup. "You wanna Wild Turkey sour?"

"Why'd they call you?"

" 'Cause my name's on the back of *Kings of Sleep*. Dedication."

"I didn't see it yet."

"She try to call you yet?"

"No."

"She will."

"Rubin, she's dead. They cremated her already."

"I know," he said. "And she's going to call you."

Gomi

Where does the *gomi* stop and the world begin? The Japanese, a century ago, had already run out of *gomi* space around Tokyo, so they came up with a plan for creating space out of *gomi*. By the year 1969 they had built themselves a little island in Tokyo Bay, out of *gomi*, and christened it Dream Island. But the city was still pouring out its nine thousand tons per day, so they went on to build New Dream Island, and today they coordinate the whole process, and new Nippons rise out of the Pacific. Rubin watches this on the news and says nothing at all.

He has nothing to say about *gomi*. It's his medium, the air he breathes, something he's swum in all his life. He cruises Greater Van in a spavined truck-thing chopped down from an ancient Mercedes airporter, its roof lost under a wallowing rubber bag half-filled with natural gas. He looks for things that fit with some strange design scrawled on the inside of his forehead by whatever serves him as Muse. He brings home more *gomi*. Some of it still operative. Some of it, like Lise, human.

I met Lise at one of Rubin's parties. Rubin had a lot of parties. He never seemed particularly to enjoy them, himself, but they were excellent parties. I lost track, that fall, of the number of times I woke on a slab of foam to the roar of Rubin's antique espresso machine, a tarnished behemoth topped with a big chrome eagle, the sound outrageous off the corrugated steel walls of the place, but massively comforting, too: There was coffee. Life would go on.

First time I saw her: in the Kitchen Zone. You wouldn't call it a kitchen, exactly, just three fridges and a hot plate and a broken convection oven that had come in with the *gomi*. First time I saw her: She had the all-beer fridge open, light spilling out, and I caught the cheekbones and the determined set of that mouth, but I also caught the black glint of polycarbon at her wrist, and the bright slick sore the exoskeleton had rubbed there. Too drunk to process, to know what it was, but I did know it wasn't party time. So I did what people usually did, to Lise, and clicked myself into a different movie. Went for the wine instead, on the counter beside the convection oven. Never looked back.

But she found me again. Came after me two hours later, weaving through the bodies and junk with that terrible grace programmed into the exoskeleton. I knew what it was, then, as I watched her homing in, too embarrassed now to duck it, to run, to mumble some excuse and get out. Pinned there, my arm around the waist of a girl I didn't know, while Lise advanced—*was advanced*, with that mocking grace—straight at me now, her eyes burning with wizz, and the girl had wriggled out and away in a quiet social panic, was gone, and Lise stood there in front of me, propped up in her pencil-thin polycarbon prosthetic. Looked into those eyes and it was like you could hear her synapses whining, some impossibly high-pitched scream as the wizz opened every circuit in her brain.

"Take me home," she said, and the words hit me like a whip. I think I shook my head. "Take me home." There were levels of pain there, and subtlety, and an amazing cruelty. And I knew then that I'd never been hated, ever, as deeply or thoroughly as this wasted little girl hated me now, hated me for the way I'd looked, then looked away, beside Rubin's all-beer refrigerator.

So—if that's the word—I did one of those things you do and never find out why, even though something in you knows you could never have done anything else.

I took her home.

I have two rooms in an old condo rack at the corner of Fourth and Mac-Donald, tenth floor. The elevators usually work, and if you sit on the balcony railing then lean out backward, holding on to the corner of the building next door, you can see a little upright slit of sea and mountain.

She hadn't said a word, all the way back from Rubin's, and I was getting sober enough to feel very uneasy as I unlocked the door and let her in.

The first thing she saw was the portable fast-wipe I'd brought home from the Pilot the night before. The exoskeleton carried her across the dusty broadloom with that same walk, like a model down a runway. Away from the crash of the party, I could hear it click softly as it moved her. She stood there, looking down at the fast-wipe. I could see the thing's ribs when she stood like that, make them out across her back through the scruffed black leather of her jacket. One of those diseases. Either they were one of the old ones they've never quite figured out or one of the new ones—the all too obviously environmental kind—that they've barely even named yet. She couldn't move, not without that extra skeleton, and it was jacked straight into her brain, myoelectric interface. The fragile-looking polycarbon braces moved her arms and legs, but a more subtle system handled her thin hands, galvanic inlays. I thought of frog legs twitching in a high-school lab tape, then hated myself for it.

"This is a fast-wipe module," she said in a voice I hadn't heard before, distant, and I thought then that the wizz might be wearing off. "What's it doing here?"

"I edit," I said, closing the door behind me.

"Well, now," and she laughed. "You do. Where?"

"On the Island. Place called the Autonomic Pilot."

She turned; then, hand on thrust hip, she swung—it swung her—and the wizz and the hate and some terrible parody of lust stabbed out at me from those washed-out grey eyes. "You wanna make it, editor?"

And I felt the whip come down again, but I wasn't going to take it, not again. So I cold-eyed her from somewhere down in the beer-numb core of my walking, talking, live-limbed, and entirely ordinary body and the words came out of me like spit: "Could you feel it, if I did?"

Beat. Maybe she blinked, but her face never registered. "No," she said, "but sometimes I like to watch."

Rubin stands at the window, two days after her death in Los Angeles, watching snow fall into False Creek. "So you never went to bed with her?"

One of his push-me-pull-you's, little roller-bearing Escher lizards, scoots across the table in front of me, in curl-up mode.

"No," I say, and it's true. Then I laugh. "But we jacked straight across. That first night."

"You were crazy," he says, a certain approval in his voice. "It might have killed you. Your heart might have stopped, you might have stopped breathing. . . ." He turns back to the window. "Has she called you yet?"

We jacked, straight across.

I'd never done it before. If you'd asked me why, I would have told you that I was an editor and that it wasn't professional.

The truth would be something more like this.

In the trade, the legitimate trade—I've never done porno—we called the raw product dry dreams. Dry dreams are neural output from levels of consciousness that most people can only access in sleep. But artists, the kind I work with at the Autonomic Pilot, are able to break the surface tension, dive down deep, down and out, out into Jung's sea, and bring back—well, dreams. Keep it simple. I guess some artists have always done that, in whatever medium, but neuroelectronics let us access the experience, and the net gets it all out on the wire, so we can package it, sell it, watch how it moves in the market. Well, the more things change . . . That's something my father liked to say.

Ordinarily I get the raw material in a studio situation, filtered through several million dollars' worth of baffles, and I don't even have to see the artist. The stuff we get out to the consumer, you see, has been structured, balanced, turned into art. There are still people naive enough to assume that they'll actually enjoy jacking straight across with someone they love. I think most teenagers try it, once. Certainly it's easy enough to do; Radio Shack will sell you the box and the trodes and the cables. But me, I'd never done it. And now that I think about it, I'm not so sure I can explain why. Or that I even want to try.

I do know why I did it with Lise, sat down beside her on my Mexican futon and snapped the optic lead into the socket on the spine, the smooth dorsal ridge, of the exoskeleton. It was high up, at the base of her neck, hidden by her dark hair.

Because she claimed she was an artist, and because I knew that we were engaged, somehow, in total combat, and I was *not* going to lose. That may not make sense to you, but then you never knew her, or know her through *Kings of Sleep*, which isn't the same at all. You never felt that hunger she had, which was pared down to a dry need, hideous in its singleness of purpose. People who know *exactly* what they want have always frightened me, and Lise had known what she wanted for a long time, and wanted nothing else at all. And I was scared, then, of admitting to myself that I was scared, and I'd seen enough strangers' dreams, in the mixing room at the Autonomic Pilot, to know that most people's inner monsters are foolish things, ludicrous in the calm light of one's own consciousness. And I was still drunk.

I put the trodes on and reached for the stud on the fast-wipe. I'd shut down its studio functions, temporarily converting eighty thousand dollars' worth of Japanese electronics to the equivalent of one of those little Radio Shack boxes. "Hit it," I said, and touched the switch.

Words. Words cannot. Or, maybe, just barely, if I even knew how to begin to describe it, what came up out of her, what she did. . . .

There's a segment on *Kings of Sleep*; it's like you're on a motorcycle at midnight, no lights but somehow you don't need them, blasting out along a cliff-high stretch of coast highway, so fast that you hang there in a cone of silence, the bike's thunder lost behind you. Everything, lost behind you. . . . It's just a blink, on *Kings*, but it's one of the thousand things you remember, go back to, incorporate into your own vocabulary of feelings. Amazing. Freedom and death, right there, right there, razor's edge, forever.

What I got was the big-daddy version of that, raw rush, the king hell killer uncut real thing, exploding eight ways from Sunday into a void that stank of poverty and lovelessness and obscurity.

And that was Lise's ambition, that rush, *seen from the inside.*

It probably took all of four seconds.

And, of course, she'd won.

I took the trodes off and stared at the wall, eyes wet, the framed posters swimming.

I couldn't look at her. I heard her disconnect the optic lead. I heard the exoskeleton creak as it hoisted her up from the futon. Heard it tick demurely as it hauled her into the kitchen for a glass of water.

Then I started to cry.

Rubin inserts a skinny probe in the roller-bearing belly of a sluggish push-me-pull-you and peers at the circuitry through magnifying glasses with miniature headlights mounted at the temples.

"So? You got hooked." He shrugs, looks up. It's dark now and the twin tensor beams stab at my face, chill damp in his steel barn and the lonesome hoot of a foghorn from somewhere across the water. "So?"

My turn to shrug. "I just did. . . . There didn't seem to be anything else to do."

The beams duck back to the silicon heart of his defective toy. "Then you're okay. It was a true choice. What I mean is, she was set to be what she is. You had about as much to do with where she's at today as that fast-wipe module did. She'd have found somebody else if she hadn't found you. . . ."

I made a deal with Barry, the senior editor, got twenty minutes at five on a cold September morning. Lise came in and hit me with the same shot, but this time I was ready, with my baffles and brain maps, and I didn't have to feel it. It took me two weeks, piecing out the minutes in the editing room, to cut what she'd done down into something I could play for Max Bell, who owns the Pilot.

Bell hadn't been happy, not happy at all, as I explained what I'd done. Maverick editors can be a problem, and eventually most editors decide that they've found someone who'll be it, the next monster, and then they start wasting time and money. He'd nodded when I'd finished my pitch, then scratched his nose with the cap of his red feltpen. "Uh-huh. Got it. Hottest thing since fish grew legs, right?"

But he'd jacked it, the demo soft I'd put together, and when it clicked out of its slot in his Braun desk unit, he was staring at the wall, his face blank.

"Max?"

"Huh?"

"What do you think?"

"Think? I . . . What did you say her name was?" He blinked. "Lisa? Who you say she's signed with?"

"Lise. Nobody, Max. She hasn't signed with anybody yet."

"Jesus Christ." He still looked blank.

"You know how I found her?" Rubin asks, wading through ragged cardboard boxes to find the light switch. The boxes are filled with carefully sorted *gomi*: lithium batteries, tantalum capacitors, RF connectors, breadboards, barrier strips, ferroresonant transformers, spools of bus bar wire. . . . One box is filled with the severed heads of hundreds of Barbie dolls, another with armoured industrial safety gauntlets that look like space-suit gloves. Light floods the room and a sort of Kandinsky mantis in snipped and painted tin swings its golfball-size head toward the bright bulb. "I was down on Granville on a *gomi* run, back in an alley, and I found her just sitting there. Caught the skeleton and she didn't look so good, so I asked her if she was okay. Nothin'. Just closed her eyes. Not my lookout, I think. But I happened back by there about four hours later and she hasn't moved. 'Look, honey,' I tell her, 'maybe your hardware's buggered up. I can help you, okay?' Nothin'. 'How long you been back here?' Nothin'. So I take off." He crosses to his workbench and strokes the thin metal limbs of the mantis thing with a pale forefinger. Behind the bench, hung on damp-swollen sheets of ancient pegboard, are pliers, screwdrivers, tie-wrap guns, a rusted Daisy BB rifle, coax strippers, crimpers, logic probes, heat guns, a pocket oscilloscope, seemingly every tool in human history, with no attempt ever made to order them at all, though I've yet to see Rubin's hand hesitate.

"So I went back," he says. "Gave it an hour. She was out by then, unconscious, so I brought her back here and ran a check on the exoskeleton. Batteries were dead. She'd crawled back there when the juice ran out and settled down to starve to death, I guess."

"When was that?"

"About a week before you took her home."

"But what if she'd died? If you hadn't found her?"

"Somebody was going to find her. She couldn't *ask* for anything, you know? Just *take*. Couldn't stand a favour."

Max found the agents for her, and a trio of awesomely slick junior partners Leared into YVR a day later. Lise wouldn't come down to the Pilot to meet them, insisted we bring them up to Rubin's where she still slept.

"Welcome to Couverville," Rubin said as they edged in the door. His long face was smeared with grease, the fly of his ragged fatigue pants held more or less shut with a twisted paper clip. The boys grinned automatically, but there was something marginally more authentic about the girl's smile. "Mr. Stark," she said, "I was in London last week. I saw your installation at the Tate."

"*Marcello's Battery Factory,*" Rubin said. "They say it's scatological, the Brits. . . ." He shrugged. "Brits. I mean, who knows?"

"They're right. It's also very funny."

The boys were beaming like table-tanned lighthouses, standing there in their suits. The demo had reached Los Angeles. They knew.

"And you're Lise," she said, negotiating the path between Rubin's heaped *gomi*. "You're going to be a very famous person soon, Lise. We have a lot to discuss. . . ."

And Lise just stood there, propped in polycarbon, and the look on her face was the one I'd seen that first night, in my condo, when she'd asked me if I wanted to go to bed. But if the junior agent lady saw it, she didn't show it. She was a pro.

I told myself that I was a pro, too.

I told myself to relax.

Trash fires gutter in steel canisters around the Market. The snow still falls and kids huddle over the flames like arthritic crows, hopping from foot to foot, wind whipping their dark coats. Up in Fairview's arty slum-tumble, someone's laundry has frozen solid on the line, pink squares of bedsheet standing out against the background dinge and the confusion of satellite dishes and solar panels. Some ecologist's eggbeater windmill goes round and round, round and round, giving a whirling finger to the Hydro rates.

Rubin clumps along in paint-spattered L. L. Bean gumshoes, his big head pulled down into an oversize fatigue jacket. Sometimes one of the hunched teens will point him out as we pass, the guy who builds all the crazy stuff, the robots and shit.

"You know what your trouble is?" he says when we're under the bridge, headed up to Fourth. "You're the kind who *always reads the handbook.* Anything people build, any kind of technology, it's going to have some specific purpose. It's for doing something that somebody already understands. But if it's new technology, it'll open areas nobody's ever thought of before. You read the manual, man, and you won't play around with it, not the same way. And you get all funny when somebody else uses it to do something you never thought of. Like Lise."

"She wasn't the first." Traffic drums past overhead.

"No, but she's sure as hell the first person *you* ever met who went and translated herself into a hardwired program. You lose any sleep when whatsisname did it, three-four years ago, the French kid, the writer?"

"I didn't really think about it, much. A gimmick. PR. . . ."

"He's still writing. The weird thing is, he's going to *be* writing, unless somebody blows up his mainframe. . . ."

I wince, shake my head. "But it's not *him,* is it? It's just a program."

"Interesting point. Hard to say. With Lise, though, we find out. She's not a writer."

* * *

She had it all in there, *Kings*, locked up in her head the way her body was locked in that exoskeleton.

The agents signed her with a label and brought in a production team from Tokyo. She told them she wanted me to edit. I said no; Max dragged me into his office and threatened to fire me on the spot. If I wasn't involved, there was no reason to do the studio work at the Pilot. Vancouver was hardly the centre of the world, and the agents wanted her in Los Angeles. It meant a lot of money to him, and it might put the Autonomic Pilot on the map. I couldn't explain to him why I'd refused. It was too crazy, too personal; she was getting a final dig in. Or that's what I thought then. But Max was serious. He really didn't give me any choice. We both knew another job wasn't going to crawl into my hand. I went back out with him and we told the agents that we'd worked it out: I was on.

The agents showed us lots of teeth.

Lise pulled out an inhaler full of wizz and took a huge hit. I thought I saw the agent lady raise one perfect eyebrow, but that was the extent of censure. After the papers were signed, Lise more or less did what she wanted.

And Lise always knew what she wanted.

We did *Kings* in three weeks, the basic recording. I found any number of reasons to avoid Rubin's place, even believed some of them myself. She was still staying there, although the agents weren't too happy with what they saw as a total lack of security. Rubin told me later that he'd had to have *his* agent call them up and raise hell, but after that they seemed to quit worrying. I hadn't known that Rubin had an agent. It was always easy to forget that Rubin Stark was more famous, then, than anyone else I knew, certainly more famous than I thought Lise was ever likely to become. I knew we were working on something strong, but you never know how big anything's liable to be.

But the time I spent in the Pilot, I was *on*. Lise was amazing.

It was like she was born to the form, even though the technology that made that form possible hadn't even existed when she was born. You see something like that and you wonder how many thousands, maybe millions, of phenomenal artists have died mute, down the centuries, people who could never have been poets or painters or saxophone players, but who had this stuff inside, these psychic waveforms waiting for the circuitry required to tap in. . . .

I learned a few things about her, incidentals, from our time in the studio. That she was born in Windsor. That her father was American and served in Peru and came home crazy and half-blind. That whatever was wrong with her body was congenital. That she had those sores because she refused to remove the exoskeleton, ever, because she'd start to choke and die at the thought of that utter helplessness. That she was addicted to wizz and doing enough of it daily to wire a football team.

Her agents brought in medics, who padded the polycarbon with foam and sealed the sores over with micropore dressings. They pumped her up with vitamins and tried to work on her diet, but nobody ever tried to take that inhaler away.

They brought in hairdressers and make-up artists, too, and wardrobe people and image builders and articulate little PR hamsters, and she endured it with something that might almost have been a smile.

And, right through those three weeks, we didn't talk. Just studio talk, artist-editor stuff, very much a restricted code. Her imagery was so strong, so extreme, that she never really needed to explain a given effect to me. I took what she put out and worked with it, and jacked it back to her. She'd either say yes or no, and usually it was yes. The agents noted this and approved, and clapped Max Bell on the back and took him out to dinner, and my salary went up.

And I was pro, all the way. Helpful and thorough and polite. I was determined not to crack again, and never thought about the night I cried, and I was also doing the best work I'd ever done, and knew it, and that's a high in itself.

And then, one morning, about six, after a long, long session—when she'd first got that eerie cotillion sequence out, the one the kids call the Ghost Dance—she spoke to me. One of the two agent boys had been there, showing teeth, but he was gone now and the Pilot was dead quiet, just the hum of a blower somewhere down by Max's office.

"Casey," she said, her voice hoarse with the wizz, "sorry I hit on you so hard."

I thought for a minute she was telling me something about the recording we'd just made. I looked up and saw her there, and it struck me that we were alone, and hadn't been alone since we'd made the demo.

I had no idea at all what to say. Didn't even know what I felt.

Propped up in the exoskeleton, she was looking worse than she had that first night, at Rubin's. The wizz was eating her, under the stuff the make-up team kept smoothing on, and sometimes it was like seeing a death's-head surface beneath the face of a not very handsome teenager. I had no idea of her real age. Not old, not young.

"The ramp effect," I said, coiling a length of cable.

"What's that?"

"Nature's way of telling you to clean up your act. Sort of mathematical law, says you can only get off real good on a stimulant x number of times, even if you increase the doses. But you can't *ever* get off as nice as you did the first few times. Or you shouldn't be able to, anyway. That's the trouble with designer drugs; they're too clever. That stuff you're doing has some tricky tail on one of its molecules, keeps you from turning the decomposed adrenaline into adrenochrome. If it didn't you'd be schizophrenic by now.

You got any little problems, Lise? Like apnea? Sometimes maybe you stop breathing if you go to sleep?"

But I wasn't even sure I felt the anger that I heard in my own voice.

She stared at me with those pale grey eyes. The wardrobe people had replaced her thrift-shop jacket with a butter-tanned matte black blouson that did a better job of hiding the polycarbon ribs. She kept it zipped to the neck, always, even though it was too warm in the studio. The hairdressers had tried something new the day before, and it hadn't worked out, her rough dark hair a lopsided explosion above that drawn, triangular face. She stared at me and I felt it again, her singleness of purpose.

"I don't sleep, Casey."

It wasn't until later, much later, that I remembered she'd told me she was sorry. She never did again, and it was the only time I ever heard her say anything that seemed to be out of character.

Rubin's diet consists of vending-machine sandwiches, Pakistani takeout food, and espresso. I've never seen him eat anything else. We eat samosas in a narrow shop on Fourth that has a single plastic table wedged between the counter and the door to the can. Rubin eats his dozen samosas, six meat and six veggie, with total concentration, one after another, and doesn't bother to wipe his chin. He's devoted to the place. He loathes the Greek counterman; it's mutual, a real relationship. If the counterman left, Rubin might not come back. The Greek glares at the crumbs on Rubin's chin and jacket. Between samosas, he shoots daggers right back, his eyes narrowed behind the smudged lenses of his steel-rimmed glasses.

The samosas are dinner. Breakfast will be egg salad on dead white bread, packed in one of those triangles of milky plastic, on top of six little cups of poisonously strong espresso.

"You didn't see it coming, Casey." He peers at me out of the thumb-printed depths of his glasses. " 'Cause you're no good at lateral thinking. You read the handbook. What else did you think she was after? Sex? More wizz? A world tour? She was past all that. That's what made her so strong. She was past it. That's why *Kings of Sleep*'s as big as it is, and why the kids buy it, why they *believe* it. They know. Those kids back down at the Market, warming their butts around the fires and wondering if they'll find someplace to sleep tonight, they believe it. It's the hottest soft in eight years. Guy at a shop on Granville told me he gets more of the damned things lifted than he sells of anything else. Says it's a hassle to even stock it. . . . She's big because she was what they are, only more so. She knew, man. No dreams, no hope. You can't see the cages on those kids, Casey, but more and more they're twigging to it, that they aren't going *anywhere*." He brushes a greasy crumb of meat from his chin, missing three more. "So she sang it for them, said it the way they can't, painted them a picture. And she used the money to buy herself a way out, that's all."

I watch the steam bead and roll down the window in big drops, streaks in the condensation. Beyond the window I can make out a partially stripped Lada, wheels scavenged, axles down on the pavement.

"How many people have done it, Rubin? Have any idea?"

"Not too many. Hard to say, anyway, because a lot of them are probably politicians we think of as being comfortably and reliably dead." He gives me a funny look. "Not a nice thought. Anyway, they had first shot at the technology. It still costs too much for any ordinary dozen millionaires, but I've heard of at least seven. They say Mitsubishi did it to Weinberg before his immune system finally went tits up. He was head of their hybridoma lab in Okayama. Well, their stock's still pretty high, in monoclonals, so maybe it's true. And Langlais, the French kid, the novelist . . ." He shrugs. "Lise didn't have the money for it. Wouldn't now, even. But she put herself in the right place at the right time. She was about to croak, she was in Hollywood, and they could already see what *Kings* was going to do."

The day we finished up, the band stepped off a JAL shuttle out of London, four skinny kids who operated like a well-oiled machine and displayed a hypertrophied fashion sense and a total lack of affect. I set them up in a row at the Pilot, in identical white Ikea office chairs, smeared saline paste on their temples, taped the trodes on, and ran the rough version of what was going to become *Kings of Sleep*. When they came out of it, they all started talking at once, ignoring me totally, in the British version of that secret language all studio musicians speak, four sets of pale hands zooming and chopping the air.

I could catch enough of it to decide that they were excited. That they thought it was good. So I got my jacket and left. They could wipe their own saline paste off, thanks.

And that night I saw Lise for the last time, though I didn't plan to.

Walking back down to the Market, Rubin noisily digesting his meal, red taillights reflected on wet cobbles, the city beyond the Market a clean sculpture of light, a lie, where the broken and the lost burrow into the *gomi* that grows like humus at the bases of the towers of glass . . .

"I gotta go to Frankfurt tomorrow, do an installation. You wanna come? I could write you off as a technician." He shrugs his way deeper into the fatigue jacket. "Can't pay you, but you can have airfare, you want . . ."

Funny offer, from Rubin, and I know it's because he's worried about me, thinks I'm too strange about Lise, and it's the only thing he can think of, getting me out of town.

"It's colder in Frankfurt now than it is here."

"You maybe need a change, Casey. I dunno . . ."

"Thanks, but Max has a lot of work lined up. Pilot's a big deal now, people flying in from all over . . ."

"Sure."

When I left the band at the Pilot, I went home. Walked up to Fourth and took the trolley home, past the windows of the shops I see every day, each one lit up jazzy and slick, clothes and shoes and software, Japanese motorcycles crouched like clean enamel scorpions, Italian furniture. The windows change with the seasons, the shops come and go. We were into the pre-holiday mode now, and there were more people on the street, a lot of couples, walking quickly and purposefully past the bright windows, on their way to score that perfect little whatever for whomever, half the girls in those padded thigh-high nylon boot things that came out of New York the winter before, the ones Rubin said made them look like they had elephantiasis. I grinned, thinking about that, and suddenly it hit me that it really was over, that I was done with Lise, and that now she'd be sucked off to Hollywood as inexorably as if she'd poked her toe into a black hole, drawn down by the unthinkable gravitic tug of Big Money. Believing that, that she was gone— probably *was* gone, by then—I let down some kind of guard in myself and felt the edges of my pity. But just the edges, because I didn't want my evening screwed up by anything. I wanted partytime. It had been a while.

Got off at my corner and the elevator worked on the first try. Good sign, I told myself. Upstairs, I undressed and showered, found a clean shirt, microwaved burritos. Feel normal, I advised my reflection while I shaved. You have been working too hard. Your credit cards have got fat. Time to remedy that.

The burritos tasted like cardboard, but I decided I liked them because they were so aggressively normal. My car was in Burnaby, having its leaky hydrogen cell repacked, so I wasn't going to have to worry about driving. I could go out, find partytime, and phone in sick in the morning. Max wasn't going to kick; I was his star boy. He owed me.

You owe me, Max, I said to the subzero bottle of Moskovskaya I fished out of the freezer. Do you ever owe me. I have just spent three weeks editing the dreams and nightmares of one very screwed-up person, Max. On your behalf. So that you can grow and prosper, Max. I poured three fingers of vodka into a plastic glass left over from a party I'd thrown the year before and went back into the living room.

Sometimes it looks to me like nobody in particular lives there. Not that it's that messy; I'm a good if somewhat robotic housekeeper, and even remember to dust the tops of framed posters and things, but I have these times when the place abruptly gives me a kind of low-grade chill, with its basic accumulation of basic consumer goods. I mean, it's not like I want to fill it up with cats or houseplants or anything, but there are moments when I see that anyone could be living there, could own those things, and it all seems sort of interchangeable, my life and yours, my life and anybody's. . . .

I think Rubin sees things that way, too, all the time, but for him it's a source of strength. He lives in other people's garbage, and everything he drags home must have been new and shiny once, must have meant something, however briefly, to someone. So he sweeps it all up into his crazy-looking truck and hauls it back to his place and lets it compost there until he thinks of something new to do with it. Once he was showing me a book of twentieth-century art he liked, and there was a picture of an automated sculpture called *Dead Birds Fly Again*, a thing that whirled real dead birds around and around on a string, and he smiled and nodded, and I could see he felt the artist was a spiritual ancestor of some kind. But what could Rubin do with my framed posters and my Mexican futon from the Bay and my temperfoam bed from Ikea? Well, I thought, taking a first chilly sip, he'd be able to think of something, which was why he was a famous artist and I wasn't.

I went and pressed my forehead against the plate-glass window, as cold as the glass in my hand. Time to go, I said to myself. You are exhibiting symptoms of urban singles angst. There are cures for this. Drink up. Go.

I didn't attain a state of partytime that night. Neither did I exhibit adult common sense and give up, go home, watch some ancient movie, and fall asleep on my futon. The tension those three weeks had built up in me drove me like the mainspring of a mechanical watch, and I went ticking off through nighttown, lubricating my more or less random progress with more drinks. It was one of those nights, I quickly decided, when you slip into an alternate continuum, a city that looks exactly like the one where you live, except for the peculiar difference that it contains not one person you love or know or have even spoken to before. Nights like that, you go into a familiar bar and find that the staff has just been replaced; then you understand that your real motive in going there was simply to see a familiar face, on a waitress or a bartender, whoever. . . . This sort of thing has been known to mediate against partytime.

I kept it rolling, though, through six or eight places, and eventually it rolled me into a West End club that looked as if it hadn't been redecorated since the Nineties. A lot of peeling chrome over plastic, blurry holograms that gave you a headache if you tried to make them out. I think Barry had told me about the place, but I can't imagine why. I looked around and grinned. If I was looking to be depressed, I'd come to the right place. Yes, I told myself as I took a corner stool at the bar, this was genuinely sad, really the pits. Dreadful enough to halt the momentum of my shitty evening, which was undoubtedly a good thing. I'd have one more for the road, admire the grot, and then cab it on home.

And then I saw Lise.

She hadn't seen me, not yet, and I still had my coat on, tweed collar up against the weather. She was down the bar and around the corner with a couple of empty drinks in front of her, big ones, the kind that come with little Hong Kong parasols or plastic mermaids in them, and as she looked up at the boy beside her, I saw the wizz flash in her eyes and knew that those drinks had never contained alcohol, because the levels of drug she was running couldn't tolerate the mix. The kid, though, was gone, numb grinning drunk and about ready to slide off his stool, and running on about something as he made repeated attempts to focus his eyes and get a better look at Lise, who sat there with her wardrobe team's black leather blouson zipped to her chin and her skull about to burn through her white face like a thousand-watt bulb. And seeing that, seeing her there, I knew a whole lot of things at once.

That she really was dying, either from the wizz or her disease or the combination of the two. That she damned well knew it. That the boy beside her was too drunk to have picked up on the exoskeleton, but not too drunk to register the expensive jacket and the money she had for drinks. And that what I was seeing was exactly what it looked like.

But I couldn't add it up, right away, couldn't compute. Something in me cringed.

And she was smiling, or anyway doing a thing she must have thought was like a smile, the expression she knew was appropriate to the situation, and nodding in time to the kid's slurred inanities, and that awful line of hers came back to me, the one about liking to watch.

And I know something now. I know that if I hadn't happened in there, hadn't seen them, I'd have been able to accept all that came later. Might even have found a way to rejoice on her behalf, or found a way to trust in whatever it is that she's since become, or had built in her image, a program that pretends to be Lise to the extent that it believes it's her. I could have believed what Rubin believes, that she was so truly past it, our hi-tech Saint Joan burning for union with that hardwired godhead in Hollywood, that nothing mattered to her except the hour of her departure. That she threw away that poor sad body with a cry of release, free of the bonds of polycarbon and hated flesh. Well, maybe, after all, she did. Maybe it was that way. I'm sure that's the way she expected it to be.

But seeing her there, that drunken kid's hand in hers, that hand she couldn't even feel, I knew, once and for all, that no human motive is ever entirely pure. Even Lise, with that corrosive, crazy drive to stardom and cybernetic immortality, had weaknesses. Was human in a way I hated myself for admitting.

She'd gone out that night, I knew, to kiss herself goodbye. To find someone drunk enough to do it for her. Because, I knew then, it was true: She did like to watch.

I think she saw me, as I left. If she did, I suppose she hated me worse than ever, for the horror and the pity in my face.

I never saw her again.

Someday I'll ask Rubin why Wild Turkey sours are the only drink he knows how to make. Industrial-strength, Rubin's sours. He passes me the dented aluminum cup, while his place ticks and stirs around us with the furtive activity of his smaller creations.

"You ought to come to Frankfurt," he says again.

"Why, Rubin?"

"Because pretty soon she's going to call you up. And I think maybe you aren't ready for it. You're still screwed up about this, and it'll sound like her and think like her, and you'll get too weird behind it. Come over to Frankfurt with me and you can get a little breathing space. She won't know you're there. . . ."

"I told you," I say, remembering her at the bar in that club, "lots of work. Max—"

"Stuff Max. Max you just made rich. Max can sit on his hands. You're rich yourself, from your royalty cut on *Kings*, if you weren't too stubborn to dial up your bank account. You can afford a vacation."

I look at him and wonder when I'll tell him the story of that final glimpse. "Rubin, I appreciate it, man, but I just . . ."

He sighs, drinks. "But what?"

"Rubin, if she calls me, is it *her*?"

He looks at me a long time. "God only knows." His cup clicks on the table. "I mean, Casey, the technology is there, so who, man, really who, is to say?"

"And you think I should come with you to Frankfurt?"

He takes off his steel-rimmed glasses and polishes them inefficiently on the front of his plaid flannel shirt. "Yeah, I do. You need the rest. Maybe you don't need it now, but you're going to, later."

"How's that?"

"When you have to edit her next release. Which will almost certainly be soon, because she needs money bad. She's taking up a lot of ROM on some corporate mainframe, and her share of *Kings* won't come close to paying for what they had to do to put her there. And you're her editor, Casey. I mean, who else?"

And I just stare at him as he puts the glasses back on, like I can't move at all.

"Who else, man?"

And one of his constructs clicks right then, just a clear and tiny sound, and it comes to me, he's right.

THE BYRDS

Michael G. Coney

Michael G. Coney is one of the three major SF figures (the others are Judith Merril and Spider Robinson) who moved to Canada in the 1970's and, of them, the most prolific writer. He lives in Victoria, British Columbia, and all except the first of his seventeen or more SF novels and the majority of his short fiction (his only collection is an early one, *Monitor Found in Orbit,* 1974) were published after his arrival in 1973. But his fiction writing had already slowed down by the publication of his ninth novel, *Brontomek* (1976), which won the British Science Fiction Award as best novel of the year. His five novels of the 1980's all share the same far future background, although two are Arthurian fantasies.

In his entry in *Twentieth-Century Science Fiction Writers,* he writes, "Each of my novels has been an experiment in style and content with one consistent trait: they are all mystery stories. Love is there too, and human psychology, and a little 'hard' science, but my main intent is to keep the reader guessing. . . . As an SF reader, my preference is for the persuasively fantastic: the 'sense of wonder' story." David Ketterer quotes Coney on writing SF where "the denouement was the result of the characters of the people concerned and their reaction to the scientific (generally sociological) premise rather than a gimmick ending based on the premise itself." Then Ketterer goes on to say, "In the best of Coney's short stories and novels, character and idea achieve this kind of integration, which the most distinctly Canadian SF aspires to."

The best of Coney is also underpinned with mature wit, irony, and humor, and his relation to SF writers such as Philip K. Dick, Brian W. Aldiss, and R. A. Lafferty in this regard is rarely mentioned. We have chosen "The Byrds" in part because it illustrates all of Coney's strengths. It is set in his hometown of Sidney, British Columbia.

Gran started it all.

Late one afternoon in the hottest summer in living memory, she took off all her clothes, carefully painted red around her eyes and down her cheeks, chin and throat, painted the rest of her body a contrasting black with the exception of her armpits and the inside of her wrists which she painted white, strapped on her new antigravity belt, flapped her arms and rose into the nearest tree, a garry oak, where she perched.

She informed us that, as of now, she was Rufous-necked Hornbill, of India.

"She always wanted to visit India," Gramps told us.

Gran said no more, for the logical reason that Hornbills are not talking birds.

"Come down, Gran!" called Mother. "You'll catch your death of cold."

Gran remained silent. She stretched her neck and gazed at the horizon.

"She's crazy," said Father. "She's crazy. I always said she was. I'll call the asylum."

"You'll do no such thing!" Mother was always very sensitive about Gran's occasional peculiarities. "She'll be down soon. The evenings are drawing in. She'll get cold."

"What's an old fool her age doing with an antigravity unit anyway, that's what I want to know," said Father.

The Water Department was restricting supply and the weatherman was predicting floods. The Energy Department was warning of depleted stocks, the Department of Rest had announced that the population must fall by one-point-eight per cent by November or else, the Mailgift was spewing out a deluge of application forms, tax forms and final reminders, the Tidy Mice were malfunctioning so that the house stank. . . .

And now this.

It was humiliating and embarrassing, Gran up a tree, naked and painted. She stayed there all evening, and I knew that my girlfriend Pandora would be dropping by soon and would be sure to ask questions.

Humanity was at that point in the morality cycle when nudity was considered indecent. Gran was probably thirty years before her time. There was something lonely and anachronistic about her, perched there, balancing unsteadily in a squatting position, occasionally grabbing at the trunk for support then flapping her arms to re-establish the birdlike impression. She looked like some horrible mutation. Her resemblance to a Rufous-necked Hornbill was slight.

"Talk her down, Gramps," said Father.

"She'll come down when she's hungry."

He was wrong. Late in the evening Gran winged her way to a vacant lot where an ancient tree stood. She began to eat unsterilized apples, juice flowing down her chin. It was a grotesque sight.

"She'll be poisoned!" cried Mother.

"So, she's made her choice at last," said Father.

He was referring to Your Choice for Peace, the brochure which Gran and Gramps received monthly from the Department of Rest. Accompanying the brochure is a six-page form on which senior citizens describe all that is good about their life, and a few of the things which bug them. At the end of the form is a box in which the oldster indicates his preference for Life or Peace. If he does not check the box, or if he fails to complete the form, it is assumed that he has chosen Peace, and they send the Wagon for him.

Now Gran was cutting a picturesque silhouette against the pale blue of the evening sky as she circled the rooftops uttering harsh cries. She flew with arms outstretched, legs trailing, and we all had to admit to the beauty of the sight; that is, until a flock of starlings began to mob her. Losing directional control she spiralled downwards, recovered, levelled out and skimmed towards us, outpacing the starlings and regaining her perch in the garry oak. She made preening motions and settled down for the night. The family Pesterminator, zapping bugs with its tiny laser, considered her electronically for a second but held its fire.

We were indoors by the time Pandora arrived. She was nervous, complaining that there was a huge mutation in the tree outside, and it had cawed at her.

Mother said quickly, "It's only a Rufous-necked Hornbill."

"A rare visitor to these shores," added Father.

"Why couldn't she have been a sparrow?" asked Mother. "Or something else inconspicuous." Things were not going well for her. The little robot Tidy Mice still sulked behind the wainscoting and she'd had to clean the house by hand.

The garish Gran shone like a beacon in the morning sunlight. There was no concealing the family's degradation. A small crowd had gathered and people were trying to tempt Gran down with breadcrumbs. She looked none the worse for her night out, and was greeting the morning with shrill yells.

Gramps was strapping on an antigravity belt. "I'm going up to fetch her down. This has gone far enough."

I said, "Be careful. She may attack you."

"Don't be a damned fool." Nevertheless Gramps went into the toolshed, later emerging nude and freshly painted. Mother uttered a small scream of distress, suspecting that Gramps, too, had become involved in the conspiracy to diminish the family's social standing.

I reassured her. "She's more likely to listen to one of her own kind."

"Has everyone gone totally insane?" asked Mother.

Gramps rose gracefully into the garry oak, hovered, then settled beside Gran. He spoke to her quietly for a moment and she listened, head cocked attentively.

Then she made low gobbling noises and leaned against him.

He called down, "This may take longer than I thought."

"Oh, my God," said Mother.

"That does it," said Father. "I'm calling the shrink."

Dr. Pratt was tall and dignified, and he took in the situation at a glance. "Has your mother exhibited birdish tendencies before?"

Father answered for Mother. "No more than anyone else. Although, in many other ways, she was—"

"Gran has always been the soul of conformity," said Mother quickly, beginning to weep. "If our neighbours have been saying otherwise I'll remind them of the slander laws. No—she did it to shame us. She always said she hated the colours we painted the house—she said it looked like a strutting peacock."

"Rutting peacock," said Father. "She said rutting peacock. Those were her exact words."

"Peacock, eh?" Dr. Pratt looked thoughtful. There was a definite avian thread running through this. "So you feel she may be acting in retaliation. She thinks you have made a public spectacle of the house in which she lives, so now she is going to make a public spectacle of you."

"Makes sense," said Father.

"Gran!" called Dr. Pratt. She looked down at us, beady little eyes ringed with red. "I have the personal undertaking of your daughter and son-in-law that the house will be repainted in colours of your own choosing." He spoke on for a few minutes in soothing tones. "That should do it," he said to us finally, picking up his bag. "Put her to bed and keep her off berries, seeds, anything like that. And don't leave any antigravity belts lying around. They can arouse all kinds of prurient interests in older people."

"She still isn't coming down," said Father. "I don't think she understood."

"Then I advise you to fell the tree," said Dr. Pratt coldly, his patience evaporated. "She's a disgusting old exhibitionist who needs to be taught a lesson. Just because she chooses to act out her fantasies in an unusual way doesn't make her any different from anyone else. And what's *he* doing up there, anyway? Does he resent the house paint as well?"

"He *chose* the paint. He's there to bring her down."

We watched them in perplexity. The pair huddled together on the branch, engaged in mutual grooming. The crowd outside the gate had swollen to over a hundred.

On the following morning Gran and Gramps greeted the dawn with a cacophony of gobbling and screeching.

I heard Father throw open his bedroom window and threaten to blast them right out of that goddamned tree and into the hereafter if they didn't keep it down. I heard the metallic click as he cocked his twelvebore. I heard Mother squeal with apprehension, and the muffled thumping of a physical struggle in the next room.

I was saddened by the strain it puts on marriages when inlaws live in the house—or, in our case, outside the window.

The crowds gathered early and it was quickly apparent that Gramps was through with trying to talk Gran down; in fact, he was through with talking altogether. He perched beside his mate in spry fashion, jerking his head this way and that as he scanned the sky for hawks, cocking an eye at the crowd, shuddering suddenly as though shaking feathers into position.

Dr. Pratt arrived at noon, shortly before the media.

"A classic case of regression to the childlike state," he told us. "The signs are all there: the unashamed nakedness, the bright colours, the speechlessness, the favourite toy, in this case the antigravity belt. I have brought a surrogate toy which I think will solve our problem. Try luring them down with this."

He handed Mother a bright red plastic baby's rattle.

Gran fastened a beady eye on it, shuffled her arms, then launched herself from the tree in a swooping glide. As Mother ducked in alarm, Gran caught the rattle neatly in her bony old toes, wheeled and flapped back to her perch. Heads close, she and Gramps examined the toy.

We waited breathlessly.

Then Gran stomped it against the branch and the shattered remnants fell to the ground.

The crowd applauded. For the first time we noticed the Newspocket van, and the crew with cameras. The effect on Dr. Pratt was instantaneous. He strode towards them and introduced himself to a red-haired woman with a microphone.

"Tell me, Dr. Pratt, to what do you attribute this phenomenon?"

"The manifestation of birdishness in the elderly is a subject which has received very little study up to the present date. Indeed, I would say that it has been virtually ignored. Apart from my own paper—still in draft form—you could search the psychiatric archives in vain for mention of Pratt's Syndrome."

"And why is that, Dr. Pratt?"

"Basically, fear. The fear in each and every one of us of admitting that something primitive and atavistic can lurk within our very genes. For what is more primitive than a bird, the only survivor of the age of dinosaurs?"

"What indeed, Dr. Pratt?"

"You see in that tree two pathetic human creatures who have reverted to a state which existed long before Man took his first step on Earth, a state which can only have been passed on as a tiny coded message in their very flesh and the flesh of their ancestors, through a million years of Time."

"And how long do you expect their condition to last, Dr. Pratt?"

"Until the fall. The winters in these parts are hard, and they'll be out of that tree come the first frost, if they've got any sense left at all."

"Well, thank you, Dr.—"

A raucous screaming cut her short. A group of shapes appeared in the eastern sky, low over the rooftops. They were too big for birds, yet too small for aircraft, and there was a moment's shocked incomprehension before we recognized them for what they were. Then they wheeled over the Newspocket van with a bedlam of yells and revealed themselves as teenagers of both sexes, unclothed, but painted a simple black semi-matt exterior latex. There were nine of them.

In the weeks following, we came to know them as the Crows. They flew overhead, circled, then settled all over the garry oak and the roof of our house.

They made no attempt to harass Gran or Gramps. Indeed, they seemed almost reverential in their attitude towards the old people.

It seemed that Gran had unlocked some kind of floodgate in the human unconscious, and people took to the air in increasing numbers. The manufacturers of antigravity belts became millionaires overnight, and the skies became a bright tapestry of wheeling, screeching figures in rainbow colours and startling nakedness.

The media named them the Byrds.

"I view it as a protest against today's moral code," said Dr. Pratt, who spent most of his time on panels or giving interviews. "For more years than I care to remember, people have been repressed, their honest desires cloaked in conformity just as tightly as their bodies have been swathed in concealing garb. Now, suddenly, people are saying they've had enough. They're pleasing themselves. It shouldn't surprise us. It's healthy. It's good."

It was curious, the way the doctor had become pro-Byrd. These days he seemed to be acting in the capacity of press-agent for Gran—who herself had become a cult-figure. In addition, he was working on his learned paper, The Origins and Spread of Avian Tendencies in Humans.

Pandora and I reckoned he was in the pay of the belt people.

"But it's fun to be in the centre of things," she said one evening, as the Crows came in to roost, and the garry oak creaked under the weight of a flock of Glaucous Gulls, come to pay homage to Gran. "It's put the town on the map—and your family too." She took my hand, smiling at me proudly.

There were the Pelicans, who specialized in high dives into the sea, deactivating their belts in mid-air, then reactivating them underwater to rocket Polaris-like from the depths. They rarely caught fish, though; and frequently had to be treated for an ailment known as Pelicans' Balloon, caused by travelling through water at speed with open mouth.

There were the Darwin's Tree Finches, a retiring sect whose existence went unsuspected for some weeks, because they spent so much time in the depths of forests with cactus spines held between their teeth, trying to extract bugs from holes in dead trees. They were a brooding and introspective group.

Virtually every species of bird was represented. And because every cult must have its lunatic fringe, there were the Pigeons. They flocked to the downtown city streets and mingled with the crowds hurrying to and fro.

From the shoulders up they looked much like anyone else, only greyer, and with a curious habit of jerking their heads while walking. Bodily, though, they were like any other Byrd: proudly unclothed.

Their roosting habits triggered the first open clash between Byrds and Man. There were complaints that they kept people awake at night, and fouled the rooftops. People began to string electrified wires around their ridges and guttering, and to put poison out.

The Pigeons' retaliation took place early one evening, when the commuting crowds jammed the streets. It was simple and graphic, and well-coordinated. Afterwards, people referred to it obliquely as the Great Deluge, because it was not the kind of event which is discussed openly, in proper society.

There were other sects, many of them; and perhaps the strangest was a group who eschewed the use of antigravity belts altogether. From time to time we would catch sight of them sitting on the concrete abutments of abandoned motorways, searching one another for parasites. Their bodies were painted a uniform brown except for their private parts, which were a luminous red. They called themselves Hamadryas Baboons.

People thought they had missed the point of the whole thing, somehow.

Inevitably when there are large numbers of people involved, there are tragedies. Sometimes an elderly Byrd would succumb to cardiac arrest in mid-air, and drift away on the winds. Others would suffer belt malfunctions and plummet to the ground. As the first chill nights began to grip the country, some of the older Byrds died of exposure and fell from their perches. Courageously they maintained their role until the end, and when daylight came they would be found in the ritualistic "Dead Byrd" posture, on their backs with legs in the air.

"All good things come to an end," said Dr. Pratt one evening as the russet leaves drifted from the trees. It had been a busy day, dozens of groups having come to pay homage to Gran. There was a sense of wrapping up, of things coming to a climax. "We will stage a mass rally," said Dr. Pratt to the Newspocket reporter. "There will be such a gathering of Byrds as the country has never known. Gran will address the multitude at the Great Coming Down."

Mother said, "So long as it's soon. I don't think Gran can take any more frosts."

I went to invite Pandora to the Great Coming Down, but she was not at home. I was about to return when I caught sight of a monstrous thing sitting on the backyard fence. It was bright green except around the eyes, which were grey, and the hair, which was a vivid yellow. It looked at me. It blinked in oddly reptilian fashion. It was Pandora.

She said, "Who's a pretty boy, then?"

* * *

The very next day Gran swooped down from the garry oak and seized Mother's scarf with her toes, and a grim tug-of-war ensued.

"Let go, you crazy old fool!" shouted Mother.

Gran cranked her belt up to maximum lift and took a quick twist of the scarf around her ankles. The other end was wrapped snugly around Mother's neck and tucked into her heavy winter coat. Mother left the ground, feet kicking. Her shouts degenerated into strangled grunts.

Father got a grip of Mother's knees as she passed overhead and Gran, with a harsh screech of frustration, found herself descending again; whereupon Gramps, having observed the scene with bright interest, came winging in and took hold of her, adding the power of his belt to hers.

Father's feet left the ground.

Mother by now had assumed the basic hanging attitude: arms dangling limply, head lolling, tongue protruding, face empurpled. I jumped and got hold of Father's ankles. There was a short, sharp rending sound and we fell back to earth in a heap, Mother on top. Gran and Gramps flew back to the garry oak with their half of the scarf, and began to pull it apart with their teeth. Father pried the other half away from Mother's neck. She was still breathing.

"Most fascinating," said Dr. Pratt.

"My wife nearly strangled by those goddamned brutes and he calls it fascinating?"

"No—look at the Hornbills."

"So they're eating the scarf. So they're crazy. What's new?"

"They're not eating it. If you will observe closely, you will see them shredding it. And see—the female is working the strands around that clump of twigs. It's crystal clear what they're doing, of course. This is a classic example of nest-building."

The effect on Father was instantaneous. He jumped up, seized Dr. Pratt by the throat and, shaking him back and forth, shouted, "Any fool knows birds only nest in the spring!" He was overwrought, of course. He apologized the next day.

By that time the Byrds were nesting all over town. They used a variety of materials and in many instances their craftsmanship was pretty to see. The local Newspocket station ran a competition for The Nest I Would Be Happiest To Join My Mate In, treating the matter as a great joke; although some of the inhabitants who had been forcibly undressed in the street thought otherwise. The Byrds wasted nothing. Their nests were intricately-woven collections of whatever could be stolen from below: overcoats, shirts, pants, clothesline, undergarments, hearing-aids, wigs.

"The nesting phenomenon has a two-fold significance," Dr. Pratt informed the media. "On the one hand, we have the desire of the Byrds to emulate the instinctive behavioural patterns of their avian counterparts. On the other hand, there is undoubtedly a suggestion of—how can I say it?—aggression towards the earthbound folk. The Byrds are saying, in their own way: join us. Be natural. Take your clothes off. Otherwise we'll do it for you."

"You don't think they're, uh, sexually *warped*?" asked the reporter.

"Sexually liberated," insisted Dr. Pratt.

The Byrds proved his point the next day, when they began to copulate all over the sky.

It was the biggest sensation since the Great Deluge. Writhing figures filled the heavens and parents locked their children indoors and drew the drapes. It was a fine day for love; the sun glinted on sweat-bedewed flesh, and in the unseasonable warmth the still air rang with cries of delight. The Byrds looped and zoomed and chased one another, and when they met they coupled. Artificial barriers of species were cast aside and Eagle mated with Chaffinch, Robin with Albatross.

"Clearly a visual parable," said Dr. Pratt. "The—"

"Shut up," said Mother. "Shut up, shut up, shut *up*!"

In the garry oak, Rufous-necked Hornbill mated with Rufous-necked Hornbill, then with Crow; then, rising joyously into the sky, with Skua, with Lark, and finaly with Hamadryas Baboon, who had at last realized what it was all about and strapped on a belt.

"She's eighty-six years old! What is she thinking of?"

"She's an Earth Mother to them," said Dr. Pratt.

"Earth Mother my ass," said Father. "She's stark, staring mad, and it's about time we faced up to it."

"It's true, it's true!" wailed Mother, a broken woman. "She's crazy! She's been crazy for years! She's old and useless, and yet she keeps filling in all that stuff on her Peace form, instead of forgetting, like any normal old woman!"

"Winter is coming," said Dr. Pratt, "and we are witnessing the symbolic Preservation of the Species. Look at that nice young Tern up there. Tomorrow they must come back to earth, but in the wombs of the females the memory of this glorious September will live on!"

"She's senile and filthy! I've seen her eating roots from out of the ground, and do you know what she did to the Everattentive Waiter? She cross-wired it with the Mailgift chute and filled the kitchen with self-adhesive cookies!"

"She did?"

And the first shadow of doubt crossed Dr. Pratt's face. The leader of the Byrds crazy?

"And one day a Gameshow called on the visiphone and asked her a skill-testing question which would have set us all up for life—and she did the most disgusting thing, and it went out live and the whole town saw it!"

"I'm sure she has sound psychological reasons for her behaviour," said Dr. Pratt desperately.

"She doesn't! She's insane! She walks to town rather than fill out a Busquest form! She brews wine in a horrible jar under the bed! She was once sentenced to one week's community service for indecent exposure! She trespasses in the Department of Agriculture's fields! You want to know why the house stinks? She programmed the Pesterminator to zap the Tidy Mice!"

"But I thought. . . . Why didn't you tell me before? My God, when I think of the things I've said on Newspocket! If this comes out, my reputation, all I've worked for, all. . . ." He was becoming incoherent. "Why didn't you tell me?" he asked again.

"Well, Jesus Christ, it's obvious, isn't it?" snapped Father. "Look at her. She's up in the sky mating with a Hamadryas Baboon, or something very much like one. Now, that's what I call crazy."

"But it's a *Movement*. . . . It's free and vibrant and so basic, so—"

"A nut cult," said Father. "Started by a loonie and encouraged by a quack. Nothing more, nothing less. And the forecast for tonight is twenty below. It'll wipe out the whole lot of them. You'd better get them all down, Pratt, or you'll have a few thousand deaths on your conscience."

But the Byrds came down of their own accord, later that day. As though sensing the end of the Indian summer and the bitter nights to come, they drifted out of the sky in groups, heading for earth, heading for us. Gran alighted in the garry oak with whirling arms, followed by Gramps. They sat close together on their accustomed branch, gobbling quietly to each other. More Byrds came; the Crows, the Pelicans. They filled the tree, spread along the ridge of the roof and squatted on the guttering. They began to perch on fences and posts, even on the ground, all species intermingled. They were all around us, converging, covering the neighbouring roofs and trees, a great final gathering of humans who, just for a few weeks, had gone a little silly. They looked happy although tired, and a few were shivering as the afternoon shortened into evening. They made a great noise at first, a rustling and screeching and fluid piping, but after a while they quietened down. I saw Pandora amidst them, painted and pretty, but her gaze passed right through me. They were still Byrds, playing their role until the end.

And they all faced Gran.

They were awaiting the word to Come Down, but Gran remained silent, living every last moment.

It was like standing in the centre of a vast amphitheatre, with all those heads turned towards us, all those beady eyes watching us. The Newspocket crew were nowhere to be seen; they probably couldn't get through the crowd.

Finally Dr. Pratt strode forward. He was in the grip of a great despondency. He was going to come clean.

"Fools!" he shouted. A murmur of birdlike sounds arose, but soon died. "All through history there have been fools like you, and they've caused wars and disasters and misery. Fools without minds of their own, who follow their leader without thought, without stopping to ask if their leader knows what he is doing. Leaders like Genghis Khan, like Starbusch, like Hitler, leaders who manipulate their followers like puppets in pursuit of their own crazy ends. Crazy leaders drunk with power. Leaders like Gran here.

"Yes, Gran is crazy! I mean certifiably crazy, ready for Peace. Irrational and insane and a burden to the State and to herself. She had me fooled at first." He uttered a short, bitter laugh, not unlike the mating cry of Forster's Tern. "I thought I found logic in what she did. Such was the cunning nature of her madness. It was only recently, when I investigated Gran's past record, that I unmasked her for what she is: a mentally unbalanced old woman with marked antisocial tendencies. I could give you chapter and verse of Gran's past misdemeanors—and I can tell you right now, this isn't the first time she's taken her clothes off in public—but I will refrain, out of consideration for her family, who have suffered enough.

"It will suffice to say that I have recommended her committal and the Peace Wagon is on its way. The whole affair is best forgotten. Now, come down out of those trees and scrub off, and go home to your families, all of you."

He turned away, shoulders drooping. It was nothing like the Great Coming Down he'd pictured. It was a slinking thing, a creeping home, an abashed admission of stupidity.

Except that the Byrds weren't coming down.

They sat silently on their perches, awaiting the word from Gran.

All through Dr. Pratt's oration she'd been quiet, staring fixedly at the sky. Now, at last, she looked around. Her eyes were bright, but it was an almost-human brightness, a different thing from the beady stare of the past weeks. And she half-smiled through the paint, but she didn't utter a word.

She activated her belt and, flapping her arms, rose into the darkening sky.

And the Byrds rose after her.

They filled the sky, a vast multitude of rising figures, and Pandora was with them. Gran led, Gramps close behind, and then came Coot and Skua and Hawk, and the whole thousand-strong mob. They wheeled once over the town and filled the evening with a great and lonely cry. Then they headed off in V-formations, loose flocks, tight echelons, a pattern of dwindling black forms against the pale duck-egg blue of nightfall.

"Where in hell are they going?" shouted Dr. Pratt as I emerged from the shed, naked and painted. It was cold, but I would soon get used to it.

"South," I said.

"Why the hell south? What's wrong with here, for God's sake?"

"It's warmer, south. We're migrating."

So I activated my belt and lifted into the air, and watched the house fall away below me, and the tiny bolts of light as the Pesterminator hunted things. The sky seemed empty now but there was still a pink glow to the west. Hurrying south, I saw something winking like a red star and, before long, I was homing in on the gleaming hindquarters of a Hamadryas Baboon.

SOLUBLE-FISH

Joël Champetier
Translated from the French by Louise Samson

Joël Champetier is the current publisher and fiction editor of *Solaris,* one of the two major French-language SF magazines published in Quebec. After working for ten years as a technician in electrochemistry, he is now a full-time writer. He has published five young adult SF and fantasy novels, beginning with *La Mer au fond du monde* (1990), winner of the Prix Boréal 1991 for best book, a collection of dark fantasy, and an adult SF novel, *La Taupe et le dragon* (1991), which tied for the Prix Boréal for 1992 for best book. Jean-Louis Trudel, writing in *The New York Review of Science Fiction,* called it "a revelation . . . it attains an exquisite balance between action, plot, science fictional speculation, extrapolation, and characterization." He has written nearly twenty SF short stories, winning the Prix Boréal twice in that category (1982 and 1991), and the Aurora Award (then called the Prix Casper) for another in 1989. Only two of his stories (and none of the award winners) have appeared in English translation, although a third, the Boréal winner for 1991, is scheduled for this year as "Heart of Iron" in the forthcoming *Tesseracts Q.*

We have selected "Soluble-Fish," which appeared in *Tesseracts* [2]. It is reminiscent of much of the British "new wave" SF of the late 1960's and of such French SF as Boris Vian's.

For weeks now, rain had been lashing against my window. The first few days, in spite of advice to the contrary, I opened the shutters. I had always hated the smell of a closed room and I just lay there languishing in memories of pleasant strolls on sunny days. But rain filtered through the shutters into the room and flooded the tiles.

I awoke to a clammy morning, hearing the moans of Onires as she sponged off the tiles.

"You shouldn't open the window when the wind is from the east."

I shivered on the wet floor and dressed, a bit ill at ease to notice that my cousin did not avert her eyes.

The water was only about ten centimetres deep, but many soluble-fish swam in it, looking like drops of mercury. It was going to rain for some time and the water would rise; soon, it would be hard to catch the fish. After several unsuccessful attempts, Guylane landed one, a sort of jelly fish that wriggled, cupped in a trembling hand. Splashing everywhere, we ran to our aunt's house: the little house with the pointed roof, perched on high pilings. We almost let go of the fish.

"Don't come in before taking your clothes off."

The fish slid soundlessly into a sand bucket. Onires lit a lamp to warm up the room.

"Don't let this fish dry here!"

My aunt's orders were, it seems, rarely to be obeyed.

We looked at the fish, which wriggled at first, but then fell quiet and motionless.

"Is it dead?"

"No. You didn't believe us?"

We spread carpets on the floor, talked and daydreamed for hours, in the warm and humid atmosphere of the workshop, for a long while unaware of the rain calling on the window pane. We soon had to go to bed. It would take days anyway.

"Can we fish some more?"

"No. Mom wouldn't like it."

Early in the dry season, we find many of these fish, all dried-up, lying in the gravel and the dust, or stuck to branches. By then it's hatching time when the rain-birds break their wrinkled skin and stretch their crystal wings.

"It's strange . . . we call them 'rain-birds' and they disappear when the rain comes. And we call them 'soluble-fish' and they only appear when there is water." Guylane looked at me, nodding in surprise at a thought he had never had before.

I looked in the sand bucket and for the first time saw a dried-up fish; its eyes and its mouth had disappeared and had melted into the wrinkles of a greyish skin, like dust.

It was one of the worst nights. I tossed and turned between clammy sheets in the illusive agony of one who waits for sleep. I thought I hadn't slept, yet Onires awakened me.

"Come."

I followed her, unable to talk to her about my dreams where her slim adolescent body haunted me. Guylane was rubbing his eyes, already tottering near the sand bucket.

"The bird will come out."

The shell had cracked hours ago. Now, pulsating within it, translucent wings were struggling to get out.

The rain-bird shivered on tiny chiselled legs; it opened a pair of soft and weak wings that would have to dry before turning into crystal. Then it opened its opaque eyes which would later dry into a liquid transparency.

Once dry, it began to fly, fragile yet graceful. The sound of a faint humming penetrated the room in answer to the drumming of the rain.

Morning found us still awake, as did my aunt who frowned when she saw the shadow of the flying bird. Onires pleaded, but to no avail. . . .

"Enough now! You disobeyed me. Get this bird out of here."

As soon as we opened the shutter, the bird slid into the grey sky. It took flight in a flutter of wings. But soon its flight was less graceful. It slowed. It was coming down now, erratically. . . .

"So soon?" I was sad and disappointed.

"The rain is like spikes on its wings. . . ."

A drop of water—which was not from the sky—rolled down my cheek. The bird gave up, stopped flapping its wings, and dove down with a muffled sound. One more soluble-fish would soon slide slowly in the thin layer of troubled waters.

MEMETIC DRIFT

Glenn Grant

Glenn Grant, the coeditor of this book, was born in London, Ontario, but now lives in Montreal. He is the founder and editor of the SF magazine *Edge Detector* and is the SF reviewer for the *Montreal Gazette*. His articles on SF have appeared in *Science Fiction Studies, Science Fiction Eye, The New York Review of Science Fiction,* and other magazines. The Canada Council awarded him an Explorations Grant to write his first SF novel, which will be called *Remote Sensing.* His short fiction has appeared in *Interzone* in the U.K., from which David Hartwell chose "Memetic Drift" to reprint.

"Speculative fiction . . . ," Grant writes, "is the lens we use to bring some clarity to the chaos around us; it's a system for redefining our world-views and our self-images. What we want is a kind of mythological edge detection, similar to the computer-processing which increases the resolution of fuzzy satellite images. If it's done well, SF can show us the big picture, yet still bring all the details into sharp focus."

Grant's desire to redefine and complexify is given free rein in this story, which suggests that Québécois nationalism is not the only centrifugal pressure that Canada may face in the near future.

> *"13.01: A meme is not replicated by words alone. Competition between meme-complexes is becoming increasingly intense, but we have no interest in resorting to evangelism or cult-tactics to gain 'converts' [see 13.3]. . . . Although actions do not, in fact, speak louder than words, they are a more subtly effective transmission vector."*
> —A Code for Nomadiks; Version 25.0 (annual updates available on the World3 Network).

Stick out my thumb, and I find myself crossing the Great Midwestern Dustbowl with a flock of sun-crazed Nomadiks, generally heading in a westward direction, without plan or destination. Half the day wasted in the hard solar infall which is the only rain here, waiting for this lift. Half the night spent staring past my reflection, past sandblasted billboards and disused silos. Not a recommended therapy for anyone just pulling out of an extended period of depression. This same desert that has finally swept over my home has now settled into my mind, grain by grain filling up the cortical folds, a thin layer of insulation against unwanted emotions.

I'm riding with the Norm Famli, a polymarriage consisting of two women, a transmale, an hermaphrodite, and two pseudochildren. All of them live in these two articulated trailer modules, carted around on the back of a mammoth surplus defense vehicle. (A GM mobile missile carrier, to be exact, auctioned off by the U.S. military when they decommissioned the MX arsenal.)

I'm one of two hitchers they picked up last night in the depopulated suburbs of Regina. The other guy, who calls himself "Scred," is a wiry geezer with a missing right canine, nasty stitchmarks up one arm, and a lot of crude jokes to tell. A few of them are even funny, but for the most part it's a dull trip. Far too much time to think.

Sometime around sunup, I notice my reflection in the window. There's a gap where my eyes should be, the shadow under the visor of my Co-op baseball cap. Only the end of my thin nose is reflected, and a twenty-year-old face that is gaunt even when I've been eating well (which I haven't), surrounded by long strands of dirty-blond hair.

Yes, I'm aware that I'm exhibiting all the symptoms of emotional shock: apathy, indifference, inexpressive staring, the whole bit. It doesn't help to have seen it happen to others, to strangers and neighbors, and to Jodi.

Jodi had to go in for observation after her parents were killed in a tornado. A year later she was off the medication and holding up fine, until the dunes swamped the pathetic encroachment barriers out behind our rented farmhouse. By ones and twos, our housemates packed up and left. Then, with an enormous sand drift engulfing the back porch, came the city's eviction notice, and the papers from the Resettlement Ministry, and the inevitable, final moving day. . . .

Eventually Jodi's aunt and uncle brought her to a hospital closer to their home in Thunder Bay. When I last saw her, a month ago, she didn't know who I was.

"Want some tea with that croissant, Fifer?" Sue sets her tray down on the table in the kitchenette where Scred and I have been sitting since midnight, getting leg cramps. "Fifer—that's your first name, is it?"

"That's right. Fifer Stenzel. And some tea would be nice. Thanks, ma'am."

Sue Norm is a tall Asian woman, eldest of the Famli, streaks of grey in her disorderly black hair, and a few crinkles around the eyes as she laughs. "Not 'ma'am,' please. Call me Sue. Or Yingsiu, if you prefer." She fills the teapot carefully, compensating as the trailer rig sways around a turn.

A couple of the other Norms are having breakfast in the small living area adjacent to the kitchen, where the TV runs a disc of a Fijian earthdub band.

Forward of that are storage shelves and overhead cupboards, haphazardly decorated with posters of obscure netbands and digital Shunga paintings. Sliding doors lead onto a low tunnel to the cab, below a warning in felt-marker: *Don't bug the driver.* Aft of the kitchen are the fresher, the shower, and the accordion-pleated passage to the second module, hung with a curtain. Famli sleeping quarters, back there.

Yingsiu pours the tea.

The first sip sets off a warning alarm, "Aw hell, this is"—then a sudden sneeze, spilling a hot mugful onto my lumberjack shirt—*"mint tea."*

"Oh, I am sorry." Sue grabs a towel, passes it to me. "You're allergic to mint?"

"And to certain trees, and cats, and"—another sneeze—"and it's my own stupid fault for not checking first." Next, an onslaught of three sneezes.

Scred is cackling hysterically. "You oughta be more careful, Fife." Grinning, he returns his attention to his *Bioregional News* fax. The top headline reads: *Secessionists Bomb Edmonton Airship Terminal.* Mopping up the spilled tea, I decide that it might not be a good idea to settle here in Alberta. More jobs out in BC, anyway.

"Yingsiu? Bad news from World3," Vicki calls from a swivel chair by the vidphone. "ResetMin just revoked our permit for Finnegan. The Christas have a monastery about one klick to the east. They filed a complaint."

"Shit. That hexes that. Left it as late as they could, didn't they?" Sue takes the other chair and slips on a headset. "What's the backup site, Larry?" Maps appear on the screen, the new destination and ETA in red. "Mount Cyprian? Great. We'll have to double back. Okay, put Sal on."

Larry, I take it, is the name of their vidphone persona, the program which handles their messages, broadcatching, and other databiz. Noel Norm calls it Larry the Lar, their protective household spirit. But Noel's a Teknik Pagan (an absurd idea, in itself) and I can't tell if she expects to be taken seriously.

On the screen, a thinly bearded face shows up in a shuddery low-angle, flowing brown hair snaking about in the breeze from the driver's window. This would be Sal Norm, somewhere up ahead of us in the box-van, seen from the dash camera. Sue explains the situation to Sal, who nods, jots down directions, and signs off.

Sue makes a few more calls, while Victoria removes her headset, sidles aft to the kitchen, and draws a cup of water from the dispenser. "What's all that about?" I ask.

"A little change of plan." She draws a felt bag out of her sweatsuit pocket, drops something blue into her palm, a capsule which she tosses back, and the water follows it. "We got word from World3—our net, y'know—that the . . . uh, Resettlement Ministry won't let us use the town of

Finnegan for a little gathering we'd planned. You ever been to one of our— no, you wouldn't have. Lotta fun, you'll see." She nods, rather Californian in speech and gesture, blond split-ends swaying into her face. (I don't know what's in the capsules she keeps downing. Maintenance doses of something, but they have no visible effect on her at all.)

"What was wrong with Finnegan?"

"Nothin'. A ghost town. Perfect, for our purposes. But there's these Christa Cultists nearby, seem to think we'd make lousy neighbors, so the ResetMin revoked our permit. Happens all the time, so we arrange for backup sites."

Another evil grin from Scred, who's been sitting across from me, reading something on his microbook. "You know those Christians. They used to say the Gypsies refused to shelter the Virgin and her child on the flight to Egypt, and for that they were cursed to wander forever. Ain't that so?"

Vicki blows hair from her eyes. "Pphh. I've heard that. They fucked up, as usual. The Romany were never Egyptians, and as far as we're concerned, it's everybody else who's *cursed to stand still*."

With that, she returns to the living area. The back of the sweatshirt reads, *Can't hack reality? Try reality-hacking*, in purple on mauve.

Turned about on the TransCanada, we head southeast from Brooks, Alberta, backtracking. After breakfast, Lyndon Norm goes to work on the plumbing system at the rear of the module, and asks me to assist. "Well, carpentry's my specialty," I tell him, "but I can turn a wrench or hold a spanner if needed."

"Specialization? Hah!" Lyndon's voice is a thin alto, an odd match for his stocky, broad-waisted frame. Somehow he manages to wedge himself into a closetful of tangled pipes and cables. The place stinks of methane and mildew. "Don't let 'em do that to ya. Hand me that bag of filters, there; thanks. You go to school?"

"Well, I applied to a few, wanted to be an architect, but . . . uh . . . I couldn't get in. Tough competition. But I was in an apprenticeship program for two years, first as an electrician, then as a carpenter. Then they cut off the funds last year, and I haven't worked since."

"Bastards—here, tighten these gaskets for me—they couldn't care less about education. So what? Do it anyway."

"Do which?"

"Become an architect, or whatever. Everything's online, isn't it? Math tutors, manuals, design standards, expert systems. Schools are just a game for rich kids anyway."

Sue's laugh again, from the kitchen. "Watch it, Fifer, that's Actuator propaganda. And they don't accept excuses."

"Damn right. Nobody's stopping you." With some difficulty, Lyndon extricates himself from the plumbing system, and replaces the service panel. "For a bunch of lazy mediabase artists, the Actuationist Transnational actually have the right idea. If I want to do something, or if I see something that needs doing, I do it. Learned a lot of electronics, automotive maintenance, metal fabrication. Like, I got tired of being Lynda Kulikosky, and now I'm not.

"Hey, thanks for the help." He picks up the toolbox and heads off to the second module. Lynda? Oh, right, those hips. First transmale I ever met.

"Damn you, I didn't see that one . . ." Noel pipes up in annoyance as Haji steals her Queen's rook. They're playing Choiss, a chess variant in which the board is defined by the players as the game progresses. She's warding off an attack from a sector of board that didn't exist five moves back. The chess pieces and board are black and red.

"Your charms and wards aren't gonna help you now." Haji tosses his head, jet-black hair (grey at the roots) spilling over his small brown face. In contrast, his opponent is pale as winter sky, probably from pigment inhibitors; a Teknik fashion, as are the jagged patterns of shaven scalp running through her crew cut.

Haji and Noel are pseudochildren, or X-youth, as they prefer to be called. Their apparently ten-year-old bodies are the results of dangerous and illegal synthetic-hormone treatments which halt most growth processes at the onset of puberty. Extended youth. But look at the crosshatching of lines around Haji's features, the cataract obscuring one iris, signs of the accelerated breakdown of an overstressed metabolism. He's not yet thirty, but I would guess that he has less than three years to live, and knows it.

I've returned to my seat by the pitted and scoured windows, trying to ignore them. Too strange, too alien. I'm not interested in how they came to be what they are, what bizarre histories brought them here. I don't care. It's all I can do to watch the dessicated landscape slide by, and try to decide on some sort of plan for myself.

All I want, really, is to find a job over in BC, and maybe a new girl to room with.

"That's a good one . . . huh." Scred puts down his book and scratches the bristles on his chin. "I got curious about these Christas, so I looked 'em up. I knew they were mostly women, but I thought they were, y'know, preparing for Jesus to come back, like most of the other kooks out there. But no, they've got an original tack: they think God is about to send us *Her only Daughter*, get it? Makes a weird kind of sense, I mean, having made such a hash of it with a male incarnation, can't hurt to try it again as a woman." He chuckles, turns off the book, folds the screen down, and pockets it. "There are worse memes, I guess."

An unfamiliar word. "Worse what?"

"Memes, you know, contagious ideas—don't they teach memetics in school anymore? Well, no, I guess these days they wouldn't want kids to . . . uh, question received ideas. Might be subversive. Huh. Well, a meme is like a gene, it exists solely to reproduce itself. Except that a meme consists of pure information, and it replicates by infecting a person's mind and inducing them to parrot it to other people, like I'm doing now. I'm trying to infect you with the Meta-meme, the meme about memes. You don't have to take it literally, it's a metaphor, right? But a damned useful one. . . ."

For the first time I regret pawning my old book and holodiscs for traveling money, and I ask Scred if he'd lend me his micro. He passes it to me: a new Zoetec model with a terabyte biomemory. I access its encyclopedia, and call up the entry on memetics. Good to have something to occupy my attention, other than that desolate New Sahel outside the window.

East of Medicine Hat, we leave the TransCanada, following an almost invisible side road into the Cypress Hills. The turnoff skirts an immense Fuji Holochrome billboard, and the glamour model's face appears to move as we pass by. Disconcertingly, her gaze follows the viewer, then she winks.

The road shortly arrives at the outskirts of Mount Cyprian, a vacant town long since picked clean by scavengers, decaying on a hillside stripped equally bare of topsoil and eroding into deep gullies. Hardly a brick left standing, even telephone poles uprooted and carted away. What remains is more of a 1:1 scale map than a town, a plan laid out in crumbling pavement and exposed foundations.

Our considerable dust plume catches up to us, swallowing the trailer as we grind to a halt on the cracked playground of a dismantled grade school. When the cloud clears I can see an assortment of eighteen-wheelers, buses, RV's, vans with campers, all scattered about the dirty streets and parking lots. Nomads wave to newcomers, hustling to erect tents, prefabs, tepees, and pressurized shelters. Fiberoptic webs are being draped between portable masts, on which satellite dishes are aimed at the southern sky, while cooking fires exchange smoke signals with the dust trails of approaching vehicles.

"Let's go, Fifer," Noel shouts, suddenly outside my window. "Link to it, we need a hand."

Right. Stretch those legs, stupid.

Out in the morning sunshine, it's already pushing thirty-five Celsius. Lyndon has unlocked a cargo section in the undercarriage of the first trailer module. All together, we haul the entire section out like a drawer, and extend the outside supports. A hefty tarp of mottled green and white polymatrix is wrestled out, exposing a densely packed trusswork underneath. Step motors begin to purr, manipulators lift the first struts into position, and everyone stands clear. These things are always fun to watch.

The dome unfolds itself with the slow grace of a rose blooming in time-lapse, triangular units linking into orderly structures, working in a spiral until the thirty-meter half-sphere encloses the entire trailer. Lyndon, Vicki, Scred, and I climb up onto the lightweight hex-pent struts, raising the tarp and snapping it into place at the hubs. Sunlight filtering through the fabric paints the interior a dappled green like the shade under the leaf canopy of an old-growth forest.

Windblown silicate particles patter against the skin of the dome, and a dust devil describes a vortex outside the threshold. The single broad doorway is high enough to admit the box-van, which has only just arrived.

We're helping to unload merchandise from the back of the van when Scred notices Sal, the driver.

"Pssst, Fife. Tell me that's not a guy in a skirt and blouse.... A lady with a beard, maybe?"

"Neither, I think." Christ, I hope none of the Norms overhear this. "Or both, rather. I mean, se's an hermaphrodite. Probably by surgery, a sex change, like Lyndon. Or maybe se was born that way. One of the Sanpharma gene-therapy kids."

We drop the cases where the display tables are being set up, and head back for another load. "Jeez, Fife, but these folks are a damned strange lot of buggers. Nice enough people, sure, but . . ."

"Yeah, I know." I warn him not to call Sal a *he* or a *she*. Instead of *he*, *him*, and *his*, they prefer to use *se*, *sem*, and *ses*. And *Ser* in place of *Mister*.

"You gotta be kidding." Shaking his head, he deposits another case. "They think they can get everybody to adopt a—a whole new set of pronouns?"

"Maybe not everybody, but . . . it sort of depends on how big this Pange movement gets. That's their name for it: Pan-genderism. They say they want to integrate the best attributes of both genders, whatever that means."

Listen to me. I've been aware of all this stuff for years, on an intellectual level, and it worries me that I'm now having difficulty dealing with the reality. Polymarriages are very rare, not to mention transmales, Panges, and X-youth, but this Famli is an exception, even among Nomads. When this gathering breaks up, in a week or two, I think I might head on to BC with some other Famli or caravan.

Haji is running a fiberoptic line out to a nearby tent, where a local comnexus is being set up. His input to the Famli business is entirely digital: poetry, hypermusic, environs, video pornography. Yes, self-produced vidporn, which shouldn't surprise me, because how else does one become an

X-youth? They often find lucrative careers in the industry, and now he's gone independent. Once again, I tell myself not to let it bother me.

The Norms immediately begin making sales, trading the fruits of their portable biosynthesis rig: pharmaceuticals, synfuels, and polymatrix fabric. You can buy such stuff for less, from industrial sources, but the Nomads prefer to purchase from each other. It's part of their Code, their meme-complex.

A hand-painted sign is lifted over the dome entrance: *NORM FAMLI, Biosynthetics and Netmedia*. Scred shakes his head at it. "Why can't you guys seem to spell anything right? What's wrong with *family*?"

"A *family* is something you're born into," Sue explains, leaning against the doorframe. "We use a kind of New Guinea Pidgin spelling when we define something a bit differently. A new word for a new meaning."

Haji has just returned with his spool of optical fiber. "Speaking of which, nobody's come up with a new name for this sinkhole. I mean, Mount Cyprian—not much of a mountain, is it?"

"Um, how about . . . Çatal Hüyük?" I suggest.

Only Sue gets it, laughing. "Yes! That's good: reinventing the city."

Noel appears from under the dome with two empty plastic water containers, and tosses one to me. "You're drafted. C'mon, we have to go pay our respects to the local genii at the well."

I stumble after her, workboots crunching on the gritty playground. "What's that, again?"

"Never mind. A little pagan humor." Her white shorts, T-shirt, and high-albedo skin throw off an amazing glare as she trots over debris from the grade school's deconstruction.

"You really into that stuff? Paganism, I mean."

"Well, not as much as Sal, who practices the Craft. Haji, he's a Chaote, and Sue is a bit of a gene-mystic, like a lot of green techs. The others are avowed atheists. Me, I like what Placidus said: *Creo quia absurdum est.*"

"Which means?"

"I believe because it is absurd."

Once again, the town has a main street, businesses, and shops. In the impromptu marketplace, crowds of Nomads kick up a yellow haze around makeshift stalls with canvas banners for billboards. *Freshly Cultured Meat and Vegetables* are advertised, sold by paunchy, squint-eyed Albertans in cowboy shirts and Stetsons, rural folk whose soil has dried up and billowed away. The proprietor of *Orb-Man Aerogel Products, Florida* must have high connections, selling zeegee materials manufactured in orbit. He probably used to operate out of a mall and live in a luxury condo, both now three meters under the rising seas.

We are all refugees. The truth of the old cliché has never fully struck home before. Here there are northerners, chased south by the Western Secessionist conflict; ex-Californians whose fault-straddling cities have lain in heaps ever since the Shocks; fallout victims from downwind of the Atlanta Fermi-IV reactor. Once these people were forced to move, they decided not to stop, and this is probably the only reason why they haven't yet been rounded up and dumped into the swarming Transfer Camps.

The authorities are out in force already, searching for proscribed bio-products, smuggled goods, and underdocumented aliens. Our societal immune systems, here to protect us from all these virulent diseases. Not only APP and Customs, but also C-SIS types (obvious in their mirrored glasses), and even a few military, from Special Counterinsurgency Units. (And what are *they* doing here?)

Noel and I take our places in line at the water truck. Across the street is Hassan's Holodome, a sixty-meter inflated geodesic, the largest in town. Today's shows: Bachant's *A Thousand and One Nights*, and *Lunar Elegy*, "Shot on location!" by the same director. (The first one is better, if only because there's less heavy breathing. Bachant is famous for her self-indulgence.)

A tap on my shoulder. "Excuse me," asks the young woman who has queued up behind me, "I don't suppose you have any organic sludge to offload, do you?"

"I . . . what?" Staring at her, baffled, I try not to laugh.

Noel steps forward and rescues me. "Yeah, I think we do. We've just arrived, so I doubt we've sold it yet. If not, it's all yours, at local market standard. I'm Noel Norm, and this is Fifer."

"Hey, great. Thanks." She quickly links to the fact that she's talking to an X-youth, rather than a stunningly precocious ten-year-old. "I'm Adriana, from Rexdaler. That's a small settlement, about twenty kilometers from here. We heard about the gathering and I was sent to get some extra organics and other stuff." An easy smile, despite the heat and the airborne grit, as she points out her pickup, a blunt-nosed Subaru parked nearby.

I can sense that she's out of her element, like myself, suddenly aware of the Earth's spin, not sure if she likes it, but trying to roll along with it. Wearing an oversized yellow jumpsuit, turned up at the ankles and wrists, she's probably close to my age though it's hard to say, with bleached blond hair cropped close, except where it sweeps over her left eye.

"I figured you were a local." Noel hands our containers to the water-seller, along with her Famli's barter card. "Next time, just get in touch with the gathering's World3 nexus. Most everything salable is on the market listings. We'd even deliver."

I hang about, feeling rather foolish and dumbfounded, as the girls work out the details of transferring the organics. Then we pick up our water and are struggling off through the crowded market. The plastic containers drip with condensation.

"What . . . what, exactly . . . is organic sludge?"

"You'll see."

With a lot of cursing and sweating, Scred and I manage to roll the monstrous tank up the ramp, onto the bed of Adriana's pickup. The stench of concentrated sewage and treatment enzymes doesn't seem so strong now. It was worse just after Lyndon had decanted the sludge from the trailer's biogas plant, before he sealed it.

Adriana wants to buy us both a drink for our efforts, which sounds like a great idea to me, but Scred checks his watch, says he'd like to have a look around the market, and takes off. So she and I stroll over to Peregrine's, a bar-tent hung with trendy bioluminescent lighting tubes. We take our beers to a table as far as possible from the sound system, which is shaking the floor with Angel Sung's latest insidious Chinapop earworm.

Adriana's telling me about Rexdaler, how they manage to live on the fringes of the Dustbowl. "It started as part of a provincial land-reclamation scheme, and grew from there. Now there's four hundred of us, and we've got a few hundred hectares of greenhouses, but we don't seem to have made much progress with the reclamation business. I can't really say, only been there for two years. I'm from Brandon, originally. . . ."

Shouldn't project my own feelings onto her, but here they are again, reflected on her face as she glances down at the table. The biolights cast a zone of green down her right side, a wash of red across her left.

"Isn't that jumpsuit just a little too big?" Good work, Fife, insult her taste in clothes.

But she laughs and tugs at a sleeve. "I know, they make me look like a scrawny kid, but I don't fit into the smaller ones. We all wear them, saves money that way. We share clothes, food, and just about everything else. It's that kind of life, at Rexdaler, we have to go without a few luxuries for the short term, and take a long-range view of things."

That kind of commitment has always impressed me. I find myself talking about my Baha'i period, in early high school, when I dropped my parent's Lutheran faith for something more universal. For a while, I enjoyed their sense of community, but I lapsed out of that as well. "Anyhow, I'm drifting off topic. You really think you can fight the climate shift, turn back the desert?"

"Well, actually . . ." She hesitates. "That's not our main concern anymore. Sure, we keep at it, the government is paying for it, but only a few of us still take it seriously. Why should we break our backs for a change that might not even come until we're dead? When Garver—that's our Chairperson—when he took over, morale was at zero, but he's given us a new purpose. He's a great guy, you should meet him."

A piercing beep from her wristwatch interrupts. "Aargh. I have to be getting back to town. We keep early hours, y'know?"

So we finish our beers and step outside.

The Earth has rolled us into her shadow, bringing Venus out of the violet dusk. The wind is still sifting through the random streets of the market. At her pickup, Adriana hesitates with the key in the door. "I really enjoyed our chat."

"Yeah, so did I."

An uncertain pause, then: "There's a good chance I'll be back again, maybe tomorrow."

"That'd be good. You know where to find me." Thinking, what's the point, idiot, you're leaving in a few days. . . .

Then she's taking those two steps, putting her hand behind my neck, and kissing me. Probably meant to be a little peck on the cheek, but it's turned into something else, and I have to hold her, simply to stay on my feet. There's a sense of desperation to it, makes me want to calm her somehow, but—

—from over her shoulder, I see a shape, a dust devil, a microtornado swirling up under a floodlamp, and Jodi is in there, trapped in a whorl of sand, stumbling blindly, crying, naked and caked with dust—

—I push Adriana away in a panic. Vaguely, I hear her asking me what's wrong, but I'm already running, tripping over tent pegs, trying to escape back to the Norms', getting lost, feeling the tears that are forced out by an upwelling of despair, guilt, and fear.

Scred finds me sitting against the doorframe of the green and white dome, trying to pull myself together.

"Jeez, man, what's got into you? You're covered in dirt." He kneels beside me and tries to check my pupils, but I push his hands away.

"I'm straight, okay? All's I had was a beer, just one." I try to tell him what I saw, but it all comes out in fragments and doesn't make a lot of sense.

"Well, shit, just sounds like a hallucination, Fife."

"Of course I was hallucinating, *I* know that. But all I had was a beer."

Scred helps me to my feet. "Sure, but you can't trust these Nomads. They could be enhancing the stuff, or somebody was filling the bar with inhalants, y'know, vaporous drugs. I've heard of places that do that. Makes people spend more, right?"

"No, Scred, really, I know what it is. It got to Jodi and now it's getting to me, man. I'm losing it—"

"Don't give me that shit. C'mon, be a man, will you? Let's go inside and watch some of Haji's vids."

Afternoon, and "Çatal Hüyük" is a chaotic blur in the harsh sunlight, a convergence zone of human advection currents. Mount Cyprian's flanks are being slowly but visibly pulverized by the wind, and everything is layered with a thin film of loess. Aeolian depositions, a poetic term I remember from Biospheric Studies.

Didn't mean to sleep in, but it was a long time before I could sleep at all, and now it's after siesta. Wandering through the market, I run into Scred, who seems hurried but wants to talk.

"Got this for ya." He hands me something in a small paper bag patterned with smiling blue snails. "Can't go see a girl without some chocolates to give her, can you? Got them from a Dutch couple, over that way. They make 'em themselves."

"Well, thanks, man. But . . . after last night . . . I kinda doubt she'll be back."

"Huh. Couldn't blame her, could ya? But, uh, isn't that her red Subaru, over there?" He points it out, across the street, gives me a thump on the back, and strides off.

It takes nearly an hour, but I manage to track her down, at a hardware-dealer's stall, where she's picking up a large coil of high-temp superconducting fiber. Today's overlarge jumpsuit is faded blue with black patches.

Always the well-conditioned prairie boy, I tip my cap. "Help you with that, miss?"

Adriana hefts the coil onto one shoulder, and tries not to smile, failing. "Didn't mean to scare you last night."

"You didn't. I mean, I think I just scared myself, is all. Acted pretty strange, didn't I?" I offer her the bag of chocolates. "Here, I . . . hope this will make up for it."

She accepts the gift, and says she has a few more purchases to make for her collective. So together we begin a slow circle through the market, and the conversation returns to where it left off last night.

"You said something about a 'new purpose' that this guy, Garver, brought about?"

She replies slowly at first, approaching a delicate subject. "It created a lot of friction . . . and most of our more religious colleagues up and left because of it. But Garver convinced the rest of us." She takes a long look at me, and becomes more fervent. "Fifer, we want to be around when all this becomes green again. In fact, we want to be alive when the next ice age happens and rolls over it all, and live to see the next interglacial after that. And we just might. We're setting up our own biostasis facility."

"A cryonics society? You're not going to *freeze* yourselves?"

"Vitrification. Not exactly freezing."

"Whatever, I still don't—"

"We've got twenty residents who aren't going to make it till the spring, Fifer. Most of them are geries, one is an X-youth like your friend Noel, but all of them are terminal. Garver doesn't trust the big cryonics firms, so we're going to care for our own. When one of us dies, they'll go into biostasis, and the rest will keep watch over them. It's a good plan, Fifer. Like Garver says: permanent death is just an obsolete meme."

"This is what all the self-sacrifice is about? What happens if they can't revive you, if they never figure it out?"

"Wake up, Fifer, the Breakthrough can't be more than five or ten years down the road. Once they can make the nanomachines self-replicate, cell repair should be a simple matter."

"Yeah, right, nanotech will work miracles; they've been saying that for decades."

Her reply is drowned out by a distorted voice over a police megaphone. Then an exchange of automatic gunfire, over by Hassan's. Very loud, close by. Everyone reacts, but it ends as abruptly as it began.

The cops are soon raising a cordon of yellow tape, isolating the large tent next to the Holodome, and pushing back curious Nomads, Adriana and I among them. Rumors are spreading through the crowd like spores hitting ripe fruit.

"Known Secessionist guerrillas, I'm not kidding. That's what I heard on the police band." The speaker is a yellow-haired Teknik with blue skin-stripes, wearing a wireless video headset, so he would be getting the news as it came in on the nex. ". . . a meeting of some kind. Must've been using the gathering as a cover. Six of them cornered by the SCI unit . . . three are dead and one wounded."

Two police vans worm their way up to the cordon. The APP clear a path through the crush of onlookers, then wheel the injured man out, belted to a stretcher. I'm more than a bit distressed when I see his face. It's Scred. There's a bloodstain seeping through the sheet over his chest, and he's writhing and hollering, either in pain or rage or both, a horrible sound, but surely they'd sedate him or something?

Scred. A West-Sep, for Christ's sake. . . .

Adriana has recognized him, too. "That was—"

"Yeah, I know, let's get out of this crowd, okay?" We manage to get across the street, but I have to stop. I feel as if reality has begun to erode like the hillside above us. I'm not sure if I can keep my footing.

Somebody has parked their rig in the intersection just to our left. The near side of the trailer is now being folded up, revealing a self-powered PA system and a backdrop which reads: *Be sure your sin will find you out.* Taking advantage of the spontaneous audience, a Retributionist preacher grabs his microphone and begins railing at everybody from this mobile platform. His magnified image then appears on a three-meter flatscreen above the stage, a live video feed from an unseen camera.

Almost unnoticed, Adriana has slipped her arm about my waist. "C'mon, let's not listen to this suckerhead. . . ."

The preacher is lunging around with a Bible in his grip, shouting about transgression, the sanctity of nature, and hiding from our guilt, but most of his congregation seems to be dispersing in boredom. Then it hits me: none of them are *memetically susceptible* or else they'd have long ago joined millions of others in the cult settlements, enslaved to one or another maniacal savior. *Selected out.*

Somewhat nervous, Adriana opens the paper bag and hands me a chocolate, then takes one out for herself. "Hey, Fifer, let's . . . let's get away from here. . . ."

I'm too fascinated to move. "Of course, these Nomads are *immune*. . . ." The only people remaining seem to be hecklers (Lyndon among them), and a few others shouting them down—"Let the man speak!"—obviously cultists planted in the crowd. Absently, I take a bite of the chocolate—

But it's a fucking *mint cream,* and I spit it out into the dirt, feeling my eyes water, histamines boiling up, the first sneeze coming on—"Asshole practical jokes"—then it hits.

As if triggered by the sneeze, the giant flatscreen image explodes into multicolored snow, and is replaced by an unclothed barely pubescent girl straddling an older man, and yes, the girl is Noel, but with long hair and tanned skin. Between sneezes, I can see audience members reacting with either horror or laughter, but the Bible-thumper onstage is unaware that his video-send has been hijacked. He goes on raving about the Lord's justice, even while the vid-pirate begins to dither with the explicit image. Now the preacher's face is superimposed, in a clumsy fashion, so that it belongs to the man under the psuedogirl.

Fistfights are breaking out in the audience between cultists and hecklers, and now the cops are moving in. Probably expecting a riot, they advance with activated staves, stunning everybody in their path. Adriana tugs at my arm, but something's just crashed into consciousness, what I've known all along—

—*they're all trying to infect my mind: the preacher, the Nomads, the Actuators and Panges, Christas and Pagans, billboard holograms, vidpornographers, Chinapop netbands, constantly abrading my defenses, trying to subvert their way inside, even Scred, even—*

—Adriana finally drags me away, down the narrow path between two camper-trailers. Wheezing and sniffling, I let her lead me along, while I experience a distinct feeling of *coming down,* like I've been beamed up on lifters all day. I remember Scred's paranoid ideas, something about inhalants, pheromones, and hormonal triggers. But, no, he couldn't have *planned* this, no way. . . .

I pull her to a halt behind the place that sells aerogel products. Just trying to remain standing, I can hear the gyros screaming in my head, maintaining stability.

Adriana wants to keep moving. "Fifer, they might've seen you with that terrorist, that Scred person. It's not safe for you to hang around here. Listen, come to Rexdaler with me. If you don't like it, you don't have to stay, just—"

A right cross and she lands on her side in the dirt. I nearly fold up from a pain in my hand like I've cracked a metacarpal, while she puts a palm to her cheek, stunned. Rasping, hoarse, I hear myself yell, "Did Garver send you here as a recruiter? Want me to spend the rest of my life nursing a stack of frozen fucking *corpses*? Fuck that!"

And by the time she's scrambled up and fled, by the time I realize what I've done, and the pain is flaring up, bringing tears, only then does it occur to me that I'm being hopelessly paranoid, that she probably had no intention of picking up anyone when she came here. But now it's far too late to explain and I doubt that I could make sense of it anyway.

Nearby, a medical chopper whines and throws up a wave of dust, carrying Scred away.

The storm front appears as a black smudge along the southern horizon, visible now from the windows of the Norms' trailer rig. The dome has been folded back into the cargo section, and the constant winds howl in the vent covers on the roof. A granular hiss across the floor as the door opens, and Sue climbs into the trailer. Despite the curtains over the doors, and the insulated windows, and the electrostatic air filters, still the sand gets in.

"Larry says we can avoid the bulk of the storm if we leave in less than half an hour." Haji gestures to the weathermap on the screen as Sue takes the other seat. "Think we can do it?" Despite the news over World3 of the sudden storm, he's still in good spirits, still high after invading the preacher's video feed over the local nex. He even caught the whole riot on disc. Chaotes, they do things like that.

Yingsiu rubs her eyes, exhausted. "We've almost finished the rec work. We'll make it."

Outside, the shelters have been coming down, tents and domes and tepees packed away. Reclamation teams have been completing the demolition of Mount Cyprian. Leaving behind no trash heaps or waste products, they adhere to the Code: they've pulled up almost all of the old unused pavement in the area, and planted gene-modified desert grasses to help fix the soil.

"What's the point?" I mutter. A monster sandstorm approaching from the south, and they're planting grass?

Although the brandykinin-blockers and syndorphins have muted the pain, I'm going to have to get somebody to look at my hand. I have this nagging vision of Adriana, driving back to Rexdaler with an ugly bruise forming under her eye. Is her home some kind of biostasis cult, or what? I imagine four hundred happy zombies, waiting to be vitrified, drugged with inhalants that have been secretly infused into their shared unisex clothing by the immortalist, Garver. It would explain why everything seemed to get more bizarre the closer I got to her, like that weird hallucination. Or am I just making excuses for myself?

I've caught Scred's contagion, his paranoia. Would he have given me mint chocolates on purpose, expecting my allergic reaction to block out the effects of the supposed aerosol drugs? And was he really here for a clandestine West-Sep conference? I don't want to think about any of it, and I can't bear to look out this damned window any longer.

Black mare's tails are stretching across the southern sky, where a featureless brown wall is consuming the horizon. The market breaks up into caravans and convoys. The last of the Norms clamber aboard, Lyndon revs up the gas-turbine engines, and we lurch back onto the road, following the boxvan. The Fuji Holochrome girl winks again as we pass by. The rig sprays her with gravel and dust.

I feel buffeted by the winds, the dust layer is being blown away, and my immune systems are faltering completely.

Picking up Scred's micro, I go to Larry's interface panel, and patch into it. I load a copy of the Code from the Norms' library into the book, then return to my seat.

The Code begins:

"1.01: Gaia has taught us a lesson in mobility. . . ."

THE RECKONING OF GIFTS

James Alan Gardner

James Alan Gardner is a technical writer in Waterloo, Ontario, who attended the Banff Writers' Clinic in 1976 and the Clarion West Science Fiction Writers' Workshop in the summer of 1989. He won the grand prize in the 1989 Writers of the Future contest, the first prize in the Canadian National One-Act Playwriting Competition in 1990, the 1991 Aurora Award for his story "Muffin Explains Teleology to the World at Large," first published in *On Spec* and then reprinted in *Tesseracts*[3]. "Reaper" was a finalist for the 1992 Aurora for best short work in English. He published four other SF stories in 1991–92 in American SF magazines, including the novella "The Young Person's Guide to the Organism," which is presently in contention for a Nebula Award from the Science Fiction Writers of America. In addition to his SF, he has written and published three nonfiction books between 1989 and 1993 on technical matters involving computers. Suddenly, it seems, Gardner is everywhere.

We have chosen his most recent story, first published in *Tesseracts*[4]. "The Reckoning of Gifts," like, for instance, Duncan's "Under Another Moon," is perhaps fantasy, perhaps science fiction. The world it is set in is not ours. Canadian speculative fiction it certainly is.

A junior cook brushes against the soup cauldron, hot, searing hot. He curses.

The kitchen noise strangles to horrified silence. Profanity is always dangerous here on temple grounds, and the danger is multiplied a thousandfold by the proximity of holy objects.

The cauldron holds the high priest's soup.

A potboy screams out the door for an exorcist, but he knows it's too late: the words have ripped the amniotic sac that protects our world from the chaos outside. Demons must be streaming in by the dozen, invisible demons who sniff once at the kitchen staff, then scatter in search of the tastier souls of the clergy. The potboy can almost see the demons—fanged, clawed, with naked female breasts—racing down the corridor, wiping their hands on the tapestries as they go by (the dyes fade, the threads ravel), pouring out into the herb garden to wither the foxgloves, to suck the soothing power from camomile and the flavor from basil, then on across the courtyard, kicking a few cobblestones loose to trip passers-by, pinching the horses of a bishop's carriage, flying unseen past the warders and into the temple proper where they will crumple scrolls, tarnish chalices, and set the bells to wild jangling. Novices in catechism class will stumble over words as the demons tempt them to remember sweet berry pies, gravied beef, and a score of other foods the holy must forswear; priests hearing confession will find themselves dreaming of the feel of sins, the satisfying crunch of a fist plunged into the face of a self-righteous parishioner, or the excitement of commanding an adulteress to disrobe; and the high priest himself, Vasudheva, voice of the gods on earth, will be swarmed by demons, engulfed by them, demons raking their claws across his heart until it shreds into tatters that toss on the winds of desire.

The junior cook faints. Others pale and scatter their clothes with salt. But the Kitchen Master simply tells everyone to get back to work. He cuffs the potboy who called for help, a good solid clout on the ear that sends the boy staggering back against a chopping block.

"The lad's too excitable," the Kitchen Master tells the exorcist who appears in the doorway. "Sorry to trouble you. Nothing's wrong."

Vasudheva, voice of the gods on earth, kneels before the Twelvefold Altar. He is indeed surrounded by a frenzy of demons. When he kisses the feet of Tivi's statue, he doesn't think of the god's power or wisdom; he thinks of the sensation of kissing, the soft pressure against his lips, the lingering contact, the ghost of sensation that remains as he slowly draws away. He longs to kiss the stone again, to kiss it over and over until his lips ache with bruising. His hand rises toward his mouth. He stops the movement in time, but in his imagination it continues, his fingers reaching his lips, caressing, stroking, flesh against flesh.

Vasudheva cannot remember what he has prayed for this past half hour. Certainly not the exorcism of his demons.

A month ago, the Assembly of Bishops assigned Vasudheva a new deacon named Bhismu: a young man of undistinguished family, chosen because he has no affiliation with the Assembly's power blocs and can therefore be trusted not to exert undue influence on the high priest. Spending time with Bhismu shows he wasn't appointed for his intellect, piety, or even willingness to work.

Ah, but he is beautiful!

His hair is a garden of soft black ringlets, his beard an effusion of delicate curls. Vasudheva's hands long to entwine themselves, oh so gently, in those ringlets and curls, to braid, to weave, to stroke. He imagines threading his fingers through Bhismu's beard, cupping the young man's chin, gazing into those clear dark eyes as he leans forward and their lips meet. . . .

Vasudheva dreams too of Bhismu's hands, strong but fascinatingly dextrous when he played the reed-pipe at the Feast of the Starving Moon. Vasudheva was hypnotized by the confident rippling fingers. He thought of nothing else far into the night, until in the bleakness of morning, he wondered if he had eaten a single bite at the feast. Scripture said the moon would starve to death, disappear from the sky forever because the high priest hadn't consumed enough on its behalf; but the moon survived, as did Vasudheva's desires.

He has never prayed for those desires to abate. He cherishes them. He relishes them.

Tonight begins the Long Night Revelries, a week of feasting and celebration in the city of Cardis. Events include the Fool's Reign, the Virgins' Dance, and the Renewal of Hearth Fires from Tivi's sacred flame, but first comes the Reckoning of Gifts in the temple's outer hall.

It's never a pleasant ceremony for the priests who officiate. The hall teems with unbathed commoners, men and women together, all clutching packages to their chests with fierce protectiveness. They jostle each other in the rush to receive blessings; they insult the Gifts of others and boast about their own. Every year fights break out, and sometimes a full-scale riot. Even if demons are loose tonight, it's hard to imagine how they could add to the usual commotion.

Vasudheva waits for Bhismu to escort him down to the hall. Not long ago, the high priest refused all help in getting around—though his quarters occupy the top of the temple's highest tower, he would climb the stairs unaided several times a day, glaring at anyone who tried to assist. Now, Vasudheva goes nowhere without Bhismu's strong supporting arm. He clings to the young man with both hands and walks as slowly as possible.

Several powerful bishops have begun overt machinations to win support in the assembly, believing there will soon be an election for a new high priest. They are men of limited imagination; they think Vasudheva has become frail.

The bishops would like to influence which Gift is chosen from the dozens presented in the hall tonight. Power and prestige ride on the choice, not to mention a good deal of gold. The laws of Cardis stifle innovation—change threatens order, and order must be maintained. No one may create a new device, a new art, a new process . . . except in preparation for the Reckoning of Gifts. In the month before the Reckoning, creators may build their inventions. On the longest night of the year, they bring those Gifts to the temple; from the dozens offered, one Gift is chosen and accepted into orthodoxy, while the others become fuel for Tivi's flame. The successful creator is fêted in all quarters of the city, honored as a benefactor of the people and a servant of heaven. The unsuccessful ones have nothing to show but ashes.

Needless to say, competition is intense. Every guild sponsors some Gift to better their lot—a new type of horse hitch offered by the cart drivers, a new way to waterproof barrels offered by the coopers—and scores of individuals also bring their offerings, some of them coming back year after year. One family of fisherfolk has sent the eldest child to the Reckoning each year for more than a century; they claim to be able to teach needles how to point north and for some reason they think the gods will be pleased with such tricks. Not so. The gods have consistently shown themselves to be pleased with the Gift accompanied by the largest under-the-table offering to the high priest. The only variation from one year to the next is whether the secret offering is made in gold, in political influence, or in the adroitness of beautiful women.

This year, Vasudheva is sure the gods smile on a type of clasp offered by the silversmiths, a clasp more secure and easier to fasten than orthodox clasps. The silversmiths have provided the high priest with several samples of work that show the virtues of the clasp: a silver necklace whose pendant is the letter V studded with sapphires; a silver bracelet encrusted with alternating emeralds and amethysts; and a silver dagger and sheath, the dagger hilt glittering with fire-eye rubies, and the sheath embroidered to show Tivi's flame.

Schemers among the bishops try to sway the gods' decision, and several believe they have succeeded . . . but the gods are in a mood to demonstrate that they speak only through Vasudheva, while upstart bishops should devote themselves to prayer instead of powermongering.

A soft knock comes at the door and Bhismu is there. Vasudheva catches his breath, as he always does when Bhismu enters the room. Sometimes the high priest thinks he has two hearts in his chest: the withered heart of an old man and the bounding, pounding heart of a youth who feels the fever of love but not the complications. If he only has one heart, it must be attuned to the hearts around him—when he's surrounded by crabbed and ambitious bishops, his heart shrivels; when Bhismu is near, his heart expands and expands until it is as large as the sky.

Bhismu asks, "Are you ready to attend the ceremony, your Holiness?"

"If they're ready for me. Are things under control?"

"Father Amaran says we have encountered no more trouble than usual, but everyone feels a strong disquiet. There have been rumors of demons."

"Rumors of demons are like mushrooms," Vasudheva says. "They spring up overnight, and the peasants feed on them."

He hopes Bhismu will laugh, but the young man only nods. He's slow to recognize jokes. It's a failing that can be overlooked.

They begin the long journey down the tower's corkscrew stairs. A month ago, Vasudheva found it awkward to descend while holding on to an arm instead of the balustrade. Now, he's completely comfortable with it. He doesn't need to concentrate on his feet anymore; he can devote his full attention to the strength of Bhismu's hands, the faint smell of his sweat, the beard so close it would take no effort at all to kiss.

"Have you ever been in love?" Vasudheva asks.

The young man's thoughts seem to have been elsewhere. It takes him a moment to collect himself. "Love? I don't know. A few times I wondered if I was in love, but it wasn't like the minstrels say. Intense. It wasn't intense. I'd spend some time with a girl—this was before I was ordained, of course—I'd spend some time and I'd feel very fond and I'd wonder, am I in love? But my father was determined for me to enter the priesthood and if he saw me becoming attached to someone, he ordered me to give her up. And I did. I always did. So I guess it wasn't love. If it really was love, I wouldn't have . . . I don't know. It's wrong to disobey your father, but if I'd really been in love . . . I don't know."

"So you've never had strong feelings for a woman?" Vasudheva asks. He is very close to Bhismu; his breath stirs wisps of the young man's hair.

"Not as strong as love. Not as strong as love should be."

"Have you ever had strong feelings for anyone?"

"I don't understand. You mean my family? Of course I love my family. You're supposed to love your family."

Vasudheva doesn't press the matter. It took him forty years to rise from an acolyte in the most crime-ridden quarter of Cardis to the supreme office of high priest. He has learned how to bide his time.

But Bhismu's beard curls invitingly. Vasudheva's demons will not wait forever.

Bishops lounge on divans in the vestry that's adjacent to the outer hall. Each wants a whispered word with the high priest; each wants to overhear the other whispers. Vasudheva forestalls their jockeying for position by sweeping past them and throwing open the thick outer door.

Screams. Shouts. Feet stamping and glass breaking.

On a night so ripe with demons, the riot is no surprise to anyone.

The door opens onto the front of the room; the stampede is surging toward the public entrance at the rear. That's why Vasudheva isn't crushed instantly. The only people nearby are two men grappling with each other, one dressed in velvet finery, the other in bloodstained buckskins, each trying to dig fingers into his opponent's eyes. Here and there within the crowd other fistfights thump and bellow, but most people are simply trying to get out, to escape the trampling mob.

Things crunch under their feet. They could be Gifts dropped in the panic, they could be bones. No one looks down to see.

Vasudheva stands frozen in the doorway. A priest staggers up to him from the hall, squeezes roughly past into the refuge of the vestry, and cries, "Close the door, close the door!" He bleeds from a gash on his forehead.

Behind the priest comes a woman, doing her best to walk steadily though her clothes hang in shreds and blood oozes from wounds all over her body. Where her arms should be, she has wings. Wings. Vasudheva steps aside for her to pass, his mind struck numb as a sleepwalker's. Bhismu drags both the woman and the high priest back into the vestry, and slams the door shut.

The noise of the riot vanishes. There is only the whimpering of the injured priest, and the heavy breathing of several bishops whose fear makes them pant like runners.

"Sit down, sit down," Bhismu says. Vasudheva turns, but Bhismu is holding out a chair to the woman. Who shouldn't even be here—women are forbidden to enter the temple beyond the outer hall.

She's a Northerner, her hair black and braided, her skin the color of tanned deerhide . . . young, in her twenties. Bhismu's age. Vasudheva can't believe anyone would find her attractive. She's too tall and bony, and her nose is crooked, as if it was broken then set haphazardly.

Vasudheva keeps his eyes off the wings. There's no doubt they're beautiful, exquisite—slim as a swift's, abundant with feathers. For a moment, Vasudheva has a vision of the bird kingdom parading past this woman, each presenting feathers for these wings: eagles clawing out sharp brown pinions, hummingbirds poking their beaks into their chests to pluck soft down the color of blood; and crows, doves, finches, jays, each offering their gifts until the woman faces a heap of feathers taller than her head, and still the birds come, geese, falcons, owls, wrens, adding to the motley pile, all colors, all sizes, herons, plovers, swallows, larks, all bowing down like supplicants before an angel.

Vasudheva shakes his head angrily. A high priest can't afford to indulge his imagination. This is no angel. This is just some woman from a tribe of savages. She killed a lot of birds, sewed their feathers into wings, then brought those wings to the Reckoning. No doubt she started the riot in the first place. Pretending to be an angel is blasphemy; the people must have attacked in outrage as she came forward for blessing.

Bhismu kneels beside her and dabs the hem of his sleeve at a wound on her cheek. He smiles warmly at her and murmurs soft encouragements: "This one doesn't look bad, this one's deeper but it's clean. . . ."

Vasudheva finds the expression on Bhismu's face unbecoming. Must he simper so? "You can help her more by getting a proper Healer," the high priest tells him. "The sooner the better. Now."

Reluctantly, Bhismu rises. For some moments, he stands like a man bewitched, gazing at the specks of blood that mar the whiteness of his sleeve. "Now," Vasudheva repeats. Suddenly the bewitchment lifts and Bhismu sprints out of the vestry and down the corridor.

"We must make the woman go back to the hall," says a voice at Vasudheva's ear. "She shouldn't be in this part of the temple."

The words echo the high priest's thoughts, but he turns and sees they come from Bishop Niravati, a man who loves to wield his piety like a bludgeon. Niravati has always been too quick to proclaim right and wrong; he conducts himself as if *he* were the voice of the gods on earth.

"She may stay here as long as necessary," Vasudheva says. Bishops must never forget who makes the decisions in this temple. "Sending her back to the hall now would be close to murder. And she's injured. Tivi commands us to minister to the sick, Niravati; did you skip catechism class the day that was discussed?"

Several of the other bishops chuckle. Good. Niravati will note who they are and later take revenge. Vasudheva foments feuds among the bishops whenever possible: dividing one's opponents is useful. And entertaining.

The woman has watched this interchange with no expression on her face. Perhaps she's in shock . . . but she gives the impression of understanding it all and simply not caring. For a baseborn woman, she's remarkably unmoved in the presence of the highest patriarchs of the faith. "What's your name?" Vasudheva asks her.

"Hakkoia."

"From a Northerner tribe?"

"From the Bleached Mountains."

Vasudheva doesn't know if this denotes a specific tribe or merely a place—his knowledge of the world outside Cardis begins and ends with the names of the bishoprics. "What happened in the hall?" he asks.

"There were fights. People threw things at me." She wipes blood from her chin.

"Why did they throw things?"

"It was demons!" the injured priest bursts out. Father Amaran. He's been huddling on a divan, hugging himself as if cold, but now he leaps to his feet and begins to babble. "Down in the kitchens . . . I can't get a straight story out of anyone but at confession . . . demons, they've released demons. In the soup."

Even Niravati drops his eyes in embarrassment. It's one thing for a priest to rail about demons to the laity, quite another to bring them up among peers. Vasudheva envisions Amaran dying years from now as a workaday priest in some remote parish, and being able to put his finger on the exact moment when he destroyed his career.

"I saw no demons," Hakkoia says in the silence that follows Amaran's gaffe. "I saw a man who was jealous of my wings. A man in the crowd—I don't know who he was. He wore fine clothes but his gift was petty and small. He stirred the others to attack me."

"Demons are deceitful," Vasudheva says lightly. "The man may have been a demon in disguise. Or someone possessed by demons." The high priest has no intention of asking Hakkoia to identify the man who attacked her. If he wore fine clothes, he was probably a noble or the representative of a guild. Arresting such a man would have repercussions. Besides, everyone could feel the tension in the air tonight. The riot was inevitable, and assigning blame is beside the point. "Niravati," he says, "help this woman take off the wings. She'll be more comfortable without them."

Hakkoia looks miserable as the wings are removed. But she says nothing.

Soon Bhismu arrives with old Lharksha, teacher of Healing to three generations of acolytes. Lharksha's silver hair is wildly tangled, and his bleary eyes blink as if he's just been roused from a deep sleep. Vasudheva can't remember Lharksha ever looking otherwise; day or night, the man always seems freshly rumpled.

"Lharksha . . ." Father Amaran begins, stepping forward and lifting his hand to the cut in his forehead. But Bhismu pulls the Healer onward to the woman and begins to inventory her wounds. Amaran looks as if he is going to demand attention; but then he subsides and slumps back onto the nearest divan.

The Healer says little as he examines Hakkoia: "Does this hurt? Lift your arm, please. Can you lift it higher? Does it hurt?" Hakkoia answers his questions in monosyllables. When Lharksha asks if something hurts, she always says no.

The others in the room say nothing. They watch avidly as Lharksha prods Hakkoia's body and smears salve on her skin. The shredded remains of her clothes are discarded; sometimes they have to be cut away with scissors when the blood has crusted them in place. The men watch. Bit by bit, her body is stripped, cleaned, clothed again with crisp white bandages. The men make no sound, except for occasionally clearing their throats.

Vasudheva watches himself watching her. He's no stranger to the bodies of women—women are frequently offered to him as bribes. Hakkoia doesn't compare to the professional beauties he has seen, and he can view her with dispassionate appraisal. The bishops, on the other hand . . . Vasudheva looks around at the hunger on their faces and chuckles inwardly. Niravati is unconsciously licking his lips. Bishops aren't bribed as often as the high priest.

Vasudheva turns toward Bhismu and sees the young man has averted his eyes.

In that moment, Vasudheva realizes that Bhismu is lost. The realization is a prickly heat that crinkles up through Vasudheva's shoulders and leaves his ears burning. He felt this way fifty years ago when he was caught stealing a coin from the poorbox. It's a feeling of guilt and pure animal desperation, the piercing desire to reverse time and erase the past few minutes.

Bhismu is in love with Hakkoia. Why else wouldn't he look? A healthy young man should relish the opportunity to see a woman naked. Even if he's zealously trying to live up to a deacon's vows, he should peek from time to time or at least show signs of temptation. But not Bhismu. His face shows neither lust nor the struggle against lust.

Bhismu in love. . . . Vasudheva averts his eyes.

"The woman may stay the night in this room," Vasudheva says, breaking the silence. Heads turn sharply toward him. "When the trouble dies down next door, collect any Gifts that are intact and arrange them at the front of the hall. Clear out the broken ones and throw them on Tivi's flame. If there have been deaths, save the bodies; I'll give them public blessing before we return them to their next of kin. In the morning. I'll judge the Gifts in the morning too. Everything in the morning." He holds out his arm. "Bhismu, take me back to my chambers."

Bhismu is reluctant to leave. As he leads the high priest away, the young man keeps glancing at Hakkoia back over his shoulder. Vasudheva thinks, *Now he looks. Couldn't he have looked before?*

Bhismu's body is still warm, his bearded cheek still inviting, but the high priest takes no pleasure in holding the young man's arm. Vasudheva needs no human escort; he is escorted by his demons who bear him up, quicken his stride, carry him along.

Vasudheva can't sleep. He paces around his desk, arguing with himself. Is Bhismu really in love? Could it just be some kind of chivalrous arousal, a reaction to the sight of a young woman in trouble? And why should a high priest be so concerned about a nobody like Bhismu? Bhismu has no brain, no political power; he's just a beard that begs to be kissed. A pretty trinket, nothing more. A high priest can't let himself get distracted by trifles.

But Vasudheva pictures Hakkoia dying. Not dying with a knife in the throat, or choking from poison, or strangled by a garotte, just . . . dying.

Vasudheva imagines the wings burning in Tivi's flame. They will sputter and crackle at first, then catch fire with a roar. The smell will be hideous.

Destroying the wings will be nearly as good as killing the woman herself, but entirely free of blame. He can imagine the look on her face as she sees the wings burn.

Sometime after midnight, Vasudheva opens the secret drawer of his desk and takes out the presents from the silversmiths. All three are exquisite, but he may have to part with one. In order for the guild's clasp to be accepted by the gods, there must be a sample downstairs in the hall. If the riot destroyed the original sample, Vasudheva must supply a new one.

Wistfully, Vasudheva toys with the necklace, the bracelet, the dagger. It will irk him to part with any of the three, but if necessary it should be the dagger—fewer gems. He'll take it downstairs and slip it in with the other Gifts. No doubt, the silversmiths will recognize the generosity of this sacrifice and offer appropriate compensation.

He finds that descending the staircase alone is more difficult than he remembers. The realization scares him; he doesn't want to depend on

Bhismu or anyone else. But no, he's not weak, just tired. He needs sleep, that's all.

As he nears the vestry, he realizes Hakkoia will be there. Why didn't he remember her before? His thoughts wander too much these days. But Hakkoia can't stop him from going to the hall. She may not even notice him; she's probably asleep.

And he has the dagger.

Vasudheva draws the blade slowly from the sheath. It glints in the light of the torches that flicker on the wall. He can't remember ever testing its blade before. He slides it along the edge of a tapestry that shows Tivi setting the temple's cornerstone at the very center of the world. The dagger effortlessly slices off a strip of cloth ornamented with dancing angels. The blade is functional as well as ornate.

Vasudheva wonders how soundly Hakkoia sleeps.

But as he steals down the corridor that leads to the vestry, he finds Hakkoia is not sleeping at all. Low voices come from the room, one male, one female. Vasudheva closes his eyes and prays that the man is not Bhismu; it may be the most fervently Vasudheva has prayed in years.

But of course, it *is* Bhismu.

They aren't in each other's arms. Both are fully dressed. Hakkoia sits on one of the divans, her spine as straight and strong as a javelin. Bhismu sits on the floor at her feet, his head leaning against her thigh. The wings lie across Hakkoia's lap like a chastity belt.

No one has heard Vasudheva's quiet approach. Standing just outside the room, he can listen to their conversation. Bhismu is describing how his father beat him for every thought or action that might have kept him out of the priesthood. Vasudheva has never heard Bhismu speak of such things; despite a month of cultivating Bhismu's trust, Vasudheva has never reaped such secrets. And Hakkoia isn't *doing* anything. She barely speaks. Her attitude suggests she is merely tolerating his attentions; her mind is elsewhere.

"I could leave the priesthood," Bhismu says. "Vasudheva is fond of me. He'll release me from my vows if I ask. He tells me all the time that I'm his favorite. He gives me presents, and. . . ."

Vasudheva steps angrily into the room. "Enough!" he shouts.

Bhismu looks up and blushes guiltily. He jerks away from the woman, and slides quickly along the floor until he's more than an arm's length from her. Hakkoia barely reacts at all; she only lifts her chin to look the high priest in the eye. Her gaze assesses him thoughtfully. Vasudheva wonders what sort of things Bhismu said about him before he arrived, but there is no time for speculation. "I am not the one who can release a deacon from his vows," Vasudheva says, glaring at Bhismu. "Only Tivi may do that. And I don't think Tivi will be inclined to grant such a dispensation to a stripling who fancies himself in love because he's seen a woman's naked flesh. Aren't you ashamed of yourself? Aren't you?"

Bhismu seems to waver on the edge of surrender. His eyes are lowered, his hands tremble. But then the hands clench and he shakes his head like a fistfighter throwing off the effects of a punch. "I haven't done anything to be ashamed of." His voice is almost a whisper, but there is no submissiveness in it. "I haven't done anything."

"What would your father think of this?" Vasudheva demands. "Alone with a woman in the middle of the night. And on holy ground!"

Bhismu cringes. But Hakkoia slaps her hand down on the divan with a loud smack. "I am not some sickness," she says. "I'm not one of these demons you talk about, the kind that you can blame but can't see. This ground is just as holy as when I arrived. If it was holy then. Why do you carry a knife?"

Vasudheva's anger surges. It's been years since someone dared to talk to him so accusingly. People like Bhismu hold him in awe; people like Niravati are too conniving to be blunt. He's on the verge of calling the warders, of consigning Hakkoia to the dungeons as punishment for her disrespect . . . but he realizes he can't do so in front of Bhismu. No violence, no cruelty, ever, in front of Bhismu.

Besides, violence is never more than a last resort. A prudent man finds other ways to eliminate problems.

"Bhismu," Vasudheva says in a calmer voice, "I think you should go to the chapel and pray."

The young man seems to have recovered some backbone, thanks to Hakkoia's words. "I haven't done anything to be ashamed of," he says again.

"Good for you," Vasudheva replies. "But I heard you talk about renouncing your vows, and that's grave business. No, no," the high priest holds up his hand to forestall a protest, "I'm not accusing you of sin. But this is something you should think about very seriously. You should be sure it's what you want, and what's best for you. For you, for your family, for everyone. That's only right, isn't it?"

"Yes," Bhismu says. He sounds like a little boy, still defiant inside but momentarily cowed. Vasudheva thinks of ruffling Bhismu's hair like a child, but he restrains his hands.

As Bhismu turns to go, Hakkoia tells him, "I'm staying with the family of Wakkatomet, the leatherworker. Elbow Street, near the Tin Market. They're Northerners; they're very glad when people come to call."

Bhismu's face blooms into a grin. He thanks Hakkoia profusely and leaves with a capering step. *He is so beautiful, so radiantly beautiful,* Vasudheva thinks. *It breaks my heart.*

"Why did you tell him where you live?" Vasudheva asks when Bhismu is gone. "You aren't interested in him."

"He said he worried about my injuries," Hakkoia answers. "He's concerned about my health. I thought he might rest more easily if he checked on me from time to time. To see that I was well."

Vasudheva conceals a smile. This is a woman he can talk to. "Lharksha is the best Healer in the city," he says. "Your health isn't in danger, believe me."

Hakkoia's eyes flick to the dagger the high priest still holds in his hand. She raises an eyebrow questioningly.

"A Gift," he tells her, "that's all. The sheath has a new type of clasp created by the silversmith's guild. I was returning it to the hall to put with the other Gifts."

"There are no other Gifts," she says. "The priest, Amaran—he told me nothing survived the rampage."

"Nothing except this dagger," Vasudheva corrects her.

"And my wings."

The wings still lie across her lap. Her hands rest on the feathers, caressing them, stroking them.

"Are the wings hard to make?" Vasudheva asks.

"My people believe that humans are born with only half a soul," Hakkoia replies. "When a child has learned how to dance, she must go in search of an animal who is willing to provide the other half. I am now of eagle blood, and flight fills my heart. I have studied the wings of every bird; I have gathered their feathers; I have learned their calls. The wings were not hard for *me* to make."

"So you intend to make yourself rich selling wings? You and your leatherworker friends?" Vasudheva shrugs. "You'll probably do well. The nobles of Cardis are always eager for novelties, and flying will certainly appeal to them. Although most of them are lazy. Is flying hard work?"

"I don't know."

Vasudheva looks at her in amazement. "You've never tried the wings?"

"I have," she answers, and the boldness in her gaze disappears for the first time. "They don't work."

Suddenly, fiercely, she stands; the wings fall off her lap and thud heavily to the floor. She picks them up, thrusts them out toward the high priest. "If they could fly, would I bring them to this stinking hateful city? Cardis law means nothing in the mountains—I would fly the peaks and valleys, and to hell with the priests who say no. But your gods . . . your holy Tivi who's terrified of new things, he's the one who's keeping me on the ground. The Queen of Eagles told me this in a dream. So I've come for Tivi's blessing and when I have it, I'll soar away from Cardis forever."

She's mad, Vasudheva thinks. No Northerner is completely sane, but this woman goes far beyond the fanatic adoration of animals for which Northerners are famed. There is no Queen of Eagles! There could be a king—certain marginal writings imply there are kings of many mammal species—but

that doesn't necessarily extend to birds. And if she expects that official recognition will make flightless wings soar . . .

Her eyes glitter too wildly. When she speaks of flying, you notice it: the
glint of obsession. Vasudheva has seen it often through the years—priests
who appear entirely balanced until you broach some subject that rouses
their lunacy. Perhaps he's that way himself about Bhismu. How often has he
told himself he is obsessed, irrational?

Thoughtfully, Vasudheva strokes his beard. "You'll leave the city?" he
asks at last.

"Like a dove fleeing from crows."

He nods. "Bring the wings to my chambers at sunrise. In the tower. The
warders will show you the way—I'll tell them to let you pass. The crowd
will be waiting in the courtyard for my announcement. I'll proclaim your
wings to be Tivi's choice and let you have your first flight from my balcony."

She hugs the wings to her chest and smiles. It is a dangerous smile, a
mad smile. "Thank you," she says. "I'll leave, I promise. Bhismu will soon
forget me."

Only years of experience let him hide his alarm at her words. She knows
too much. Bhismu, innocent Bhismu, must have told her enough that she
could deduce how Vasudheva feels. The dagger is still in his hand . . . but
sunrise will be soon enough. If the wings work, she leaves; but the wings
will not work. Vasudheva knows how little magic there is in Tivi's blessing.

The silversmiths will be annoyed when their Gift is not chosen; but they
can be mollified. A big order of new chalices, bells, censers. Silver soup
bowls for the acolytes, silver plates for the priests. He nods to himself, then
sheaths the dagger and tucks it inside his robe.

"Tivi's grace on you," Vasudheva says to Hakkoia.

"Thank you," she says again.

After telling the warders to escort Hakkoia to his tower before sunrise,
Vasudheva stops by the chapel. All the candles have burned out; the only
light is Tivi's flame, flickering in the enormous hearth at the front of the
sanctuary. The rest of the room is in blackness.

Bhismu lies before the flame, sound asleep. There's a smile on his face;
no doubt he dreams of Hakkoia, but Vasudheva can forgive him for that.
The more Bhismu loves her, the more her death will shake him and the more
comforting he'll need.

He looks so vulnerable.

Without warning, a wave of passion sweeps over Vasudheva's heart,
and he is bending to the ground. Bhismu will never feel it, a kiss on the
cheek, the beard, one kiss stolen in the night, flesh, lips, and yes! Bhismu's
curls are soft, and warmed by Tivi's own flame. The kiss is like a sacrament,

holy, blessed. Another kiss, this time on the lips . . . but no more, no more, he'll wake up, one more, it doesn't matter, he's sleeping so soundly. . . .

Something rustles in the back of the chapel, and Vasudheva is immediately on his feet, peering into the shadows. Is there someone on the bench in the farthest corner? Vasudheva strides down the aisle, his entire body trembling with rage. Reluctant to wake up Bhismu, he whispers, "Who are you?" with a piercing harshness.

"Duroga, sir, your Holiness," a voice whispers back. "Junior cook down in the. . . ."

"What are you doing here?"

"Praying, your Holiness." The whisper is full of fear.

"In the middle of the night? More likely, you came to steal. What did you want? The sacramental silver?"

"No, your Holiness, no! I'm praying. For forgiveness. I burned myself on the soup cauldron and I said a very bad word. The word released demons, I know it did. The riot was all my fault. And everyone acting so oddly, it's the demons making everyone—"

Vasudheva slaps the cook's face, once, very hard. His palm stings after the blow and the stinging feels good. "You listen to me, junior cook," Vasudheva says. "You did not release any demons. If demons exist at all, they have more important things to do than flock about when some peasant burns his thumb. Understand?" He grabs the front of the cook's robe and shakes the man. Duroga's teeth clack together with the violence of the jostling. "You want to hear something? You want to hear?"

And Vasudheva begins to curse. Every profanity learned as a child, every foul oath overheard in the vicious quarters of Cardis, every blasphemy that sinners atoned for in the confessional, words tumbling out of the high priest's mouth with the ease of a litany, all tightly whispered into Duroga's face until the cook's cheeks are wet with spittle and his eyes weeping with fear. The words spill out, here before Tivi's own hearth, the most sacred place in the universe and so the most vulnerable . . . but no demons come, not one, because hell is as empty as heaven and the void hears neither curses nor prayers. Vasudheva knows; he's been the voice of the gods on earth for twenty-three years and not once has he spoken a word that didn't come from his own brain, his own guts, his own endless scheming. Wasn't there a time when he prayed that some god would seize his tongue and speak through him? But the first thing ever to seize his tongue is this cursing, on and on until he can no longer draw enough breath to continue and he releases the cook, throws him onto the floor, and gasps, "Now let me hear no more talk of demons!"

Without waiting for a reaction, Vasudheva staggers out to the corridor. His heart pounds and his head spins, but he feels cleansed. Duroga must meet with an accident in the near future, but it can wait, it can wait. Vasudheva has kissed Bhismu, has dealt with Hakkoia . . . has faced his demons. Climbing the tower steps his soul flies upward, dragging his feeble body behind. His soul has huge wings, and as he reels into his chambers, he has a vision of the bird kingdom parading past him, each presenting feathers for those wings: eagles, hummingbirds, crows. . . .

A loud knocking comes at the door. Vasudheva wakes, aching in every bone. He has spent the night on the floor; he never reached the bed. Now the room is quickening with pre-dawn light, grey and aloof. Vasudheva shivers, though the day is already warm.

The knocking comes again. Vasudheva pulls himself to the bed. Off with the robe he still wears, a quick rumpling of sheets, and then he calls out, "Come in."

Bhismu enters. Vasudheva's smile of greeting for the man dies as Bishop Niravati and the cook Duroga enter too.

"Good morning, your Holiness," Niravati says. The bishop's voice has none of its usual tone of feigned deference. "Did you sleep well?"

"Who is this?" Vasudheva asks, pointing at Duroga, though he remembers the cook quite clearly.

"His name is Duroga," Niravati says. "Last night he came to me with a disturbing tale about demons. Demons which he thinks have possessed high-ranking officials of our temple."

"He claims to be able to sniff out demons?"

"No, your Holiness, he's merely a witness to their work. He saw a great deal in the chapel last night." Niravati glances toward Bhismu. "A great deal."

"I was there," Bhismu says. "I saw nothing."

"You were asleep." Niravati smiles, a smile gloating with triumph. "You slept through quite a lot."

"Well, if you really think there are demons loose," Vasudheva says, "call out the exorcists." He tries to sound mocking, but doesn't succeed. The trapped feeling burns in his ears again, guilt and desperation.

"I've already called the exorcists," Niravati says. "But I thought I should come directly to you on another important matter. You asked the warders to escort that woman Hakkoia to your chambers this morning. . . ."

Bhismu looks startled. "You did?"

"Her wings are Tivi's chosen Gift this year," Vasudheva replies. "No other Gift survived. I thought it would please the people to see her fly from my balcony."

"No doubt it would be exciting," Niravati says. "But with so much concern about demons, surely it's rash to let a woman visit your room. The laity is not in a mood to accept . . . deviations from common practice."

Vasudheva knows he must rebuke Niravati now, immediately. To hesitate for another second will prove he's afraid. (Does Niravati know about the kisses? He must. Bhismu lay in the light of Tivi's fire; Duroga could see everything.)

But Vasudheva *is* afraid. The people are used to the clergy sporting with women—order an ale in any tavern of Cardis, and you'll hear a joke about lascivious priests before your glass is empty. Such joking is good-natured, almost fond. However, to be caught kissing a man . . . of course, there would be no trial, no public punishment, for a high priest could not be convicted on the word of a junior cook. But there would be insolence from the novices; too much salt in every meal; clothes that come back dirty from the temple laundry; conversations that fall silent as the high priest enters the room.

He couldn't stand that. He couldn't stand a world that did not respect or fear him.

Vasudheva sighs heavily. "You have a point, Niravati. Hakkoia will have to fly from some other height. Perhaps the bell tower of the City Council?"

Niravati shakes his head. "The people are gathering in the courtyard below us. They expect you to announce the Gift from your balcony here. That's the tradition."

"*I* could wear the wings," Bhismu says suddenly.

"No!" Vasudheva's voice cracks.

"But I could!" the young man insists. "I want to. For Hakkoia's sake."

"An excellent idea," Niravati says, clapping Bhismu on the shoulder. "I should have thought of it myself."

"She talked to me about flying," Bhismu says excitedly. "She says she has eagle blood. The way she spoke of eagles . . . as if she were in love with them . . . please, your Holiness, let me fly in her place."

"Yes, let him," Niravati says. "It would show your . . . good faith."

Vasudheva looks at Bhismu's eager face and remembers warm curls, soft lips. "All right," the high priest says. "Go get the wings."

He turns away quickly. Another second, and Bhismu's grateful expression will wring tears from the high priest's eyes.

"People of Cardis!"

The rim of the sun is emerging over the rooftops. Only those in the tower can see it; five storeys lower, the city is still in shadow. But men and women crowd the courtyard, their heads craned up to watch the high priest's balcony. Every onlooker wears some small finery—a new ribbon in the hair, a patch of bright cloth sewn on the shirt directly over the heart.

Hakkoia must be in the crowd somewhere, but Vasudheva doesn't see her. His eyes water; he can't focus on any of the faces below.

"People of Cardis!" he repeats. "As you may have heard, many of the intended Gifts were destroyed last night in a terrible commotion. A commotion we believe was caused by demons."

At Vasudheva's back, Niravati murmurs, "That's right."

"But through Tivi's heavenly grace," Vasudheva continues, "one Gift was spared. That Gift is the one that the gods have chosen to accept this year. A Gift that is nothing less than the gift of flight!"

Bhismu steps onto the balcony, arms high and outspread to show the wings he wears. The crowd stirs with wonder as the feathers catch the dawning sunlight, catch the soft breeze blowing down from the hills. Bhismu glistens like dew, so pure, so clean.

Vasudheva can see Bhismu's arms tremble as they try to support the weight of the wings. The wings will never fly.

Bhismu grins, eager to leap out over the crowd. He waggles a wing to someone; it must be Hakkoia, though Vasudheva still can't pick her out. Bhismu no doubt intends to fly a few circles around the tower, then land at the woman's feet.

He is so beautiful.

Vasudheva lifts his hand to touch the young man's hair. As simple as that, a totally natural gesture. Bhismu turns and smiles; he must think it's a sign of encouragement.

Niravati clears his throat disapprovingly. "Your Holiness . . ." he murmurs.

And suddenly, Vasudheva is angry, righteously angry, at Niravati, at himself, at all those who try to lever people away from love. All the scheming conniving bishops, and others like Bhismu's father who trample over affection on their way to meaningless goals. Love demands enough sacrifices in itself; no one should impose additional burdens. One should pay the price of love and no more.

And no less.

Vasudheva touches Bhismu's arm. "Take the wings off," he says. "Give them to me."

A stricken look of betrayal crosses Bhismu's face. "No!"

"You can have the second flight. Warders!"

They grab him before he can jump. One warder looks at Niravati for confirmation of Vasudheva's command; already the bishop has followers under his thumb. Let him. Let him have the whole damned temple. "Give me the wings!" Vasudheva roars.

They slide onto his arms like musty-smelling vestments, each as heavy as a rug. Vasudheva can barely lift his arms. A warder helps him up to the balcony's parapet.

Vasudheva would like to turn back, just for a moment, and say something to Bhismu, something wise and loving and honest. But that would only burden his beloved with confusion and guilt. Best to leave it all unsaid.

"With wings like these," the high priest calls out to the crowd, "a man could fly to heaven."

He laughs. He is still laughing as he leaps toward the rising sun.

THE CAULDRON

Donald M. Kingsbury

Donald M. Kingsbury moved to Montreal in 1948 to study at McGill University and between 1956 and 1986 taught math there. He had imbibed the essences of Golden Age SF (characterized by the stories editor John W. Campbell published in *Astounding* in the 1940's and 1950's—the work of Isaac Asimov, Robert A. Heinlein, L. Ron Hubbard, and others) and managed to sell one story to Campbell in 1952. He also became involved, as did Campbell, A. E. Van Vogt, and many others, in L. Ron Hubbard's Dianetics movement, later Scientology, from which he was ultimately excommunicated. Then, in 1978–79, three striking hard SF novellas were published in *Analog* (*Astounding* retitled), all reprinted in Best of the Year volumes, and one, "The Moon Goddess and the Son," was nominated for the Hugo Award in 1980, later becoming the kernel of his second novel in 1986.

His first novel, *Courtship Rite* (1982—U.K. title: *Geta*), established him as a major figure in science fiction, confirmed by a Hugo Award nomination for best novel. It was compared favorably to Frank Herbert's *Dune*, the most popular SF novel of modern times. Almost all his work shares a common future history, which he is still expanding and developing. The major exception is his third novel, *The Survivor*, which is set in the "known-space" future history conceived by Larry Niven and has been published only in a collection of shared-world stories, *The Man-Kzin Wars IV* (1991). Regardless of the publishing setting, *The Survivor* is an inexorably powerful and logical SF novel of future war.

"The Cauldron" is an excerpt from a novel in progress, tentatively titled *The Finger Pointing Solward*, which takes place five hundred years later than the events of *Courtship Rite*. While lacking final polish, it has the energy, imaginative power, and ambition of Kingsbury's best work.

For strategic reasons it was necessary that the Getans use human soldiers to fight on the human world of Enclad. Being biologists they manufactured their soldiers as one might manufacture any other item of military equipment. Their factory lay far from any sun, at the confluence of the *Remeden Drift* and a wisp of stars that the human foe called *The Finger Pointing Solward*.

It hung in space, a black sphere, pimpled by troop ships loading for the trip to Omicron Samekh, layered inside like an onion, Getan administrators crowding its surface where time was normal, overseeing the cauldron below that, layer by layer, gradiently dropped from normal time to a seething one hundred seconds per second where the troops were born and forged. A new soldier went from conception to fully trained adulthood in eighty days. The tailored warriors carried many Getan genes, for the Getans had once been human, but their mother-genes were Encladian, they looked Encladian, they could breed with Encladians and they carried only forty-six chromosomes. A soldier had no mother or father; he was raised by a fighting family. The older soldiers of the family guided the younger soldiers and nursed the babies. Their gospel came from the tales of *The Forge of War.* "Then Judah went up and the Lord gave the Canaanites and the Perizzites into their hand; and they defeated ten thousand of them at Bezek." Each of the families was named after an ancient battle on the planet Earth. Tuagi had been a soldier of the family of Bezek for all of the five thousand days of his preadolescence. Tuagi Bezek.

Tuagi never remembered a time when he had not been in command of his own training program. Obedience required only that he make for himself a balanced path toward the Art of Action. Indolence was not tolerated by his older brothers, neither was he allowed to neglect body or senses or mind. Failures were culled. Other than that he was on his own.

His life had been the cyclic honing of those three cardinal edges which every warrior had to wield—body and senses and mind. He took the path toward a strong, swift, limber body. He took the path which developed eyes that saw and ears that heard and fingers that felt. He took unquestioningly the path giving him the kind of mind that put together winning moves.

With serious eyes he would attach accelerometers to his limbs and practice for kilosecs to break one of his own speed records. He belonged to a group of five who were using dancing to bring that speed under coordinated control. Sometimes he would spend days in the sense-perception labs. He could identify every kind of tree that grew on Enclad and he could tell how much adrenaline was in a man's blood by watching the faint pulsing at his throat. He knew by sight the meanings of all the common nonverbal gestures and nuances of facial expression used on Enclad and was adept at duplicating most of them.

Tuagi's hobby was shaping weapons, and whenever he could, horseback riding in the cauldron's slower higher levels. He had made English longbows, a Mongol bonebow, and a Byzantine crossbow. His older brother Kartiel Bezek had helped him machine an ancient M-1 rifle and taught him how to take its recoil against his small shoulders. A good mind was capable of good workmanship. He wanted to get together a team to build a Sopwith Triplane, for which he had the plans, but there was no place to fly it in the caves of their gigantic training base which hung in the dark of space leagues from any sun.

Instead he built a flying scale model, one and a half meters long. He spent days at the microscope machining and assembling the engine and machining the tiny working Vicker's guns, and further days at the wind tunnel testing its flying capabilities. He felt an affection toward the triplane because a (simulated) flight of these Sopwiths had once strafed a cavalry brigade of his, decimating it while he was leading a charge in the simulator. The surprise had taught a very arrogant young soldier a lesson he was not liable to forget.

Cavalry had held a romantic fascination for Tuagi since, as a young child, he had admired the horse of one of the officer historians and that gentleman had spent an afternoon teaching him how to shoot his bow from horseback in the Byzantine style which the general Belisarius had used so effectively against the lance-equipped cavalry of the Goths.

His discovery of equestrian warfare made a sudden centaur out of him. He spent time at the forge drawing wire and crafting his own chain mail while his brothers merely hammered out swords and what-not. He became a horse trainer. He watched cavalry thrillers for entertainment and spent days in the very realistic horse-battle simulator (which smelled of manure and sweat) where he was able to kill a variety of foes from horseback or, if he wasn't skillful enough, was himself mock-killed in some painful fashion and ejected from the simulator for the rest of the day.

In time he graduated to the study of cavalry tactics and had to direct his cavalry forces in vast simulated battles. He became very good at it. He could direct cavalry under Roman or Medieval or Napoleonic constraints with a flair that earned him attention. He began to boast.

Amused, his Getan teachers, who lived in the slowness of the cauldron's rim, put him in command of a German cavalry brigade on the French battlefield in 1914—against tanks which he wasn't expecting since they hadn't been invented in 1914 though the technological base for them existed. He got slaughtered. Like all cavalry officers before him who loved horses, he defended his brigade fiercely during the battle postmortem. Smiling, his instructors gave him a second try. That was the time he had been strafed by four Sopwith Triplanes who came and went—at a time when *he knew* the British were flying only unarmed and truculent pushers. At the visual display on his console he had cried.

The key concept wasn't horses, it was mobility. What is the best kind of mobility that your technology can give you? For a while he became an avid student of Heinz Guderian, the German who first developed the concept of the Panzer Division and the tactics to go with it and put them brilliantly to use in the invasion of Poland in 1939 and of France in 1940. But once Tuagi thought that he understood mobility, he found himself in command of the Roman Xth Legion during the siege of Masada in ancient Judea. There he was in the desert against an impregnably fortified and well supplied rock. Mobility was meaningless.

In time he learned that his distant Getan officers would always do that to him. As soon as he had mastered some strategic concepts he would find himself in a simulated battle where no tactical solution known to him could work. In the game rooms with the computers Tuagi began to expect the unexpected. It might be a replay of some ancient battle on Earth that required knowledge of the military constraints of the time, or it might be a battle from one of the fourteen mock worlds which had been programmed each with their own peculiar constraints, but whatever the tactical situation, always there was the promise of surprise.

The Getan training officers didn't believe in teaching their soldiers how to fight the war on Enclad, they believed in teaching strategic concepts which were usable at any time and any place from any technological base.

Each member of the Grand Army of Geta was a dedicated individual, but it was made very clear to him that individualistic behavior was not always appropriate. Sometimes a soldier had to function as a well-coordinated piece of a machine whose operation was on a scale vaster than he could comprehend. And so every few hundred days the Bezek Family was drafted into a group task and Tuagi had to obey his orders with precision. One never knew what the task was going to be. But the grueling pressure of any of the group operations provided Tuagi with a level of excitement he never felt while he was on his own. Would the Bezeks heap honors upon themselves? The smiles of his older brothers, the friendly clout, the singing when they had all come through together was something he relished.

Disobedience was unthinkable. Once, long ago, on a desert operation in the battle simulator with a squad of mature brothers, he had been unable to keep up—the heat of the two suns, the wind, the struggle had been too much. He was still only a small child, the smallest body in his squad. Rebellion flashed to his mind and out of him rose a monumental temper tantrum.

"Ah, we have the makings of a temperamental gigolo!" exclaimed his comrades lewdly. "A delight for the girls!"

With bawdy chuckles they suggested that if he didn't shape up immediately and bring honor to the family, he would be culled as a soldier and sent off to service the Female Army, there to earn his life with his penis. They detailed the horrors to come. He would have to kiss women on their mouths or on their bottoms or on their toes all day long. He'd have to wear perfume and curl his hair and read poetry while he stared into their eyes with adoration. He'd have to whisper that he loved them while he nibbled their ears. He'd have to let women soldiers dress and undress him and fondle his body, and let his body be bought and sold among them as they chose. And if he failed in those arduous duties . . . well, there was always the stewpot.

They discussed the size of the bonus paid by each of the Female Families for a fresh young boy who was too genteel to make it as a soldier and how much they thought the Bezeks could get for Tuagi. How they argued and scrapped! Four of them inflicted upon him the indignity of measuring the length of his penis. The bigger it was, the better the bonus, they said. They bemoaned the fact that it was the smallest in the unit.

He chose the fury of the suns and reshouldered his duty with silent resentment. He decided that he did not like girl soldiers, even though he had never met one. He'd die under the melting humidity of the double suns before he'd let a girl touch his penis! Stoically he tried to keep up and when he did not complain, he found that the older boys understood and helped him through his exhaustion. Later, when the Bezeks were commended for a brilliant performance, he became proud that he had been able to stay with the men in the simulator. He was tough enough to be a soldier.

He equated women with his fear of failure and put them out of his mind. But try as he might he was never really able to get away from thoughts of the mysterious sex. He had never met one of them, yet they constantly appeared in the military simulations in the most awkward of places like in the middle of burning buildings where he had to respond to their ghost images. If he did not meet some computer standard, he was recycled through the ordeal again and again. They were everywhere.

Tuagi's perception studies usually consisted of things like how to see through camouflage but could just as easily turn into lessons requiring discrimination between the moods of different Encladian women as shown by shifts of muscle tension on their faces.

Worse, part of his training consisted of learning the typical strategies used by Encladian women to attract and hold their men. If you were stupid enough to do something that annoyed the simulated woman, you had to talk to her all over again. Absorbing such belief structures was torture.

He grew. His voice deepened and the down on his body became hair but when his older brothers discussed women or a particularly delightful whore he left for elsewhere. He was more content at the stables or at some new game to sharpen his body or perceptions or mind. Mostly the topic of women bored him. He endured their appearance in the simulations. So he was taken by surprise when the Bezeks went on maneuver with a unit of the Female Army and he ended up in a foxhole with a real armed girl who looked exactly like the Encladian girls whose psychology he'd had to memorize in the simulation units. The resemblance was striking, even under the helmet and the light combat armor.

She didn't act like an Encladian girl though; she had the swiftness and grace and toughness of a Bezek—until an unplanned lull in the battle when they were pinned down and had to hold their position lying in the mud with nothing to do but wait. Mischievously her voice transformed into an Encladian accent and her mannerisms softened into the mold he had met so often in the simulations. She was flirting with him! He had a traitorous desire to seduce her.

She just laughed. "You oaf! You're wasting your time. They're all virgins!"

Before he could respond, the battle resumed. His foxhole companion re-transmogrified into a lean attack weapon, they moved out, covering each other, and he never saw her again.

And girls kept coming up in his study of history. It seemed that every great warrior had been suckled by a mother.

Not Tuagi. Tuagi was born of the ectogenetic tanks on level 115 from a witch's brew of chromosomes smuggled out of Enclad and distilled by the Getan engineers. He had neither seen nor been touched by any woman. His earliest memory was being held against the hairy chest of one of his bearded Bezek brothers and pissing all over him. His brother had jerked Tuagi up and away, laughing. That was all there was to that memory. Emotionally his brothers had been everything to him.

Avoiding thoughts about women became more and more difficult. The more he suppressed them, the more he dreamed. In the dreams he would always meet one of his Encladian mothers. They were always his age or younger. That was part fantasy, part take-it-for-granted physics. He knew he was growing up inside a time-accelerated cauldron. He was growing from newborn to man in only eighty Encladian days. It was possible that his chromosomes might have been smuggled out of human space dozens of kilodays ago, packaged in nitrogen-frozen ova, their donor long dead. But it was also possible that they had been taken from Enclad only after the first Getan beachheads.

Sometimes the dream of that contact with a mother was a nightmare. She would reject him like all of Enclad had rejected the soldiers who had already landed. Sometimes it was a peaceful meeting. Then he would be eating grapes with her on a mountainside or grooming her horse.

Once in his dream his mother came to him with a face from a standard training sequence on Encladian emotions. "Come!" He had been helpless to resist her beckon. She took him into a situation maze that forced on him her love and rage, her fear and grief, warmth and hatred, petulance and despair, exultation and serenity, mercy and pettiness. In that maze he had killed her friend, saved a son, bought her a dress, reclaimed her eyesight, cynically betrayed her, comforted her, refused to talk to her when she pleaded with him, tended her while she was sick and cursing him, each thing right on top of the next. He had been hard put upon to find the right responses.

Then at the end of the maze she had told him with no emotion at all: "You will never conquer me! See, I am unafraid of any emotion you can create in my soul." Then she had handed him a sword. And he was so afraid of the sword he woke up.

It was because of his love for horses that he met the whore Elieta. He was often at the cavalry stables. Brother Kartiel came into the stall to watch him groom his favorite mare. Tuagi was surprised to see him. Kartiel was into infantry tactics and communication and had never been known to give an animal a second glance. True to form he was watching Tuagi and not the mare.

"Ah, as soon as I spied you here, I knew you were my man. Where else could I find a handsomer, more deserving virgin who loves horses? I told myself: Tuagi Bezek, my faithful brother, will do this one last favor for me before I am shipped off to Enclad."

Tuagi grinned without changing the pace of his currying. He had not the slightest notion of what his brother desired, but was willing to let his imagination speculate outrageously. "That's an obscene idea, me knocking up a horse just to amuse a one-balled veteran like you."

"A horse!" Kartiel raved with horror. "Here I am, I've come all the way from the antipodes to offer to you the magnificent Elieta as a parting present out of my love for you, and you just stand there and call her a horse." He patted the mare. "Elieta has a cave that would put this huge animal to shame."

Tuagi, suddenly, was too embarrassed to speak.

"Come," said Kartiel. "I ship out tomorrow. We see her now. The mare can wait."

Tuagi shook his head without looking at his brother. "Let me handle the women my way," he replied coldly. "I'll be ready for them when I'm ready for them. I haven't finished my training yet. You don't have to do me any favors."

Kartiel roared. "Do you want to land on Enclad and disgrace all Bezeks by not knowing the difference between a sword and a sheath? When I was your age I'd already had twenty women, old ones and little girls fresh out of the tank." He smiled. "Listen, stew meat, I'm not doing *you* a favor, I'm doing *her* a favor." He took the comb out of Tuagi's hand and guided the boy irresistibly out of the stalls. He sat him down at a heavy wooden table carved with the signs of soldiers long gone, and poured two mugs of ale.

"I'm fond of that wench, Tuagi. I'd take her with me if I could. She'd come if she could—I think. But it's not possible. She's going to die here in the cauldron. It's hard for us to really understand in our guts, but out there"—he pointed with his mug and slopped ale—"out there where we're all going, time flows a hundred times slower than inside the Base. I'll just be getting my ground legs on Enclad, just be getting used to belonging to a regiment rather than a family, three hundred days will have passed for me—and her?"

Kartiel paused and sighed. "In that time she'll have matured into a little old lady and maybe withered away. In this place time is a flying demon. I'm leaving tomorrow. Thirty Encladian days after I debark, some troop transport will bring you in, but you're not going to be a kid anymore. You'll be a man with a beard, as old as I am. How can we conceive of how fast time is moving here? Do you know what I'm going to do when I get to Enclad? I'm going to look up Jolly Barak Bezek—he was before your time. He taught me how to shit in a pot and I'd get so mad at him I'd pick up the shit and try to throw it in his face. He was a father and mother to me—and now he's fighting on Enclad and I'm as old as he is."

Kartiel raised his mug. "To time." Then he drank. He rubbed the inscriptions on the wooden table. "So for me and Elieta it is goodbye forever. I asked her what she wanted as a going-away present. Whores are strange. You'll find out. There isn't any master plan to their life. They get excited about something and a while later it is something else. Elieta just discovered horses. She wants to learn to ride. I promised I'd get someone to teach her how to ride. You're going to do that for your brother, and if by chance you get your wick dipped in wax and set on fire, just relax and enjoy the flame. I want you to take care of her. I'll meet you at the Ganatil spaceport thirty of my days from now, three thousand of your days from now, and you're going to tell me exactly how well you've taken care of her or I'm going to put your glass balls in a gravel crusher. Your memory won't be so good by then—but my memory will be fresh. Now bottoms up on that ale. I'm making out a four-day pass for you and you're getting your glass balls melted down. Come on."

"How can you tell she'll like me?"

Kartiel roared with laughter. "She's a whore! Of course she'll like you! What else has she got to do with her time but like you!"

Kartiel took Tuagi through the labyrinth that was the whore's quarters, which had been designed unlike any other section of the Base. The only rapid transportation was by bicycle along winding shrub-lined tunnels that occasionally opened up into small parks. Mostly you had to walk. Corridors ended abruptly. A hidden stairwell would take you down to some entertainment district or perhaps to a plaza of restaurants where there were pretty hostesses to drink with you.

After a zigzag course they came up into a small courtyard with a tree and a garden. Ten apartments faced the courtyard: five on the ground floor and five on the second floor with balconies. One woman was sitting on her balcony and Tuagi knew instantly she was Elieta from her reaction. She smiled at Kartiel with full lips shaped for smiling, stood up and went inside. Hair flowed to her waist and she wore a loose robe vertically striped—vermilion, white, with smaller stripes of gold and blue.

Tuagi followed behind his brother, up the stairs, glad that he did not have to meet this woman alone. A greenhorn had better go into combat with a veteran at his side. He was wryly amused that he had suddenly assumed the mental attitude he always did in the battle simulator when he was presented with a tactical problem for which he had no ready solution. As the door opened and he saw Elieta begin her smile, he was wondering what kind of decision General Guderian would be making.

But her radiance was all for Kartiel. "I didn't think you'd make it! I thought you were gone!" Tuagi she had placed leagues away from their embrace, and he became an astronomer deducing facts from spectral line and photograph.

She had a face typical of the Encladian women he had studied—the cheekbones of the Akirani, a touch of Christmas in the subdued curling of her rich hair, the hint of a Kartan jawline. But the way her nose smoothly met her forehead seemed more like the nose of the Getan officers he knew. Certainly she came of standard soldier stock. He saw that she was older than Kartiel—at least twice Tuagi's age—every quality of her face had the rubbed polish of experience. He noticed the way her fingers moved in Kartiel's hair. Those weren't the gestures of any Encladian woman from any training sim he had ever seen. Enclad was stiffer, more restrained than this woman would ever be. His mothers back on Enclad, whoever they were, would never be so free.

He glanced at her apartment. Here was the richness and balance of a long-perfected battle plan—a fortress of a bed, screens that seemed to provide privacy, but to the tactical eye looked more like traps to intrigue the unwary into ambush, and everywhere the loot of some carefully conceived conquest designed to fill a corner with exactly the right object. His eyes touched successively the pale green glass goblets handcrafted by an enchanted soldier, the carved chair, the open electronic circuitry shimmering in the delicate colors of gas-kiln glazes worth a fortune not because of the accuracy of resistor or module but because of their beauty and arrangement.

"Heartsweet, I brought you a present," Kartiel smiled, and Tuagi saw that it was the same smile he used for his younger brothers.

For the first time Elieta's eyes enveloped Tuagi. "Him?" And the energy of her smile explored his body while she looked at his face. "How cute." She came over to him, gently touching the top button of his tunic as if she meant to open it. "May I unwrap my present now?" It was the softest hand that had ever touched him, yet he felt its enormous force pressing on him. In a disturbing way he couldn't seem to measure the direction of the force. "How long may I keep him?"

"I gave him a four-day pass." Kartiel was grinning. "I'm not sure he could survive longer than that."

"Oh! But can *I* survive that long near him without losing my mind? He's gorgeous."

"He's *not* gorgeous. He's my cavalry fanatic. He's going to teach you how to ride a horse."

Instantly her energy deserted Tuagi and again he was left leagues away from her. "You remembered! Oh . . . Mug-face, you remembered! You gave me exactly what I wanted. I'm surprised. I really am. I didn't think you would." She was holding Kartiel. "Horses! I'm so frightened of those beasts." She began to undress herself, to Tuagi's horror; he hadn't gotten over his drills in Encladian morality. "Frightened but awed by their beauty. I so want to ride one. Do you think they'll let me ride through the Black Forest?"

"No, but Tuagi will arrange it. Sometimes we have to put it over on the cannibals." He was referring to their Getan officers. "We Bezeks work together when it is a good cause. You'll have to wear a uniform. Have to pass you off as a soldier. Too bad we can't pass you off as Female Army. At the moment I can't think of a way to hide those cantaloupes"—he saluted one of her breasts with an affectionate cup—"but my brother is more cunning than I am at camouflage."

"Why do you have to go?" Her voice was petulant. "You're somebody who really loves me!"

She was already half nude. Tuagi didn't know whether it would be more strategic to leave or to stay. None of his studies of military-civilian morality were applicable here. Physically paralyzed, his mind lingered on the graceful way the line of her waist flared into her hips, not like a man at all. Kartiel caught his emotion of discomfort and nodded to him a subliminal gesture that all Bezeks knew how to read. It meant: *it's her skirmish, let her control it her way.*

So he did nothing. He watched her move Kartiel to the bed and snuggle him while she cried. He stood as if he were evaluating a strange new weapon. In time Elieta noticed him and called him over. She motioned for him to sit down and took his hand, rubbing it seriously. Shooting people was easier.

"When can we go horseback riding?" she asked innocently while Kartiel kissed her neck.

"Tomorrow." Slowly, gently he moved a finger against her thigh so she wouldn't notice.

"I told you I'm a little afraid of horses. They're such enormous brutes."

"I'll give you Field Marshal Keitel. We call him that because he does everything you tell him to do. A very easy horse."

"Would you do me a favor?"

"Anything," he agreed. Kartiel was grinning at him. Tuagi was just grinning foolishly.

"I'm in charge of a little girl—she's a hellion. She's disoriented right now. We just received her from the Female Army. I don't know why she wasn't making it as a soldier and I couldn't care less. I'd like you to take her out for a few kilosecs. Be nice to her. Bring her back at the seventy-third kilosec. That's when Mug-face here has to go. We can talk then." Unobtrusively she had trapped his finger against her thigh and wouldn't let it go. "Domat!"

"Yes, madam," said the robutler from a speaker in the wall.

"Ask Wefia to come here."

"Yes, madam."

Memories were stirring in Tuagi. "Were you once a soldier?" he asked Elieta.

She laughed. "Heavens, no! I came out of the womb-tanks feet first, legs spread apart ready for action. Girls like Wefia are a problem. She's already two kilodays old; reorientation at that age is a trauma. We don't get many 'broken cannon' anymore, less now than a few generations ago." She paused, then added sternly, "By the way—no sex—she's young and under-developed physically. It would hurt her." The woman's voice was as stern as that of any Getan officer.

Elieta sat up when Wefia came in and kissed the child on the forehead. "I'd like you to meet Tuagi Bezek. You're to take him out and entertain him till he brings you back."

"Yech."

"Wefia!"

"Sure I'll take him around." She went over and picked up one of the delicately blown goblets.

"Wefia, you don't have to touch that."

She set it down. "Come, soldier Bezek." Tuagi followed her out the door. "Have a good fuck," she shouted over her shoulder. Tuagi glanced back at Elieta and found her rolling her eyes.

"Do I have to wear shoes?" Wefia asked in the courtyard. She looked up at him with brown eyes and a pug nose, patiently.

"I don't care what you wear."

Suddenly smiling, she took off her shoes and hid them in the flower garden. Her robe was translucent, revealing her body in the same shape as that of a young boy. She was obviously uncomfortable in the filmy stuff. Tuagi could see that she'd rather be in a combat uniform.

She took three of his fingers in an iron grip. "I'm supposed to hold your hand. It's supposed to be sexy or something. Lesson number one." She jerked her thumb toward the apartment. "Do you like her?"

"A lovely woman," said Tuagi diplomatically.

"She's not a woman. She couldn't even shoot a rifle. She drools over horses and if you set her on top of one she'll fall off on her head!"

"Well, well, well," said Tuagi.

"Let's go down here. We'll probably get lost. I've only been here seven days. Do you know your way around Skintown?"

"I'm lost already."

"So you've been staying away from these crazy women? You're a smart man. I've never seen so many crazy women in my life!" She looked up at Tuagi and rolled her eyes in imitation of Elieta. "That Elieta!" Then, pulling her robe up around her hips, she disappeared down the stair ramp. When he

rounded its curve, he found her sitting on the bottom stair gazing absently
at the plaza scene. He sat down beside her and sneakingly took three of her
fingers in an iron grip.

"What would you like to do, old man? I have *orders* to entertain you. We
could do it in the trees or over there on a tabletop."

Tuagi was imagining her in a frying weapons carrier on a frying desert
under two frying suns and thinking that she would be doing well for a little
soldier.

"Thirsty?"

"I could take you to a place where a naked lady will serve you beer.
That's something you'll never see on Enclad. There aren't enough crazy
women on all of Enclad to do that. Not *one*, I'll bet."

"Suits me. Let's go."

She took him across the plaza via a circuitous route through the bushes.
"Sometimes you can flush some gushers kissing in here." She giggled and
held her hand over her mouth to suppress the sound. They emerged on a
windy terrace overlooking a fountain. A woman wearing scanty beads came
over to their cushions and low table. Wefia ordered a bowl of eggnog with a
double rum. She stared at the waitress as she left. "I'm the one who needs
the double rum. That's what I'm going to grow up to be. Yech. Look at those
lovely buttocks. I don't want you to miss the entertainment. I'll bet you'd
rather be in a trench."

He stared at her. She stared back at him levelly. He wondered what you
said to a little girl like this. It was totally beyond his experience.

"Do you have a penis?" she asked casually.

"Why ask a question like that?"

"It's whore talk. Whores talk like that all the time. They're so nimby-
bimby they drive me crazy already."

"What would you like to talk about?"

"Rifles."

"Ah," he said, lighting up. "You're a rifle buff?"

"I was," she said sadly.

"Ever made a rifle?"

"No," she said, lighting up. "Did you?"

"Yeah, an M-1. Got good at shooting it, too. Made my own cartridges. I
still have it. Maybe you'd like to shoot it—it's got a wicked kick."

"Gee," she said.

"What's your favorite rifle?"

That started her off. The more she drank of the eggnog the more eloquent
she became. She had an amazing fund of knowledge about early gunpow-
der weapons, some of it obviously biased by Akiran sources. She spoke
often of the *tanegashima*, the name given by the Japanese to firearms after the
island where Portuguese traders first appeared.

Finally he interrupted her. "Would you like to make one; bore the barrel yourself, everything?"

She looked stricken. "They wouldn't let me."

He chuckled. "There's always a way to get around the cannibals."

Later when they were walking along the plaza together, Wefia leaped up on a table and flung herself on him for a piggyback ride. She held her arms awkwardly around his head and leaned over to whimper in his ear, "Will you be my sister?"

For a moment he didn't understand. But of course. She wouldn't know what "sister" really meant. She only knew she'd lost her whole family of sisters and was now living with women whose behavior she couldn't comprehend. He was a soldier. Her sisters were soldiers. "Sure I'll be your sister."

Her hug tightened. "I'm a dangerous sister to have. Very dangerous. I real-killed three of my sisters. That's why the Vicksburgs don't like me anymore. I'll be careful not to kill you."

Tuagi knew what kind of a whore Wefia would grow up to be. She'd never like women. But men she would love. The men she would know would be soldiers and soldiers she could understand.

They returned to the apartment by kilosec-73. Elieta handed him a message from Kartiel. "See you soon with a beard," it read, the traditional farewell from a soldier to his younger brothers.

"He's sweet," she said melancholically. "I made him promise to remember me for the rest of my life—just as a joke. I'm sorry to be so sad. It's not good. Usually I'm very gay."

"If you want to be alone . . ."

"Anything but being left alone right now. Don't leave me. Wefia, we'll take Tuagi to the baths."

It was very different from the barrack showers, a running stream with pools and bathers and waterfalls. Wefia splashed around while Elieta quietly soaped his body, humming to herself. This, Tuagi thought, would be what it was like to have a mother. He wondered at that recurring fantasy of his.

The way the Getans created men made motherhood meaningless. Still, all the soldiers of history had been born from women. He remembered the image of the mother of Alexander the Great praying at the altar of her gods for them to give her son the powers of a warrior general. Closing his eyes, he tried to imagine Elieta as his mother and couldn't.

He rinsed himself in a falling spray and allowed his two women to towel him dry. They wouldn't let him dress. They dragged him back through the streets naked, Elieta laughing and hailing her friends, Wefia clinging tightly to his hand, only once leaving him to rescue her shoes among the flowers.

Wefia, the soldier, had a fight with Elieta when she was dismissed. "I'm staying! I'm a whore, too! We can put him between us!"

Tuagi reached out and held her until her tears wore out. "I'll see you tomorrow after I show Elieta the horses. We can start working on that rifle. Think about the one you want to make."

"I want to stay here," she sniffled.

"Ah, little sheath, it would never do. I'm a virgin and you're a virgin. We wouldn't know which end the bullet came out. Wait until I have a lot of experience and then you will sleep with me alone."

With great dignity she left his lap. "Good night, whore Elieta. Good night, soldier Bezek." Then she kicked the bed, lifted up her robe, and ran away.

"My. She likes you."

"That's because I like her."

"All she needed was a man. That's all we all need." The seductress was silent for a long time. She played some music. Again she was leagues away from him. He didn't mind. She sat cross-legged on the bed, nude, playing her flute with the music. Time stood still and went on forever. He felt like a man, even if his thoughts were still rattled. Women weren't all that different from soldiers.

He found her huge picture book of horses, famous horses, unknown horses caught by a hundred artists with and without their riders. She crept beside him on the bed and he put his arm around her.

"Look at that one! He's so *wild*. Look at those eyes and his head!" She held the book out.

"Would you like to ride him?"

She trembled in his arms.

"He's an Arabian stallion."

"Is it true that Catherine the Great of Russia died trying to make love to a stallion when the structure holding him above her bed collapsed?"

Tuagi cracked up.

"But did she!"

He shook his head helplessly.

"All you men know about is wars! You don't know any of the interesting things!"

Her hand reached out and the lights began to fall and flicker softly in some unpredictably sensual rhythm. She pushed the book away in a dismissing fashion that left her by herself on her belly, head away from Tuagi, tempting him. He slid over beside her, wracking his brain for dialogue from the simulations.

"Hello," he said.

"You're sure you're a virgin?" she said to the wall.

He thought about kissing her and didn't know if he dared. He had never kissed a woman before. Slowly he touched his lips to her back and rubbed his face against the smoothness of it. "Yeah."

She pulled him closer. "Let's just snuggle for a while. It's better if we make it last. Touch me. Do anything."

With one round buttock in the palm of his hand he found himself wondering about the exact nature of his relationship to the fifty thousand women of Enclad who, unknowingly, had acted as the seed group for the Grand Army. Why should he be thinking that? If Kartiel was right about sex, by now he should be lying here overwhelmed by lust.

She took his head in the crook of her arms, smiling, legs locked around him so that he couldn't get away. "There's a mystery about you. Tell me what it is."

"Nothing."

"Tuagi, I've been around soldiers too long and you wouldn't believe the number of virgins I've had. Something is on your mind. Tell me. No matter how silly it sounds, tell me."

He evaded Elieta's request. "Do you know who your mother was?" he asked instead.

"Tuagi!" She laughed. "Tuagi! You know I don't have a mother. I came out of the tanks just like you!"

"I've often wondered who *my* mother was."

"But you don't have a mother!"

"Don't be silly. Everyone has a mother."

"Except us."

"The Getans are very careful with genetics. They know every gene in each of us and where it came from! They know everything!"

"Tuagi! Your mother was murdered when she was a baby for her artificially matured ovaries. Then she was butchered and added to some recipe up in the officers' mess. What are you talking about!"

"I don't mean *that* one. Four generations back we came from Enclad, our mothers did, grandmothers, whatever."

"Four generations is a long time. That's fifteen mothers if you go that far back—and with genetic splicing and dicing it could be even more."

"Or less. Have you ever thought that those remote great-grandmothers of yours are still alive on Enclad? They are. Some of them would be younger than you are."

"So? I remind you of your mother?" Elieta was amused.

"No. It's just that women make me think of that. I've seen more women today than I have in my whole life, except in pictures. It's a queer thought but when I go to Enclad I dream of meeting one of my mothers—just to satisfy something in myself. It will make the dreams go away, to meet one of my mothers while I'm awake."

"So ask around. Find out who they are!"

"It's impossible. The genetic data are in the main information vaults. Locked solid."

"I've often heard you soldiers boast that you can outflank the cannibals."

"A covert horseback ride in the Black Forest and cracking the main computers aren't the same problem." He was reminded that he was only a beardless youth.

She pondered his difficulty for six seconds. "I'll tell you what to do, little boy. The Encladian political system is based on computer games and on cheating the computers. So your officers will let you study computers—they'll want you to study them. After a while you'll know enough to crack the vaults. Now isn't that a good scheme?" She laughed at her own intelligence. "If you find out who your mother is, tell me about my father."

"I know some of that story."

"Oh?"

"All of our fathers are from the Clan of Itraiel, which has been bred for military intuition. The Base is crawling with them."

"Oh, manure! The Getans have never won a war! Have you read about the campaign on Enclad so far? It's a farce! How could *they* breed for military intuition! This whole war thing is a farce!"

"I work in their training devices every day. Military intuition they have."

"Do you trust them?"

"Yes. Implicitly. I've never met a single case of corruption or incompetence in any of the Getans I've known. I've never met the officer who won't knock himself out for me if I have a problem."

"They *ate* your real mother when she was still a baby."

"So? Babies aren't human until they have memories."

"If you were hungry, you young cannibal, would you eat me?"

It was a ridiculous question. She was a mature woman with obvious kalothi—but he was learning that whores didn't always speak sensible things. Absurd questions required absurd answers. He smiled. "You'd be a bit tough. Just feel the muscle tone in your thighs. You might make a good stew if you were pickled in wine for a ten-day."

"Shall we sleep?"

"No, I'm filled with lust."

"Still thinking about your mother?" she jabbed. "All fifteen of them at once?"

Kartiel was so right. You felt different and talked differently when you lay with a woman. He felt very mature. He tried to think of some phrase that Encladian men used to appease their women. "How long has it been since a man told you that you are the most beautiful woman in the universe?"

"Not since earlier this evening!"

Then she melted in his arms. It was strange that such a silly phrase should work and get the effect he desired. He felt tenderly toward this whore who could pick his mind as if she had a cord into his brain, and he wondered why it had taken him so long to come here. Presently he was no longer a virgin.

Tuagi never mentioned again to anyone his obsession with his mothers. But he began to make a serious study of computers. He unraveled computers methodically, learning how to program the political games that Encladians played with them, learning how to cheat them, and cheatproof them.

Nine hundred days after commencing his studies he was ready. The central vault, he found, was impregnable, but the desks used by Getan officers were not. He faked a disease that had many genetic symptoms. A curious officer decrypted his genetic file into a desk's temporary storage. He blocked the erase, duplicated the records, then repaired the erase. It was as simple as that. But it took four hundred more days to crack the file code since the recording was designed for direct input into a Getan's peculiar brain.

Tuagi's genetic map was anomalous. Forty percent of his genetic material was of diverse Getan origin. He had a total of eleven Encladian mothers but thirty-two percent of his genes came from only one of them. That puzzled him until he traced back his record through four female developmental generations (all of whom had been destroyed as infants during the oval decanting). The favored mother had many characteristics that showed amazing survival potential under the contingencies placed upon them by the Getan genetic engineers. A very unusual woman.

Her background was ordinary. She had been born on an obscure Akiran planet of moderately superior parents and had migrated to Enclad as a youth. Her pictures showed her to be of pure Akirani stock, Kiromashoi branch. The records indicated that ova had been taken from her covertly while she was still physically maturing into womanhood. She was one of the earlier donors and her genetic material had been widely used in soldier stock. Tuagi made a rough calculation on her age and came out with a figure of less than ten kilodays, younger than Elieta. He destroyed the stolen records, but kept the pictures. He certainly *looked* like her son.

Kyojida Nachirami.

He knew who his senior mother was! Promptly he dreamed about her. It was a nightmare. In his dream he met her after debarking at Enclad's Ganatil spaceport and told her every detail of his life, and she coldly reported him to the Getan Command for disobedience and with stern faces they shipped him back to the cauldron to become a gigolo for the Female Army.

But when he woke up he found it wasn't true. He stared at her pictures. There was such intelligence in the way she moved. Was he in love with her? That was silly. Was he obsessed? Yes. Was it only a crush? Perhaps. He was a trained soldier with a single purpose, to take Enclad and with his brothers lay the foundation for a Getan conquest that would last a megaday. But there would be an interesting side trip crossing his purpose.

Somewhere on that newly terraformed world he would locate his mother—come Nova or Kelvin's darkness. When he found her she would tell him what it was like to grow up free without a destiny. Perhaps, perhaps he would kiss her on the cheek. That shouldn't be such a hard task for a soldier who was the equivalent of any general who had ever walked the face of ancient Earth.

Happy Days in Old Chernobyl

Claude-Michel Prévost

Translated from the French by John Greene

Claude-Michel Prévost was born in Haiti and moved to Quebec in 1979, and from thence to Vancouver, where he now lives. He considers himself a Canadian writer, or a New World writer, and identifies with both British Columbia and Quebec. His mentor was Élisabeth Vonarburg; she was the first to appreciate and publish his work when she was editing *Solaris*. Rather than identify himself as a "science fiction writer," he says that he is a writer who happens to write SF; he is proud of his SF, but does not feel limited to it, and cites Doris Lessing as an important role model in this respect. When asked what got him into writing SF, he replies: "Anger. I wasn't happy with the way things were in the world outside. So science fiction was a way to escape inside, to imagine a world that was perhaps better. I am often prone to pessimism about the way things are going."

He holds a Bachelor of Commerce degree and an Advertising Certificate, and is currently a marketing consultant with his own business, specializing in helping companies integrate new technologies into the marketing process. He is also writing erotica and an interactive Hypercard stack on voodoo.

In this story, there's Michel. Michel with his pale skin despite three months of sun. Michel floating in his parka, pink gums, cracked glasses, weak wrist on the machete. Michel watching me dig in silence, he's hunched against a dead tree trunk, shivering from time to time, like a rabbit. I put on his earphones, and he's listening to Pink Floyd, *"Dark Side of the Moon."* He is Michel Langlois.

In this story, there's Daniel. Daniel chuckling in front of the Macintosh screen, nose to nose, dirty hair in his face, he was staring at the screen and chuckling softly in the fluorescent lab light, CHOM was going *dididi, dididii, dididiii,* he was jigging the mouse like an epileptic with withdrawal symptoms, *just you wait, sluuuut, just you wait,* and he brought into being a whole galaxy of RNA molecules, a colony of jellyfish children, a pink marshmallow chain-saw dancing the cha-cha on Broadway, cane in hand like the old Looney Tune cartoons . . . Daniel, his bass guitar was as heavy as a flamethrower, he named it Slut, and he'd whip the strings of the Gibson on the apartment roof, with his paranoid Bugs Bunny silhouette ready to dive down the light well. His cage was at the top of fifty-six steps of a madman's staircase, and at the entrance the aquarium walls tilted at a thirty-five-degree angle. Every night for exactly twenty-seven nights, *twenty-seven,* he screamed with laughter over it in the cafeteria, every night at two A.M. sharp, he ran silently over the roof, adjusted the anti-aircraft battery of the Yamaha Fender, yelled *Viva Casa!!* out over Sherbrooke Street blue in the mist, and *BALLOUNG,* volume at 15, *BALLOOOUNG,* a single note, a single howl made the neighbourhood taaaake off. The entire H2V 2K8 sector. And you could see them landing, eyes in painful trance, falling out of bed after two tough seconds of bewildered levitation. His next-door neighbour was starting to give him suspicious looks. Hi, Daniel.

At Bordeaux jail he had FUCK tattooed on his skull, starting from the left temple, a red scar slipping down onto the forehead at the verge of the hair; he came back with the tattoo, the clap, two front teeth gone and that way of looking without seeing, of slipping his personal bubble between other people's, trying not to identify anything. The thunderscan was crackling over a picture pirated from Penthouse, but his pixels were hurting, he never used the least dot of orange any more, and now only coke helped him keep up his self-esteem in front of the screen. But in our tribe he was Wolfgang Megahertz or Daddy Satellite, he took a deep breath, lifted both arms over his head, and his fingers burned up the bakelite consoles. He was the one who took us from orbit to orbit over the sleeping mountains, who traced the monotonous rounds of an RCA spy satellite, the trill of a submarine drowsing off Ceylon, the low frequency grumbling of a B-52 scratching the gold of early morning. Even in bed, he searched for the quiver of other cells, his ear right up against the federal channels, *just you wait, slut, just you wait;* and when the day would end red and black, red with dust and with sleep in the eyes, black with rage and exhaustion after sixteen hours of panicked marching, when everyone was watching the glow on the other side of the mountain in exhausted silence, he was the one who tickled out Radio Amsterdam, *No woman no cry, no, woman, no cry.* And who made us laugh with the Voice of America, that sort of nervous laugh that makes your head shake, that finally forces your lungs to open. And who made us shiver when a voice whispered: *friends, we call as friends . . .*

Daniel Megahertz, Daniel Rainville. His moment of glory was when we spent three minutes embracing the members of SHAZAM, the pirate researchers of M.I.T., riding a couple of micro-hairs off the signal of Radio Canada International. Daniel Rainville. In this story, he's the one who will join the loggers of ENGATE ONE, who will slip into one of the armed convoys toward the cities of the South. His favourite hero was, no, is, Doctor Spock: *no feelings, man, no feelings.*

Hi, Daniel.

In this story, there's Aldridge. Aldridge Clearwater, the duke of cool springs, Aldridge who opens his soul wide when he walks in the forest, bazooka on his back, and who recites his doctoral thesis to the raccoons while he feeds them. He can look at the stars and name them, one by one, by their real names. Aldridge taught us to eat roots and berries, to open our third eye when brute fatigue begins to win, to breathe in sync with the ferns while the patrolling troops' boots march by our cheeks. He's the one who sniffs out the trail of McLOEDGER's soldiers, who silently watches the tiny trucks on the mountainside, who slides his heron body among the supposedly invulnerable gasoline tanks, among the immigrant workers gathered around the recreation trailers. He stuffed his hiding places in the hollow of century-old trunks, near mossy creeks smelling of mint, in warrens of needles capped by rocks. He knows the tiniest corners of the cathedrals of this forest, the smallest clearing where bearcubs play, he knows how to ask the trees for rest and energy, he's crossed every carpet of branches and leaves covering the damp trail the Indians traced. Aldridge has been here for twelve years and eight eternities, eight seasons of loud and cluttered prime-time. Back then, he wasn't called Aldridge, he wasn't Aldridge yet. He seemed like just one of those loners with the high dry foreheads who can't stand more than three people at once. Every time he went into town, when he turned his feet toward the guard of walls, he could feel his heart stifling with the first suburbs, tied down by ribbons of road, so he bought a cabin in the middle of nowhere and a satellite dish, and he kept doing his geology research while cultivating his two acres of ganja. The cabin quivered in the sunlight, in harmony with the firs; the logging companies' trucks looked like DINKY TOYS driven by ants, their camps were still nothing but pimples on the mountains' skin; a pirate radio hummed from the Aleutians, and *Romeo and Juliet, tam, ta-tam-tatam, Samson and Delilah, tam, ta-tam-tatam,* and Aldridge had a monumental tranquility. Until eight summers ago.

When the EARTH NOW fanatics sat on the explosives in front of the sniggering loggers, Aldridge agreed to grow up. That day, that third day, one of the eight kilo charges just went off. The foreman pleaded not guilty, the company hired the best lawyer in Vancouver. Accident. Technical defect. Sometimes Aldridge talks to me about the kid who blew up, he describes the birch slope quiet in the breeze, the arms closed around the dynamite sticks, embracing them while the boy leaned back against the tree, you could see him in all the binoculars, his breathing as calm as a November river. He describes the arms closing, then opening. Aldridge has already killed three supervisors, blown up two supply dumps, smashed millions of dollars worth of McLOEDGER equipment. He built around the camps an insubstantial web of informers and fears, retreats and traps, and we patiently write terror on the convoys in letters of quick ambushes at sloping corners, with ink of deadly raids on trailers guarded by throat-slit sentinels. No, I'm not talking about Afghan fighters with calm peregrine-falcon eyes, I'm not even talking about Fatheh, martyrs listening to the tanks rolling over their ruined walls, even if it is true that for all of us the evening news has a taste of the inevitable. All I know is my Leica lens faithfully holding to the driver's head, searching for the spot between the eyes, under the yellow and gold helmet, searching patiently and charitably; all I know is the mines exploding on the road still muddy with snow, roughly standing up the giant Crane, the head hitting the back partition before slumping on the wheel, the Jeep flipping over in a red and blue howl while the whole mountain grumbles; all I know is forced marches, open eyes seeing nothing, wild goat plunges through cold sticky branches, while the Huey Cobras rake the landscape, with the stubborn patience of infuriated wasps, their thermal scanners full of venom. Aldridge Clearwater. He taught us to shoot and to breathe, he showed us the tombs of the village of Saida, nicely lined up in the main street, pushed out of line by ferns and wild-cherry roots. Fifty-eight tombs with no inscription, which became our pilgrimage.

Aldridge will continue the story in the woods. He will continue to be the woods, he can change himself into an eagle, a crow, a trout, a weasel. Aldridge will continue to call up the cells from the city, to come and get us one by one against the walls bleached by the searchlights: his name shines in our concrete despair, every day wilder, every day stronger, despite his repeated deaths, despite the ever-victorious new military contingents. Someone else will come to take my place beside him, will relearn the use of his eyes, will roll naked and whimpering in the grass. Aldridge Clearwater. My master. My brother.

In this story, there are the dead. Stories always need bodies to fill up the background, shovel-loads, truck-loads, container-loads, to scratch their heads over. Suzanne is the one with the blonde hair and the little-girl hips, her small fatigue-dirty face sticking out of the sleeping bag. Suzanne died in the first burst, I heard the dotted line. Bernard screamed for an hour, he yelled insults, he said the gas was getting inside his helmet. Bernard already had gangrene, his left leg stank sweet from the fourth day: the sliver went in deep, then decomposed immediately, as if it had been programmed. We had been on the lookout for a week: a thinly-disguised Chinook dropped thousands of booby traps over the firs, false twigs, false gossamer. Even the moss is phony, your hand swells up like a balloon. So there are Suzanne, Bernard, Mario; Mario died about five days earlier stepping on an anti-personnel mine. Tired head-of-the-class look, trained as a group leader, Export-A cigarettes. Suzanne, Bernard, Mario, nice and juicy, nice and dead, their swollen bits are in my memory awaiting burial.

In this story there are lots of bodies. I am digging in the name of a Mount-Royal of corpses rotting in the corner of some waiting-room, who disappear leaving only a few spots of vomit on the sidewalk one Thursday night toward two A.M., who pretend to leaf through the magazines they can't read in the heat of the *Varimag* and who feel their hands trembling when they look at the plastic cheese packages with their inflexible yellow plastic tags. I'm thinking of RED SCREAM and their anti-Catholic charades on the billboards of CYBERG at U.Q.A.M., of the anarchist cells of Vancouver, FRAGILE, KHARTOUM, of the butch karatekas of the EVE network who learned to take apart their Uzis in an old pool hall; I am digging in the name of the punk commandos of the SCHIZOID SHRIMPS, silent on their skateboards while the river waters blazed, I'm digging in the name of two pages of dead who preceded us in this forgotten corner of B.C. Bodies of all shapes, of all ages, bodies that still walk around and wait for the bus without even realizing they're already dead. *Choose your favourite shit, because, yes, yes, today, on special in the bargain basement, there are exceptional deals on large volumes, national or continental format, in the maximum bestiality mixture.* I'm digging the grave at top speed, Michel has drool running over his chin, he's gently wagging his head and singing to himself. Dawn will come soon, a few crows pass overhead softly with muffled wing-beats. His hair still smells of gas, you'd think he'd gone swimming in it. In this story, Michel will be the last body. But you know as well as I do that stories go on . . .

We buried Michel this morning. He was gently drooling, hugging his knees, shivering while he watched us dig. Aldridge gave him water, he had to show him how to drink without choking, he lay there with his mouth open and water running out. May this be a lesson to the urban cells, drops of mercury between concrete blades: urban guerilla is the only solution. Even if it's the only false solution.

Because in the cities at least you have the impression you're accomplishing something, you can melt into the belly of the crowd as soon as the sirens go off, you can rub your skin against someone before putting your loneliness back on. At least in the cities you can discuss, lecture, criticize in smoky university cafeterias, meetings smelling of hash and French tobacco, unmade beds on the floor against gargling old hot-water heaters. You can write harsh editorials flagellating your enemies, ridiculing those poor dogmatic, unconscious, lobotomized retards. At least in the cities you can affirm *We are the Pure, We have the Truth, it's you who are off the rails,* and you can dream of your personal Utopia while you're spray-painting a billboard . . .

At least in the cities rage has some variety, the adrenaline is stronger. You can identify the precise spot or the exact moment that will make you grind your teeth, clench your fists and grimace your hatred, covering up with a facial tic or an absent look. You can sniff the odour of approaching cataclysm, decipher the code of the big lie in the inkspots on your fingers, and especially get ready for the good days with a detached look, knowing that in fact when the boots start marching, when the rockets whistle out of Place Ville-Marie, that in fact *we're going to have fun, we'll be heroes, we knew it was coming, we're going to soar like crazy, we're going to live one hundred percent . . .*

Since we decided to leave the metro sewers, we've been getting shot down, group after group, co-op after co-op, cell after cell, commune after commune. We've been shooting ourselves down, in our own dogmatic struggles, our socio-sexo-economico-political affiliations, our nauseated partisan solo actions, too proud and too pure to use the enemy's weapons. I know that the last white tribes, in the east of the island, were decimated in a wave of brutal violence, it took long enough to get two quickly-forgotten press releases. Nobody thought of analyzing the water; anyway, the camera team belonged to a McLOEDGER station, and the water table lies under McLOEDGER land. I know that Radio-Cadaver has stopped broadcasting since the pink trawler recorded the crimes on Lake Superior. And I know that my shit is still drying on my thighs after last night's attack.

We never saw anything. Absolutely nothing. The first grenade rolled right in among our warm bodies, splattered *KAVOOOUM* all its shrapnel in a white and purple crown. Bernard was still lifting his head to look for his glasses when the tracers sizzled yellow through the campsite. The heavy machine gun firing from prone position coughed three arpeggios, low, deep, the burst had the same heavy softness as Suzanne's hiccups, our shadows burned red in the shrieking night. Didn't see a damn thing. Aldridge was already moving off to the left, I've never crawled so fast, I've never crawled so hard. The second grenade fell at the feet of the sleeping bags near one of the bracelets and the gas whistled out. I kept calling my mother, the stones battered my chin and my cheeks, I was spitting in my mask feeling the warmth of my shit, the valley was singing blue in the moonlight, yellow in the gas, I was strangling on my sobs and my saliva, a whole forest of eyebrows were judging me. Bernard stopped making noises a little after that. When the last drips had dried in the earth and the wind, I returned to the campsite, going a long way round, centimeter by centimeter, bush by bush. Daniel was single-mindedly putting his transmitter back together; Aldridge was staring at a black hole in the empty mountain. Michel had his mask around his neck, smiling, the idiot hadn't even put his mask on, his infra-red bracelet had saved him from the tracers and he hadn't even put his mask on. His eyes were starting to go dull, his head was flopping on his neck. The MERCKZ laboratories are the elite of the pharmaceutical industry; the Alzheimer virus was cranked up to the eighth power.

Accelerated degenerescence.

I was forgetting the bad guys. There's always a bad guy who won't pull in the same direction, who persists in thinking that his drums beat the best doctrine. The lawyer, spokesman for the natives, drowned in his car. Coca-Cola buying out Warner Brothers. The IBM commandos in partnership with the Japanese zabuki killers. The takeover of Amnesty International by an angel-faced consortium. The first graft of a transmitting device in a juvenile delinquent's skull. The raging F18s ripping apart the clip of the national anthem. The guard dogs at the turnstiles in the Metro, pensively fingering their nightsticks as the blacks go by. The indifferent satellite zooming in on the boat people's raft. The first union lobotomy of an Australian miner. The bad guys keep it up and sign their work. And nine times out of ten they win hands down.

In this story, the bad guy is McLOEDGER. The pride of the Canadian west, one of the glories of the new imperialism with big Kennedy brother's face, 3.28 billion dollars in sales, 138.56 million dollars profit. Pulp and paper, real estate, poultry, biotechnology, space research, eighteen ocean liners, two satellite communications companies, twenty-three specialized magazines, thirteen TV stations covering the six biggest markets . . . McLOEDGER is docile firs that grow three times as fast, plasmic computers calibrating hydroponic crops, logging camps shaving my mountains, layer after layer, skin after skin. It's electricity produced for half the province, with its own clinics, its own portable villages, its own social workers, its travelling exhibitions of neo-impressionist paintings and its own hired killers, Mozambique vets. McLOEDGER is a magnificent logo on a background of corporate advertising and sponsorship, its head offices a crystal needle in the heart of Edmonton, its roots plunging into every stock exchange, every cutting edge of technology, every bus heading for the factories before the sun's even up . . .

And somewhere in the great crystal needle, up at the top of the cloud-defying building, someone has just placed a magnetic card on an old mahogany desk, in a room with stained-glass windows, a card that whispers to the busy gentleman that one of his elite androids has just bought it . . .

It took us three hours to find it. Aldridge was sitting on his heels, humming a one-note tune, losing the thread in the wind, then catching it again, the same low note resounding in his chest. I began the dosage of pills and injections, carotene, two thousand milligrams, Ecstasy 3.2, three hundred milligrams, psilocybin, three capsules of five hundred milligrams, codeine, twenty milligrams, LSD-26, four capsules, caffeine, twenty-five milligrams. The camp was burning itself out among the respectful firs, an owl watching us think about nothing amid the corpses. The thermos had caught a bullet, there were only a few drops of tea left. I joined Aldridge on his rock, sat on my heels looking at the lemon-yellow moon, patiently waited until I found the frequency of his mantra in the shapes of the clouds, until the notes of our hatred were sounding in my throat, until my breathing was slow and strong like the breastbone of a grizzly, until the woods were breathing through the pores of my fingers, the beehive of my lungs. Then we stood up, we took off our clothes, and we set out to kill.

Three hours picking our way through friendly branches, sniffing odours, listening to the advice of the fireflies who lit our way. Three hours to find our trail through the total black, the leaves radiated magnesium, the branches caressed my sweat, the twigs remained quiet beneath my feet. Three hours to slip between the ever-vigilant sporadic searchlights, scrutinizing every frequency and every radiation, but they couldn't make out my aura floating from bush to bush, they couldn't penetrate the patience which had permitted me to smash the head of the cop by the Metro turnstile an eternity ago. Three hours to drift as far as the chill of tungsten and steel, eyes in the night came to tell me *no, that way, it's over that way,* even the trees narrated the Cartesian path to its radium battery. The rockets were heavy on the plates of its left shoulder, the exoskeleton supported, besides the machine-gun, a grenade launcher and a low frequency harmonics detector. Light arms, for a teleported mission, from one of the military Chinooks. Three hours to find myself face to face with a seventeen-year-old killer, asleep in his composite carcass, eyes closed behind the electronic visor embedded in the plexiglass mask. The antenna was quivering gently in the breeze, and the yellow and gold logo was waiting for the day which would soon dawn . . .

An eagle passed over my head, silently, no slippage of air over his mute feathers. Behind me, Suzanne, Bernard, Mario, Jean-Marc, all my friends had joined me and were waiting. The killer was sleeping, standing against a tree, all his senses awake, his black coverall giving no reflections at all. Polarized Mylar: that's why our own harmonics sensors had picked nothing up. So the hackers of the Boomerang group were right: the new models of android had finally left the United Technologies hangars, they were already operational on the trails of the Sertao exploited by Volkswagen, with the police commandos sweeping over the campus of Kim Sung II University; the antenna kept turning in the cold air, diligent and imbecilic. The eagle inscribed a broad circle over the head of the killer, without the slightest sound, I heard him say: *now.* And the talons plunged into the visor, perforated the wide-open retinas, the eagle lifted the android two meters off the ground, all its circuits frenzied, crying like a baby, eyelids pierced, and dropped it on its back, crunch, a wounded monster. And I was already on it, fist tight, fist of cement, jumping, jumping, beating it down in one long howl until I felt the softness of the earth again, until the gargling stopped . . .

Aldridge and me, the eagle and the grizzly, we went back to the camp. The dawn was gentle on my face, the wind washed our tiredness away. Somewhere in the crystal a magnetic card . . .

We buried Michel this morning, near the rocks overhanging the glacial lake where we all used to bathe. A copter was patrolling in the distance, looking for smoke. A third column was completing the encirclement, the crash of trees echoed from valley to valley. We had one day of life left, two if the marijuana growers decided to counterattack, seeing their crops burn in spite of the unofficial agreements; three if the army took the trouble to elaborate a big televised lie to justify six battalions armed to the teeth chasing after our bedbugs. Daniel would join the loggers, he would melt into the 35 dismal zombies waiting for the convoy to take them to the whores of

Edmonton. He'd memorized the phone number of a dusty bookstore which would lead him to Calgary, and from there to Halifax, Montreal, Amsterdam, and finally from there to Oslo. This route used to be the stations of the cross of the women of the Thirteen network, back when the anti-abortionists were having public burnings . . .

Bye, Daniel.

Michel was already in the final stages; we had to clean him, roll him in a blanket and hug him, putting off the moment as long as possible. Daniel had been gone for an hour, and we hadn't heard any shots.

I masturbated him slowly, patiently, his head was on my shoulder and he was looking at the mountains; he came with a sob, his sperm was old, yellow and cold, old. Then Aldridge kissed him, and I was the one who pulled the trigger . . .

That's the story. These pages were found in the private diary of a Greenpeace guerillero, when he tried to pass Forward Post B34 with false papers. It seems that as he showed his transportation pass he was whistling "Happy days are here again." . . .

PITY THE MONSTERS

Charles de Lint

Charles de Lint lives in Ottawa and is a musician and a major fantasy writer, popular worldwide. He is also the publisher/editor of Triskell Press in Ottawa, which publishes fantasy. His most famous novels include *Moonheart, Greenmantle,* and *The Little Country.* He has published nearly forty books since 1979. His central work is characterized by the intrusion of the fantastic into a gritty, real-world (usually Canadian) setting. "There is no doubt," says *Twentieth-Century Science Fiction Writers,* "that Charles de Lint is currently one of the most popular and prolific writers currently producing fantastic literature. . . . He has succeeded in fusing the kingdoms of Faery with modern Canadian landscapes, producing a variety of urban fantasy, which can be very satisfying to those who reject the notion that all such stories require a greenwood setting."

"My prime interest as a writer," de Lint says, "is to explore the complexities of human relationships through mythic/folkloric material against a mostly contemporary urban setting. I see the juxtaposing of the two as a way of exaggerating the dichotomy of our relationships with each other and our environment."

De Lint rarely strays into SF territory (he has written only one SF novel, *Svaha*) as he does, somewhat ambiguously, in this story. "Pity the Monsters" is reprinted from an anthology entitled *The Ultimate Frankenstein.*

We Are Standing in the Storm of Our Own Being.
—*Michael Ventura*

"I was a beauty once," the old woman said. "The neighborhood boys were forever standing outside my parents' home, hoping for a word, a smile, a kiss, as though somehow my unearned beauty gave me an intrinsic worth that far overshadowed Emma's cleverness with her schoolwork, or Betsy's gift for music. It always seemed unfair to me. My value was based on an accident of birth; theirs was earned."

The monster made no reply.

"I would have given anything to be clever or to have had some artistic ability," the old woman added. "Those are assets with which a body can grow old."

She drew her tattery shawl closer, hunching her thin shoulders against the cold. Her gaze went to her companion. The monster was looking at the blank expanse of wall above her head, eyes unfocused, scars almost invisible in the dim light.

"Yes, well," she said. "I suppose we all have our own cross to bear. At least I have good memories to go with the bad."

The snow was coming down so thickly that visibility had already become all but impossible. The fat wet flakes whirled and spun in dervishing clouds, clogging the sidewalks and streets, snarling traffic, making the simple act of walking an epic adventure. One could be anywhere, anywhen. The familiar was suddenly strange; the city transformed. The wind and the snow made even the commonest landmarks unrecognizable.

If she hadn't already been so bloody late, Harriet Pierson would have simply walked her mountain bike through the storm. She only lived a mile or so from the library and the trip wouldn't have taken *that* long by foot. But she was late, desperately late, and being sensible had never been her forte, so there she was, pedaling like a madwoman in her highest gear, the wheels skidding and sliding for purchase on the slippery street as she biked along the narrow passageway between the curb and the crawling traffic.

The so-called waterproof boots that she'd bought on sale last week were already soaked, as were the bottoms of her jeans. Her old camel hair coat was standing up to the cold, however, and her earmuffs kept her ears warm. The same couldn't be said for her hands and face. The wind bit straight through her thin woolen mittens, her cheeks were red with the cold, while her long, brown hair, bound up into a vague bun on the top of her head, was covered with an inch of snow that was already leaking its wet chill into her scalp.

Why did I move to this bloody country? she thought. It's too hot in the summer, too cold in the winter . . .

England looked very good right at that moment, but it hadn't always been so. England hadn't had Brian whom she'd met while on holiday here in Newford three years ago, Brian who'd been just as eager for her to come as she had been to emigrate, Brian who walked out on her not two months after she'd arrived and they had gotten an apartment together. She'd refused to go back. Deciding to make the best of her new homeland, she had stuck it out surprisingly well, not so much because she led such an ordered existence, as that she'd refused to run back home and have her mother tell her, ever so patronizingly, "Well, I told you so, dear."

She had a good job, if not a great one, a lovely little flat that was all her own, a fairly busy social life—that admittedly contained more friends than it did romantic interests—and liked everything about her new home. Except for the weather.

She turned off Yoors Street onto Kelly, navigating more by instinct than vision, and was just starting to congratulate herself on having completed her journey all in one piece, with time to spare, when a tall shape loomed suddenly up out of the whirling snow in front of her. Trying to avoid a collision, she turned the handlebars too quickly—and the wrong way.

Her front wheel hit the curb and she sailed over the handlebars, one more white airborne object defying gravity, except that unlike the lighter snowflakes with which she momentarily shared the sky, her weight brought her immediately down with a jarring impact against a heap of refuse that someone had set out in anticipation of tomorrow's garbage pickup.

She rose spluttering snow and staggered back towards her bike, disoriented, the suddenness of her accident not yet having sunk in. She knelt beside the bike and stared with dismay at the bent wheel frame. Then she remembered what had caused her to veer in the first place.

Her gaze went to the street, but then traveled up, and up, to the face of the tall shape that stood by the curb. The man was a giant. At five-one, Harriet wasn't tall, and perhaps it had something to do with her low perspective, but he seemed to be at least seven feet high. And yet it wasn't his size that brought the small gasp to her lips.

That face . . .

It was set in a squarish head which was itself perched on thick broad shoulders. The big nose was bent, the left eye was slightly higher than the right, the ears were like huge cauliflowers, the hairline high and square. Thick white scars crisscrossed his features, giving the impression that he'd been sewn together by some untalented seamstress who was too deep in her cups to do a proper job. An icon from an old horror movie flashed in Harriet's mind and she found herself looking for the bolts in the man's neck before she even knew what she was doing.

Of course they weren't there, but the size of the man and the way he was just standing there, staring at her, made Harriet unaccountably nervous as though this really was Victor Frankenstein's creation standing over her in the storm. She stood quickly, wanting to lessen the discrepancy of their heights. The sudden movement woke a wave of dizziness.

"I'm dreadfully sorry," she meant to say, but the words slurred, turning to mush in her mouth and what came out was, "Redfolly shurry."

Vertigo jellied her legs and made the street underfoot so wobbly that she couldn't keep her balance. The giant took a quick step towards her, huge hands outstretched, as a black wave swept over her and she pitched forward.

Bloody hell, she had time to think. I'm going all faint. . . .

Water bubbled merrily in the tin can that sat on the Coleman stove's burner. The old woman leaned forward and dropped in a tea bag, then moved the can from the heat with a mittened hand.

Only two more bags left, she thought.

She held her hands out to the stove and savored the warmth.

"I married for money, not love," she told her companion. "My Henry was not a handsome man."

The monster gaze focused and tracked down to her face.

"But I grew to love him. Not for his money, nor for the comfort of his home and the safety it offered to a young woman whose future, for all her beauty, looked to take her no further than the tenements in which she was born and bred."

The monster made a querulous noise, no more than a grunt, but the old woman could hear the question in it. They'd been together for so long that she could read him easily, without his needing to speak.

"It was for his kindness," she said.

Harriet woke to the cold. Shivering, she sat up to find herself in an unfamiliar room, enwrapped in a nest of blankets that carried a pungent, musty odor in their folds. The room itself appeared to be part of some abandoned building. The walls were unadorned except for their chipped paint and plaster and a cheerful bit of graffiti suggesting that the reader of it do something that Harriet didn't think was anatomically possible.

There were no furnishings at all. The only light came from a short, fat candle which sat on the windowsill in a puddle of cooled wax. Outside, the wind howled. In the room, in the building itself, all was still. But as she cocked her head to listen, she could just faintly make out a low murmur of conversation. It appeared to be a monologue, for it was simply one voice, droning on.

She remembered her accident and the seven-foot tall giant as though they were only something she'd experienced in a dream. The vague sense of dislocation she'd felt upon awakening had grown into a dreamy kind of muddled feeling. She was somewhat concerned over her whereabouts, but not in any sort of a pressing way. Her mind seemed to be in a fog.

Getting up, she hesitated for a moment, then wrapped one of the smelly blankets about her shoulders like a shawl against the cold and crossed the room to its one doorway. Stepping outside, she found herself in a hall as disrepaired and empty as the room she'd just quit. The murmuring voice led her down the length of the hall into what proved to be a foyer. Leaning against the last bit of wall, there where the hallway opened up into the larger space, she studied the odd scene before her.

Seven candles sat in their wax on wooden orange crates that were arranged in a half circle around an old woman. She had her back to the wall, legs tucked up under what appeared to be a half-dozen skirts. A ratty shawl covered her grey hair and hung down over her shoulders. Her face was a spiderweb of lines, all pinched and thin. Water steamed in a large tin can on a Coleman stove that stood on the floor in front of her. She had another, smaller tin can in her hand filled with, judging by the smell that filled the room, some kind of herbal tea. She was talking softly to no one that Harriet could see.

The old woman looked up just as Harriet was trying to decide how to approach her. The candlelight woke an odd glimmer in the woman's eyes, a reflective quality that reminded Harriet of a cat's gaze caught in a car's headbeams.

"And who are you, dear?" the woman asked.

"I . . . my name's Harriet. Harriet Pierson." She got the odd feeling that she should curtsy as she introduced herself.

"You may call me Flora," the old woman said. "My name's actually Anne Boddeker, but I prefer Flora."

Harriet nodded absently. Under the muddle of her thoughts, the first sharp wedge of concern was beginning to surface. She remembered taking a fall from her bike . . . had she hit her head?

"What am I doing here?" she asked.

The old woman's eyes twinkled with humor. "Now how would I know?"

"But . . ." The fuzz in Harriet's head seemed to thicken. She blinked a couple of times and then cleared her throat. "Where are we?" she tried.

"North of Gracie Street," Flora replied, "in that part of town that, I believe, people your age refer to as Squatland. I'm afraid I don't know the exact address. Vandals have played havoc with the street signs, as I'm sure you know, but I believe we're not far from the corner of Flood and MacNeil where I grew up."

Harriet's heart sank. She was in the Tombs, an area of Newford that had once been a developer's bright dream. The old, tired blocks of tenements, office buildings and factories were to be transformed into a yuppie paradise and work had already begun on tearing down the existing structures when a sudden lack of backing had left the developer scrambling for solvency. All that remained now of the bright dream was block upon block of abandoned buildings and rubble-strewn lots generally referred to as the Tombs. It was home to runaways, the homeless, derelicts, bikers, drug addicts and the like who squatted in its buildings.

It was also probably one of the most dangerous parts of Newford.

"I . . . how did I get here?" Harriet tried again.

"What do you remember?" Flora said.

"I was biking home from work," Harriet began and then proceeded to relate what she remembered of the storm, the giant who'd loomed up so suddenly out of the snow, her accident . . . "And then I suppose I must have fainted."

She lifted a hand to her head and searched about for a tender spot, but couldn't find a lump or a bruise.

"Did he speak to you?" Flora asked. "The . . . man who startled you?"

Harriet shook her head.

"Then it was Frank. He must have brought you here."

Harriet thought about what the old woman had just said.

"Does that mean there's more than one of him?" she asked. She had the feeling that her memory was playing tricks on her when she tried to call up the giant's scarred and misshapen features. She couldn't imagine there being more than one of him.

"In a way," Flora said.

"You're not being very clear."

"I'm sorry."

But she didn't appear to be, Harriet realized.

"So . . . he, this Frank . . . he's mute?" she asked.

"Terrible, isn't it?" Flora said. "A great big strapping lad like that."

Harriet nodded in agreement. "But that doesn't explain what you meant by there being more than one of him. Does he have a brother?"

"He . . ." The old woman hesitated. "Perhaps you should ask him yourself."

"But you just said that he was a mute."

"I think he's down that hall," Flora said, ignoring Harriet. She pointed to a doorway opposite from the one that Harriet had used to enter the foyer. "That's usually where he goes to play."

Harriet stood there for a long moment, just looking at the old woman. Flora, Anne, whatever her name was—she was obviously senile. That had to explain her odd manner.

Harriet lifted her gaze to look in the direction Flora had pointed. Her thoughts still felt muddy. She found standing as long as she had been was far more tiring than it should have been and her tongue felt all fuzzy.

All she wanted to do was to go home. But if this *was* the Tombs, then she'd need directions. Perhaps even protection from some of the more feral characters who were said to inhabit these abandoned buildings. Unless, she thought glumly, this "Frank" was the danger himself. . . .

She looked back at Flora, but the old woman was ignoring her. Flora drew her shawl more tightly around her shoulders and took a sip of tea from her tin can.

Bother, Harriet thought and started across the foyer.

Halfway down the new hallway, she heard a child's voice singing softly. She couldn't make out the words until she'd reached the end of the hall where yet another candlelit room offered up a view of its bizarre occupant.

Frank was sitting cross-legged in the middle of the room, the contents of Harriet's purse scattered on the floor by his knees. Her purse itself had been tossed into a corner. Harriet would have backed right out of the room before Frank looked up except that she was frozen in place by the singing. The child's voice came from Frank's twisted lips—a high, impossibly sweet sound. It was a little girl's voice, singing a skipping song:

Frank and Harriet, sitting in a tree
K-I-S-S-I-N-G

*First comes love, then comes marriage
Here comes Frank with a baby's carriage*

Frank's features seemed more monstrous than ever with that sweet child's voice issuing from his throat. He tossed the contents of Harriet's wallet into the air, juggling them. Her ID, a credit card, some photos from back home, scraps of paper with addresses or phone numbers on them, paper money, her bank card . . . they did a fluttering fandango as he sang, the movement of his hands oddly graceful for all the scarred squat bulk of his fingers. Her makeup, keys and loose change were lined up in rows like toy soldiers on parade in front of him. A half-burned ten dollar bill lay beside a candle on the wooden crate to his right. On the crate to his left lay a dead cat, curled up as though it was only sleeping, but the glassy dead eyes and swollen tongue that pushed open its jaws gave lie to the pretense.

Harriet felt a scream build up in her throat. She tried to back away, but bumped into the wall. The child's voice went still and Frank looked up. Photos, paper money, paper scraps and all flittered down upon his knees. His gaze locked on hers.

For one moment, Harriet was sure it was a child's eyes that regarded her from that ruined face. They carried a look of pure, absolute innocence, utterly at odds with the misshapen flesh and scars that surrounded them. But then they changed, gaining a feral, dark intelligence.

Frank scattered the scraps of paper and money in front of him away with a sweep of his hands.

"Mine," he cried in a deep, booming voice. "Girl is mine!"

As he lurched to his feet, Harriet fled back the way she'd come.

"The hardest thing," the old woman said, "is watching everybody die. One by one, they all die: your parents, your friends, your family. . . ."

Her voice trailed off, rheumy eyes going sad. The monster merely regarded her.

"It was hardest when Julie died," she went on after a moment. There was a hitch in her voice as she spoke her daughter's name. "It's not right that parents should outlive their children." Her gaze settled on the monster's face. "But then you'll never know that particular pain, will you?"

The monster threw back his head and a soundless howl tore from his throat.

As Harriet ran back into the room where she'd left Flora, she saw that the old woman was gone. Her candles, the crates and stove remained. The tin can half full of tea sat warming on the edge of the stove, not quite on the lit burner.

Harried looked back down the hall where Frank's shambling bulk stumbled toward her.

She had to get out of this place. Never mind the storm still howling outside the building, never mind the confusing maze of abandoned buildings and refuse-choked streets of the Tombs. She just had to—

"There you are," a voice said from directly behind her.

Harriet's heart skipped a beat. A sharp, small inadvertent squeak escaped her lips as she flung herself to one side and then backed quickly away from the shadows by the door from which the voice had come. When she realized it was only the old woman, she kept right on backing up. Whoever, whatever, Flora was, Harriet knew she wasn't a friend.

Frank shambled into the foyer then, the queer lopsided set of his gaze fixed hungrily upon her. Harriet's heartbeat kicked into double-time. Her throat went dry. The muscles of her chest tightened, squeezing her lungs so that she found it hard to breathe.

Oh god, she thought. Get out of here while you can.

But she couldn't seem to move. Her limbs were deadened weights and she was starting to feel faint again.

"Now, now," the old woman said. "Don't carry on so, Samson, or you'll frighten her to death."

The monster obediently stopped in the doorway, but his hungry gaze never left Harriet.

"Sam-samson?" Harriet asked in a weak voice.

"Oh, there's all sorts of bits and pieces of people inside that poor ugly head," Flora replied. "Comes from traumas he suffered as a child. He suffers from—what was it that Dr. Adams called him? Dissociation. I think, before the accident, the doctor had documented seventeen people inside him. Some are harmless, such as Frank and little Bessie. Others, like Samson, have an unfortunate capacity for violence when they can't have their way."

"Doctor?" Harriet asked. All she seemed capable of was catching a word from the woman's explanation and repeating it as a question.

"Yes, he was institutionalized as a young boy. The odd thing is that he's somewhat aware of all the different people living inside him. He thinks that when his father sewed him back together, he used parts of all sorts of different people to do so and those bits of alien skin and tissue took hold of his mind and borrowed parts of it for their own use."

"That . . ." Harriet cleared her throat. "That was the . . . accident?"

"Oh, it wasn't any accident," Flora said. "And don't let anyone try to tell you different. His father knew exactly what he was doing when he threw him through that plate glass window."

"But . . ."

"Of course, the father was too poor to be able to afford medical attention for the boy, so he patched him up on his own."

Harriet stared at the monstrous figure with growing horror.

"This . . . none of this can be true," she finally managed.

"It's all documented at the institution," Flora told her. "His father made a full confession before they locked him away. Poor Frank, though. It was too late to do anything to help him by that point, so he ended up being put away as well, for all that his only crime was the misfortune of being born the son of a lunatic."

Harriet tore her gaze from Frank's scarred features and turned to the old woman.

"How do you know all of this?" she asked.

"Why, I lived there as well," Flora said. "Didn't I tell you?"

"No. No, you didn't."

Flora shrugged. "It's old history. Mind you, when you get to be my age, everything's old history."

Harriet wanted to ask why Flora had been in the institution herself, but couldn't find the courage to do so. She wasn't even sure she *wanted* to know. But there was something she had no choice but to ask. She hugged her blanket closer around her, no longer even aware of its smell, but the chill that was in her bones didn't come from the cold.

"What happens now?" she said.

"I'm not sure I understand the question," Flora replied with a sly smile in her eyes that said she understood all too well.

Harriet pressed forward. "What happens to me?"

"Well, now," Flora said. She shot the monster an affectionate look. "Frank wants to start a family."

Harriet shook her head. "No," she said, her voice sounding weak and ineffectual even to her own ears. "No way."

"You don't exactly have a say in the matter, dear. It's not as though there's anyone coming to rescue you—not in this storm. And even if someone did come searching, where would they look? People disappear in this city all of the time. It's a sad, but unavoidable fact in these trying times that we've brought upon ourselves."

Harriet was still shaking her head.

"Oh, think of someone else for a change," the old woman told her. "I know your type. You're filled with your own self-importance; the whole world revolves around you. It's a party here, an evening of dancing there, theatre, clubs, cabaret, with never a thought for those less fortunate. What would it hurt you to give a bit of love and affection to a poor, lonely monster?"

I've gone all demented, Harriet thought. All of this—the monster, the lunatic calm of the old woman—none of it was real. None of it *could* be real.

"Do you think he *likes* being this way?" Flora demanded.

Her voice grew sharp and the monster shifted nervously at the tone of her anger, the way a dog might bristle, catching its master's mood.

"It's got nothing to do with me," Harriet said, surprising herself that she could still find the courage to stand up for herself. "I'm not like you think I am and I had nothing to do with what happened to that—to Frank."

"It's got everything to do with you," the old woman replied. "It's got to do with caring and family and good Samaritanism and decency and long, lasting relationships."

"You can't force a person into something like that," Harriet argued.

Flora sighed. "Sometimes, in *these* times, it's the only way. There's a sickness abroad in the world, child; your denial of what's right and true is as much a cause as a symptom."

"You're the one that's sick!" Harriet cried.

She bolted for the building's front doors, praying they weren't locked. The monster was too far away and moved too slowly to stop her. The old woman was closer and quicker, but in her panic, Harriet found the strength to fling her bodily away. She raced for the glass doors that led out of the foyer and into the storm.

The wind almost drove her back inside when she finally got a door open, but she pressed against it, through the door and out onto the street. The whirling snow, driven by the mad, capricious wind, soon stole away all sense of direction, but she didn't dare stop. She plowed through drifts, blinded by the snow, head bent against the howling wind, determined to put as much distance as possible between herself and what she fled.

Oh god, she thought at one point. My purse was back there. My ID. They know where I live. They can come and get me at home, or at work, anytime they want.

But mostly she fought the snow and wind. How long she fled through the blizzard, she had no way of knowing. It might have been an hour, it might have been the whole night. She was shaking with cold and fear when she stumbled to the ground one last time and couldn't get up.

She lay there, a delicious sense of warmth enveloping her. All she had to do was let go, she realized. Just let go and she could drift away into that dark, warm place that beckoned to her. She rolled over on her side and stared up into the white sky. Snow immediately filmed her face. She rubbed it away with her hand, already half-frozen with the cold.

She was ready to let go. She was ready to just give up the struggle, because she was only so strong and she'd given it her all, hadn't she? She—

A tall dark figure loomed up suddenly, towering over her. Snow blurred her sight so that it was only a shape, an outline, against the white.

No, she pleaded. Don't take me back. I'd rather die than go back.

As the figure bent down beside her, she found the strength to beat at it with her frozen hands.

"Easy now," a kind voice said, blocking her weak blows. "We'll get you out of here."

She stopped trying to fight. It wasn't the monster, but a policeman. Somehow, in her aimless flight, she'd wandered out of the Tombs.

"What are you doing out here?" the policeman said.

Monster, she wanted to say. There's a monster. It attacked me. But all that came out from her frozen lips was, "Muh . . . tacked me . . ."

"First we'll get you out of this weather," he told her, "then we'll deal with the man who assaulted you."

The hours that followed passed in a blur. She was in a hospital, being treated for frostbite. A detective interviewed her, calmly, patiently sifting through her mumbled replies for a description of what had happened to her, and then finally she was left alone.

At one point she came out of her dozing state and thought she saw two policemen standing at the end of her bed. She wasn't sure if they were actually present or not, but like Agatha Christie characters, gathered at the denouement of one of the great mystery writer's stories, their conversation conveniently filled in some details concerning her captors of which she hadn't been aware.

"Maybe it was before your time," one of the policemen was saying, "but that description she gave fits."

"No, I remember," the other replied. "They were residents in the Zeb's criminal ward and Cross killed their shrink during a power failure."

The first officer nodded. "I don't know which of them was worse: Cross with that monstrous face, or Boddeker."

"Poisoned her whole family, didn't she?"

"Yeah, but I remember seeing what Cross did to the shrink—just about tore the poor bastard in two."

"I heard that it was Boddeker who put him up to it. The poor geek doesn't have a mind of his own."

Vaguely, as though observing the action from a vast distance, Harriet could sense the first officer looking in her direction.

"She's lucky she's still alive," he added, looking back at his companion.

In the days that followed, researching old newspapers at the library, Harriet found out that all that the two men had said, or that she'd dreamed they had said, was true, but she couldn't absorb any of it at the moment. For now she just drifted away once more, entering a troubled sleep that was plagued with dreams of ghosts and monsters. The latter wore masks to hide the horror inside them, and they were the worst of all.

She woke much later, desperately needing to pee. It was still dark in her room. Outside she could hear the wind howling.

She fumbled her way into the bathroom and did her business, then stared into the mirror after she'd flushed. There was barely enough light for the mirror to show her reflection. What looked back at her from the glass was a ghostly face that she almost didn't recognize.

"Monsters," she said softly, not sure if what she felt was pity or fear, not sure if she recognized one in herself, or if it was just the old woman's lunatic calm still pointing an accusing finger.

She stared at that spectral reflection for a very long time before she finally went back to bed.

"We'll find you another," the old woman said.

Her tea had gone cold but she was too tired to relight the stove and make herself another cup. Her hands were folded on her lap, her gaze fixed on the tin can of cold water that still sat on the stove. A film of ice was forming on the water.

"You'll see," she added. "We'll find another, but this time we'll put her together ourselves, just the way your father did with you. We'll take a bit from one and a bit from another and we'll make you the perfect mate, just see if we don't. I always was a fair hand with a needle and thread, you know—a necessary quality for a wife in my time. Of course everything's different now, everything's changed. Sometimes I wonder why we bother to go on. . . ."

The monster stared out the window to where the snow still fell, quietly now, the blizzard having moved on, leaving only this calm memory of its storm winds in its wake. He gave no indication that he was listening to the old woman, but she went on talking all the same.

CARPE DIEM

Eileen Kernaghan

Eileen Kernaghan has lived in British Columbia all her life and operates a used bookstore in the Greater Vancouver area, Neville Books. She has published three fantasy novels, *Journey to Aprilioth*, *Songs from the Drowned Lands* (which won the Aurora Award—then called the Casper—in 1985), and *The Sarsen Witch*, and a book on reincarnation, all from Berkley Books in the U.S. She has also published speculative poetry and SF short stories in a number of Canadian magazines and anthologies, including *Ark of Ice* and the *Tesseracts* volumes.

"Carpe Diem" is from *Tesseracts*³.

"**I**'d better get going." Angela sweeps up hat, gloves, U-V shield, air monitor from the foot of Martha's bed. "Meditation class in half an hour." She is always in a hurry, even for these daily sessions that are supposed to slow her down, teach her to relax. Already, at thirty, there are faint stress-lines around her mouth. "See you in a week. Is there anything you need?" She hovers in the doorway, waiting for Martha to ask, as usual, for magazines, or shampoo, or dental floss.

Martha says, on a sudden crazy impulse, "Yes—a bottle of Bushmills." She enjoys seeing Angela's eyebrows go up, her mouth stiffen. "A great big one, a forty-ouncer, if you can still buy such a thing. Oh, and a carton of cigarettes."

Angela gives Martha a tight-lipped smile. She is annoyed, but indulgent—an adult dealing with a wilful two-year-old. Martha feels a quick stab of resentment. She is neither young enough nor old enough to be treated like this. Well, my girl, she thinks, you'll soon enough be in my shoes. When the time comes, all the exercise and clean living in the world won't save you from Assessment.

Angela has her hat on, and one glove. "I'll bring you some apple juice," she promises, predictably. "And you other ladies? Can I get you anything?"

Martha's roommates glance up—June from her knitting, Dorothy from the inevitable copy of *Christian Health*.

"Nothing for me, thank you." Dorothy places a faint but perceptible emphasis on the "thank." She has a high, nasal, vaguely British voice that sets Martha's nerves on edge.

Encouraged by Martha's small act of rebellion, June winks, and leers. "Well, dear, since you ask . . . how about something about six-foot-two, that looks good in tight jeans?"

There is an awkward silence. Angela, pretending not to have heard, zips up her other glove. Dorothy is sitting bolt upright, holding her magazine like a U-V shield in front of her face. Even Martha is uncomfortable. June always goes that fraction of an inch too far, stepping over the thin line between the risque and the merely vulgar. Her notoriety is spreading, on this and other floors. She flirts outrageously with male examiners, and is said to have called the head counsellor a silly cow.

"June is indiscreet," Dorothy has more than once remarked, in June's absence. Martha's mother, plainer-spoken, would have called her common.

When Angela is out of earshot, boots clicking briskly towards the elevator, June says, "She's a pretty girl, your daughter."

"Well, not my daughter, actually," Martha tells her. "My husband's daughter, by his first wife." She is not sure why she is bothering to explain the distinction. "My late husband," she adds. Widowed and childless, she thinks, with a sudden sick lurching of her heart. Things like that mattered, when it came to Assessment.

June says, "No offense, mind, but if that was my daughter I'd give her a good whack on the bum." Martha takes no offense. She knows exactly what June is talking about. She is fond of June—fond of her irreverence, her boisterous, good-natured vulgarity, her shameless defiance of the rules. June's own daughters—big, cheerful, loud-voiced, blonde women, younger versions of June—bring her candy bars, which she hides between the mattress and the springs. Martha hears the furtive rustling of the wrappers, late at night.

"What's the use of being alive," June wants to know, "when you have to give up everything that makes life worth living? A short life and a merry one, that's what my daddy used to say. Did I tell you about my dad? He was fifty-three when he passed on. His heart just plain gave out—and small wonder. Nearly three hundred pounds when he died, bacon and eggs every day, cream in his coffee, two packs of cigarettes, half a quart of whiskey after supper . . ."

Dorothy, turning a page of *Christian Health*, allows herself a ladylike snort. Martha hopes this unfortunate piece of family history has not been recorded in June's file.

"Mind you," says June cheerfully, "that wasn't what killed him. When he died he was drunk as a newt in bed with Sally Rogers from next door, who wasn't a day over eighteen."

Martha laughs. It's hard to stay depressed with June in the next bed. "Gather ye rosebuds while ye may," Martha says.

"Come again?"

"A poem. 'To the Virgins, to Make Much of Time.' By Herrick, I think—one of those fellows, anyway. Second-year English. It was a catch-phrase around our dorm." Martha closes her eyes, drawing the lines bit by bit out of the deep well of the past.

Gather ye rosebuds while ye may,
Old time is still a-flying:
And this same flower that smiles today,
Tomorrow will be dying . . .

She falters. "Damn. I wish I could remember the rest of it."

"Well, I never was much of a one for poetry," June says. "Though I didn't mind a Harlequin once in a while. But that, what you just said, makes good sense to me."

"It did to us, too," says Martha, remembering, with affection and astonishment, her eighteen-year-old self.

At three A.M. Martha wakes from an uneasy doze. She has not slept well since she came here; and tomorrow she faces a battery of tests. She tells herself there is no need to worry. She hasn't touched sweets for fifteen years, or butter, or cream, or cigarettes. Nor, in spite of her joke about the Bushmills, alcohol. Seven years ago she gave up meat. She is only slightly overweight—better than being underweight, according to her doctor, who keeps up on the latest studies. She walks everywhere, takes megavitamins, exercises, practises biofeedback and meditation, checks her blood pressure daily; is as scrupulous as Angela in the use of U-V shield and air monitor. There is, perhaps, a little breathlessness on the stairs; a trace of stiffness in her finger-joints. An occasional absent-mindedness. Normal enough, surely, for a woman of sixty. Nothing to worry about. Certainly nothing to warrant Reassignment.

Her throat is dry, and her heart is beating faster than it should. She repeats a mantra in her head. Health. Joy. Peace. Sleep. Other words, unsummoned, creep into her mind.

That age is best which is the first,
When youth and blood are warmer;
But being spent, the worse, and worst
Times still succeed the former.

She wants a drink. She wants a cigarette. She wants to get out of this place. Lying wide-eyed and fearful in the aseptic dark, she listens to the small mouse-like rustle of candy wrappers.

Martha lies back on her pillows, staring at the posters on the opposite wall. They remind her of the samplers in her grandmother's drawing room. "Healthiness is Next to Godliness." "A Healthy Mind in a Healthy Body." "A Megavitamin a Day Keeps the Doctor Away." She is exhausted by the daylong pokings and proddings and pryings, the sometimes painful and frequently embarrassing invasions of her person. She admires, without daring to imitate, June's cheerful rudeness to counsellors and examiners; her steadfast refusal to co-operate. Only Dorothy seems unaffected by the tests. She wears the smug and slightly relieved look of a schoolgirl who knows she has done well on her math final.

June turns on the TV. Martha realizes, with some surprise, that it is New Year's Eve. A pair of talking heads are discussing the Year 2000. With the end of the millennium only twelve months away, the media are obsessed with predictions, retrospectives. It is hard for Martha to imagine what may lie around that thousand-year corner. She finds it odd—and in a curious way exciting—that by a mere accident of birth she may live to see the next millennium.

"The biggest New Year's Party in a thousand years," says June, when the commercial comes on. Her voice is wistful. "I always did like a good party."

Martha smiles at her, remembering that she was fond of parties too, when she was younger. There seems so little point in them now.

"Perhaps," she says, "we will be allowed a glass of champagne."

June chuckles. "Maybe one small glass. The last for a thousand years."

That's enough to set them off. They take turns describing what they will eat and drink on the Eve of the Millennium—a stream-of-consciousness recitation of forbidden delights.

"Chocolate mints," says June. "Pecan pie. Truffles."

"Amaretto cheesecake," Martha adds. "Christmas pudding with rum sauce. Tawny port."

Pointedly, Dorothy puts on her earphones. Martha and June, caught up in their game, ignore her.

"Fish and chips. Bangers and mash." "Guinness stout. Roast suckling pig." "Crab croquettes and oyster stew."

It's so long since Martha has eaten anything unwholesome, she has to stop and think. "Sour cream and hot mango chutney." Then—an inspiration—"Sex-in-the-Pan."

"Sex in anything," says June, and howls with laughter.

Dorothy seems to take their foolishness as a personal affront. Lips pressed into a thin line, she thumbs rapidly through a fresh copy of *Christian Health*.

They sit up to see the New Year in, and afterwards Martha sleeps soundly, even though there are tests scheduled for the morning. These ones don't sound too awful. Blood-sugar again, cholesterol check, an eye and ear exam; and—absurdly, it seems to Martha—tests for the various sorts of social diseases.

Still, she is awake hours before the first robots rumble down the hall with breakfast. She knows, instantly, that something is wrong. She sits up, switches on her overhead light. In the far bed, Dorothy is heavily asleep. The other bed, June's bed, is empty.

The bathroom, Martha thinks; but no, the door is ajar and the light is out. Could June have been taken ill in the night? A sudden heart attack, like her father? Has Martha somehow slept through lights, buzzers, running feet, the clatter of emergency equipment? But when that happens, don't they always draw the bed curtains?

Dorothy is awake. "Where's June?" she asks immediately, smelling trouble.

Martha shakes her head. She feels on the edge of panic. Should she push her bell? Call for a counsellor? Go out and search the corridors?

And then suddenly June is back, waltzing into the room in boots, hat, coat, humming gently to herself. The cloud of cheap perfume that surrounds her is not strong enough to drown the smell of liquor.

"June, where have you been?" Martha realizes, to her dismay, that she sounds like a mother interrogating a wayward teen-aged daughter.

June grins and pulls off her toque. "Should old acquaintance be forgot," she sings, "and never brought to mind . . . I went to a New Year's party."

Dorothy gives a snort of disbelief. "How could you have gotten out of the building?"

"Who was to stop me? Only robots on night shift, and one duty counsellor. Only reason nobody walks out of here, is nobody thinks to try."

She flops across her bed, arms outflung, short skirt riding up over pale plump knees. After a moment she sits up and tries, unsuccessfully, to pull off her boots. "Oh, shit, Martha, can you give me a hand?"

She slides down on the mattress so that both feet are dangling over the edge. Kneeling on the cold tiles at June's feet, Martha takes hold of the left boot and tugs hard. It's a frivolous boot—spike-heeled, fur-cuffed, too tight in the calf. Dorothy watches in outraged silence.

Martha rocks back on her heels as the boot comes off with a sudden jerk. She hears June give a small, contented sigh.

"Oh, Christ, Martha, what a ball I had! There's this little club on Davie . . . I wish you'd been there too, there were these two guys . . ." June sighs again, as the other boot comes off. "But I knew you wouldn't come, there was no use asking, you're too afraid of old creepin' Jesus, there . . ."

Dorothy, white-faced with fury, stalks into the bathroom and slams the door.

"June, what did you do?" Martha hears her voice rising, querulously; and thinks, I sound like my mother did; I sound like an old woman.

"Christ, honey, what didn't I do? I drank. I ate. I danced. I smoked." Her s's are starting to slur. She rolls over, luxuriously, and adds something else which is muffled by her pillow.

"I beg your pardon?" Martha asks.

June sits up. Loudly enough to be heard at the end of the hall, she announces, "I even got laid."

"Shhh," Martha says, instinctively. Then, "June, how could you? All the tests we have to take today—blood sugar, cholesterol . . ."

"AIDS," says Dorothy grimly, through the bathroom door.

"Oh, June. Oh, my dear." Martha is just now beginning to realize the enormity of what June has done.

There are footsteps in the corridor as the dayshift arrives. Martha feels like crying. Instead, she searches through June's bedside drawer for comb, make-up, mouthwash; and silently unbuttons June's coat.

On Wednesday the test results are announced. One at a time they are called to the Chief Examiner's office for their reports. Dorothy returns, smug-faced and unsurprised, and puts on her street clothes. Martha's name is called. Sick and faint with anxiety, she makes her way through the maze of corridors. She has passed, but with a warning.

June is gone for a long time. "I thought from the first," Dorothy remarks, as she waits for the Chief Examiner to sign her out, "that June lacked any sense of self-respect."

Martha doesn't often bother to contradict Dorothy's pronouncements, but this time it seems important to set the record straight. "You don't mean self-respect," she says. "You mean self-preservation."

Then the door opens, and June comes in. She has applied her blusher and lipstick with a heavy hand; the bright patches of red look garish as poster-paint against the chalk-white of her skin. She stares blankly at Martha as though she has forgotten where she is. Gently, Martha touches her arm.

"June? What did they say?"

"Nothing I didn't already know." June's voice shakes a little, but her tone is matter-of-fact. "Sugar in the blood—incipient diabetes. Gross overweight. High cholesterol count. Hypertension. Just what you'd expect."

"They can treat all those things. They don't have to Reassign you."

June shrugs. "Not worth it, they say. Bad personal history. And there's my pa."

"Quite right," says Dorothy. How Martha has learned to loathe that prim, self-congratulatory voice. "If people won't take responsibility for their own health . . ."

"Better to get it over with," June says. "It'd be no fun at all, hanging around for Reassessment."

And then—awkwardly, and oddly, as though it is Martha who is in need of comfort—she pats Martha's shoulder. "Never mind, Martha, love, that was a hell of a good party the other night. And there's something I want you to remember, when your time comes. Once you know for sure, once you make up your mind to it, then you can spit in their eye, because there's bugger-all more they can do to you."

Dorothy pins her hat on her grey curls and leaves. Martha's papers are signed; she could go too, if she wished, but she has decided to stay with June. She knows she won't have to wait long.

Soon they hear the hum of trolley-wheels at the end of the hall. Martha holds June's hand.

"Listen, the news isn't all bad," June says, with gallows humour. "The kidneys are still okay, and the lungs, and a few other odd bits. There's quite a lot they can Reassign. Maybe to some pretty young girl. I like that idea a lot."

Then the trolley is wheeled in.

"A short life and a merry one," says June. She winces slightly as the counsellor slips the needle into her arm. "Remember to drink a glass of bubbly for me, at the big party."

Martha nods, and squeezes June's hand as June slides away.

Esther Rochon

Translated by Lucille Nelson

Esther Rochon lives in Montreal and turned to writing after studying mathematics. Her first SF novel, *En hommage aux araignées* (1974), is in fact the second novel of a trilogy, the first volume of which has been published only in German as *Der Träumer in der Zitadelle* (1977). She became a major figure in francophone Canadian SF and has three times won the Grand Prix de la Science-fiction et du Fantastique (for *L'Épuisement du soleil* [1985], *Coquillage* [1986], and *L'Espace du diamant* [1990]). The last of these books, her fifth novel, completed her trilogy. Her collection of short fiction, *Le Traversier*, was published in 1987.

David Ketterer, in his *Canadian Science Fiction and Fantasy*, says, "it was *Coquillage* (which also won a Prix Boréal [translated as *The Shell*, 1990]) that first gained Rochon mainstream attention. This extraordinary SF fable, which describes how a man and his son become intimately involved in a tortured love affair with a monster, a shellfishlike alien, achieves a most effective ambivalence of desire and repugnance." He goes on to say, "Influenced by her interest in Eastern religions and philosophies, Rochon's work is further characterized by a musical tone, irony, a clear vision of evil, and an astonishing ability to find the beautiful."

Clearly, Rochon works for the most part independent of the traditions of American SF. Her work is poetic, fantastic, on the border between fantasy and SF in a manner very different from the speculative fiction of her anglophone Canadian peers.

Walking in the dirty slush along the half-cleared sidewalks of Côte des Neiges Road, a string of Xils flickering around me, some as high as skyscrapers, I ask myself what people think of us as they inch along in rush hour traffic. They've rolled up their windows, afraid a ravenous Xil will shoot out a sucker to siphon off their blood. And they're right. Anyway, it's the law. Every so often you see signs that read "Passage de Xils/Xils Crossing," with a skull and crossbones underneath. In the area around Forest Hill, which has fallen on hard times, the few inhabitants only go out in cars or body suits.

Because I am a Guardian I have no protection.

When I was a girl, no one lived in Montreal, which for years had been a Xil hunting ground. Then, as they still do, they played around in the marshes of the Town of Mount Royal, flashing between this world and another perhaps slightly more their own. They killed the people in the city when they arrived, except those who fled (what traffic tie-ups on the bridges!). I lived on the back river with my parents, in one of the hastily constructed refugee camps. I went to school in Saint-Eustache.

From time to time a helicopter would fly over Montreal, nostalgically surveying the abandoned city infested with derisive and blood-thirsty Xils. No one knew how to begin living there again. Many tried, since the resources of the metropolis were essential to the province's economy. It was only when the Xils attacked New York that a way was found: there people were more resourceful; the situation didn't get out of hand. Body suits were invented. They noticed that the Xils never went into houses where the doors and windows were tightly closed; it was as though Xils didn't perceive interiors. They shared their discovery with us since our economic interests are off-shoots of theirs. The army, well protected, went into Montreal to clean up the streets and prepare the return of the exiles, while the factories started manufacturing body suits. My parents were glad to come back to the Island, even though their neighbourhood—Hochelaga-Maisonneuve—had been declared uninhabitable. After our return I went walking around there. The officials refused to let it be renovated, probably because it's such a nice area. They preferred to pile people on top of each other in large buildings where the anti-Xils and anti-asocial controls were easier to enforce. Whatever the reasons, we set up camp in Place Ville Marie, in huge old office buildings lit by fluorescent lights.

You could spend weeks without going outside: schools, stores, work, everything was located in the same gigantic building. Occasionally a horde of Xils would materialize on Dorchester Boulevard, right under our windows; some looked like dinosaurs, others like spaghetti. They flickered to change shape; that's how they swallowed people up. I admired them and at the same time found them stupid. I was ten years old.

Later, by myself, I started to go out. The body suit was comfortable, especially in winter. Walking: in the sleet, among the Xils. I went as far as the port, afraid of being raped by men as well as being attacked by Xils. Even so I left the body suit open. But nothing happened to me; my fears weren't realized. I went to the port, to the edge of the river the Xils wouldn't cross: were they afraid of open spaces? Once, I crossed over by way of the Jacques Cartier bridge. How glad I was to be on the other side. I was expected in Montreal so I went back, stopping halfway to put on my helmet. A herd of Xils had gathered at the beginning of the bridge. Every year they were getting more stupid. The cars honked. The Xils, like dumb animals, stayed on the ramp and the middle of the median, waving their hands about (those that had them) or playing in the litter. Furious, a woman got out of her car to insult them. They moved away from her. I couldn't get over it: she had no protection and they hadn't killed her.

A while later the Guardian Organization started and I joined up. We don't wear body suits. That way it's easier for the Xils to pick us out. It's somewhat dangerous; there are accidents. It attracts loners. Soon I'll be twenty-five years old. I've been a Guardian for six years and I've never been hurt. It's a question of paying attention, using the whistle or, if necessary, the whip.

As a teenager I despised both the Xils and those who feared them. I haven't changed much. As I walk along Côte des Neiges Road, on my left, in their cars, are the despised people; on my right, flickering wildly, the equally despised Xils. Ill-tempered, I protect them from each other, perpetuating a petty world of bureaucrats and secretaries. So the expansive recklessness of the Xils does not mix with the narrowness of people. So the intelligence of people does not mix with the stupidity of Xils. I am a Guardian. I am paid to prevent contact. So Xils and people can coexist without knowing each other. How trivial.

I like to walk. Montreal weather agrees with me. That's what led me to take this job. I blow on the whistle a few times to keep a large pink Xil shaped like a balsam pine from going among the cars. They obey me because they know I'll feed them. My body would give them only a little food; by following me, obeying me, they can get much more, every day. Stupid, yes, but not so stupid they don't know what's in their own best interest.

They change shape too much; I never recognize them. I don't know how many there are altogether. Perhaps they are all part of a single being, who enters our world in several different places, just as my fingers easily penetrate the water in a bowl. This being undoubtedly pays little attention to the activities of its body-parts immersed in our world. One can imagine it chatting with its neighbour: what we see as Xils, shapechangers, in continual motion, are in reality the hairs on its leg, voracious ones in this species. Or those of its genitals. Now there's a thought, to screw this evening.

My Xils are like kids in daycare who, lost in daydreams, blindly follow their daydreaming monitor. People daydream in the traffic jam beside me. Côte des Neiges daydreams.

Good thing the day's winding up. I put my Xils out to pasture in the cliff-side field near Guy, where the autoroute meets up with Dorchester Boulevard. Nice spot. It was clear, you could see as far as the United States. Some took to the air. Every so often they like music. A group gathered around a transistor radio that I stuck in the snow. From my chilly little hut I looked over my band of loafers: idle Xils that have lost their ferocity. I guard them, just in case. Two or three were dancing.

There are other Guardians in Montreal, one for each neighbourhood. We have a union. We're poorly paid, so we're mostly women. I doubt the people in the cars have more interesting jobs. A city of civil servants, kept in place by bogeymen: Xils, bosses, and various fears parrotted by the media. Inane. Each weekend we make up love stories, or literary squabbles, or something else, to convince ourselves we exist: "I'm hurt," "I'm angry," and so on. My secretary friends spend their paychecks on clothes. I don't expect that one day the world will get more real. Daydreams, complaints; if my reality is not here, where is it?

At the entrance to the cemetery I turn right. Some of the Xils give little sharp cries; they spread out in the empty space in front of the graves. They know the road. A protective belt of old willows will soon screen us from the traffic.

Other Xils, led by other Guardians, join us. We meet in front of a building dominated by a cement cross, on the hillside, and we wait, shivering. A few humans surrounded by a crowd of Xils. Music plays. Snow and electric guitar. The Xils dance, lighting up in the dusk. Below in the main arteries of Côte des Neiges rush hour is ending.

Seven o'clock. The doors of the old crematorium open. The corpses from the day, on stretchers, are rolled outside. For Xils, like people, it's time for supper. But not for Guardians.

I go home while the first Xils, satiated, fall asleep, fly away or disappear. I live nearby, in Rockhill. I'll make myself some chicken soup.

A long time ago, in books, on the radio and in school, people talked about our greatness, the dignity of Man. I have even read authors who found something noble in the situation of people here. It's flattering, but it's not what I've seen. Xil or human, I know no one worthy of respect. Perhaps we would inspire it if we could learn how to do it. I would like that, but it's impossible. I live on an island of pettiness. Wind and snow make me dream of heroism. They are awe-inspiring. Not me. But sometimes . . .

In a little bit (why not?) I'll dress up like a secretary; I'll put on an outfit that pleases me: tragic colours and scarves that float in the wind. I'll go to the Xils, alone in the middle of the night. I'll wake up one or two if possible, offer them sunflower seeds or french fries, like squirrels. Or perhaps some wine. It's about time we hung out together. They, like Montreal, are beautiful. Some have webbed feet, others look like needles that have just been threaded.

I'll wear my purple coat. They will flicker in violet and bright red. At night, in the winter, the sky is pink. The snow in the cemetery is sprinkled with ashes from the office-tower incinerators, forever burning our mountains of garbage. If the Xils don't recognize me and take fright, my blood will be one more bright colour in the landscape, my body will be their sustenance. The crows returning from the south will join them in the dawn. I think however they will know who I am, that at least, if we can't talk, we can be beautiful together.

STOLEN FIRES

Yves Meynard

Yves Meynard, like Jean-Louis Trudel and Élisabeth Vonarburg, is a well-known ambassador for francophone SF at conventions across Canada and in the United States. He lives just south of Montreal in Longueuil, and has recently completed a Ph.D. in Computer Science.

Since 1986 he has published more than twenty-five SF stories in French and English, mostly in the magazines *Solaris* and *imagine.* . . . He was one of the three finalists for the 1992 Grand Prix de la Science-Fiction et du Fantastique Québécois, and he was the winner of the 1993 Grand Prix, for the entirety of his published work in 1993. His novella, "L'Enfant des Mondes Assoupis" ("Child of the Sleeping World"), won the 1992 Aurora Award for best short work in French. The short story "Convoyeur d'âmes" ("Soul-carrier") won the 1993 Boréal Award. He was coeditor, with Claude J. Pelletier of Ianus Publications, of the original SF anthology *Sous des soleils étrangers* and of two books by Daniel Sernine (the two-volume collection of Sernine's Carnival sequence, which includes the story in this book).

In either language, his fiction typifies a tendency in Québécois SF towards lyricism and extended metaphor, verging on allegory.

"Stolen Fires" was originally written for Glenn Grant's magazine, *Edge Detector*.

Rails have been set to cincture the world, east to west to east, along the equatorial lowlands. There are many other lines, in all directions. Only this one runs forever, looping back upon itself.

On the rails, in the middle of the region the toponymists have named New Caucasus, a train is running, in the direction of Sternstadt, the hub of the network. The train is several hundred cars long: from one end of it you can barely see the other.

Its locomotive is a screaming woman. Steel hair sweeps back from her steel eyes; steel arms piston at her sides; her gaping steel mouth howls as it devours the thick air.

She roars over the rails at a terrific pace. It is as if she wanted to outrace the setting sun; indeed, she nearly does. The already sluggish passage of the World's furnace through the heavens is slowed fourfold: sunsets last more than a full workshift.

Apart from the steel woman, who may or may not count, there is only one living being aboard the train: a man, who spends the voyages in the control cabin built at the back of the locomotive, where the organic lines of her body flow into rectangular contours. For long Hours, the man works, checking and rechecking the status of the energy systems, feeding the furnace the fuel it demands, wiping the glass dials clean with a moistened cloth. One Hour in every four he may rest. At those times, he usually sits quietly and drinks vodka, which is allowed so long as it is not done to excess. The man needs very little sleep. Also, he has no name. The former is essentially a consequence of the latter.

Wasps and vipers, fangs and stings, the bite of alcohol after a long Day's work. For this Hour, the man without a name sits atop the metacoal tender and watches the angels fly alongside the train.

Why they do it he does not know. Every voyage, as soon as he has left Sternstadt behind the horizon, they appear. Where they come from he cannot tell. It is almost as if they were escorting him. Their stiff wings beat rapidly, but they fail to keep pace with the train's progress.

The man enjoys watching them. He knows they do no harm. He feels a touch of pity for them, of embarrassment for the grueling pace he sets. Sometimes he toys with the idea of slowing down the train, if only for a brief while, so that they will be able to keep up with it. Perhaps they would appreciate his kindness, he tells himself. But he never entertains this thought for long: after a short time, he begins to feel pain in his head, and busies himself with the locomotive to make the ache stop.

He has, after all, a schedule to maintain; how could he think of running late?

The man chases away that idea and returns to his contemplation of the angels. One of them is very close, indeed closer than he has ever seen one come. It is a large male, full of the strength and temerity of all young men. It is actually flying faster than the train is running. It advances (for all its speed, it seems almost to crawl), flying low above the wagons. It is so very close . . . It has reached the edge of the tender! The man stares in disbelief as the angel grasps the rail with its hands and feet, and climbs aboard.

The man without a name is stunned. He eases down from the pile of golden-red metacoal, approaches the angel. He is careful and slow, not wanting to scare it away. But the angel does not seem timid; it remains immobile, only its thin chest heaving with breath, as it watches the man (its eyes are entirely black, with a smoky gleam in them from the sun).

The man is close to the angel now. He marvels silently at its face, whose incredibly falcate nose and deep wrinkles belong to a fairy-tale crone; at the mating-hooks protruding from its haunches; at the design on its chest, a set of whitish lines on the blue scales, like a ritual scar: a tilted lemniscate struck by a broken diagonal.

The angel still watches the man, without a quiver, or a sign of fear; it runs the long fingers of one hand through its mop of feathery hair (all six of its digits have four joints). And then it speaks.

—Are you a man of words?

The man's jaw goes slack. He had never thought that angels could talk—although perhaps, once, someone he only dimly recalls might have told him something about it; but certainly he never believed.

—I look for a man of words, says the angel. I will hear a story. Tell me a story, Other (its voice is like the wind whistling through the branches of the hag-pines that line the railway).

A story? The request is even more surprising than the fact of the angel speaking.

—What . . . which story do you mean? the man says stupidly.

As he speaks, the man without a name feels a slight ache in his brain. Then he stands quite still, and tells himself—clearly, in words that echo loudly through his head—that this is the end of his shift, that he has a full Hour to himself, that nothing he does hurts the Company in any way. And after a moment the pain goes away, like water drunk by a patch of dry sand—diffused, but still wholly there, under the surface.

—A story, any story, the angel has been saying with apparent urgency. Tell me a story, Other.

The man hesitates; but the request is not for something forbidden, and he does not wish to refuse if it means the angel will go away. So he nods slowly, sits down amidst the nuggets of metacoal. The angel smiles as if with relief (its teeth are thin, numerous, and pointed) and sits likewise. It folds its stiff butterfly wings so that they offer as little surface to the wind as possible. Were it to deploy them fully, thinks the nameless man, the wind of their passage would propel the angel backwards and away in an instant.

Now the man thinks of asking a price for the storytelling. But what could the angel give him—and what does he need that the Company does not provide? He cannot even ask for an exchange of names, lacking one of his own. So, somewhat gracelessly, he begins:

—This is a story from long ago. I heard it from someone on the railway, I think. I don't remember when.

The angel hunches its head forward on its long neck and clutches a nugget of metacoal in its spidery hands. The man without a name begins his tale.

THE TALE OF THE YOUNG MAN AND HIS LOVE

Not long after the Company came to the world, there was a young man who lived in one of the cities of the plain.

In those Days, the mantle of the World still had holes in it: there were many places in the World which would poison you if you went there un-protected. The young man's father was a monitor: his duty was to check the poisoned places, to gather data for the life-weavers, those who planned the mantle's growth, its slow conquest by assimilation. The young man's mother had been one of the life-weavers. She had died many years back, from a native illness that had escaped from the glass tubes where she had been studying it.

The young man went to school at a lyceum of high repute in Sternstadt, thousands of kilometers away from his home, so that he could rarely return home. Before his mother's death, the young man had looked forward to those infrequent visits; too much so he felt. When he became an adult, he might be called on to leave his home for a new one halfway across the world; and so strong ties were discouraged by the Company.

But now he feared his return home, for after his mother's death, his father had grown slowly but thoroughly insane. In all ways now he acted as if his wife had never died, and this terrified the young man, who began to find excuses not to come. After a while, he realized that his father did not need any justification from him for his absences, and he ceased to bother. And in some way that was worse than all of his father's madness.

Now when the young man was twenty, a year away from the Employment Examinations, he fell in love. It isn't very surprising that his love was the exact opposite of his father's. His mother had been a quiet and dependable woman, and his father's love for her a quiet and dependable thing. The young man fell in love with a vain young woman whose future as an Employee was doubtful; he quarrelled with her all the time, only to make up in tears before the Day was half-done.

In his own painful way, he was probably happy.

Not long after he met the young woman, the young man began to neglect his studies. The Day of the Examination approached, and he failed to prepare properly: he scored less than ever before. His mentors warned him as sternly as they could; but he did not listen. In desperation the mentors tried to call the young man's father, to make him talk sense into his son; but he was away on a mission.

He never came back.

His body was found in one of the poisonous areas, not far from his lifter. A spine from a needlegaunt had struck though a fault in his xenosuit's fabric: the venom had killed him in an instant.

Everyone was sad at the news: the young man's father had been a good Employee, even after his wife's death. Everyone thought there would be a full funeral, as always for those Employees who die in the line of duty. But the investigation revealed that the damage to the fabric had been deliberate. The death was ruled to be a suicide. The young man's father was cremated and all his wealth reverted to the Company, as its laws said it must. It was also decreed that his name would not be written on the Pioneer's Monument.

Something happened to the young man then, like the phase-shift that announces a fusion engine has gone into self-generating mode. All of a sudden, he returned to his studies. He did not seem to be making any special efforts, but at the Examination, his marks were the highest the lyceum had seen in a generation.

He was admitted into the ranks of the Employees, but this was not the end of his rise. One of his few friends said his intelligence had "bloomed like a flame" and now he would have said it wanted to devour the whole world of knowledge. The young man took the most demanding courses, and passed them easily; he made several brilliant suggestions on the research problems where he was put as an assistant; in his spare time, he designed improved life-weaving machines.

They called him a genius. The Company put him on the Planetology program, with the master planners for the development of the World. No one else had ever achieved those ranks so young; his reputation was made, his wealth was assured. The stigma of his father's madness and death had been washed from him.

The one thing that reflected poorly on him was his continuing relationship with the frivolous young woman: as anyone would have foretold, she had failed to become an Employee. She was immensely below his status, yet he remained with her, despite their incessant quarrels. His money supported her. And after all, it was a minor thing: geniuses are allowed to be eccentric, and some people said it reflected well on him, to be supporting a young woman who otherwise would have been drafted into the Reproduction Corps.

So the young man was set for the future, and *his* name was certain to be carved deep on the Monument. No one could have foretold what was to happen.

The young man was right at the peak of his career; he was involved in nearly every project at the highest level, which meant he knew many of the secrets of the Company. That was when he rebelled. He had never forgiven the Company for its ruling on his father's death; and now he intended to make war on it.

With his wealth, he had built a hidden castle in the mountains, where no one could find him; he fled to it in a stolen flier, along with tons of equipment. The young woman went along with him.

From the castle, he waged war with the Company. In all the places he had worked, he had left software-bombs to irretrievably destroy data, or mechanical ones that would wreck priceless experiments, if not entire laboratories. But he didn't stop there. He blew up the rail network that linked the cities. He introduced chaos into the computers that controlled the automated outposts. He had even brought genetic equipment with him, and with it he tried to undo the efforts of the life-weavers, by adapting the local life to compete with Man-life, by creating diseases to attack the plants, and microorganisms that changed the atmosphere back to what it had been.

For years he fought his war; he did terrible damage to the Company, and they could not stop him. But then something else happened that hadn't been foretold. The young woman fell sick. It was a sickness the young man couldn't cure. Only the Company could heal her.

And so he communicated with the Company. He made a deal with it: if it saved his love, he would stop his war and give himself up.

The Company agreed; and its word was binding. It saved the young man's love in the way that only it could have saved her; so the young man surrendered.

He thought the Company would punish him by killing him, but the Company could not take his life. Instead, it forgave him: it took him back as an Employee, and the young woman as well.

And they lived happily ever after.

The man falls silent. The angel watches him fixedly, the lump of metacoal still held tightly in its hands. Feeling a sudden spasm of unreasoned fear— water moistening the surface of the sand—the man rises to his feet, goes forward to check on the locomotive.

But all is well. In the depths of the furnace, the metacoal nuggets catalyze the cool fusion of light nuclei; as they become exhausted, they disaggregate and fall to a fine powder that is evacuated and dispersed beneath the engine, coating the rails as with gold dust. The hopper is full, the reaction temperature squarely within the green portion of the alarm spectrum, the cybersystem murmurs softly "all is well." The nameless man is not needed; he is still on his Hour-long break. The sun will not set for a long time yet.

He returns to the tender. To his surprise, the angel is still there. Dimly the man feels there may yet be something to be accomplished. What more does the angel expect?

—Now I will tell you a story, Other, says the angel. (Its face is set in a strange expression that might be sadness, or even grief.)

The man settles down uncomfortably. He does not think he wants to hear a story. He thinks of telling the angel this, but holds his tongue. He realizes that the angel is not paying him back, but rather that he is bound to listen to its tale, that *he* is the one making the payment.

THE TALE OF THE ANGEL

Some of us were present when the Others first came to Earth, in ships of metal that flew without wings. We were puzzled, and somewhat afraid. A few conquered their fear and went to observe more closely, perhaps to speak with the Others, if they should know how to speak.

Those were captured and put in cages. The Others did not listen to their talk, they only talked amongst themselves, and then they cut their prisoners with metal knives and wounded them with needles. Later, our captive brethren escaped; when they bore their tale to the rest of us, it was decided never to approach the Others again.

At first we thought it would be easy; but the Others grew in numbers, as more and more dropped down from the sky; and they built castles of metal and surrounded them with gardens under glass.

And soon something strange happened: the land around the castles of the Others became poisonous. Plants withered, animals died, and when we ventured there, we could not breathe the air for long.

What could we do to change things? There was nothing that could be done to the metal and glass of the men. So we retreated to the high mountains, where the air was thin, but still pure. And from the mountaintops we watched the Others spread onto the world like a bloodstain.

One day a ship without wings came to one of the mountains where we lived. Many were afraid and said this was the end, the Others had come to take us all and cut us apart with their metal. Many said nothing but gathered up their hunting bows and their best blades.

The ship was not so large as the first ones we had seen. It landed on a plateau and a door opened in its side, like a hut's. An Other walked out, and it was naked. Several of us had come out of their caves and they now pointed their bows at it and drew.

The Other looked them in the eye, calmly. Then it spoke. It said, in the male mode, What do you want with those weapons? Please do not harm me. Do you speak?

Later we understood he did not know the meaning of the words he had spoken. He had merely repeated the sounds one of our captive brethren had made when he had tried speaking with the Others who were about to cut them. Thus we would know he was the Prophet.

We began to talk with him. He pointed at himself and gave his name, which is too holy to repeat. We gave him our own names, and then he made a gesture and a second Other came out of the ship. She was his mate. And thus it all began. It proceeded slowly, but we had all of Time.

Eventually we understood one another. The Prophet told us why the Others were the Enemy. He explained how the poisoning would one day kill all of us. He said he had come to teach us the Other's magic, if we would learn it. That this way we could fight them. He used a word: sabotage. He said that the castles were fragile, that the metal way for trains could be destroyed, that we could regain our land one day.

We knew that he was holy, for nothing he said made sense, and at the same time, we felt it was deeply true. So we let him live and began to learn from him.

It took years. He taught us better ways to count, and to measure distances, and so many other things our souls could not hold them all. Every day, he taught us. He filled us with the magic of the Others, and when we were full, we started the war.

What we liked best was to make bombs, to place them next to the castles or the rails, and to make them explode. Soon the Others installed weapons that threw bullets at us, but they could not protect all the rails, and where they were not protected we destroyed them easily.

Careful as we were, many of us were injured by the Others' defenses, and some died. So we began to make young again, to readjust our numbers.

One day the Prophet went to witness one of our young being made into an adult. When we performed the Time rite, he inquired what we did.

We answered, We do not know how the Others do it, but this is how we make her undying.

He repeated, Undying? But all things grow old and die.

At this we were stunned. But *we* do not, we said. Don't the Others know how to work that magic?

He had us explain. We showed him our magic, how we changed a person's twin fires with our souls, how we made them keep always in balance, neither one devouring the other. He was amazed. He named our magic *psychokinesis*. He demanded that we prove our claims.

So we did. We showed him how we could make a leaf wither with our souls, driving one of its fires hard and repressing the other. We showed him the rock mice, how by reaching with our souls we could make them die or live longer, although it demanded more effort and more care, as they were very different from us.

The Prophet went away into the ship by himself then, even his mate could not speak to him. When he came out, he began to explain more things to us. The way stuff is made of tiny balls and how our souls made them shake, and how the shaking changed the fires in ourselves. And when he was sure we understood as much as we could, he asked us to make him eternal.

We were very worried that it might not work; but he had showed us many things that explained how the Others were different from us, and so those whose souls were strongest among us gathered and performed the rite of Time.

It worked. After it was done, the Prophet looked inside himself with the machines he had brought and said he would live forever.

At this his mate grew frightened; she said things to him in their language, which many of us spoke by that time. She accused him of leaving her to die, and many other things. He answered he did not want her to be exposed to the risk, because he did not want to be parted from her. He was holy: what he said was both very right and very wrong.

In the end he did the only thing he could do, and our wise ones performed the rite on the Prophet's wife.

But with her, it failed. There are little strings in the middle of the cells, where life resides. The strings of the Wife's cells were unravelling, falling apart into little bits. It was a thing that sometimes happens with our kind: we call it the Rot. Once it starts the only merciful thing to do is to destroy the affected one. But the Prophet would not lose his wife. He used all the magic he had, but he could not stop the unravelling.

So, in desperation, he went inside the ship, and spoke to the Enemy to bargain with them. He would give himself up to them, forever end his war, if they agreed to save his mate. The Enemy swore to the compact.

I remember how it was just before he left us. He held his Wife in his arms as he carried her inside the wingless ship. She was white as snow; her flesh was coming loose in clumps. He took her inside, then he came back to speak to us. His words made no sense, and too much. His eyes leaked water as he spoke. He asked us to forgive him, as if he had done something wrong. And to continue the war, never to stop. And then he spoke of a future when we would live at peace with the Enemy, a time which he had seen inside his soul. And then he stopped suddenly, and retreated inside the flyer, took off and went to the Enemy.

He was very holy.

The Enemy was true to their word. They had promised they would save his mate; but the Rot was too far upon her, her body's destruction could not be halted. So they worked their magic, and took her soul and put it into a metal box.

And then they took their full vengeance on the Prophet. They did not kill him; instead, they opened his head and maimed his brain, to shackle his soul. They made him their slave, and put him in charge of running the trains that we used to sabotage, because they knew we could not destroy the tracks that he would be crossing.

And so they think they will win. But they will not. We fight on. We will not stop. *We will live forever.* He will live forever. We wait for him. He will come back to us. We have all of Time.

The nameless man stares at the angel. He does not understand the story. But he knows that he should not have listened to it. All the pain that he had held dispersed under the sand is bubbling to the surface.

He puts his hands to his head. His eyes are full of tears. He staggers away from the angel, going to the control cabin, going to his duties, going to make the pain stop.

He hears the great stiff wings being deployed behind him; as the angel is swept away by the wind of their passing, it shrieks, like someone dying in pain.

The nameless man stumbles into the cabin. He turns to the meters and gauges, checks and rechecks every one, performs a hundred minute adjustments by hand. The pain is slowly loosing its hold on him as he drowns in his work. The man flops the switch that allows communication with the cybersystem.

—Increase speed, he tells it. I want maximum!

—Understood and complying, the cybersystem replies in a toneless voice.

He opens the hatch to the hopper and shovels metacoal inside until the hopper is brimming. He shuts the hatch, checks the meters again, attentive to the slow movements of the needles, the flickering of the blue digits, as the train gathers yet more speed. Through a window he sees the steel arms become a blur of motion. The howl of the wind gathered inside the mouth rises to a near-shriek.

Night has fallen. The pain has left him now. He cannot clearly remember what caused it—perhaps he fell asleep on his break and neglected his tasks. That cannot be allowed. He must never run late. He has a duty to the Company.

The cybersystem indicates all is well. The nameless man goes out into the night, to breathe cooler air. He sits down on a small gray-painted metal seat. He reaches for the bottle and takes a slug of vodka, stoking the furnace of his body. He absently scratches the scar that cinctures his skull, left to right to left. On the horizon, the hard pinpricks of light of Sternstadt have become visible. The train roars on; the woman who is the locomotive swallows the night with her screaming mouth.

RETRIEVAL

John Park

John Park moved from England to Vancouver in 1970 as a graduate student and in 1976 published his first SF story professionally, in *Galaxy*. In 1978 he attended the Clarion SF writers' workshop in Michigan and later that year moved to Ottawa, where he has become a partner in a scientific consulting firm. His SF career to date includes only six stories, three of them in *Tesseract* anthologies, and three of them in the 1990's, which bids fair to be his most productive decade as a writer.

"Retrieval" is reprinted from *Tesseracts* [2].

Outside, they were playing cricket on Stockhausen Square. In his office on the second floor of the gutted museum, the man with the burned face pushed aside the battered electronic device he had been examining and turned to watch. The square was surfaced with gravel, except for a patch of earth in which a black, leafless poplar stood at deep midwicket. The man could remember the tree dying, long after everything had collapsed, its leaves streaming away in a morning gale.

He watched Durkheim, the epileptic, take three skipping strides and bowl. The far wicket was an empty drum of cleaning fluid. In front of it, Ramsay, the helicopter pilot, jabbed forward with part of a door-frame as a bat, but the tennis ball broke past his elbow, and was taken head-high behind the wicket. From the two-dozen players there was not a sound or a hint of excitement. The man told himself as usual that the fact that they were playing at all was a good sign.

He picked up the set of identity cards he had made, and began the game of choosing his identity for the month. C. L. Staples, the university lecturer? Larry D. Herbert, the painter? F. Edward Morgan, back from the East? Eliot T. Stearns, the ex-bank-clerk. That would do. The game, begun when he had tried renaming the ruined streets and buildings, was losing its attraction. Today it reminded him of what was lost.

The device at his elbow seemed to pluck at his memory. It had been scavenged from the ruins the evening before, and he had not had time to do more than glance at it before he slept. But then a dream had woken him, and vanished, leaving a blurred memory of a man's face. He had lain in the dark, afraid to move, thinking he was still in the hospital, with the pain about to return.

He opened an old coffee jar and took out the prosthetic skin he used to build up the ruin of his left cheek. As he worked, he examined his face in the driving mirror from a VW bus. Whatever name he attached to it, it remained a stranger's face with an unknown past. He wondered what it had looked like, what it had smiled at, when its smile had been more than a grimace.

He glued on his left eyebrow and pulled a black leather glove over his shrivelled left hand. Finally he scooped his leather overcoat from the back of the chair, checked the Beretta in the right pocket, and was ready.

Outside, at the foot of the fire-escape, he was met by a red-bearded man carrying a repeating shotgun. Stearns nodded to him. "All ready, Sammy," he said, and took one more look across the square. The sun broke through thin cloud, and the jagged shadow of an office tower fell across the players as they changed ends. "They look happy enough for the moment. You're sure Colin knows the water truck's due?"

Dumb Sammy grinned and nodded.

"Okay then, let's go." Stearns could see the cloud shadows on the grey hills beyond the city, and, closer, the fractured dome of the town hall gleaming in the sun. With Sammy at his shoulder he walked briskly, with only a slight limp, whistling Jagger and Richard's "Satisfaction."

They came to the public library. A battered Renault electric was parked in the lot, a spare battery strapped to its rear bumper. "It looks as if Ernst is punctual for once," Stearns remarked. He glanced quickly along the empty street. "Okay, let's go in."

He pushed the front door open, and they walked past the looted shelves to the office. Ernst's equipment was there on the chipped wooden desk, between the arm chairs, and the usual two alkaline batteries were on the floor beside it; but the man waiting for him was new. Stearns let Sammy go ahead of him, and slipped his hand into his pocket. "Ernst," he said, "that's the best facial I've seen in years. A whole-body job, too? In these days? I'd never have known you without the toys."

The man came slowly to meet him. He was middle-aged and stocky, with grey hair and a clipped moustache. He wore a leather-patched green anorak that was frayed enough to show the bullet-proof Kevlar lining.

"Ernst has been—discommoded," the man said. "Nothing serious, but he asked me to take over for the time being." He held out part of a torn fifty-franc note. "You can call me Cavendish."

Stearns pulled out his wallet and compared his half of the banknote to Cavendish's. He nodded. "Okay, Sammy. Just wait outside and see we're not disturbed, please. Glad to meet you," he said to Cavendish. "My name is Stearns. On this occasion."

"Ah," the man murmured, "old habits." Stearns frowned, but Cavendish was examining a list on a clip-board. "Now, you're the customer for the special, I understand."

Stearns nodded, and Cavendish took a green plastic thermos from a tool box behind the desk and handed it over. "Enough for two, right?"

The flask was filled with crushed ice, in which a screw-top phial was packed. Stearns picked up the phial in his fingertips, examined the serial number etched into the glass and the seal on the neck, then put it back in the ice. "Defrosted today? Okay. Now, what about the rest?"

"Ernst's quite a sick man, actually." Cavendish drew a fingertip along one of the gouges in the desk. His wrist quivered and the finger went white around the nail. "He had to go to a lot of trouble to get that for you."

Stearns put the thermos down. "Well, well, well. After all these years. Did Ernst mention to you that I've got twenty-six in permanent aftershock who need the stuff, that one's epileptic, and another three need heroin?"

"Actually, all he mentioned was that you needed the special rather badly."

Stearns frowned. "If Ernst is developing capitalist ambitions, I'm afraid he's either too early, or much too late."

"Whatever." Cavendish began tapping his fingers on the desk. "If you want the rest, I have a slightly different arrangement to offer."

Stearns sighed. "The good Ernst, for all his faults, is not one to welsh on a deal. But I'm not sure how he reacts to being cut out by his partners. Maybe you'd know that?"

"I know what I just told you."

"Then there's no problem, is there? Shall I call Sammy in to help you pack up? Maybe we'll meet again in more congenial circumstances."

Neither of them moved. "Interesting," Cavendish said at last. He reached down and put an egg carton containing a dozen ampoules packed in blue foam plastic on the desk. "You're quite committed to these people, aren't you? Have you been here all along?"

"Only as long as I can remember," Stearns said, and began checking the ampoules. Finally he nodded. "Now we've finished our little courtship dance, perhaps we can get on with the main business." He dragged one of the arm chairs back against the desk and sat down. He reached up and peeled back his hairpiece, revealing the metal insert in his scalp. "Perhaps you can help me here? I assume you've seen one of these before. It's just the housing and sensor guide for the memory packs. Bring the sensor head over here and position it—there, that's right. Now all you have to do is enter number eleven on the keyboard—"

"—and press the little red button."

Stearns closed his eyes; his right hand clenched, his jaw quivered. A minute passed. Then he sat back and smiled weakly. "There we are. I'm sure Ernst would want you to enter the check codes to make sure I haven't cheated you."

Cavendish worked at the keyboard. "That other deal I mentioned. I have a client interested in certain information that may pass your way. If you come across it, it could be to both our advantages."

Stearns raised his eyebrow.

"The code name was Viking," Cavendish went on. "I can give you a hexadecimal reference."

After Cavendish had read off the reference, Stearns closed his eyes, leaning forward with his arms stiff. "I may have something, a cross-reference. Maybe—I'm not sure—" He shook his head and sat up. "It's gone, if there was anything—" He broke off, and looked at Cavendish. "I've seen you before."

Cavendish peered at him, his eyes suddenly hard. "Have you now? I'm not sure I can say the same."

"I've changed," Stearns muttered.

"Hm. Do you know where you've seen me?"

"No. It's gone now. Just a flash of something. A dream."

"Interesting. Do you get these flashes often?"

"No. I wish I did. It might mean my memory was coming back."

"You may be fortunate as you are. After the plagues, and some of the things that followed, not many illusions about human worth or dignity survived. But—we have to keep on going, don't we? So—keep an ear to the ground, and if you hear anything about Viking, let me know."

Stearns waited until Cavendish had loaded his equipment into the Renault and driven away before he came out to meet Sammy. He handed over the package of ampoules. "Off you go, now. Get this back safe. Colin knows what to do."

Stearns walked north for a block, then stopped at the corner where the salvage crew was working. They were clearing rubble from the remains of an office building. The side walls and rear were smoke-blackened but intact; the front had collapsed into the street. The foreman was looking at the motor of a blue Ford that had been under the rubble.

"Afternoon, Carl," Stearns said. "What have we got?"

"Not much today, looks like. We'll tear the motor out and have a look, but the oil's been gone for a long time. We got the radio out, though. Pretty chewed up, but some of the boards still look good." He went over to a bundle of sacking and handed the radio to Stearns. "Werner started this find, when he picked up that other thing in the stairwell with his metal detector. Thought he'd tripped over another bloody Claymore at first."

Stearns handed the radio back. "Ship this back to my office and I'll check it out tonight. I haven't had time to look at the other one yet. If you can't see much else that's easy to get at, you'd better wrap it up; I'd like to put the team on clearing some of the warehouses by the bridge. We might have better luck there. I've got to be going now. I'll see Werner gets credit for the find."

He walked on, his left leg starting to drag, and came to a limestone-and-slate motor hotel, still largely intact in its concrete lot. At the lobby entrance he saw a BMW electric cycle pushed among the yellow weeds by the door. He frowned, then clumped up the steps and went in. From the broken window, the usual splash of light fell across the registration desk; but the two chairs behind it were empty. As he hesitated, his hand slipping into his right pocket, a woman in black cycle leathers moved from the shadows in the far corner. She was of medium height, with straight brown hair and she carried a machine pistol easily at her side, its muzzle aimed a couple of metres in front of Stearns's feet.

"It's cold for April this year," he said, feeling ridiculous.

"And no lilacs are blooming," she completed, and clipped the gun to her belt. "Right you are, but I've learned to be careful with a new customer. What's the matter? Oh—you were expecting Adrienne. She's—not going to make it. Trouble last month. You know."

"I can imagine."

"Anyway, I've got the data you wanted, and as far as we're concerned, the deal's still on." She paused. "Did you know her well?"

"Well? I'm not sure." He swallowed. "I looked forward to when she came through here, but it's been so quiet here that you forget. . . . Today's full of surprises." The fingers of his right hand were gripping his gloved wrist. "She won't be back at all? That'll be hard to get used to."

She nodded. "It's still hard to lose someone, even now, after all this. I've got some medicinal alcohol on the bike. You want a slug?"

He shook his head and took out the thermos. "Won't mix with this."

"I've got a recorder with me. We could use that if you'd rather."

"No. No. Those things start to mash my brains if they're not perfectly tuned. Electric feet scuttering through my mind. Can we talk a bit first, though? I'm not ready yet."

They talked. Her name was Megan. She had a husky voice and rather coarse features, and she carried two gigabytes of RAM implanted in her head. Talking of fortified villages and water-powered assembly lines in a ruined cathedral, she leaned forward, gesturing with stiff wrists and curved fingers. There was something wrong with her right hand. They compared stories of agricultural projects, outdated maps and new perimeter defences. When she laughed, as she did finally, she was almost silent, falling back in her chair, open-mouthed, while her cheeks went red and her nose white.

"God," she said, sitting up and shaking her head. "Mass hysteria, just the two of us. The last few weeks were worse than I'd realized." She lay back in the chair again and looked at her hands. "The past keeps coming back, doesn't it. Someone I used to know . . . I'd assumed he was dead; I'd almost managed to forget he'd existed. Then just a couple of days ago, a new database came onto the circuit. It has an old security classification: secret projects and who was working on them. His name was there, and where he had been working; and when this job came up, I took it, even though I was due for a break, because it would take me here, and I could be where he'd lived."

She was sombre again and went on quietly: "Memories. Some of them are more real than what's around me, but I can't trust them. Have you noticed there's always some leakage, some cross-talk between what's in the implants and your own memories. At least, I think that's the trouble. He once told me that was it; he said you could make use of it if you knew how. Memories change on me—it scares me, I don't want to say it—and I dream, or I remember, but I can't see him. Or I see him, but it's someone else. Sometimes he changes while I remember. That's what frightens me. Supposing he hadn't died, and I found him, and we didn't know each other?"

Stearns shook his head. "I can't believe people change that easily. I think you're worrying too much."

"I know, I know, I'm old enough to know better. But still . . ." She shrugged and then smiled. "You're a good listener. I've needed to talk. You ready now?"

He nodded. "There's a room through there. The light's about right, and there's even a bed."

She followed him. When she hung her jacket on the door handle, he saw that the right sleeve of her work shirt was worn through at the elbow, and her arm was prosthetic. The false skin had hardened and was flaking away at the joint. As they sat, his gloved hand brushed that elbow.

They sat facing each other on the bed. There was enough light to see her eyes clearly; the irises were grey. He opened the thermos, took out the phial and broke the seal. Loading the hypo-spray he shook his head. "I thought I wouldn't be able to get it this time. I thought I'd have to give it up for the neurovaccine."

"But you didn't have to. So it's all right."

Her hands moved down the front of his shirt, unfastening buttons. When her fingers reached his belt and began loosening it, he put the spray gun down and took her hand away.

"No use," he said softly, his eyes closed. "Burned." He picked up the hypo. "Just this now."

They injected each other at the base of the neck and waited, her left hand resting loosely on his right.

The first change was always visual, as details forced themselves into prominence: a grey hair at her temple, the crease at the corner of her mouth, two red veins in her eye. Then his hearing sharpened, so that their heartbeats and breathing filled the room with muffled thunder. As he became aware of it, the syncopation smoothed away. Breath came with breath, pulse beat with pulse. He felt veins swell and relax. Air pushed down into his lungs, lifting the ribcage, pressing down the diaphragm, opening each alveolar sac like a bud.

She parted her lips and sang. Starting from an inhumanly precise B-flat, the sound broke and shivered into a hail of notes, too fast to be consciously controlled or apprehended. The sounds and the grey aureoles of her eyes filled his senses. He floated disembodied on a river of numbers that surged into an abyss of dark. When the song ended and the abyss was filled, he reached into his body and let his own song spill out. The river poured through him, molecular switches firing neurons, shaping puffs of air into sound. He orbited twin grey suns in a void that sang.

At the end, their bodies slackened, the world came back, their foreheads touched. They closed their eyes and slept.

He knew he was dreaming. Cavendish turned from the map on the wall and pushed a blue folder across the desk toward him. . . . An incandescent light bulb was reflected in the froth-ringed liquid in Stearns's beer mug. Beside him, a folded newspaper had been left between a beer mat and the ash-tray. Casually he picked it up, felt for the envelope inside. . . . He was staring up at the twin flourescents in the white ceiling, wondering if his head should feel different after the operation, how long it would take to learn to use the implants. He tried to sit up, and the ceiling cracked and turned brown, the lights became dim unshaded incandescents, and he screamed with the return of pain and the stink of burned flesh. . . . He was up on the second floor, pushing discs through the eraser. Beside him was a box of documents for the incinerator and a ten-litre can of petrol. His hands were shaking and he worked so that he could watch the doorway and the stairs. . . . It was dark with just the embers from the fireplace, and his arms were full. They were standing, he and she, turning together, so that the snow on the cars outside passed across his gaze, then the bookshelves under the Escher print, the stereo that had turned itself off, the dark hallway, the window again, moonlight and shade, turning, until his eyes closed and there was just her weight in his arms, her hair against his cheek.

Megan's hands, the warm and the cold, shook him awake. It was late afternoon and his throat was stiff.

She took her hand from his shoulder. "You okay? I've got to be going soon."

"I was remembering things, perhaps. Some of them hurt." He swung his feet to the floor. "You're right, you know—how can you trust memories like that? Still . . . before you go, could you tell me the hex reference for that secret project of yours?"

She told him, and he nodded. "I think I expected that. I'd like to look at some of that database you mentioned. Could we arrange something?"

"I'm not sure. I'd have to ask when I get back."

"Yes of course." He followed her to the door. "I'll make the usual arrangements when I know what we've got to offer."

"Fine," she said. "I'll see you then."

"Travel safely."

"Take care."

They started to shake hands, then moved closer and held each other stiffly for a few moments. She put on her jacket and walked out to the motor cycle. Stearns listened to her ride away, then turned and made his way back to see the end of the cricket match on Stockhausen Square.

That evening in his office in the museum, he turned to the device that the salvage team had found: a grey metal box with interface sockets and a small keyboard and display. It looked military. That meant triply-redundant software storage; and when he removed the cover plate, the circuitry looked intact. So there was a chance it would still work. With his storage batteries connected to the oscilloscope and pulse-tester, he worked by the light of two oil lamps, using the mirror from the VW to illuminate the device. He noted the serial number, traced the circuitry, then closed his eyes. A frown of concentration appeared on his face, his jaw slack, his lips slightly parted. After a moment, he nodded and bent to pull a catalogue from a box under his bench. He opened it at the page he wanted and checked the diagram there against the device in front of him. He inhaled sharply and nodded. "An easy-out. That's what we used to call them—"

He stopped breathing. Carefully he put the catalogue down. He closed his eyes and clenched his teeth, then slowly repeated, "That's what we used to call them, when . . . That's what *we* used to call them when, when—" He moistened his lips. There was sweat on his forehead. "That's what *we* . . ." He shuddered and shook his head, and sat for a few moments, breathing heavily. Then he sighed and bent over the work again.

He replaced the cover, brought out a length of optical cable and coupled the easy-out to his implants. He adjusted the voltage regulator in series with his batteries and connected it to the device, and began entering commands through its keyboard. After a few minutes, he paused, frowning; then he nodded and continued.

A spasm went through him. He gasped, and his body twisted and arched in the chair. A scream started to force itself out through his teeth, and then his hand jerked the power cable free.

He slumped back in his seat and shivered. Outside the window, beyond his lamps, the last red was fading from the sky, and two stars were visible. He remembered grey eyes and data-song echoing through his mind. Two guards with shotguns walked across Stockhausen Square on their way to the bridge checkpoint. Their footsteps crunched across the gravel, slapped on concrete, and receded into their own echoes. Stearns reconnected the easy-out and began again.

In the library, Stearns examined the ampoules Cavendish had brought. As he checked the serial numbers, he remarked, "I may be able to get something for you on that Viking project. But I'd want something special for it."

"That's reasonable. It's a valuable property."

Stearns put the package down. "As we both know." He looked at Cavendish for a moment. "I found someone who remembers something about it, but the memory is associated with trauma. It's going to be difficult to recover. He was hurt while he was trying to destroy the research records, after the balloon started to go up. Someone was on his track and must have caught him at the last minute."

"I've no doubt several parties were quite anxious to get hold of information about it."

"And some of them are still in business?"

"No doubt," Cavendish said impassively. "Now, what is it you—or your associate—wants in exchange?"

"A security file," Stearns said, "with a list of personnel working on that project. I want to see the personal files. And"—he looked into Cavendish's eyes—"there must have been a counterespionage file, with the identities of known agents, the ones likely to be looking for such information. I think it would be interesting for me to see that too. Don't you?"

Cavendish linked his fingers together and looked down at the backs of his hands. "It might be interesting, if you are interested in the past for its own sake. It might also be more distressing than it's worth. The situation has changed somewhat, after all. People's motives change. Even though they may keep on performing the same little manipulations, what's inside them changes, erodes, wears itself out. You might be disappointed in what you find."

"Can you bring me the files next time, or not?"

"I won't pretend I can't get them." Cavendish closed his eyes and sighed. "Yes, it might be interesting to let you see them. I think we can arrange something on that basis."

Stearns was setting up a recorder in the lobby of the motel when Megan arrived. "We're a bit short of time today," he said. "I've arranged a meeting for both of us later this afternoon, and there's something I want to discuss with you, so I'd rather use this for once."

"Okay. I imagine you know what you're doing."

Stearns bent over the recorder, tuning it. "I looked in at the hospital last night," he remarked. "Roger Finlay stepped on a mine two days ago, and we've got him on antiobiotics. . . . My first memories are there—the pain, and looking up at that ceiling. I was lying in that bed waiting for the universe to finish with me, and one day, Charlotte asked me to help with the evening meal." He paused and abstractedly checked and rechecked a setting. "I hadn't thought I could walk that far, but I did it. And then I was fetching water, washing dishes—until one day I stumbled over some technical manuals and found we had enough information to start repairing things. Then I started to realize what could be done with just a bit of organization. I had just discovered I could still use the implants and store what I'd read, when old Ernst turned up, offering to trade. . . . That's all I know about myself for sure. That's all I am now."

He looked up from the recorder. "It's good to see you again," he said, and hesitated. "This man you were looking for—you know the project he was working on was military, it could still be used if the data became available?"

"I know people are still interested in finding it. How much do you know about it?"

"Not much more than that—at the moment." He hesitated again, then asked abruptly, "If you found this man alive, and you were sure it was him—you'd still know all about him, where he was born, who his friends were, what books he read—everything?"

"I have to believe that. Yes."

"What would you do if you found he'd been killed, or badly injured by someone?"

"I'd try to find out who did it."

Stearns nodded. "As I said, we have an appointment later." He moistened his lips. "And what if he'd lost his memory? If he was—disfigured."

She looked at him, then swallowed and closed her eyes. "I don't know," she whispered. "I'd have to be sure."

Stearns nodded and started connecting his implants to the recorder. "Right. Let's get this business out of the way then."

They sat facing each other and made the data transfer. He disconnected from the recorder and waited for her to check her data and do the same. Then he reached down and put the easy-out on the table. "Will you help me with this? You've seen one of these before? It carries enough lock-picks and brute-force probes to read practically anything you can store, if you know how to use it. I want you to use it on me. There's something in me that won't come out, something to do with that project, and I want you to keep this thing operating until we get it."

"Why can't you use it yourself?"

"I tried working it from the keyboard. The memories are buried under some trauma. It hurts when I go near them. I lose control of it then."

"All right," she said slowly. "You want me to hook into it directly?"

"Yes. I'll probably show some signs of discomfort. You'll have to ignore them."

She used the optical cable to interface with the control port, and he linked himself to the probe terminal. They began.

The first time he screamed, Sammy burst in with his shotgun levelled, and they had to stop so that Stearns could explain. Then they continued.

Finally she whispered, "I think that's the best I can do," and slumped in her chair. "Has it worked?"

He was sprawled across the table, panting. He levered himself up and dragged the cable from his scalp. His artificial cheek was livid against the pallor of the rest of his face. He pushed himself to his feet. "Come on," he muttered. "We're going to be late."

She followed as he picked up his coat and limped to the door. "Has it worked?"

"I don't know."

Sammy followed, and Stearns hurried them past the library to the building where the salvage crew had been working. The stairwell was almost clear of rubble, and Stearns scrambled up to the second floor. "It's safe enough. Come on." He turned through an empty door-frame and began heaving at smoke-blackened masonry. "Help me with this, will you." Sammy joined him, and a slab of plasterboard cracked and slid out of the way.

Stearns looked down, gasping. "There." Just inside the door lay what might almost have been a pile of old sticks, brown and charred, and a broken ceramic bowl with fragments of metal. "There," he repeated. "That's all there is now. We can bury him. Let's go down."

Megan followed him without speaking, and the pressure of her silence made him start to explain. "He was destroying the documentation when I caught him. I must have been in a hurry, because I didn't have time to use a recorder. I'd immobilized him and was using the easy-out to feed straight into my implants. He'd hidden the data, the Viking data, behind layers of defences. Some of the last ones were just sets of his own memories, including those of what he'd just been doing. Before I realized what I was getting, I broke through into the Viking files. I got some of the data, but the last defences triggered. The easy-out almost shorted, but I didn't quite have my brain fried because most of the power surge must have been directed into his last defence, the one that blew the back of his skull away. I think there was a can of petrol open nearby. . . ."

Megan did not look at him. "So now you know who you are."

"I know what I did. I know who I was working for. . . . Come on." He headed back toward the motel.

Cavendish met them on the way. "I've got the information you wanted."

He looked from Stearns to Megan and back. "I don't think we've been introduced. But something tells me you've just made a discovery."

"We found a body, that's all," Stearns muttered. "I think you know whose it was better than I do." He looked quickly at Megan, but she was staring vacantly past his shoulder.

"So now you know the price of the past," Cavendish said. "Makes it harder to maintain self-sacrificial postures, doesn't it? If you'd known what happened in those years, you'd have known that there's no part of us we cherish so much that we can't be made to betray it."

"Right," Stearns said, stepped close. He pinned Cavendish's arm with his gloved hand, and with his right pressed the muzzle of the Beretta to the back of Cavendish's neck.

Cavendish inhaled sharply. His eyes flickered, then his face went blank, his shoulders sagged. "All right," he whispered. "It's time. Perhaps you should be the one."

Stearns's hand began to tighten. He saw Cavendish sprawled among the dusty weeds, his skull a broken chalice. He snarled and pushed Cavendish away. "Find yourself another henchman." He dragged air into his lungs, held it, and then breathed out heavily. "When you bring the next shipment, I want an extra stock of antibiotics. Twice the usual load. We've got a casualty here. Okay?"

Cavendish massaged the back of his neck. "I could tell you your name. I could find out where you were born."

"Leave this batch with Sammy. And remember the extra antibiotics. Next time."

Stearns watched Cavendish walk slowly back to the Renault, Sammy two paces behind. At his shoulder, Megan said, "I've got to go. The bike's still at the motel."

"Right." He did not look at her. "Will you be back?"

"Maybe. I don't know."

"All right."

When she had gone, he went back and looked at the burned building. Ghosts of flames prickled over his skin. Always, the body remembered what the mind could forget. *Body or brain*, he thought: *two of us died there.* He traced the join where his artificial cheek met his skin, and thought of metal sockets in a skull. He remembered arms, real and prosthetic, equally firm against his back, and moonlit snow, and red embers in the fireplace of a darkened room. . . . *And one of us lives.* He turned and began to walk back to the museum on Stockhausen Square.

Outport

Garfield Reeves-Stevens

Garfield Reeves-Stevens is from Toronto and has been an active participant in SF Canada. He has written several novels of SF and horror fiction; with his wife Judith, two *Star Trek* novels, *Memory Prime* and *Prime Directive*, both best-sellers; an ecological thriller; and a series of fantasy novels, *The Chronicles of Galen Sword*. While devoting his principal efforts to novels, he has written a number of short stories, including "Outport," which was originally done for Lesley Choyce's anthology, *Ark of Ice*.

You can smell the ice and you can smell the fear and sometimes the fear's so strong you can't tell one from the other. And sometimes, it's just the excitement of the passengers who don't know enough to be afraid yet. Going into the outports. What's left of them. Looking for the survivors.

"Never did know why they called them *survivors*." Burl Finn asks the question. He's an American. They all are, seven of them this time, the passengers. Only ones who can afford the trip. Only ones desperate enough to want to take it. This one, Burl, made his money building the dykes around Florida. A lot of them did. Getting rich not by making something new but by saving what was old. There's too much that's old left in this world.

Burl's drinking beer from a small can in his huge gloved hand. He's a big man. They all are. Food's easy to get down south. Not like St. John's where we sailed from. Not like the outports where we're going. Things still grow outside down south, under the UV nets at least. Burl drinks some more and then he belches. The sound's swallowed by the mist and the pulse of the ship's engines churning. But the stink of the ice and the fear is overcome for the moment.

" 'Cause they're still here," I say, close enough to the truth. I don't like Burl. I don't like any of them. But I'm leaning on the railing with him just the same, watching the sea out here grey and thick, carved by the ship's bow like molten glass, almost solid. I can believe that someone might walk across this water. I wish someone would. It would be an easier path to salvation than what I'm doing now.

"Not for long," Burl says, sort of snorting. He horks down what's left of the beer like he's cleaning out his nose through the back of his throat, like the beer's part of him, some liquid made by his body that he's reclaiming, recycling. The plastic can splinters easily in his glove and he tosses the shards over the side, and they spin like ice crystals all the way down. If there were fish left out here, those shards probably would've killed a few, when they'd tried to swallow them. But that's nothing to worry about anymore. The Banks aren't what they used to be and most of the fish are long since sucked up into the factory ships that used to sweep these waters worse than the ice does now.

There're fish inshore of course. Lot's more than there used to be, too, back when the outports were real fishing villages, not any ever big enough to be towns, not without roads, no way in and out in the winter. It's just that those inshore fish can't be caught. Not by the survivors anyway. They've got too much else to think about. Too much else to do. Getting ready for a summer when the ice won't melt at all. Supposed to be soon now. Winter all the time.

Burl doesn't care about any of that, though. Not that I've tried telling him what it used to be like, the way my father and mother told me it was. I've tried telling them before, other passengers, other trips, but they never were much interested. Used to bother me then, when I was younger and I thought it was important that they understand what was going to happen to them, when it happened to them. But it doesn't anymore. Makes it easier, really. Part of the process.

We stand there for a long while till Linda gives me a call from the cabin. Shore's coming up, she says. Can't hear the breakers in the fog, not over the engines, but the cliffs of Newfoundland like black clouds are suddenly there, a storm front roiling up, solid, twisted, puckered like something that's grown in place, like some of the plants down south that still hold out on their own, without protection, no matter what the UV does to their DNA. They know about DNA in the outports. The survivors know what's important. If they didn't, they wouldn't be survivors, would they?

Linda cuts back on the engines and we almost coast. She's looking for markers, something familiar. Can't use the radar or fix on the NavStars with the Maritime Command in the same waters. The big red ships, all metal and composites, with brilliant white lines across their hulls blinding like ice when the sun breaks through the fog, they don't really care about us, as long as we don't rub their noses in it. They know what we say we're doing, and they know what it is we really do, and either way you look at it, it's illegal. But if you look at it just one particular way, you can't say it's wrong. And after the summer comes when the ice won't melt at all, who's going to care?

"Should we get the stuff ready?" Burl asks. The black wall of rock has changed his mood, made the beer courage go away.

"Leave it be for a while, yet," I tell him. "Maritime Command's got better things to do than search us if they find us out here, but if we've got the guns on deck, they won't have any choice but to board us and take us in."

Burl nods at that. I know he's relieved. Jerry Bright, his partner, is still belowdecks, sleeping off last night. Jerry's not nervous, not like Burl. Jerry fought in the Mex-American. When he gets drunk enough, he tells us he was first across the Rio Grande, first to march into Mexico City. Wish I had a dollar for every American I've met said he was the first to do those things. I could buy another boat or ten. A couple of others are belowdecks with him. I saw them using their knives to cut crosses into the soft ends of bullets to make them break apart when they hit. The others are in the galley complaining about the cold. And this the summer.

"I hear sometimes it's easy," Burl says after a while.

I pretend to not know what he's talking about.

"You know," he says, "that they know how bad things are getting so they, they just like, leave the children there, on the shore, and you just have to leave something in exchange. You know, guns, food, even whiskey."

"Yeah, I've heard that, too," I tell him. It calms him down a bit. Burl wasn't in the Army, but he knows there's a hell of a difference between a Mexican regular and what he's going to find out on those rocks. The Mexicans were fighting for a wasteland, stripped bare by the exodus from Central America, fried by the sun, scourged by disease. It was a country already lost and no matter what the American politicians said, it wasn't a police action to restore order to their neighbour to the south, it was a war to keep the starving millions on their own side of the border until nature had run her course. The Mexicans didn't have a whole lot of reason to fight. They'd already lost.

Of course, nature doesn't stand a chance out on those rocks and Burl knows it. The survivors aren't fighting for a wasteland. They've been a colony, a Dominion, a colony again. Even been another country's province for awhile. But the land never changed through all of that. And the people never changed. They're fighting for a future, same as always. And as long as the ice keeps ploughing down from the north, keeps the mist and the fog in the air to shield this place from the UV, there will be a future here. Something new, like the name says.

And by being new, that makes it something that Burl and Jerry and none of their countrymen can understand. I've seen it happen to them. Their thoughts are like their country now, constrained by dykes that will never withstand the thousand-year patience of the sea. Their dreams are walled in by armed borders that might, for now, be keeping disease out, but just as certainly choke off what little life remains within, a tourniquet applied too tight and too late. At some level the Americans know that.

At some level their government lets enough of them out beyond their iron borders to search for the life they know they need. Searching here, in Australia, through what's left of the EC. Just like the Maritime Command lets my boat cross the Banks, the US Coast Guard blinks when men like Burl and Jerry slip out to sea. Looking for survivors, they say. But in Australia, and through what's left of the EC, all they ever find are those who *have* survived and now are only waiting without purpose. Out here, they find those who *are* survivors, and still survive. None of my passengers has ever understood that difference until it was too late.

Linda angles the boat closer toward the shore and now the breakers sound over the barely idling engines. Burl grabs the railing hard as we rise and fall with the growing grey swells.

"Are we getting close?" he asks.

"Seems so," I say, though the bright patch of fog that's the sun is still high enough over the cliffs that I know we won't be setting off for an hour or two. I tell Burl so.

"It's better at night?" he asks.

"That's right," I say. "Especially for the children."

That always works on these passengers. After all, they say, that's what they're doing it for. Never for themselves. Never for the adoption bounties. Not even any mention of their country's gene pool slowly evaporating in the heat of a century's worth of toxic, mutagenic pollution. This is *all* for the children, they say, the poor, poor children, thinking that the children of the outports need rescuing from their bleak dismal life among the rocks and the ice, as if for some reason they'd enjoy the new and better bleak and dismal life of a country that already has begun to live by night, afraid of the sun, choking on its own waste, its own past, inflicting genetic instability to the point of sterility to all that were trapped within the delimiting borders first forged by geography, now set even more immutably within a fixed inertial intellect.

Burl stumbles away from the railing toward the cooler and pulls another can of beer from the coldpacks. As if keeping the beer exposed to the air wouldn't keep it cold enough, as if just the fact that it is summer is enough to require beer to be chilled. They do that a lot, I've found, ignoring reality for what they *know* is real.

"Watcha see, Linda?" I call out.

Through the window of the cabin I see Linda wave one hand ahead and down, flashing three fingers. I track the cliffs according to her instructions and spot the grey smudge of what we call Old Mike's cabin, the first of the landmarks we need to find our way. The cabin is in ruins, really, little more than a bleached jumble of timber atop the rocks. But it lets us know we're close to Dunder's Cove.

"That where we're going?" Burl asks, beer in hand. I can tell the difference between the stink of ice and fear now. He's truly scared. As if he knows what's going to happen.

"Just an old shack," I tell him and he believes me. It's easier. "Lots of old things on the cliffs out here."

"But you know where we are, don't you?"

I nod. There's not much left to hide from him anymore.

"So there's an outport near?" He likes that word. Uses it a lot. Maybe it sounds alien to him, as if the trip has taken him to another planet, as if he won't be facing humans, as if that makes it easier, too.

I nod again.

Burl stares at the cliffs and the fog. I wonder if they remind him of the walls he's built against the sea down south, and how useless those walls will be. "How do you find them?" he asks me.

That's one of the things still to hide, until we get close to shore and the sun gives way to night. My passport doesn't say so, and I've learned a mainland accent, but I know how to find the outports because I was born here. Because my mother and father were born here, as were their own. Because the folds of these cliffs are the folds of my skin and the crash of the breakers is the pounding of my heart and because the ice that's ploughing down from the north in unending sheets that soon will defeat the summer for the next ten thousand years is my soul. Cold, perhaps, with features hidden, but more enduring than the sea it engulfs.

Burl waits for my answer, knowing I have one, but Jerry's down below with the guns and the others are cutting their bullets into dum-dums and we're not yet in position so I can't tell Burl what he wants to know.

So I tell him, "Sometimes you see a boat, a dory, going into the outports. Old and creaky, tied up some places, dragged up in others, usually hidden, not very well. Sometimes you see just splinters from where the ice took hold. Sometimes you see a building, too, like that one. Most of them are wood, like the boats, dragged over from the west, the valleys, back when what roads there were, were clear, when there were still forests."

Burl nods in time to the rise and the fall of the deck. I like to think he senses the life of the land and the sea here. Something he's not familiar with. Something new.

I tell him that the real outports are long since flooded. That the buildings we see are the ones that were built high enough. Scattered like barnacles across black rocks all craggy and sculpted and ragged. As if the ice took hold of the land once and splintered it, too. Eventually, the ice will reach to Florida. I see Burl understands that, that he knows the true worth of his useless dykes, though he says nothing.

"Sometimes you see lots of buildings," I tell him, and this is true. You see them underwater. When there's not much ice. Whole villages caught like paintings melting in rain. Rippling a bit where the water's clear. Disappearing softly, with no lines, no borders or boundaries, where the water's murky. Those buildings, trapped like that, quiet and still, make me think of waiting. The feeling of waiting, looking down off the side of the boat with the passengers. There have been a great many Burls over the years. I haven't liked any of them. Though sometimes, I have felt sorry for a few. I don't know yet if I will feel sorry for this Burl.

Burl looks over the railing, beer held forgotten in his hand, as if trying to peer beneath the waves and the years, trying to see the past. Typical, I think. They used to walk those ghost streets, narrow, twisting, the first survivors did. Their parents, anyway, before the ocean rose up, swallowing the outports like the factories swallowed the fish. Lobsters live in those streets now, scuttling, and crabs. And the fish. Lots of fish inshore where the factories can't get them, lazy schools of them weaving through the streets like flocks of slow birds, silvery white reflections of the gulls that used to follow the factories, back when there were gulls.

"Why do they do it?" Burl asks.

"Do what?" But I know what he means.

"Just give them up."

"Give what up?"

"The children," he says.

I stare at the cliffs. We're getting closer to where we need to be. "They don't give them up, Mr. Finn. You've got guns," I remind him.

"But you said, sometimes, they just, they just leave the children there, for the ships to take."

"I said, I've heard the stories."

"Then they don't?" he asks. "Leave the children?"

Sometimes, I find it painful to be around these people. "Under current conditions, what would you do?"

"I'd do what was best for the children."

"I assure you that that is what they do, too."

The poor man smiles in relief. That's another common trait among them, the stubborn insistence that there's only one way of looking at things. Their way. I don't try and set him straight.

By the time the patch of sun has passed behind the cliffs, all the passengers are gathered on the foredeck, sidelit by running lights. Four have blackened their faces with camouflage paint. They're the ones used to be in the Army. All of them wear laden equipment belts, local transponders, and carry their rifles. All of them pose like commandos prepared to take on a vicious enemy. But they're only doing this for the children.

Linda and I keep them occupied with a transponder and weapons drill while John and Eleanor wrestle with the launching gear aft, dropping the dinghy into the dark water with enough splashing and grinding of winch gears to drown out the other sounds from the ocean.

We check the transponders twice so that no one will lose his way, we tell them. Linda starts talking about using the handheld infrareds to see where the fires have been burning. The passengers listen attentively, in love with their technology.

"Above all, be safe," Linda tells them. "Don't fire unless you have to." But by the intensity of their eyes, we see that the four with the painted faces have no intention of restraining themselves. To them, this is not an adoption run, this is not an attempt to rescue the poor children of the decaying world to bring them to safety within Fortress America. This is a hunt, pure and simple, a make-good for the killing fields lost now that Mexico is uninhabitable. They're right, of course, but they have the wrong idea of who is to be the hunted.

Linda looks to me but John still hasn't given the signal from the winch. "Let's check those safeties one more time," I tell them. "We want this to go as smoothly and as quickly as possible."

Burl gurgles with a beer laugh. "So you can get back home and spend all the money we paid you!"

I laugh with them, though the money's already spent and what it bought is sitting in the hold.

I hear the winch grind for a moment when I know it shouldn't. Eleanor stands by the aft railing, lit by a floodlight fastened to the top of the cabin. She flashes two fingers.

"The dinghy's almost ready," I say. Then I tell them that the sea is choppy and I'd feel a whole lot safer if they'd just unload until we hit shore. Stop any chance of an accidental discharge.

One of the men with a painted face is unhappy at the suggestion but I point out that everyone on shore will be hiding away from the cliffs. No one's going to attack while we're in the dinghy, heading for land. He hears the truth in my voice and reluctantly disarms his weapons.

By now, of course, the Dunder's men have worked their way up the netting from their dory. I sense them moving in the shadows of the unlit half of the ship as Linda and I wave our disarmed passengers aft, keeping them distracted.

The Dunder's men are silent but they make no other attempt to hide now. Their dingy white jackets and pants, padded thickly for insulation and protection, almost glow in the darkness of the deepening night. Even their faces are encased in white sacks. An old tradition brought back to life to forestall any identification, in case any passengers escape.

But no passengers ever escape.

Burl goes down easily with one blow. The rest except for two ex-soldiers follow in seconds. Those two men whirl at the first sign of the silent attack, assuming positions of martial arts combat.

But they are not facing other soldiers. They're facing pale apparitions who scream at them with wailing indrawn breaths, even as they swing their bladed pikes.

One ex-soldier goes over the railing and hits the sea. I mourn the loss of his equipment, but the cold will claim anyone in that water within minutes and I have long ago learned to respect the cold and give it its due.

The other ex-soldier goes cleanly, his final breath leaving his severed trachea like a mummer's wail, bubbling just a bit at the end like Burl finishing a beer.

The attack takes less than thirty seconds. The passengers hadn't been expecting it, so of course it is easy.

We work the rest of the night offloading the supplies we bought with the passengers' payments. Book disks. Tools. Seeds for the greenhouses. The transactions were all in cash so there are no records and no trail. Burl and Jerry and the five others will be just another group of Americans who have slipped illegally from their country to disappear in the dying world. Perhaps, as sometimes happened, a brother or friend will come looking for them. And when and if that happens they will have no difficulty in hiring a ship to take them up through the ice, searching the outports. This land, this sea, this ice, my home, is admirably efficient in dealing with those who don't respect it.

I explain this to Burl as he sits tied on the deck, just as the sun rises, a pale glow in the mist. Without his beer, Burl looks more frightened than ever. He cringes when Linda says everything's been offloaded.

"What happens to us now?" he asks. His lips are tinged with blue. It's the summer and it's getting that cold.

"You get offloaded, too," I tell him. I help him to his feet. He is unsteady. "You'll finally get to see an outport."

"What happens then?" His teeth are chattering. This is not his climate, not his world. He really might as well be on another planet, or from one.

"That's up to the doctors," I explain. The other passengers are being led to the railing. If they have cooperated, then the Dunder's men untie their hands to let them climb down the rope ladder to the dory more easily.

"Why doctors?" he asks. I don't know yet if I should untie Burl's hands. The ship rocks up and down with the swells, the pulse of life.

"To see what you can add to the community, Mr. Finn. It's very small, very self-contained, and sometime soon is liable to be cut off by a winter that will last for centuries."

He tells me he doesn't understand what I'm saying.

"Contributions to the gene pool," I tell him. "We've found that not all of you are as badly affected as you think. In time, given a proper diet, a rest from contaminants, there's a chance that you'll produce healthy sperm again."

"You're going to *breed* us?" He seems shocked by the suggestion.

"You've taken so much from this world, Mr. Finn. Isn't it time you put something back?"

His cheeks go splotchy, angry red against the stark white of his skin. "And if I can't? If I *can't*?"

I'm always surprised when they don't figure it out for themselves. "One way or another, you will," I tell him. "Food's hard to get up here. But we do get it."

He trembles badly, tied hands resting on the rail. I watch his eyes as they go to the sea, as if they look beneath its grey surface, struggling to find ghost cities of the past, as if he knows that the past is his only future. And in that moment, I sense something more about Burl Finn, something hidden. Perhaps he's had an operation, perhaps an accident or exposure to something so toxic that his gametes will never run clean and error free. Whatever, he seems to know that there will only be one way he will give something back to the world. I think of him sucking on his beer, as if he were recycling his own fluids.

"Why?" he asks.

I know that he knows the answer, but I tell him anyway. "For the children. For the future."

"But like this?"

"Like what?" I ask him gently.

His wide, panicked eyes are so easy to read. Kidnapping, they say, theft, murder, cannibalism. A dozen other terms of one world's horror. Another world's necessity.

"*This!*" he says by way of briefer explanation. "How can you?"

I didn't like him throughout the trip, and standing with him by the railing, with no more reason to hide anything at all from him, my mission done, I find that I still don't like him. But I do, at last, feel sorry for him. I look at the slow pulse of the sea long enough that his eyes are drawn to it as well, and at that moment, I cut through the rope that binds his hands, giving him his final freedom. The dory creaks below us, beneath the waiting rope ladder. The fog is rose and yellow with the dawn.

"We're not jetsam, not dredges, not the forgotten waiting for our time to be over," I tell him. "We're not like you are." I step back from him, knowing what he must do even before he does. "We are survivors. Always have been. And will be."

Tears freeze to his cheeks in the cold wind of this summer morning. There's ice nearby, beyond the fog, closing in, inexorable, enduring. "What about me?" He forms the words but doesn't say them.

I shake my head. "You might have been able to ask that once. Perhaps. But no longer."

A Dunder's man, impatient, wails up from the dory, white arm waving Burl down and down.

Burl doesn't look at me again. I smell the ice waiting offshore. And his fear. This time, they are the same again, brought into balance.

Burl Finn goes over the railing, spinning like a large shard of something old and fragile. And when he hits the thick grey surface of the water, it parts for him, drawing him down to the ghost streets of the outports that so fascinate him. I wonder if in his last moment he thinks that there still might be an escape for him, that the water might hold and that he might walk upon it. Sometimes, I get that impression from my passengers. That that's the type of people they think they are.

But not this time.

He leaves only a ripple, and only for an instant. And then there is only the splash of the sea against the boat's hull as the Dunder's men push off with the last of my passengers, heading for shore.

I wave a final time to them, then signal Linda to swing us out.

The sun almost breaks through the fog then, and on the wind that comes to me, I scent the continent of ice that grows out there, coming from the north, invincible.

I stand at the railing, eager to meet it.

It smells like home.

JUST LIKE OLD TIMES

by Robert J. Sawyer

Robert J. Sawyer is Canadian Regional Director of the Science Fiction and Fantasy Writers of America and *The Canadian Encyclopedia*'s authority on science fiction. He has written and narrated documentaries on SF for CBC radio and reviewed for *The Globe and Mail*. He is the author of six science fiction novels, all published in the U.S. since 1990, and a number of short stories that have appeared in magazines and original anthologies in Canada and the U.S. since the early 1980's. *Golden Fleece* (1990), his first novel, expanded from a 1988 magazine story, won the Aurora Award for best long-form work in English in 1991. "Just Like Old Times" first appeared in the original anthology *Dinosaur Fantastic* and was reprinted in *On Spec*. It is the epitome of the clever, entertaining science fiction that is the hallmark of Sawyer's work.

The transference went smoothly, like a scalpel slicing into skin.

Cohen was simultaneously excited and disappointed. He was thrilled to be here—perhaps the judge was right, perhaps this was indeed where he really belonged. But the gleaming edge was taken off that thrill because it wasn't accompanied by the usual physiological signs of excitement: no sweaty palms, no racing heart, no rapid breathing. Oh, there was a heartbeat, to be sure, thundering in the background, but it wasn't Cohen's.

It was the dinosaur's.

Everything was the dinosaur's: Cohen saw the world now through tyrannosaur eyes.

The colours seemed all wrong. Surely plant leaves must be the same chlorophyll green here in the Mesozoic, but the dinosaur saw them as navy blue. The sky was lavender; the dirt underfoot ash gray.

Old bones had different cones, thought Cohen. Well, he could get used to it. After all, he had no choice. He would finish his life as an observer inside this tyrannosaur's mind. He'd see what the beast saw, hear what it heard, feel what it felt. He wouldn't be able to control its movements, they had said, but he would be able to experience every sensation.

The rex was marching forward.

Cohen hoped blood would still look red.

It wouldn't be the same if it wasn't red.

"And what, Ms. Cohen, did your husband say before he left your house on the night in question?"

"He said he was going out to hunt humans. But I thought he was making a joke."

"No interpretations, please, Ms. Cohen. Just repeat for the court as precisely as you remember it, exactly what your husband said."

"He said, 'I'm going out to hunt humans.' "

"Thank you, Ms. Cohen. That concludes the Crown's case, my lady."

The needlepoint on the wall of the Honourable Madam Justice Amanda Hoskins's chambers had been made for her by her husband. It was one of her favourite verses from *The Mikado*, and as she was preparing sentencing she would often look up and re-read the words:

> *My object all sublime*
> *I shall achieve in time—*
> *To let the punishment fit the crime—*
> *The punishment fit the crime.*

This was a difficult case, a horrible case. Judge Hoskins continued to think.

It wasn't just colours that were wrong. The view from inside the tyrannosaur's skull was different in other ways, too.

The tyrannosaur had only partial stereoscopic vision. There was an area in the centre of Cohen's field of view that showed true depth perception. But because the beast was somewhat wall-eyed, it had a much wider panorama than normal for a human, a kind of saurian Cinemascope covering 270 degrees.

The wide-angle view panned back and forth as the tyrannosaur scanned along the horizon.

Scanning for prey.

Scanning for something to kill.

The Calgary Herald, Thursday, October 16, 2042, hardcopy edition: Serial killer Rudolph Cohen, 43, was sentenced to death yesterday.

Formerly a prominent member of the Alberta College of Physicians and Surgeons, Dr. Cohen was convicted in August of thirty-seven counts of first-degree murder.

In chilling testimony, Cohen had admitted, without any signs of remorse, to having terrorized each of his victims for hours before slitting their throats with surgical implements.

This is the first time in eighty years that the death penalty has been ordered in this country.

In passing sentence, Madam Justice Amanda Hoskins observed

that Cohen was "the most cold-blooded and brutal killer to have stalked Canada's prairies since *Tyrannosaurus rex . . .*"

From behind a stand of dawn redwoods about ten metres away, a second tyrannosaur appeared. Cohen suspected tyrannosaurs might be fiercely territorial, since each animal would require huge amounts of meat. He wondered if the beast he was in would attack the other individual.

His dinosaur tilted its head to look at the second rex, which was standing in profile. But as it did so, almost all of the dino's mental picture dissolved into a white void, as if when concentrating on details the beast's tiny brain simply lost track of the big picture.

At first Cohen thought his rex was looking at the other dinosaur's head, but soon the top of the other's skull, the tip of its muzzle and the back of its powerful neck faded away into snowy nothingness. All that was left was a picture of the throat. Good, thought Cohen. One shearing bite there could kill the animal.

The skin of the other's throat appeared gray-green and the throat itself was smooth. Maddeningly, Cohen's rex did not attack. Rather, it simply swiveled its head and looked out at the horizon again.

In a flash of insight, Cohen realized what had happened. Other kids in his neighbourhood had had pet dogs or cats. He'd had lizards and snakes—cold-blooded carnivores, a fact to which expert psychological witnesses had attached great weight. Some kinds of male lizards had dewlap sacks hanging from their necks. The rex he was in—a male, the Tyrrell paleontologists had believed—had looked at this other one and seen that she was smooth-throated and therefore a female. Something to be mated with, perhaps, rather than to attack.

Perhaps they would mate soon. Cohen had never orgasmed except during the act of killing. He wondered what it would feel like.

"We spent a billion dollars developing time travel, and now you tell me the system is useless?"

"Well—"

"That is what you're saying, isn't it, professor? That chronotransference has no practical applications?"

"Not exactly, Minister. The system *does* work. We can project a human being's consciousness back in time, superimposing his or her mind overtop of that of someone who lived in the past."

"With no way to sever the link. *Wonderful.*"

"That's not true. The link severs automatically."

"Right. When the historical person you've transferred consciousness into dies, the link is broken."

"Precisely."

"And then the person from our time whose consciousness you've transferred back dies as well."

"I admit that's an unfortunate consequence of linking two brains so
closely."

"So I'm right! This whole damn chronotransference thing is useless."

"Oh, not at all, Minister. In fact, I think I've got the perfect application for
it."

The rex marched along. Although Cohen's attention had first been arrested
by the beast's vision, he slowly became aware of its other senses, too. He
could hear the sounds of the rex's footfalls, of twigs and vegetation being
crushed, of birds or pterosaurs singing, and, underneath it all, the relentless
drone of insects. Still, all the sounds were dull and low; the rex's simple ears
were incapable of picking up high-pitched noises, and what sounds they did
detect were discerned without richness. Cohen knew the late Cretaceous
must have been a symphony of varied tone, but it was as if he was listening
to it through earmuffs.

The rex continued along, still searching. Cohen became aware of several
more impressions of the world both inside and out, including hot afternoon
sun beating down on him and a hungry gnawing in the beast's belly.

Food.

It was the closest thing to a coherent thought that he'd yet detected from
the animal, a mental picture of bolts of meat going down its gullet.

Food.

*The Social Services Preservation Act of 2022: Canada is built upon the prin-
ciple of the Social Safety Net, a series of entitlements and programs designed
to ensure a high standard of living for every citizen. However, ever-increas-
ing life expectancies coupled with constant lowering of the mandatory retirement age have placed an untenable burden on our social-welfare system and,
in particular, its cornerstone program of universal health care. With most
taxpayers ceasing to work at the age of 45, and with average Canadians living to be 94 (males) or 97 (females), the system is in danger of complete
collapse. Accordingly, all social programs will henceforth be available only
to those below the age of 60, with one exception: all Canadians, regardless of
age, may take advantage, at no charge to themselves, of government-spon-
sored euthanasia through chronotransference.*

There! Up ahead! Something moving! Big, whatever it was: an indistinct
outline only intermittently visible behind a small knot of fir trees.

A quadruped of some sort, its back to him/it/them.

Ah, there. Turning now. Peripheral vision dissolving into albino nothingness as the rex concentrated on the head.

Three horns.

Triceratops.

Glorious! Cohen had spent hours as a boy poring over books about dinosaurs, looking for scenes of carnage. No battles were better than those in which *Tyrannosaurus rex* squared off against *Triceratops,* a four-footed Mesozoic tank with a trio of horns projecting from its face and a shield of bone rising from the back of its skull to protect the neck.

And yet, the rex marched on.

No, thought Cohen. Turn, damn you! Turn and attack!

Cohen remembered when it had all begun, that fateful day so many years ago, so many years from now. It should have been a routine operation. The patient had supposedly been prepped properly. Cohen brought his scalpel down toward the abdomen, then, with a steady hand, sliced into the skin. The patient gasped. It had been a *wonderful* sound, a beautiful sound.

Not enough gas. The anesthetist hurried to make an adjustment.

Cohen knew he had to hear that sound again. He had to.

The tyrannosaur continued forward. Cohen couldn't see its legs, but he could feel them moving. Left, right, up, down.

Attack, you bastard!

Left.

Attack!

Right.

Go after it!

Up.

Go after the *Triceratops.*

Dow—

The beast hesitated, its left leg still in the air, balancing briefly on one foot.

Attack!

Attack!

And then, at last, the rex changed course. The ceratopsian appeared in the three-dimensional central part of the tyrannosaur's field of view, like a target at the end of a gun sight.

"Welcome to the Chronotransference Institute. If I can just see your government benefits card, please? Yup, there's always a last time for everything, heh heh. Now, I'm sure you want an exciting death. The problem is finding somebody interesting who hasn't been used yet. See, we can only ever superimpose one mind onto a given historical personage. All the really obvious ones have been done already, I'm afraid. We still get about a dozen calls a week asking for Jack Kennedy, but he was one of the first to go, so to speak. If I may make a suggestion, though, we've got thousands of Roman legion officers cataloged. Those tend to be very satisfying deaths. How about a nice something from the Gallic Wars?"

The *Triceratops* looked up, its giant head lifting from the wide flat gunnera leaves it had been chewing on. Now that the rex had focussed on the plant-eater, it seemed to commit itself.

The tyrannosaur charged.

The hornface was sideways to the rex. It began to turn, to bring its armoured head to bear.

The horizon bounced wildly as the rex ran. Cohen could hear the thing's heart thundering loudly, rapidly, a barrage of muscular gunfire.

The *Triceratops*, still completing its turn, opened its parrot-like beak, but no sound came out.

Giant strides closed the distance between the two animals. Cohen felt the rex's jaws opening wide, wider still, mandibles popping from their sockets.

The jaws slammed shut on the hornface's back, over the shoulders. Cohen saw two of the rex's own teeth fly into view, knocked out by the impact.

The taste of hot blood, surging out of the wound . . .

The rex pulled back for another bite.

The *Triceratops* finally got its head swung around. It surged forward, the long spear over its left eye piercing into the rex's leg . . .

Pain. Exquisite, beautiful pain.

The rex roared. Cohen heard it twice, once reverberating within the animal's own skull, a second time echoing back from distant hills. A flock of silver-furred pterosaurs took to the air. Cohen saw them fade from view as the dinosaur's simple mind shut them out of the display. Irrelevant distractions.

The *Triceratops* pulled back, the horn withdrawing from the rex's flesh.

Blood, Cohen was delighted to see, still looked red.

"If Judge Hoskins had ordered the electric chair," said Axworthy, Cohen's lawyer, "we could have fought that on Charter grounds. Cruel and unusual punishment, and all that. But she's authorized full access to the chronotransference euthanasia program for you." Axworthy paused. "She said, bluntly, that she simply wants you dead."

"How thoughtful of her," said Cohen.

Axworthy ignored that. "I'm sure I can get you anything you want," he said. "Who would you like to be transferred into?"

"Not who," said Cohen. "What."

"I beg your pardon?"

"That damned judge said I was the most cold-blooded killer to stalk the

Alberta landscape since *Tyrannosaurus rex*." Cohen shook his head. "The idiot. Doesn't she know dinosaurs were warm-blooded? Anyway, that's what I want. I want to be transferred into a *T. rex*."

"You're kidding."

"Kidding is not my forte, John. *Killing* is. I want to know which was better at it, me or the rex."

"I don't even know if they can do that kind of thing," said Axworthy.

"Find out, damn you. What the hell am I paying you for?"

The rex danced to the side, moving with surprising agility for a creature of its bulk, and once again it brought its terrible jaws down on the ceratopsian's shoulder. The plant-eater was hemorrhaging at an incredible rate, as though a thousand sacrifices had been performed on the altar of its back.

The *Triceratops* tried to lunge forward, but it was weakening quickly. The tyrannosaur, crafty in its own way despite its trifling intellect, simply retreated a dozen giant paces. The hornface took one tentative step toward it, and then another, and, with great and ponderous effort, one more. But then the dinosaurian tank teetered and, eyelids slowly closing, collapsed on its side. Cohen was briefly startled, then thrilled, to hear it fall to the ground with a *splash*—he hadn't realized just how much blood had poured out of the great rent the rex had made in the beast's back.

The tyrannosaur moved in, lifting its left leg up and then smashing it down on the *Triceratop*'s belly, the three sharp toe claws tearing open the thing's abdomen, entrails spilling out into the harsh sunlight. Cohen thought the rex would let out a victorious roar, but it didn't. It simply dipped its muzzle into the body cavity, and methodically began yanking out chunks of flesh.

Cohen was disappointed. The battle of the dinosaurs had been fun, the killing had been well engineered, and there had certainly been enough blood, but there was no *terror*. No sense that the *Triceratops* had been quivering with fear, no begging for mercy. No feeling of power, of control. Just dumb, mindless brutes moving in ways preprogrammed by their genes.

It wasn't enough. Not nearly enough.

Judge Hoskins looked across the desk in her chambers at the lawyer.

"A *Tyrannosaurus*, Mr. Axworthy? I was speaking figuratively."

"I understand that, my lady, but it was an appropriate observation, don't you think? I've contacted the Chronotransference people, who say they can do it, if they have a rex specimen to work from. They have to back-propagate from actual physical material in order to get a temporal fix."

Judge Hoskins was as unimpressed by scientific babble as she was by legal jargon. "Make your point, Mr. Axworthy."

"I called the Royal Tyrell Museum of Paleontology in Drumheller and asked them about the *Tyrannosaurus* fossils available worldwide. Turns out there's only a handful of complete skeletons, but they were able to provide me with an annotated list, giving as much information as they could about the individual probable causes of death." He slid a thin plastic printout sheet across the judge's wide desk.

"Leave this with me, counsel. I'll get back to you."

Axworthy left, and Hoskins scanned the brief list. She then leaned back in her leather chair and began to read the needlepoint on her wall for the thousandth time:

My object all sublime
I shall achieve in time—

She read that line again, her lips moving slightly as she subvocalized the words: "I shall achieve *in time . . .*"

The judge turned back to the list of tyrannosaur finds. Ah, that one. Yes, that would be perfect. She pushed a button on her phone. "David, see if you can find Mr. Axworthy for me."

There had been a very unusual aspect to the *Triceratops* kill—an aspect that intrigued Cohen. Chronotransference had been performed countless times; it was one of the most popular forms of euthanasia. Sometimes the transferee's original body would give an ongoing commentary about what was going on, as if talking during sleep. It was clear from what they said that transferees couldn't exert any control over the bodies they were transferred into.

Indeed, the physicists had claimed any control was impossible. Chronotransference worked precisely because the transferee could exert no influence, and therefore was simply observing things that had already been observed. Since no new observations were being made, no quantum-mechanical distortions occurred. After all, said the physicists, if one could exert control, one could change the past. And that was impossible.

And yet, when Cohen had willed the rex to alter its course, it eventually had done so.

Could it be that the rex had so little brains that Cohen's thoughts *could* control the beast?

Madness. The ramifications were incredible.

Still . . .

He had to know if it was true. The rex was torpid, flopped on its belly, gorged on ceratopsian meat. It seemed prepared to lie here for a long time to come, enjoying the early evening breeze.

Get up, thought Cohen. *Get up, damn you!*

Nothing. No response.

Get up!

The rex's lower jaw was resting on the ground. Its upper jaw was lifted high, its mouth wide open. Tiny pterosaurs were flitting in and out of the open maw, their long needle-like beaks apparently yanking gobbets of horn-face flesh from between the rex's curved teeth.

Get up, thought Cohen again. *Get up!*

The rex stirred.

Up!

The tyrannosaur used its tiny forelimbs to keep its torso from sliding forward as it pushed with its powerful legs until it was standing.

Forward, thought Cohen. *Forward!*

The beast's body felt different. Its belly was full to bursting.

Forward!

With ponderous steps, the rex began to march.

It was wonderful. To be in control again! Cohen felt the old thrill of the hunt.

And he knew exactly what he was looking for.

"Judge Hoskins says okay," said Axworthy. "She's authorized for you to be transferred into that new *T. rex* they've got right here in Alberta at the Tyrrell. It's a young adult, they say. Judging by the way the skeleton was found, the rex died falling, probably into a fissure. Both legs and the back were broken, but the skeleton remained almost completely articulated, suggesting that scavengers couldn't get at it. Unfortunately, the chronotransference people say that back-propagating that far into the past they can only plug you in a few hours before the accident occurred. But you'll get your wish: you're going to die as a tyrannosaur. Oh, and here are the books you asked for: a complete library on Cretaceous flora and fauna. You should have time to get through it all; the chronotransference people will need a couple of weeks to set up."

As the prehistoric evening turned to night, Cohen found what he had been looking for, cowering in some underbrush: large brown eyes, long, drawn-out face, and a lithe body covered in fur that, to the tyrannosaur's eyes, looked blue-brown.

A mammal. But not just any mammal. *Purgatorius,* the very first primate, known from Montana and Alberta from right at the end of the Cretaceous. A little guy, only about ten centimetres long, excluding its ratlike tail. Rare creatures, these days. Only a precious few.

The little furball could run quickly for its size, but a single step by the tyrannosaur equaled more than a hundred of the mammal's. There was no way it could escape.

The rex leaned in close, and Cohen saw the furball's face, the nearest thing there would be to a human face for another sixty million years. The animal's eyes went wide in terror.

Naked, raw fear.

Mammalian fear.

Cohen saw the creature scream.

Heard it scream.

It was beautiful.

The rex moved its gaping jaws in toward the little mammal, drawing in breath with such force that it sucked the creature into its maw. Normally the rex would swallow its meals whole, but Cohen prevented the beast from doing that. Instead, he simply had it stand still, with the little primate running around, terrified, inside the great cavern of the dinosaur's mouth, banging into the giant teeth and great fleshy walls, and skittering over the massive, dry tongue.

Cohen savoured the terrified squealing. He wallowed in the sensation of the animal, mad with fear, moving inside that living prison.

And at last, with a great, glorious release, Cohen put the animal out of its misery, allowing the rex to swallow it, the furball tickling as it slid down the giant's throat.

It was just like old times.

Just like hunting humans.

And then a wonderful thought occurred to Cohen. Why, if he killed enough of these little screaming balls of fur, they wouldn't have any descendants. There wouldn't ever be any *Homo sapiens.* In a very real sense, Cohen realized he *was* hunting humans—every single human being who would ever exist.

Of course, a few hours wouldn't be enough time to kill many of them. Judge Hoskins no doubt thought it was wonderfully poetic justice, or she wouldn't have allowed the transfer: sending him back to fall into the pit, damned.

Stupid judge. Why, now that he could control the beast, there was no way he was going to let it die young. He'd just—

There it was. The fissure, a long gash in the earth, with a crumbling edge. Damn, it *was* hard to see. The shadows cast by neighbouring trees made a confusing gridwork on the ground that obscured the ragged opening. No wonder the dull-witted rex had missed seeing it until it was too late.

But not this time.

Turn left, thought Cohen.

Left.

His rex obeyed.

He'd avoid this particular area in future, just to be on the safe side. Besides, there was plenty of territory to cover. Fortunately, this was a young rex—a juvenile. There would be decades in which to continue his very special hunt. Cohen was sure that Axworthy knew his stuff: once it became apparent that the link had lasted longer than a few hours, he'd keep any attempt to pull the plug tied up in the courts for years.

Cohen felt the old pressure building in himself, and in the rex. The tyrannosaur marched on.

This was *better* than old times, he thought. Much better.

Hunting all of humanity.

The release would be *wonderful*.

He watched intently for any sign of movement in the underbrush.

STARDUST BOULEVARD

Daniel Sernine

Translated from the French by Jane Brierley

Daniel Sernine is one of the most important French Canadian SF writers, and certainly the most prolific. His first SF story was published in 1975 in *Requiem* (now *Solaris*) and since then he has published seventy-six more stories and thirty books, including six collections of horror/fantasy, three collections of science fiction, two science fiction novels, one anthology, thirteen juvenile SF and fantasy novels, and three children's books. He is the editor of *Lurelu,* a magazine about children's literature, and of a line of juvenile novels, and is a member of the editorial staff of *Solaris.* He is active as a lecturer, reviewer, and critic. His many literary awards include the Prix Dagon (1977), the Prix Solaris (1982), the Canada Council Award in Children's Literature (1984), the Prix Boréal (twice in 1992, for best short story and best book), and the Grand Prix de la Science-Fiction et du Fantastique Québécois (1992). It is worth noting that the French Canadian SF community has been immeasurably advanced since the mid-1970's by the existence of two regularly published SF magazines, without which careers such as Sernine's might not have been supportable. In that sense, the francophone SF community in Quebec has a longer tradition than the anglophone Canadians, but is less accessible to the rest of the SF world because of the language barrier. One hopes that the forthcoming *Tesseracts Q,* a full volume of translations, will accelerate the communication between the two Canadian SF communities inagurated in *Tesseracts.*

"Stardust Boulevard" is the first of six short stories and novellas written by Daniel Sernine between 1980 and 1989, all set in a never-ending Carnival in a postcataclysmic North American city, unnamed, but presumably Montreal. The whole cycle was collected and published in two volumes. This story, from *Tesseracts,* is the only one of them thus far published in English. "Influences on these stories," Sernine writes, "can be tracked to Ballard's *Vermillion Sands,* Ridley Scott's *Blade Runner,* the clip of Anderson & Vangelis' 'Friends of Mr. Cairo,' the careers of Québécois racing-car pilot Gilles Villeneuve and American rock star Jim Morrison, black-and-white detective movies of the forties, Doors and Eagles songs from the seventies, as well as the general mood and certain events of the 'peace and love' era—and Sernine's feeling of having missed something great because he was too quiet and a few years too young."

Morning. Fountain Place. The square is in shadow and will remain so for long hours yet, because buildings border it on three sides. As I sit in the shade looking up at a boundless blue sky, the fresh morning air soothes the fevers of the night.

The Place is deserted. It couldn't be otherwise: the morning calm, the morning mood implies solitude. I'd be startled to see someone else here. I wonder—was it possible to find yourself alone like this, to *feel* alone, at peace, in the days when there were billions of people on this planet?

My cough reverberates sharply between the façades.

It's so vast here, the wind blows so freely I find it hard to imagine that it was once unbearably crowded; perhaps not in this neighbourhood of tall buildings and esplanades.

The concrete rim I'm sitting on is still cool from the night. I don't remember deciding to sit down. That's one of the benefits of being stoned: you don't have to decide what you'll do or say; some apparently independent mental mechanism looks after it.

Running water. The soft gurgle is that of city water rather than a brook. It rises within a thin glass wall and streams down the outer surface. With a little imagination it might be a curtain of water. From one level to another it has been cascading for decades, polishing the surfaces and rounding off the rough edges. I can't find it in my heart to resent the person who dreamt up these concrete blocks, these rectilinear falls and square pools, a century ago. They have a beauty of their own.

The tall façades are lifeless. Just as well. The only time I saw them in motion they were bending over to grab me. Very unpleasant. Now they are empty, deserted. Not a face at any of the windows, not a curtain fluttering; there must be apartments that no one's gone into for decades. I don't know whether the architect who created this apartment complex had imagined it fully occupied; it can't ever have been the case, anyway, since that was around the time of the Big Sweep. Now only the last two or three floors are lived in. And sometimes one of the unoccupied apartments—when teenagers from the lower town feel like a change of scene.

Well, what do you know. I'm not alone any more. Someone is coming down from one of the top floors by a rope fastened to a balcony. Maher Stelson, of course, unless someone else has had the same idea. He could use the elevator to do his shopping and take his daily exercise, but the rope is . . . more fitting.

Except that one of these days he's going to go splat on the esplanade. Blood and brains all over the place. That'll keep us amused for a while. Nice of him.

In the meantime I'm going in. I'm no longer alone with my morning.

Caught up in a farandole, a great motley caterpillar that gets longer with every wriggle. I was stoned before I came, and here I am on Stardust Boulevard cavorting under the Carnival lanterns without really meaning to.

Cavorting. . . . Perhaps finding. . . .

It isn't very crowded—it never is, even if nearly the whole town is here—but the blare of the loudspeakers is deafening: music, laughter and exclamations, excited voices. You get used to the contradiction of hearing the noise of a lively crowd when there isn't one; anybody not in the know would put it down to being stoned.

A little hand, tepid, soft, slightly limp, takes mine on the left. I turn and see a small woman behind me, a girl perhaps. She's simply dressed: fringed jacket over a flowered blouse. Curly, blond locks over a white face and a sad smile. Deep, shadowed eyes that look elsewhere.

The hand holding my right is icy. The woman is tall and slender; greendelight has turned her into a double-jointed marionette. I see her capering about, pliable bones going every which way. She seems to be able to do anything with her body and still hold together by some miracle. Her face is mauve underneath the pink frizz, three green ovals surround her mouth and eyes. I can't see her costume clearly; lots of veils and feathers, a train streaming out behind her as she rushes along. But her eyes . . . her eyes when she turns around and looks right through me, laughing wildly . . . I break the chain and leave the farandole.

I begin working my way against the flow of the parade. I'll be able to see everyone this way. And perhaps I'll find what I'm looking for.

Image after image. I don't see them come, I don't see them go. I live only in a very finished present that excludes all continuity. To keep it that way, I light up another joint.

The pageant goes on. Characters the size of elephants, escaped from a vial of greendelight. Floating in front of a brilliantly lit UFO, a large alien advances, toga white, hair silver, face blue with an enigmatic beauty. Around him little green men dance in a circle.

Here comes a grotesque lunar excursion module made of balsa wood and silver paper, supported by two trotting legs emerging from its blast pipe. Half a dozen ungainly midgets in space suits bounce around it with the comic slow-motion of astronauts.

A huge, silky dove, washbasin white, skims the ground. I pass under one of its stiff, slowly beating wings, coming out with my hair covered in confetti-sequins thrown by the Priestesses of Peace, their eyes perpetually turned heavenward.

Here is Christ. On his big cardboard cross he's laughing his head off while some skinheads in orange togas prance around him with cymbal and fife.

The balloons have passed by. I watch them go, then turn to find myself face to face with a dragon.

It undulates, a thing of crepe paper and streamers with a fabulous head—a real oriental demon. It spits fire and people draw back, shrieking, excited.

A woman surges forward, twirling in the space cleared by the dragon's breath. It's the junkie I just left, the green and mauve one. Her laughter is demented, her eyes more glittering than ever. The long veils swirl around her, and the rosy hair looks as though electrified by a Van de Graaff generator.

People fall silent and watch. A reeling drunk bumps into the nearest loudspeaker stand and knocks it over. A resonant sputter: the music, laughter and exclamations drop a tone.

She dances, dances, a whirling dervish, twisting and turning, an eddy of colour.

In front of the dragon's head.
That stops its progress and undulates where it stands.
Its ferocious eyes trained on her.
She dances, spins.
Throws herself down on her knees, back arched, arms thrown wide, throat prof-
fered beneath the smoking muzzle.
With a roar of flame, it blasts.

I'm hazy about the time, but there's no mistaking the sun's noonday glare. I would have thought I'd sleep longer, and yet here I am outdoors again, still stoned, but coughing a little less.

Beneath the burning sun the city stretches out in lawns and esplanades, its harmonious buildings rising almost everywhere. All these uninhabited architects' challenges, these sculptural dwellings of glass and concrete, have become monuments. Or memorials?

Their pinnacles pierce the clear sky like blades.

On the esplanade—which one? they have names, I think—Chris and Maryse are seated on the concrete border of an immense square flower bed in the full sunlight.

Should I go up to them? They don't seem to be arguing—even that is too much.

I move forward.

As I walk towards them they remain motionless, apparently silent, looking vaguely at the horizon.

Something is placed between them. What? A candle.

Maryse becomes aware of my presence and recognizes me. A smile—tender? knowing?—lights her thin, angular face.

I draw near.

The candle is lit. In full sunlight. This mania for messages! I don't think I'll stay long.

Stardust Boulevard. The Carnival plays on. The cafés are on a parallel artery,
Bloomgarden Street. Why this name? The only things blooming are the café terraces
and, behind heavy doors at the foot of staircases, the dens.

No festoons of lights over the street here, only lamps on the café walls.

I come out of Life on Mars. *I'd only found John, Guy and Cornelius, all three*
already half-stoned. We talked for a bit, with long pauses, like old buddies. Then I
left them.

Moonlight Café. Faces I've seen before, a few I actually know. I pick a small
table on the second terrace, the one overlooking the street on the corner of the Ca-
rouseway.

O'Reilly's doublewhammy. Nothing better for my cough. The first shotglass
still makes me wince. But the others slide down easily, and their heat decongests my
lungs.

The Carnival music penetrates even here, of course. And the laughter, the exclamations, the excited voices. Powerful loudspeakers.

Now and then the sound of a firecracker, the faint whiff of laughing-gas. Occasionally, bubblelights go by, chased by children shrill with fatigue. It's late.

The Carouseway is not lit. At the end of this dark trench I can see a slice of Stardust Boulevard. Like a stage set from the very back of the theatre. Brilliantly lighted.

Sarabandes. A cavalcade. But there is more noise than there are people. I muse on what Carnivals must have been like before the Big Sweep, when there were millions and millions of people in the cities. New Orleans! Venice! Quebec! Nice! Trinidad! Rio! It must have been delirious. I've never seen anything like that; it's hard to imagine. . . . But it must have been hell to make them come to that decision. I'm not one to complain about the Big Sweep, anyway. How could you—how did you—merely survive in this city when there were a thousand times more people? It's beyond comprehension, like trying to picture the immensity of the galaxy. In any case, no one complains about the Big Sweep these days, not even old people; they're just glad to be able to breathe freely.

The thing is, if the Big Sweep had really succeeded there'd be no Earthlings left.

"Munchies, mister?"

Why not? The boy is perhaps twelve, thirteen. Dark-haired, pretty. His made-up eyes have an equivocal look. He carries his munchies in a basket like a flower girl her roses. I select a yellow one.

"Munchies? Munchies?"

He moves off, threading his way between the tables. I look away.

Well, now. There's a face I've seen recently. On the first terrace, the one at street level. Beside the wrought-iron railing. Alone at a table.

The blond from the farandole.

That mop of hair like pale seaweed gathered on the shore. Bizarre: one long, curled strand; one long, frizzed strand; one curled; one frizzed. Two panels of alternating threads drape a pale, so pale, face.

Dark, unfathomable eyes.

Something strange. I can't put my finger on it.

Flickering. The girl and her table are flickering like a candle flame in a draft. The munchy is working.

I look towards the Boulevard. The lighted scene stands out like a series of frames on a film strip.

More inflatable allegories. A large, rotund tree. Then another and another, prancing along. Next a cohort of flowers, their faces indistinguishable at the centre of their corollas.

Now I see only one frame at a time. The receding ones fade out behind one another, away from the present. The coming images are still blurred, transparent, ahead of reality.

Everything radiates gold. The golden gleam of the torches. The golden lightbulbs

*in the illuminated wreaths. The gold lamé of some of the costumes. The sousaphones
and tubas of a brass band.*

*My camera eye reverts to the terrace. The pale-faced little blond has left. Is that
her disappearing down Bloomgarden Street? Too bad.*

The munchy is already losing its potency. It's just candy.

Another shot of doublewhammy and I'll be off to the Straynight Cabaret.

The sky has changed. No, not the sky: it has stayed blue, limpid. But what
must be a wind of very high altitude is pushing big white clouds along. It
creates an atmosphere, a very special light, a continual contrast between
chiaroscuro and full sun. I don't like this weather; the light is too harsh, too
brusque in its variations, and I feel threatened, uncomfortable. Such days
put me in a very odd mood. Not really depressive, a sort of aggravated consciousness. Of time fleeting. Time wasted. Of dabblings leading nowhere.
Of the inanity of doing anything.

Uptown, where the daring but empty buildings are—empty, but carefully maintained for aesthetic reasons—robot-sweepers stream along the esplanades and automatic mowers whirr in the parks. On the lawns the idlers
flourish. In Century Park I catch sight of Philip underneath the great trees.

Philip passes the time making art objects.

They're fine. You can't deny the things he does are fine. They're difficult
to describe. Sculpture? They're more like three-dimensional collages.
Stained glass and precious stones assembled on delicate metal frames.

He's just finished one and is showing it in the park. Standing on its gran-
ite pedestal it looks to me like a cylinder in shades of sapphire, amethyst and
garnet, set in silver. Apparently it's supposed to sing as well, at dawn and
dusk. Rapid variations of light and heat activate chords memorized in the
very structure of crystal and gems.

I stop beside the artist in front of the pedestal.

"Has it got a title?"

"I'm open to suggestion."

He's almost bald, with a greying beard. And yet he's not so old. But
burnt out. Why? Because he's put too much of himself into his works?
They're stale as dregs. Or so it seems to me. But perhaps that's the way he's
made. Who am I to judge?

"So—what do you suggest?"

I think of the candle in full sun.

"Leisure Society."

I don't think he appreciates it. I move away.

Seated on the edge of the man-made lake, a little girl searches gravely in
her bag of marbles. She's having fun. Is she having fun? Perhaps; she's too
young to be bored. She's having fun throwing them in the pond to make
circles.

Passing close to her I notice that the marbles are jewels. Emeralds, diamonds, rubies, roughly cut.

They make a very ordinary plop as they hit the water.

The dens.

Smoky, sewer-dark.

Syncopated flashes above the sweaty, gleaming torsos, dancing, dancing. The music is a solid block. And a powerful rhythm, making the room a monstrous, engorged heart.

But it's a trick: the room is tiny, the walls covered with mirrors. The crowding is an illusion, a few dozen seem like several hundred. Sometimes you find that after fifteen minutes of ardent looks, the face you're eyeing is your own. Cruising yourself: the height of narcissism! Or just schizo.

In the dens the looks are heavy, the hands insistent. Here is a woman—or is it? Here is a man—or is it? Doubt blossoms in the shadows. The couples that form and leave give rise to the wildest speculation. For many, the doubt continues until they're in bed. And even after.

I haven't found what I'm looking for.

Haven't even been able to get near the bar to have a drink.

I saw the little munchy-vendor, but someone carried him off. Too bad.

An eddy among the surrounding people brings me face to face with an Erymaean—well, I'm not sure whether he's an Atropian, a Psychaean, a Dissident or God knows what. I've never been able to figure out all these parties. But in general you can recognize Erymaeans by their subtly tragic expression, by their air of purposefulness. They haven't that vacuous look we Earthlings get from being idle. But it's something very subtle, something you feel rather than see.

This one really looks the part. There are people like that; Philip, for instance. They really have—or else they contrive to have, consciously or not—the face that corresponds to their calling or station. The stereotype.

He's clothed in black with simple silver embroidery. Some Erymaeans like sombre colours. And he is sombre: black hair greying at the temples; serious eyes surrounded by a network of fine lines; thin, pale lips from having smiled too little; a lean face with something aristocratic in its features.

I wonder what he's doing here? I wouldn't have thought that Erymaeans frequented dens. But no doubt he's here for a reason.

He's already behind me, out of my line of vision.

I'm leaving because the smoke really isn't helping my cough.

The air in the street seems cold, making me shiver. This isn't very healthy either. The night closes behind me, peopled with furtive shadows.

Probing hands in the den have given me a furious desire to screw. Let's go to the woods.

* * *

In the azure sky the moon is in its first quarter. Its texture by day is not at all the same as by night: this crescent, this demi-circle, looks as insubstantial as mist. Hard to believe it's a globe of rock, especially the part you can't see— invisible, therefore transparent?—and yet it's tangible. But you see the clear blue of the sky where you know the other half of the globe exists. Come to think of it, do you *know*? Doesn't its existence depend on the light it receives—and if not lighted, then non-existent? If the blue of the sky were *behind* the moon, you'd see a white crescent and the rest of the globe in black. Therefore the blue of the sky is *in front* of the moon: but that's also an illusion, merely the effect of light and optics. Everything is illusion, Philip would say. Except that he deludes himself with words. I've tried to deceive myself with empty arguments, tried to make them dizzyingly metaphysical, but it doesn't work: the moon is still there, concrete, whole, I *know* it. Even when smoking I'm not able to make reality abstract, to escape.

Amusing to think that the people of Argus are perhaps behind the transparent, immaterial portion of the moon; a tiny dot in the blue sky, to the left of the first quarter.

Now why did I think of Argus? Is the city still inhabited? They haven't anything left to observe: the Earthlings are so quiet, so inoffensive, since becoming a mere handful, no longer obliged to fight over land and resources. Are the underground halls of Argus deserted? Or are they haunted too, like our cities, by a few people whom leisure has rendered hollow, shallow, without ties—mere party balloons. Has boredom overtaken the Erymaeans? What a joke: to be condemned to idleness by Peace on Earth, their *raison d'être* since time immemorial.

A hand touches my arm before I reach Stardust Boulevard. I turn my head: the Erymaean of a moment ago. A Psychaean, I now observe; the breeze has lifted a lock of hair from his temple, revealing the small triangular interface.

He scrutinizes me intently, as though to scan not my mind but my soul, if in fact I have one.

I submit to his scrutiny without flinching, and, funny thing, I imagine the contrast between the black diamonds of his hard, piercing eyes with their clear-cut irises, and my own as they must be at the moment: washed-out blue seeping into the rosy-veined whites, as though melting in the water that constantly bathes my eyes.

Everything about him seems clear cut: his elegant but sober costume, his precise way of speaking, his intensity. It's the intensity, I think, that I envy; I feel I'm always . . . blurred, vague.

"Are you happy?"

What's he getting at? And that almost solicitous air, as though he really cared about my happiness, about the happiness of us Earthlings. They've always been concerned about us.

Just curiosity? More than that. Is he conducting a sociological survey? His question seems more like a heartfelt cry.

"I'm okay," I answer. "I can't complain."

"But still—don't you sense . . . something missing, some uneasiness?"

Some uneasiness! I should ask him to spend a few days inside my head; then he'd see. Some uneasiness. . . . Yes, perhaps: to live is an uneasiness. But I'm not about to unburden my soul to him in the midst of the thronging Carnival crowd—we've reached the Boulevard and its merrymaking. I answer by telling him what I'm missing most.

"Right now what I want most is a good screw."

"There must be something else. . . ."

"So long, buddy. At least try to have a little fun."

I think I've disappointed him. No, not really disappointed. Hurt. He carries a burden of hurt that I've made a bit heavier, just a bit. But he could have stopped anyone in the street and got the same sort of answer, or an even more curt retort. For a moment I think of turning back and saying, "You shouldn't worry about us; we're okay like this, I suppose. There's no way we'd want to live like they did in the last century."

I look behind me. He's standing where I left him, scanning the merrymakers with a sombre eye. He's not going to interrogate anyone else. It was just something that came over him all of a sudden; he spotted me—perhaps I also look very much the part.

Poor guy. I'd rather be me than you, with all those gloomy thoughts festering in your head. Is it remorse? You should have a fix of greendelight; it'd do you good, make you forget.

A cortège of inflatable myths hides him from view: great country bumpkins swollen to bursting, girls in peasant skirts and ankle-boots, pink with health. I bump into someone—I should look where I'm going—and then a really clever juggler by the roadside makes me forget all about the Erymaean.

Not really, though; who can forget the Erymaeans?

I've lost the moon and here I am, alone again, between two long buildings that form an artificial canyon. The shade is cool at the end of the day.

This is the silence I like. I don't think anyone lives here.

The slice of sky is blue, with a few fast-moving, grey-bellied clouds. I stop and look up. I like it when there are clouds. You'd think the tops of the buildings were moving against a steady background of sky. Like standing at the bowsprit of a ship. Dizzying, even when you haven't had anything. When you're stoned, it's better to stretch out on the concrete; it creates the perfect illusion.

Time passes unnoticed.

Children's voices. I turn to look, propping myself up on one elbow.

Over there in the square. Two or three kids on low-slung tricycles, the ones with a huge front wheel and gears. The fun is in skidding around corners, but at those speeds it's dangerous. The kids are helmeted and swathed in elbow guards and kneepads.

One of them heads in my direction.

I watch him coming the length of the canyon.

Quite effective.

He jams on the pedals, braking at my feet. I've risen.

"Come and see, mister. Aeros."

He turns on a dime; look at the way he handles that cycle! And off he goes. I run after him, feeling like a teenager with my beat-up running shoes, my jeans and T-shirt. I feel the wind in my long hair—a bit stiff; I'll have to see about washing it.

I pass the little guy, but by the time he catches up with me on the square I'm doubled over with a coughing fit. The other kids—are there four?—watch me without a word.

"How old are you?" finally asks a little girl with yellow ribbons.

It's not the one with the jewels. This one's even younger.

"Twenty-two, I think."

I look up at the sky: two aeros. Who had talked of going up? Charles, I think. And the girl who was with him last time . . . Vonda? It doesn't matter, anyway. Their aeros are high up, you can't hear them. It's mainly the vapour trail that shows they're there. They make patterns, arabesques. Symbols? I'm not stoned enough to read anything into it.

I find they're delaying, dragging out the show. The children have already started pedalling and shouting.

"How old are you?"

It's the same kid.

"I just told you."

"Have you a mom?"

"Everyone has."

"And a dad?"

"Must have."

"And a little brother?"

"Yes."

The crafts have stopped their somersaults.

"How old is he?"

"He's dead."

"How old was he?"

I really think they're getting ready for the grand finale.

"How old was he?"

"Sixteen."

Yes, there they go, letting off all the remaining smoke charges. Red, as it should be.

"How did he die?"

Two thick red lines converge on a huge field of azure.

"How did he die?"

I raise my arm and point.

"Like that."

Short and sharp. Head on.

Did I *see* the aeros break up a fraction of a second before the explosion? Bravo! Not surprising their somersaults were a bit slow, with a payload like that.

The flash has tinged the cloud-bellies pink, hundreds of metres above. Pink, green, a hint of silver in the falling debris. A beautiful combination.

The smoke lasts for quite some time, white as real cloud but with a glow underneath.

I'll have to find out if that was Charles. I didn't think he was up to such a good performance.

A Carnival night without fireworks wouldn't be the same. Pyrotechnics have certainly improved since the ancient Chinese, but I don't think the ritual of exclamations has changed. The oohs! and ahs! of the spectators are those of my grandparents on public holidays. I don't think you ever get tired of it. Except that fireworks can't fill your whole life.

In Century Park at the end of Stardust Boulevard I find a good place to look up at the sky. I should have taken two munchies from the little vendor just now in the Moonlight Café. They're best when you're watching fireworks.

Among the heads lit up by the explosions I see a light gold one. The girl with the curly-frizzy-curly hair. Her head is lowered, her pale face in shadow. And her eyes are two wells of darkness.

Still the same sad, fixed smile.

I realize that unconsciously I've been looking for her.

She manoeuvres her way between the people and animated sculptures, walking purposefully towards the park woods. She's taken off her sandals and lets her feet drag on the grass. Waves of whistling rockets—the kind that don't go very high and form a curtain of colours—silhouette her against the light, a frail outline on a luminous ground, her head a fluffy halo.

I stay a moment to watch the sprays, the showers of gold, the bursts of colour, the fleeting comets, the small, blinding suns.

Then I climb the gentle slope as far as the woods.

The echo of Carnival fades as you go beyond the first line of trees. Even the explosions are somewhat subdued. The flashes filter through the young leaves, lighting the scene in snatches. People leaning against the trees, or strolling, hands in their pockets.

As you penetrate the wood, the human density increases. There are almost as many people as on the Boulevard. They scrutinize each other as they pass, but the darkness only allows them an impression. Guys? Girls? Men? Women? Everything is in the way they walk, linger, turn their heads to look intently at one another.

Hands furtively probing to check or make contact. Hands gently pushed away, or grasped and held.

Murmurs. Friends meet, recognize each other, light up a joint, part to continue the round.

From the thickets come whispers, sighs, raucous breathing.

In the heart of the woods is where it happens. In couples. Leaning against trees, stretched out beside a bush or one kneeling while the other stands. In clusters on the grass, confused movements, soft slitherings, glimpses of white skin when a flash lights up the sky. Passersby meld, separate, in incessant rotation.

Gasps, sucks, hisses.

I don't enter into the orgy, not for now, at any rate. You can't always control what's happening; my anus is still sore from being buggered yesterday evening because I was too stoned to get myself out of a tangle of arms and legs.

I go back to the less thriving section.

And there, in front of me, is the little blond again.

Perhaps she's what I'm looking for?

She looks at me steadily, deeply. The fixed smile on her pale face makes me uncomfortable.

My hand seeks hers. Slim and warm. Soft, slightly limp. Like in the farandole.

Almost blindly we reach a bank and lie down on it.

That pathetic smile, that unmoving face. . . .

I bring mine close to hers.

With a rapid movement she lifts hers off.

Her mask.

My lips touch hers before I've had time to see her real face. My fingers find it slim, angular, firm-skinned. And the eyes that open when I open mine are the black holes that I wanted to sink into.

Her blouse opens on slight breasts. How old is she, then?

Awkward rubbings and squirmings. Our jeans are off at last, our legs find each other, entwine, our bodies roll.

The damp triangle is not blond. I look up, see a dark head with short hair. The wig is on the grass, near my T-shirt rolled up in a ball. The fireworks have stopped.

The rest happens as usual. Even stoned, I come right away—the hands in the den really turned me on—but I keep it up until she shudders and lies quiet.

I've heard those stifled little cries before.

We go on for a moment, giving pleasure to our bodies that came here for this purpose. But it isn't as if the little blond were . . . what she seemed.

But just what am I looking for? It's pathetic: I don't even have a clear idea. And when I find it, if there is anything to find, it will be vague, uncertain. Am I actually looking for someone? That would be too easy: I might end up finding someone, there aren't that many of us. A mirage, then, that will always elude my grasp just when I think I've caught it?

I'm asking too many questions. There are times like this, especially after making love, when my mind becomes cruelly lucid despite the smoke I inhale.

It doesn't last, fortunately, and the next day I take up where I left off.

The girl and I get dressed. She puts her wig back on, but not her mask. We head towards the edge of the woods.

Her hand feels for mine. I take it. Soft and warm, but now her clasp is firm.

A little before reaching the open area of the Park, those vast lawns planted with singing sculptures, we stop for a last kiss. Passionate, as is often the case here, expressing the tacit closeness, the almost pathetic moment of great tenderness, the complicity of two absurd lives that, for the space of an embrace, have sought to reach something together.

Already our bodies move away from each other. Her hand grasps mine hard, and I return the pressure. Then we drop hands and, without looking back, I walk towards Stardust Boulevard where the Carnival hasn't yet run out of steam.

I think that was Maryse.

At twilight people stroll on the promenade overlooking the lower town. If we were in a seaside resort this would be the boardwalk along the ocean front, with bonfires on the dunes, cocktails on the villa patios, with poets, actors and artists.

Here there are also poets, actors and artists, and this evening most of them will go down to Stardust Boulevard to play among the Carnival characters, masked and music-making, to recite their verses on the café terraces, to dance and show their fine bodies in the dens.

I lean on the balustrade, my head swimming a little, my stomach churning.

The Boulevard is lighting up for the Carnival, but all I can see are the images of this day. The aeros and Charles, my little sixteen-year-old brother. Chris and his candle lighted in full sun.

Maher Stelson is dead. I saw him sprawled on the concrete when I went home just now to shower and change. Blood and brains splattered all over the place, as I'd pictured. Greendelight sometimes gives you premonitions. Too bad he did it when I wasn't around. In fact, it seems that no one saw it happen: the body was lying alone, still warm. Poor Stelson. Climbing up and down his rope every day for months on end—it was a good idea—and then to flub his exit line like that. . . .

There's a planetary show tonight. Before going down to the Carnival I'll stay on the promenade for a while and watch, since it's beginning in a minute.

And not a munchy vendor in sight.

The ships have all lit up at once. There must be at least twenty in translunar orbit.

They form a four-pronged star. That pulses and fades. Hey, look at that! They make a line that must stretch halfway across the sky. A vast, synchronized movement, from east to west, like a bow drawn across the firmament. Then the ships close up.

What speeds they must be doing!

Energy beams! From one ship to another, a line of bluish, vibrating lights. A good start, if they're going to stay up for an hour.

It might have been an interesting job. Astronaut. Of course, it's no big deal, just entertainment for idlers. But all the same, to see good old Earth from up there. Now it's done by remote control and they don't need pilots. They wouldn't have picked me anyway; my health isn't good enough.

I'm impatient to see the Northern Lights. Nothing beats it, whatever else they try. Especially when one doesn't have to live up north to see it.

Strange how the best things never last and leave you feeling let down. . . . Yesterday it was that little blond with the sad smile who succeeded in making herself desirable simply by appearing here and there during my trip. The planetary show just now; unforgettable, yes. But I'm already off my high.

Broadgate Street, and no one's going uptown. We're all going in the same direction, towards Stardust Boulevard, towards the cafés and the dens. In little groups, in couples, and alone; there's something to look at and enjoy, in any case.

Tonight again I'll search among the masks and costumes, among the inflatable myths. Beneath the festoons of light, the torches and Chinese lanterns, the bubblelights.

The loudspeakers are already broadcasting music, laughter and exclamations, excited voices.

A particularly violent coughing fit brings my supper up. Just as well, I won't have anything on my stomach. I'd better go by the Moonlight Café *early, though, and have a shot of O'Reilly's doublewhammy.*

The people going down talk of nothing but the planetary show.

"That Catherine Wheel!"

"And the laser battle!"

True, it was a success.

Trainers cross the street with enormous tigers on leashes. Those eyes! Those green eyes! Awesome!

Small circles of four dancers form, chasing each other like links from a broken necklace. A circle opens for me. I stick my joint between my lips and take the two proffered hands.

Tonight again I'll search among the café terraces and in the smoke of the dens. On the grass and among the trees of Century Park.

On Stardust Boulevard the Carnival plays on.

BALLADS IN 3/4 TIME

Robert Charles Wilson

Robert Charles Wilson came to Canada at the age of nine and has lived there continuously—in Toronto, Nanaimo, and Vancouver—ever since. He has been publishing science fiction novels since the late 1980's, all seven from Bantam/Doubleday Books in the U.S., including the most recent, *Mysterium* (1994). His first novel, *A Hidden Place* (1986) marked him as a significant new writer and garnered comparison to the work of Theodore Sturgeon. Two of his books have been selected as Notable Books of the Year by *The New York Times Book Review*, and two were finalists for the Philip K. Dick Award (for a distinguished work of science fiction published as a paperback original in the U.S.).

He writes: "My fondness for science fiction and my fondness for my adopted country are parallel passions. Both have lapsed from time to time. I sometimes travel beyond the borders of both, sometimes with a sense of relief. But I keep coming back. Isn't that the definition of home?" The *Science Fiction Encyclopedia* says of his works: "He expresses with vigor and imagination the great Canadian theme (for the sense of being on the lonely side of a binary has sparked much of the best Canadian SF) of geographical alienation."

He lays claim only to four short stories, all published in science fiction magazines in the late 1980's, of which this is one.

I remember how it was that night we decided to kill Toby Torvis.

It was an average night at Toby's Roadhouse out on Route 16. Probably you don't know Toby's, but you know some place like it: slat roof and gravel parking lot and halide lights that draw the summer bugs in big old clouds, freight trucks whooshing in from the Route and settling down on their repellor shields like dogs curling up to sleep; inside, the drummer and the fiddler and the guitarman up on a wood stage with colored spotlights slung from the rafters and a blue haze of smoke and noise and—this night—me out front dishing up "Rose of Cimarron" or "Tennessee Waltz" in a gingham dress like the preachers' wives wear on TV (only sexier about the neckline). I am, of course, a Phony Girl, a Lonely Nell. My given name is Idella; there is no last.

Toby's Place belonged to Torvis: Toby Torvis, a beer barrel of a man who hated his customers and hated us who worked for him even more. From the stage I could see him shadowing Jack the barman, making sure the drinks weren't too generous. Sometimes Torvis shaved the service so tight it drove customers away, saving nickels and dimes at the expense of dollars. But Torvis didn't care. For a man like that, being miserable is its own reward.

And I could see Lafe, too, as the stage lights dimmed and the band unplugged for a break.

Lafe is the other Phony here, a Barroom Cowboy. He has his own table next to the jukebox. Sometimes I'd see him shooting pool, all by himself because the clientele wouldn't play with him; more often he'd be doing his bounden duty, sweet-talking some half-drunk and goggle-eyed country girl till she was pink in the face and damn near swooning.

It's in the nature of the work we do.

Lafe is handsome as a holostar, and I am, I guess, pretty enough, and we liked each other a lot. I admired his big jaw and his twinkly blue eyes, his razor-creased trousers and his starched white shirt. Right at that moment I wanted to go sit with him—share that dingy round little table with him and sit together proud and contented. But of course, Torvis wouldn't allow it. We had our jobs to do. So I climbed down from the stage and went and sat at my own table, drinking cold tea from a whiskey glass and lighting up a big welcome-howdy smile I did not feel when a feed wholesaler name of Cortney pulled up a chair by my side.

"Pretty girl," he sighed. "My, but you a pretty girl."

I was not so depressed that I could not appreciate a man who calls me that. This one was fat and wore big Buddy Holly glasses; but I like a man who calls me "girl" or "woman." The prissy ones get real upright about it.

It was coming on 1:00 A.M., and I had done a final set, when Cortney got around to the inevitable suggestion. I pointed out the plain silver band round his ring finger and said, "You're a married man, ain'tcha?"

And he blushed very prettily and began a sob story. And so it goes. I paid not much attention.

Over at the other table, Lafe had attracted a mousy woman with gristly cords up her neck and hair like a leaky hayrick. He flashed me one long, careless look, and I returned it . . . we were done before either Whole Human noticed a thing. But it was unprofessional. And I think Torvis might have seen.

Before long I was back in my trailer in the rear lot of the Place, listening to the roar of the traffic on the Route while this man Cortney worked off the memories of his wife. He was sweet and excitable, and it didn't take too long. When he finished, we performed the ritual: he pulled his pants on and said how he loved me but he's got a woman and three kids; and I got teary but tough and told him I understood, making it sound like I really didn't.

And he went home consoled and self-congratulatory, and isn't that the purpose of it all?

That's what they told us, at least, down on the Farm.

It was half past two, and I desperately wanted to sleep; but old Torvis came knocking at the door and rousted me up.

He stood there with his hands on his big belly and his eyebrows humped up like two caterpillars. "There's men inside," he said, "who would like to meet you."

"Aw, come on, Mr. Torvis. In my contract it says—"

"You work for me," he said, "or you don't. That's the long and short of it. So get your flabby ass back into that pretty little dress and get inside."

He's wrong about the contract, but there was nothing I could do about it. As a Fake Person, I don't have what you call recourse to the law. It made me spitting mad, and I thought again of my roommate from the Flesh Farm, Laurel Anne, and how she had one day thrown a pot full of chicken noodle soup right in the face of our Dialect Coach. How good Toby Torvis would look drenched in chicken stock and noodles! But I did what he said.

When I stepped down, there was a ruckus over by Lafe's trailer. A Jealous Husband banging on the door and kicking at the siding. A big one, drunk enough to be mean. Torvis just watched, chewing a fat cigar.

The door swung open. First the wife stumbled out, staring at her husband with big admiring eyes. Then he pushed her behind him, and Lafe came down.

The Jealous Husband said a lot of nasty things and then punched Lafe right in the face.

Lafe fell down. Lafe is big, but he can't do much to protect himself: they wrote that into his wet program. Wouldn't do to have an outraged Fake beating up some hapless Whole Human. That is not in the scenario.

The human man stalked away with his wife.

I wanted to run over to Lafe, but Torvis dragged me back into the Place. That's bad business sense, too, not taking care of his investments.

All for naught. The action had pretty much died down inside. A trucker bought me tea till he collapsed.

Out back, I helped Lafe into my trailer and sponged his bruises.

"Torvis told him," Lafe said sadly. "I mean, I'm prepared to face this sort of thing. But I'm supposed to be safe in the trailer. Torvis told him where I was."

"He's a mean rotten son of a bitch," I said, holding Lafe's pretty face in my two hands, sponging it. "We oughta kill him."

And I saw the light go on in Lafe's eyes.

Laurel Anne, I thought, you would be proud of me now!

Well, it's all so much like a sad old song, isn't it! The songs I sing every night, which come down to one song, which is the Cheater's Blues. And how much we expect from this life, and how much we get.

The word on us Fakes and Phonies is that we do a service to the true and good order of things. Torvis reminded us of that now and then, though in a leering, nasty tone of voice. Didn't matter. I believed him. The TV preachers talk about the sacred values of the Family, and Love and Marriage and the Happy Ending, and I believe them, too.

But the devil is in Whole Humans like a stain that won't wash out; and we (Phonies like Lafe and me) are here to ensure that those bad impulses don't do permanent damage. Say a married man like that nice Mr. Cortney needs to sow some wild oats. A thing like that could ruin his entire life, set him on the road to Sin Black as Night . . . unless he comes to me.

I give him all he's longing for, not just the physical aspect but the lingering looks and the heartbreak and the little good-byes that stab and burn. And in the morning he can go back to his wife and negotiate forgiveness from her and the Lord. And I don't suffer because I have no human soul.

Lafe performs much the same service for women like, presumably, Mr. Cortney's wife; except that an irate husband has the option of punching him out. Another service we provide.

Happy to Serve was the motto at the backwater Georgia flesh farm where I was bred. Job satisfaction is burned into my neocortex, along with the Role I perform. What with all that, I guess I should have been happy, right? And was I?

Oh my Lord, no.

Lafe and I discussed this one Tuesday night in my trailer. Torvis had closed up and gone home, and there were crickets chirping away in the hour before dawn. "We're not getting anywhere," Lafe said, his eyes half open in the dark. "And we're not getting younger. If we had a decent contract, we might have been able to buy ourselves out by now. Buy our freedom and maybe take out a franchise on some roadhouse of our own somewhere." The standard dream. "But Torvis leeches away our salaries on his so-called expenses. And we get screwed." In any sense of the word.

"But, Lafe, if we actually—you know—"

I could not bring myself to say it.

"I've got it all figured out," Lafe said. "Torvis is vulnerable because of what he is. He's an old bull with no family that'll speak to him and no friends and no possessions but the Place. And I know where he keeps his records. We kill him, and I'll doctor the books to make it look like we bought him out and he just moved on. We get all we want all at once." His eyes were like saucers, and he hugged me. "You and me together, Idella."

It's forbidden for Fakes to marry. Marriage is a sacred institution, and we were grown in vats like meat, not born. But if we owned the Place, or appeared to, nobody would say boo if we shared a back room.

And I thought again of Laurel Anne. My best friend back at the Farm, she had kept me up late hours whispering all sorts of sedition. How Fakes were just as good as people, and how it didn't matter how we were born; that we had the same needs and rights as Whole Humans, even in spite of the wet programming they read into our skulls. It wasn't fair, she said, to make us live out Roles all our lives, Lonely Nells and Barroom Cowboys and Pretty Boys and all. We had our rights, and someday we would rise up and demand them.

Well, this was not quite that. But it was something.

"O.K.," I said. "But I couldn't—I don't think I could—"

"It's all right, my love," Lafe said, still holding me. "I understand. I'll do it. I'll kill him."

And I thought for some reason of that old ballad they taught me back at the Farm:

> But I've treasure of the promise
> That you made me in the lane
> When you said we'd be together
> When them roses bloom again . . .

First time we tried, it was less than a week later.

It was an average night. I did my two sets with the band and kept a customer happy. Guy named Idaho Charlie rode the mechanical bull for twenty-five minutes, and would of rode longer except his bladder ruptured. The take was good, the till was busy, and the beer was flowing like—well, beer.

We had no specific plan, but I knew the tension had been building up in Lafe; he was tight as a piano wire. He had gone so far as to snub a couple of customers, drinking by himself and looking hostile. Torvis had dressed him down for it earlier in the day. But Lafe had not reformed, and now Torvis appeared long enough to hail him into his office with a rude and contemptuous gesture.

Lafe stood up and took a last sip of real whiskey—steeling himself, I thought excitedly. It would not be uncommon for Torvis to hide in that office until all the Whole Human employees had packed up and gone home: Torvis was a secret drinker on top of everything else. So there would be no bad appearances if Lafe picked this moment to put an end to our torment.

I was onstage for my last set of the evening. I stumbled through the ballads and moaners dutifully, but I could not conceal my anxiety. The drummer complained that I was rushing the tempo. I apologized and jumped down, waiting for Lafe to emerge.

Lafe did not.

Time passed. A burly out-of-towner in a Teamsters uniform settled down opposite me. "You're the Nell," he said gruffly, "right?"

I told him to buzz off. I purely dislike Whole Humans who treat me like some kind of prostitute. I am a Lonely Nell; the program won't run right unless the customer is maybe a little bit in love with me. Silly one-night love, maybe; misplaced yearning, sure, drunken affection . . . but not this mean-tempered randiness. If Torvis had been around, I might have had to comply. But maybe Lafe had solved that problem already.

When I couldn't wait any longer, I went to the door of Torvis's back office. Maybe Lafe was dead, I thought, stricken. Maybe Torvis had killed him. Maybe they had killed each other.

The door was unlocked.

I opened it a crack and saw Torvis slumped across his desk.

I slid inside.

Lafe was there, white as a ghost, trembling, a big kitchen knife in his hand—

But the blade was clean.

"He's drunk," Lafe groaned. "He passed out while he was talking. Oh, Idella . . . I should have done it . . . but the programming . . . I just *can't* . . ."

I saw that he was on the brink of tears, and in spite of the disappointment, my heart went out to him. Poor Lafe! That's the deepest kind of conditioning a Fake Person gets, the conditioning that prevents a Barroom Cowboy from committing violence. A Cowboy is different from a Nell: some men wouldn't tolerate his behavior even from a Fake, if not for the fact that he posed no threat at all.

But conditioning is not perfect; I had hoped Lafe would be able to break free long enough to kill Torvis.

Apparently not.

I pried the knife gently out of his hand and tucked it into the deep pocket of my skirt. "Come on, baby." And I led him, still trembling, back to his trailer.

Torvis had begun to snore.

It cast the whole project into doubt.

Laurel Anne had belabored this point often back at the Flesh Farm. What we are, she said, is what we *want* to be, and to hell with the Roles. Wet programming impresses only a tendency on the brain, she said, not an obligation. Most times what we are programmed to be is what we expect to be, and so we fall into the habit of complicity. But there is always a choice.

So said Laurel Anne. But I thought of Lafe, reduced almost to tears with the knife in his hand, helpless.

We did not speak of it. But the issue remained between us like a weight. When I could think of nothing else to do, I called up Laurel Anne's name and code from the Artificials Directory and got her most recent address and terminal number: a barroom in L.A.

I had to steady my hand to punch out the numbers. I had not seen Laurel Anne in twenty years. We had corresponded a little, but that trailed off after a time, though we still got off Christmas cards some years. Would she even recognize me?

But then her face was all over the CRT, somewhat wrinkly and careworn, but the same old Laurel Anne for all that, really still awful pretty. I smiled bravely, but when she said *"Idella?"* I could not hold in the tears any longer. I guess I didn't know myself just how much I had been suffering. "Honey," she said, "what's wrong with you?"

So I told her the basic stuff about Torvis and how I wasn't making any money or getting any younger. There's not a whole lot of options for an aging Nell. The best I could hope for would be maybe nursemaiding a crèche-lot of kids out on some farm; the worst did not bear thinking about.

Laurel Anne clucked appreciatively. "I know what you mean. It's not much better where I am. You just gotta face it, kiddo: the game is rigged in favor of the house. I can't help much, but if you need some cash—"

"Lord, Laurel Anne, I didn't call you to cadge money off you!" And I thought how nice she kept her pure blonde hair. Her own color.

She creased her eyebrows. "What, then? Not that I mind chatting, God knows. It's your nickel."

I told her about Lafe.

She sucked in her breath. "Idella, that's dangerous stuff. A Cowboy— wow! They're not the most *reliable* types in the world, you know what I mean?"

"Oh, Lafe's O.K. He's loyal. You know what you told me about Programming and all. No; Lafe's not the problem. See—"

And I explained about our little plan.

She was silent for a long time after I finished. I wondered for a sickening moment if she had changed beyond redemption, if maybe the world had broken her down—maybe this was *not* the Laurel Anne I remembered from the Farm.

But then her consternation lifted like a cloud passing from in front of the sun, and she smiled a big wicked smile that made her look twenty years younger. "Honey," she said, "my advice to you is—what the hell. *Go for it.*"

I laughed and she laughed.

"Lafe's a problem, though," I said. "His Cowboy conditioning. He can't bring himself to *hurt* the old son of a bitch."

"There's two solutions I can think of," Laurel Anne said.

"Yeah?"

"Well—first off, keep in mind *you're* not a Cowboy."

I saw what she meant. "Oh, but—no, I couldn't—I have my own conditioning, you know—"

She waved it away. "There's another possibility. I guess this Lafe of yours isn't up to *direct* violence. But maybe you can make some arrangements. You understand? See that ol' Toby has an accident. That way Lafe doesn't have to be there when it happens."

I sighed happily. "Laurel Anne, you are a genius."

She grinned again. "Just happy to get in on the action."

We chatted awhile; then Laurel Anne said, "O.K., gotta go." And she added something wicked and obscene.

"Invite me to the wedding," she said.

Lafe and I sat up late making plans.

"Very bright girl, this Laurel Anne," he said.

"Oh Lafe, do you suppose it'll really work?"

"I don't see why not."

"And we'll have the place?"

"Sure thing."

"You and me? Together?"

"For eternity," he said, and kissed me so sweetly I could have cried.

We used a length of steel wire Lafe extracted from an old holoset in the junk pile Torvis kept back behind the Place. He greased it so it wouldn't shine in the dark.

Torvis had beer delivered in big steel kegs once a week. He stored them in the cold room down under the Place, a nasty timber and concrete basement with the floorboards of the barroom creaking and swaying above it. Here was the crux of the plan: every Friday night, providing he was sober enough to do so, Torvis would go down into that hole to count the kegs. "Consumption's up," he would say, grousing because he'd have to put in a bigger order; or, "Consumption's down," grousing 'cause business was off.

Friday before he arrived, we snuck in through his office and down a ways into that lightless place where the beer was kept. The stairway was rickety and narrow and smelled of old malt. First Lafe unscrewed the light bulb at the bottom so it would look to have burned out. Then he came back up to the second stair or so. He had bought some of those steel eyehole screws from the hardware store up in Lawson. He drove one into the supports at each side of the stair. Then he threaded the steel wire between them, tying it off as tight as he could. Then he twisted the screw eyes a couple more times each until the wire hummed like the high E string on an electric guitar. He gave it a final slick of shoe polish, and we backed to the top of the stairway.

The wire was invisible.

Lafe was shaking; I held his hand.

"This is it, girl," he whispered. "This is our ticket. Keep your fingers crossed."

It was a nervous night, you might imagine. I felt elated, optimistic, sick—all at once. I suppose I was feeling some of what Lafe must have felt when he hovered over the body of Torvis with that big meat knife in his hand. Back at the Farm there was a motto we heard almost as often as *Happy to Serve*, which was *You Can't Cheat Fate*. Maybe that is so, I thought. But you can by God *try*. I sang, up there on the stage with the band behind me, the same old songs that are precisely the story of my life, Loved and Lost and the Guy Who Left Me Behind; but I sang them, I would pledge, with a special poignancy that night. Let Me Be in Your Arms Tonight, I sang (and Lafe smiled his big white smile, all alone at his table); I Shouldn't But I Love You; This Is Sin But It Feels So Good.

Oh yes.

Torvis did not appear in public that night.

We had been for a couple of weeks circulating rumors among the staff that he was planning to sell out. I suppose those rumors accelerated during the evening. Any ordinary evening, Torvis usually appeared at least once to guarantee that the bar was churlishly tended, or to badger the waitresses and put his fat hands on their behinds.

But he did not.

Time passed and after a while everybody went home and it was not long before dawn, and still Torvis had not appeared.

The entrance to the cellar is strictly through Torvis's private office.

I looked at Lafe; Lafe looked at me.

"He could be drunk," Lafe whispered.

"We have to know," I said. "We have to at least *know*."

So we tiptoed through the dark and silent, sawdust-scattered barroom to Torvis's door. Which was not locked.

It was dark inside.

I found the light switch.

Torvis was sitting there, grinning like a maniac, the trip wire dangling in his hand.

"Well, by God, it *would* be you two." He waved us in, almost a friendly gesture. "There's nowhere to run to, so you might as well sit and chat for a time."

Lafe entered the room stiff-legged, eyes wild, as if his brain weren't firing on all cylinders. And me behind, hot in the face, angry and scared both at once.

Torvis perched on the edge of his desk, one hand curled around a bottle of Southern Comfort. There was a bruise on his cheek and some blood around one ankle, so I guessed the trip wire had worked—just not well enough. He had fallen down the stairs, but it hadn't killed him. And now he knew.

"Well, well, well. I guess I should have expected this. You buy cheap Fakes, you get what you pay for." He laced his link-sausage fingers across the belly of his yoke shirt. His string tie was askew. "I should have knowed."

"We didn't—" Lafe stammered hopelessly; "—you don't think—"

And I fingered the knife I had been carrying in my big dress pockets since I prized it out of Lafe's hand that day.

"Don't make it worse," Torvis said, turning grim for the first time. "Wouldn't have worked anyhow. I guess you thought you could take over the Place. Kill me and take over the Place and live as if you were real people. Hah! Oh, you *could* of killed me, I guess, if this chickenshit plan had worked out. Killed me without *facing* me, 'cause you can't do *that*—just some underhanded trick. But even if it worked, where are you?"

His hand lingered about the telephone terminal. I guessed he was going to call the local Artificials Board, and we would be processed dogfood, me and Lafe both, before the next nightfall.

"Because you're *not* human," Torvis said gleefully. He grinned, his face like a big beet-red Halloween pumpkin. "There's the flaw! It all comes out in the Programming, don't it? You can't dodge a Program!"

You Can't Cheat Fate.

I guess it was the words that set me off: made me think of the Farm, and of Laurel Anne, and of poor Lafe's programmed helplessness. Torvis had already started punching out numbers on the terminal, chuckling crazily to himself, when the knife came down. Again. And again. In *my* hand.

We hid him in that cold, dark basement back of the beer kegs.

"Got a surprise for you," Lafe said one night after the ruckus had died down and we were alone in the Place again. *Our* Place, as I had lately begun to think of it.

"Surprise?" I asked.

And he opened up the front doors in a grand gesture, and Laurel Anne waltzed in.

Comes to the same thing, seems to me. We play out our roles, and we want what we're so often promised: our One True Lover, our Happy Ending.

I thought all this while I cried into Laurel Anne's pretty blond hair. Lafe said, "She needed a job. We need a new Nell. And we can pay her double salary until she buys herself free."

I looked at her. She nodded, grinning. " 'Course," she said, "that's not the *main* reason I'm here."

"The main reason—?"

"Didn't want to miss your wedding."

I wept all over again.

Laurel Anne sang "When Them Roses Bloom Again," alone up onstage in the empty barroom, and Lafe and I said the vows about forsaking all others and death do us part and so forth, and he put a Cracker Jack ring on my finger; and he was my cowboy bridegroom and I was his jukebox bride.

* * *

Well, business picked up after that. Torvis was unmissed and unmourned. Lafe took over accounting. Laurel Anne stood in as Nell, though I continued to sing the songs every night.

The sad old songs. The ballads in waltz time.

Sad and true. Fate is a tricky and mean opponent, they seem to say; he sneaks up from behind.

I stood up onstage and watched them glide across the dance floor.

My old friend and my true love. His hand was on the shoulder of her taffeta gown, his other hand pressed her tight, and his eyes—those gorgeous Cowboy eyes!—were all lit up with love.

While the band played in 3/4 time.

(Learning About) Machine Sex

Candas Jane Dorsey

Candas Jane Dorsey is one of the mature writing talents to have emerged in the last decade from Canadian SF. She is currently president of the Writers Guild of Alberta, and concurrently president of SF Canada (Speculative Writers Association of Canada, of which she is a founder). A former social worker and teacher, she had worked in freelance writing and editing in Edmonton, Alberta, the city of her birth, and published three books of poetry before her first SF book, a collection of her stories: *Machine Sex and Other Stories* (1988). Another collection, of erotic poetry, appeared in 1992. Only six of the thirteen stories had been published prior to the collection, and four of those had appeared in little magazines, not in SF publications. The blurb on the small-press trade-paperback first edition of her collection promised "a brilliant new voice in SF" from the publishers of the *Tesseracts* series. And indeed the stories, such as "Sleeping in a Box" (which won the 1989 Aurora Award for best short-form work in English), "Willows," and the title story here reprinted, fulfilled that promise.

She writes: "In 1994 Dorsey's publishing history transcends the mundane literally, when a short story ["Johnny Appleseed on the New World"] is included on a CD-ROM travelling on a spaceship to Mars. Fame and posterity thus assured, Dorsey is now working on fortune—as well as a new book of short fiction, a novel, and a nonfiction book on sex and society." Dorsey, like Andrew Weiner, Terence Green, and Margaret Atwood, seems more influenced by feminist than traditional hard SF, more influenced by British than U.S. SF. She is one of the central figures in speculative fiction (as distinct from American SF) in Canada. Her attitudes are further illuminated by the essay elsewhere in this book.

A naked woman working at a computer. Which attracts you most? It was a measure of Whitman that, as he entered the room, his eyes went first to the unfolded machine gleaming small and awkward in the light of the long-armed desk lamp; he'd seen the woman before.

Angel was the woman. Thin and pale-skinned, with dark nipples and black pubic hair, and her face hidden by a dark unkempt mane of long hair as she leaned over her work.

A woman complete with her work. It was a measure of Angel that she never acted naked, even when she was. Perhaps especially when she was.

So she has a new board, thought Whitman, and felt his guts stir the way they stirred when he first contemplated taking her to bed. That was a long time ago. And she knew it, felt without turning her head the desire, and behind the screen of her straight dark hair, uncombed and tumbled in front of her eyes, she smiled her anger down.

"Where have you been?" he asked, and she shook her hair back, leaned backward to ease her tense neck.

"What is that thing?" he went on insistently, and Angel turned her face to him, half-scowling. The board on the desk had thin irregular wings spreading from a small central module. Her fingers didn't slow their keyboard dance.

"None of your business," she said.

She saved the input, and he watched her fold the board into a smaller and smaller rectangle. Finally she shook her hair back from her face.

"I've got the option on your bioware," he said.

"Pay as you go," she said. "New house rule."

And found herself on her ass on the floor from his reflexive, furious blow. And his hand in her hair, pulling her up and against the wall. Hard. Astonishing her with how quickly she could hurt how much. Then she hurt too much to analyse it.

"You are a bitch," he said.

"So what?" she said. "When I was nicer, you were still an asshole."

Her head back against the wall, crack. Ouch.

Breathless, Angel: "Once more and you never see this bioware." And Whitman slowly draws breath, draws back, and looks at her the way she knew he always felt.

"Get out," she said. "I'll bring it to Kozyk's office when it's ready."

So he went. She slumped back in the chair, and tears began to blur her vision, but hate cleared them up fast enough, as she unfolded the board again, so that despite the pain she hardly missed a moment of programming time.

Assault only a distraction now, betrayal only a detail: Angel was on a roll. She had her revenge well in hand, though it took a subtle mind to recognise it.

Again: "I have the option on any of your bioware." This time, in the office, Whitman wore the nostalgic denims he now affected, and Angel her street-silks and leather.

"This is mine, but I made one for you." She pulled it out of the bag. Where her board looked jerry-built, this one was sleek. Her board looked interesting; this one packaged. "I made it before you sold our company," she said. "I put my best into it. You may as well have it. I suppose you own the option anyway, eh?"

She stood. Whitman was unconsciously restless before her.

"When you pay me for this," she said, "make it in MannComp stock."

She tossed him the board. "But be careful. If you take it apart wrong, you'll break it. Then you'll have to ask me to fix it, and from now on, my tech rate goes up."

As she walked by him, he reached for her, hooked one arm around her waist. She looked at him, totally expressionless. "Max," she said, "it's like I told you last night. From now on, if you want it, you pay. Just like everyone else." He let her go. She pulled the soft dirty white silk shirt on over the black leather jacket. The compleat rebel now.

"It's a little going away present. When you're a big shot in MannComp, remember that I made it. And that you couldn't even take it apart right. I guarantee."

He wasn't going to watch her leave. He was already studying the board. Hardly listening, either.

"Call it the Mannboard," she said. "It gets big if you stroke it." She shut the door quietly behind herself.

It would be easier if this were a story about sex, or about machines. It is true that the subject is Angel, a woman who builds computers like they have never been built before outside the human skull. Angel, like everyone else, comes from somewhere and goes somewhere else. She lives in that linear and binary universe. However, like everyone else, she lives concurrently in another universe less simple. Trivalent, quadrivalent, multivalent. World without end, with no amen. And so, on.

They say a hacker's burned out before he's twenty-one. Note the pronoun: he. Not many young women in that heady realm of the chip.

Before Angel was twenty-one—long before—she had taken the cybernetic chip out of a Wm Kuhns fantasy and patented it; she had written the program for the self-taught AI the Bronfmanns had bought and used to gain world prominence for their MannComp lapboard; somewhere in there, she'd lost innocence, and when her clever additions to that AI turned it into something the military wanted, she dropped out of sight in Toronto and went back to Rocky Mountain House, Alberta, on a Greyhound bus.

It was while she was thinking about something else—cash, and how to get some—that she had looked out of the bus window in Winnipeg into the display window of a sex shop. Garter belts, sleazy magazines on cheap coated paper with Day-Glo orange stickers over the genitals of bored sex kings and queens, a variety of ornamental vibrators. She had too many memories of Max to take it lightly, though she heard the laughter of the roughnecks in the back of the bus as they topped each other's dirty jokes, and thought perhaps their humour was worth emulating. If only she could.

She passed her twentieth birthday in a hotel in Regina, where she stopped to take a shower and tap into the phone lines, checking for pursuit.

Armed with the money she got through automatic transfer from a dummy account in Medicine Hat, she rode the bus the rest of the way ignoring the rolling of beer bottles under the seats, the acrid stink of the onboard toilet. She was thinking about sex.

As the bus roared across the long flat prairie she kept one hand on the roll of bills in her pocket, but with the other she made the first notes on the program that would eventually make her famous.

She made the notes on an antique NEC lapboard which had been her aunt's, in old-fashioned BASIC—all the machine would support—but she unravelled it and knitted it into that artificial trivalent language when she got to the place at Rocky and plugged the idea into her Mannboard. She had it written in a little over four hours on-time, but that counted an hour and a half she took to write a new loop into the AI. (She would patent that loop later the same year and put the royalties into a blind trust for her brother, Brian, brain damaged from birth. He was in Michener Centre in Red Deer, not educable; no one at Bronfmann knew about her family, and she kept it that way.)

She called it Machine Sex; working title.

Working title for a life: born in Innisfail General Hospital, father a rodeo cowboy who raised rodeo horses, did enough mixed farming out near Caroline to build his young second wife a big log house facing the mountain view. The first baby came within a year, ending her mother's tenure as teller at the local bank. Her aunt was a programmer for the University of Lethbridge, chemical molecular model analysis on the University of Calgary mainframe through a modem link.

From her aunt she learned BASIC, Pascal, COBOL and C; in school she played the usual turtle games on the Apple IIe; when she was fourteen she took a bus to Toronto, changed her name to Angel, affected a punk hairstyle and the insolent all-white costume of that year's youth, and eventually walked into Northern Systems, the company struggling most successfully with bionics at the time, with the perfected biochip, grinning at the proper young men in their grey three-piece suits as they tried to find a bug in it anywhere. For the first million she let them open it up; for the next five she told them how she did it. Eighteen years old by the phoney records she'd cooked on her arrival in Toronto, she was free to negotiate her own contracts.

But no one got her away from Northern until Bronfmann bought Northern lock, stock and climate-controlled workshop. She had been sleeping with Northern's boy-wonder president by then for about a year, had yet to have an orgasm though she'd learned a lot about kinky sex toys. Figured she'd been screwed by him for the last time when he sold the company without telling her; spent the next two weeks doing a lot of drugs and having a lot of cheap sex in the degenerate punk underground; came up with the AI education program.

Came up indeed, came swaggering into Ted Kozyk's office, president of Bronfmann's MannComp subsidiary, with that jury-rigged Mannboard tied into two black-box add-ons no bigger than a bar of soap, and said, "Watch this."

Took out the power supply first, wiped the memory, plugged into a wall outlet and turned it on.

The bootstrap greeting sounded a lot like Goo.

"Okay," she said, "it's ready."

"Ready for what?"

"Anything you want," she said. By then he knew her, knew her rep, knew that the sweaty-smelling, disheveled, anorectic-looking waif in the filthy, oversized silk shirt (the rebels had affected natural fabrics the year she left home, and she always did after that, even later when the silk was cleaner, more upmarket, and black instead of white) had something. Two weeks ago he'd bought a company on the strength of that something, and the board Whitman had brought him the day after the sale, even without the software to run on it, had been enough to convince him he'd been right.

He sat down to work, and hours later he was playing Go with an AI he'd taught to talk back, play games, and predict horse races and the stock market.

He sat back, flicked the power switch and pulled the plug, and stared at her.

"Congratulations," she said.

"What for?" he said; "you're the genius."

"No, congratulations, you just murdered your first baby," she said, and plugged it back in. "Want to try for two?"

"Goo," said the deck. "Dada."

It was her little joke. It was never a feature on the MannComp A-One they sold across every MannComp counter in the world.

But now she's all grown up, she's sitting in a log house near Rocky Mountain House, watching the late summer sunset from the big front windows, while the computer runs Machine Sex to its logical conclusion, orgasm.

She had her first orgasm at nineteen. According to her false identity, she was twenty-three. Her lover was a delegate to MannComp's annual sales convention; she picked him up after the speech she gave on the ethics of selling AIs to high school students in Thailand. Or whatever, she didn't care. Kozyk used to write her speeches but she usually changed them to suit her mood. This night she'd been circumspect, only a few expletives, enough to amuse the younger sales representatives and reassure the older ones.

The one she chose was smooth in his approach and she thought, well, we'll see. They went up to the suite MannComp provided, all mod cons and king-size bed, and as she undressed she looked at him and thought, he's ambitious, this boy, better not give him an inch.

He surprised her in bed. Ambitious maybe, but he paid a lot of attention to detail.

After he spread her across the universe in a way she had never felt before, he turned to her and said, "That was pretty good, eh, baby?" and smiled a smooth little grin. "Sure," she said, "it was okay," and was glad she hadn't said more while she was out in the ozone.

By then she thought she was over what Whitman had done to her. And after all, it had been simple enough, what he did. Back in that loft she had in Hull, upstairs of a shop, where she covered the windows with opaque Mylar and worked night and day in that twilight. That night as she worked he stood behind her, hands on her shoulders, massaging her into further tenseness.

"Hey, Max, you know I don't like it when people look over my shoulder when I'm working."

"Sorry, baby." He moved away, and she felt her shoulders relax just to have his hands fall away.

"Come on to bed," he said. "You know you can pick that up whenever."

She had to admit he was being pleasant tonight. Maybe he too was tired of the constant scrapping, disguised as jokes, that wore at her nerves so much. All his efforts to make her stop working, slow her down so he could stay up. The sharp edges that couldn't be disguised. Her bravado made her answer in the same vein, but in the mornings, when he was gone to Northern; she paced and muttered to herself, reworking the previous day until it was done with, enough that she could go on. And after all what was missing? She had no idea how to debug it.

Tonight he'd even made some dinner, and touched her kindly. Should she be grateful? Maybe the conversations, such as they were, where she tried to work it out, had just made it worse—

"Ah, shit," she said, and pushed the board away. "You're right, I'm too tired for this. *Demain.*" She was learning French in her spare time.

He began with hugging her, and stroking the long line along her back, something he knew she liked, like a cat likes it, arches its back at the end of the stroke. He knew she got turned on by it. And she did. When they had sex at her house he was without the paraphernalia he preferred, but he seemed to manage, buoyed up by some mood she couldn't share; nor could she share his release.

Afterward, she lay beside him, tense and dissatisfied in the big bed, not admitting it, or she'd have to admit she didn't know what would help. He seemed to be okay, stretched, relaxed and smiling.

"Had a big day," he said.

"Yeah?"

"Big deal went through."

"Yeah?"

"Yeah, I sold the company."

"You what?" Reflexively moving herself so that none of her body touched his.

"Northern. I put it to Bronfmann. Megabucks."

"Are you joking?" but she saw he was not. "You didn't, I didn't. . . . Northern's *our* company."

"My company. I started it."

"I made it big for you."

"Oh, and I paid you well for every bit of that."

She got up. He was smiling a little, trying on the little-boy grin. No, baby, she thought, not tonight.

"Well," she said, "I know for sure that this is my bed. Get out of it."

"Now, I knew you might take this badly. But it really was the best thing. The R&D costs were killing us. Bronfmann can eat them for breakfast."

R&D costs meant her. "Maybe. Your clothes are here." She tossed them on the bed, went into the other room.

As well as sex, she hadn't figured out betrayal yet either; on the street, she thought, people fucked you over openly, not in secret.

This, even as she said it to herself, she recognised as romantic and certainly not based on experience. She was street-wise in every way but one: Max had been her first lover.

She unfolded the new board. It had taken her some time to figure out how to make it expand like that, to fit the program it was going to run. This idea of shaping the hardware to the software had been with her since she made the biochip, and thus made it possible and much more interesting than the other way around. But making the hardware to fit her new idea had involved a great deal of study and technique, and so far she had had limited success.

This reminded her again of sex, and, she supposed, relationships, although it seemed to her that before sex everything had been on surfaces, very easy. Now she had sex, she had had Max, and now she had no way to realize the results of any of that. Especially now, when Northern had just vanished into Bronfmann's computer empire, putting her in the position again of having to prove herself. What had Max used to make Bronfmann take the bait? She knew very clearly: Angel, the Northern Angel, would now become the MannComp Angel. The rest of the bait would have been the AI; she was making more of it every day, but couldn't yet bring it together. Could it be done at all? Bronfmann had paid high for an affirmative answer.

Certainly this time the bioware was working together. She began to smile a little to herself, almost unaware of it, as she saw how she could interconnect the loops to make a solid net to support the program's full and growing weight. Because, of course, it would have to learn as it went along—that was basic.

Angel as metaphor; she had to laugh at herself when she woke from programming hours later, Max still sleeping in her bed, ignoring her eviction notice. He'll have to get up to piss anyway, she thought; that's when I'll get him out. She went herself to the bathroom in the half-dawn light, stretching her cramped back muscles and thinking remotely, well, I got some satisfaction out of last night after all: the beginnings of the idea that might break this impasse. While it's still inside my head, this one is mine. How can I keep it that way?

New fiscal controls, she thought grimly. New contracts, now that Northern doesn't exist any more. Max can't have this, whatever it turns into, for my dowry to MannComp.

When she put on her white silks—leather jacket underneath, against the skin as street fashion would have it—she hardly knew herself what she would do. The little board went into her bag with the boxes of pills the pharmaceutical tailor had made for her. If there was nothing there to suit, she'd buy something new. In the end, she left Max sleeping in her bed; so what? she thought as she reached the highway. The first ride she hitched took her to Toronto, not without a little tariff, but she no longer gave a damn about any of that.

By then the drugs in her system had lifted her out of a body that could be betrayed, and she didn't return to it for two weeks, two weeks of floating in a soup of disjointed noise, and always the program running, unfolding, running again, unfolding inside her relentless mind. She kept it running to drown anything she might remember about trust or the dream of happiness.

When she came home two weeks later, on a hot day in summer with the Ottawa Valley humidity unbearable and her body tired, sore and bruised, and very dirty, she stepped out of her filthy silks in a room messy with Whitman's continued inhabitation; furious, she popped a system cleanser and unfolded the board on her desk. When he came back in she was there, naked, angry, working.

A naked woman working at a computer. What good were cover-ups? Watching Max after she took the new AI up to Kozyk, she was only triumphant because she'd done something Max could never do, however much he might be able to sell her out. Watching them fit it to the bioboard, the strange unfolding machine she had made to fit the ideas only she could have, she began to be afraid. The system cleanser she'd taken made the clarity inescapable. Over the next few months, as she kept adding clever loops and twists, she watched their glee and she looked at what telephone numbers were in the top ten on their modem memories and she began to realise that it was not only business and science that would pay high for a truly thinking machine.

She knew that ten years before there had been Pentagon programmers working to model predatory behaviour in AIs using Prolog and its like. That was old hat. None of them, however, knew what they needed to know to write for her bioware yet. No one but Angel could do that. So, by the end of her nineteenth year, that made Angel one of the most sought-after, endangered ex-anorectics on the block.

She went to conferences and talked about the ethics of selling AIs to teenagers in Nepal. Or something. And took a smooth salesman to bed, and thought all the time about when they were going to make their approach. It would be Whitman again, not Kozyk, she thought; Ted wouldn't get his hands dirty, while Max was born with grime under his nails.

She thought also about metaphors. How, even in the new street slang which she could speak as easily as her native tongue, being screwed, knocked, fucked over, jossed, dragged all meant the same thing: hurt to the core. And this was what people sought out, what they spent their time seeking in pick-up joints, to the beat of bad old headbanger bands, that nostalgia shit. Now, as well as the biochip, Max, the AI breakthrough, and all the tailored drugs she could eat, she'd had orgasm too.

Well, she supposed it passed the time.

What interested her intellectually about orgasm was not the lovely illusion of transcendence it brought, but the absolute binary predictability of it. When you learn what to do to the nerve endings, and they are in a receptive state, the program runs like kismet. Warm boot. She'd known a hacker once who'd altered his bootstrap messages to read "Warm pussy." She knew where most hackers were at; they played with their computers more than they played with themselves. She was the same, otherwise why would it have taken a pretty-boy salesman in a three-piece to show her the simple answer? All the others, just like trying to use an old MS-DOS disc to boot up one of her Mann lapboards with crystal RO/RAM.

Angel forgets she's only twenty. Genius is uneven. There's no substitute for time, that relentless shaper of understanding. Etc. Etc. Angel paces with the knowledge that everything is a phrase, even this. Life is hard and then you die, and so on. And so, on.

One day it occurred to her that she could simply run away.

This should have seemed elementary but to Angel it was a revelation. She spent her life fatalistically; her only successful escape had been from the people she loved. Her lovely, crazy grandfather; her generous and slightly avaricious aunt; and her beloved imbecile brother: they were buried deep in a carefully forgotten past. But she kept coming back to Whitman, to Kozyk and Bronfmann, as if she liked them.

As if, like a shocked dog in a learned helplessness experiment, she could not believe that the cage had a door, and the door was open.

She went out the door. For old times' sake, it was the bus she chose; the steamy chill of an air-conditioned Greyhound hadn't changed at all. Bottles—pop and beer—rolling under the seats and the stench of chemicals filling the air whenever someone sneaked down to smoke a cigarette or a reef in the toilet. Did anyone ever use it to piss in? She liked the triple seat near the back, but the combined smells forced her to the front, behind the driver, where she was joined, across the country, by an endless succession of old women, immaculate in their Fortrels, who started conversations and shared peppermints and gum.

She didn't get stoned once.

The country unrolled strangely: sex shop in Winnipeg, bank machine in Regina, and hours of programming alternating with polite responses to the old women, until eventually she arrived, creased and exhausted, in Rocky Mountain House.

Rocky Mountain House: a comfortable model of a small town, from which no self-respecting hacker should originate. But these days, the world a net of wire and wireless, it doesn't matter where you are, as long as you have the information people want. Luckily for Angel's secret past, however, this was not a place she would be expected to live—or to go—or to come from.

An atavism she hadn't controlled had brought her this far. A rented car took her the rest of the way to the ranch. She thought only to look around, but when she found the tenants packing for a month's holiday, she couldn't resist the opportunity. She carried her leather satchel into their crocheted, frilled guest room—it had been her room fifteen years before—with a remote kind of satisfaction.

That night, she slept like the dead—except for some dreams. But there was nothing she could do about them.

Lightning and thunder. I should stop now, she thought, wary of power surges through the new board which she was charging as she worked. She saved her file, unplugged the power, stood, stretched, and walked to the window to look at the mountains.

The storm illuminated the closer slopes erratically, the rain hid the distances. She felt some heaviness lift. The cool wind through the window refreshed her. She heard the program stop, and turned off the machine. Sliding out the backup capsule, she smiled her angry smile unconsciously. When I get back to the Ottawa Valley, she thought, where weather never comes from the west like it's supposed to, I'll make those fuckers eat this.

Out in the corrals where the tenants kept their rodeo horses, there was animal noise, and she turned off the light to go and look out the side window. A young man was leaning his weight against the reins-length pull of a rearing, terrified horse. Angel watched as flashes of lightning strobed the hackneyed scene. This was where she came from. She remembered her father in the same struggle. And her mother at this window with her, both of them watching the man. Her mother's anger she never understood until now. Her father's abandonment of all that was in the house, including her brother, Brian, inert and restless in his oversized crib.

Angel walked back through the house, furnished now in the kitschy western style of every trailer and bungalow in this countryside. She was lucky to stay, invited on a generous impulse, while all but their son were away. She felt vaguely guilty at her implicit criticism.

Angel invited the young rancher into the house only because this is what her mother and her grandmother would have done. Even Angel's great-grandmother, whose father kept the stopping house, which meant she kept the travellers fed, even her spirit infused in Angel the unwilling act. She watched him almost sullenly as he left his rain gear in the wide porch.

He was big, sitting in the big farm kitchen. His hair was wet, and he swore almost as much as she did. He told her how he had put a trailer on the north forty, and lived there now, instead of in the little room where she'd been invited to sleep. He told her about the stock he'd accumulated riding the rodeo. They drank Glenfiddich. She told him her father had been a rodeo cowboy. He told her about his university degree in agriculture. She told him she'd never been to university. They drank more whiskey and he told her he couldn't drink that other rot gut any more since he tasted real Scotch. He invited her to see his computer. She went with him across the yard and through the trees in the rain, her bag over her shoulder, board hidden in it, and he showed her his computer. It turned out to be the first machine she designed for Northern—archaic now, compared with the one she'd just invented.

Fair is fair, she thought drunkenly, and she pulled out her board and unfolded it.

"You showed me yours, I'll show you mine," she said.

He liked the board. He was amazed that she had made it. They finished the Scotch.

"I like you," she said. "Let me show you something. You can be the first." And she ran Machine Sex for him.

He was the first to see it: before Whitman and Kozyk who bought it to sell to people who already have had and done everything; before David and Jonathan, the Hardware Twins in MannComp's Gulf Islands shop, who made the touchpad devices necessary to run it properly; before a world market hungry for the kind of glossy degradation Machine Sex could give them brought it in droves from a hastily-created—MannComp-subsidiary—numbered company. She ran it for him with just the automouse on her board, and a description of what it would do when the hardware was up-graded to fit.

It was very simple, really. If orgasm was binary, it could be pro-grammed. Feed back the sensation through one or more touchpads to pro-gram the body. The other thing she knew about human sex was that it was as much cortical as genital, or more so: touch is optional for the turn-on. Also easy, then, to produce cortical stimuli by programmed input. The rest was a cosmetic elaboration of the premise.

At first it did turn him on, then off, then it made his blood run cold. She was pleased by that: her work had chilled her too.

"You can't market that thing!" he said.

"Why not. It's a fucking good program. Hey, get it? Fucking good."

"It's not real."

"Of course it isn't. So what?"

"So, people don't need that kind of stuff to get turned on."

She told him about people. More people than he'd known were in the world. People who made her those designer drugs, given in return for fa-vours she never granted until after Whitman sold her like a used car. People like Whitman, teaching her about sexual equipment while dealing with the Pentagon and CSIS to sell them Angel's sharp angry mind, as if she'd work on killing others as eagerly as she was trying to kill herself. People who would hire a woman on the street, as they had her during that two-week nightmare almost a year before, and use her as casually as their own hand, without giving a damn.

"One night," she said, "just to see, I told all the johns I was fourteen. I was skinny enough, even then, to get away with it. And they all loved it. Every single one gave me a bonus, and took me anyway."

The whiskey fog was wearing a little thin. More time had passed than she thought, and more had been said than she had intended. She went to her bag, rummaged, but she'd left her drugs in Toronto, some dim idea at the time that she should clean up her act. All that had happened was that she had spent the days so tight with rage that she couldn't eat, and she'd already cured herself of that once; for the record, she thought, she'd rather be stoned.

"Do you have any more booze?" she said, and he went to look. She fol-lowed him around his kitchen.

"Furthermore," she said, "I rolled every one of them that I could, and all but one had pictures of his kids in his wallet, and all of them were teenagers. Boys and girls together. And their saintly dads out fucking someone who looked just like them. Just like them."

Luckily, he had another bottle. Not quite the same quality, but she wasn't fussy.

"So I figure," she finished, "that they don't care who they fuck. Why not the computer in the den? Or the office system at lunch hour?"

"It's not like that," he said. "It's nothing like that. People deserve better." He had the neck of the bottle in his big hand, was seriously, carefully pouring himself another shot. He gestured with both bottle and glass. "People deserve to have—love."

"Love?"

"Yeah, love. You think I'm stupid, you think I watched too much TV as a kid, but I know it's out there. Somewhere. Other people think so too. Don't you? Didn't you, even if you won't admit it now, fall in love with that guy Max at first? You never said what he did at the beginning, how he talked you into being his lover. Something must have happened. Well, that's what I mean: love."

"Let me tell you about love. Love is a guy who talks real smooth taking me out to the woods and telling me he just loves my smile. And then taking me home and putting me in leather handcuffs so he can come. And if I hurt he likes it, because he likes it to hurt a little and he thinks I must like it like he does. And if I moan he thinks I'm coming. And if I cry he thinks it's love. And so do I. Until one evening—not too long after my *last* birthday, as I recall—he tells me that he has sold me to another company. And this only after he fucks me one last time. Even though I don't belong to him any more. After all, he had the option on all my bioware."

"All that is just politics." He was sharp, she had to grant him that.

"Politics," she said, "give me a break. Was it politics made Max able to sell me with the stock: hardware, software, liveware?"

"I've met guys like that. Women too. You have to understand that it wasn't personal to him, it was just politics." Also stubborn. "Sure, you were naive, but you weren't wrong. You just didn't understand company politics."

"Oh, sure I did. I always have. Why do you think I changed my name? Why do you think I dress in natural fibres and go through all the rest of this bullshit? I know how to set up power blocs. Except in mine there is only one party—me. And that's the way it's going to stay. Me against them from now on."

"It's not always like that. There are assholes in the world, and there are other people too. Everyone around here still remembers your grandfather, even though he's been retired in Camrose for fifteen years. They still talk about the way he and his wife used to waltz at the Legion Hall. What about him? There are more people like him than there are Whitmans."

"Charlotte doesn't waltz much since her stroke."

"That's a cheap shot. You can't get away with cheap shots. Speaking of shots, have another."

"Don't mind if I do. Okay, I give you Eric and Charlotte. But one half-happy ending doesn't balance out the people who go through their lives with their teeth clenched, trying to make it come out the same as a True Romance comic, and always wondering what's missing. They read those bodice-ripper novels, and make that do for the love you believe in so naively."

Call her naive, would he? Two could play at that game. "That's why they'll all go crazy for Machine Sex. So simple. So linear. So fast. So uncomplicated."

"You underestimate people's ability to be happy. People are better at loving than you think."

"You think so? Wait until you have your own little piece of land and some sweetheart takes you out in the trees on a moonlit night and gives you head until you think your heart will break. So you marry her and have some kids. She furnishes the trailer in a five-room sale grouping. You have to quit drinking Glenfiddich because she hates it when you talk too loud. She gets an allowance every month and crochets a cozy for the TV. You work all day out in the rain and all evening in the back room making the books balance on the outdated computer. After the kids come she gains weight and sells real estate if you're lucky. If not she makes things out of recycled bleach bottles and hangs them in the yard. Pretty soon she wears a nightgown to bed and turns her back when you slip in after a hard night at the keyboard. So you take up drinking again and teach the kids about the rodeo. And you find some square-dancing chick who gives you head out behind the bleachers one night in Trochu, so sweet you think your heart will break. What you gonna do then, mountain man?"

"Okay, we can tell stories until the sun comes up. Which won't be too long, look at the time; but no matter how many stories you tell you can't make me forget about that thing." He pointed to the computer with loathing.

"It's just a machine."

"You know what I mean. That thing in it. And besides, I'm gay. Your little scenario wouldn't work."

She laughed and laughed. "So that's why you haven't made a pass at me yet." She wondered coldly how gay he was, but she was tired, so tired of proving power. His virtue was safe with her; so, she thought suddenly, strangely, was hers with him. It was unsettling and comforting at once.

"Maybe," he said. "Or maybe I'm just a liar like you think everyone is. Eh? You think everyone strings everyone else a line? Crap. Who has the time for that shit?"

Perhaps they were drinking beer now. Or was it vodka? She found it hard to tell after a while.

"You know what I mean," she said. "You should know. The sweet young thing who has AIDS and doesn't tell you. Or me. I'm lucky so far. Are you? Or who sucks you for your money. Or josses you 'cause he's into denim and Nordic looks."

"Okay, okay. I give up. Everybody's a creep but you and me."

"And I'm not so sure about you."

"Likewise, I'm sure. Have another. So, if you're so pure, what about the ethics of it?"

"What *about* the ethics of it?" she asked. "Do you think I went through all that sex without paying attention? I had nothing else to do but watch other people come. I saw that old cult movie, where the aliens feed on heroin addiction and orgasm, and the woman's not allowed orgasm so she has to O.D. on smack. Orgasm's more decadent than shooting heroin? I can't buy that, but there's something about a world that sells it over and over again. Sells the thought of pleasure as a commodity, sells the getting of it as if it were the getting of wisdom. And all these times I told you about, I saw other people get it through me. Even when someone finally made me come, it was just a feather in his cap, an accomplishment, nothing personal. Like you said. All I was was a program, they plugged into me and went through the motions and got their result. Nobody cares if the AI finds fulfilment running their damned data analyses. Nobody thinks about depressed and angry Mannboard ROMs. They just think about getting theirs."

"So why not get mine?" She was pacing now, angry, leaning that thin body as if the wind were against her. "Let me be the one who runs the program."

"But you won't be there. You told me how you were going to hide out, all that spy stuff."

She leaned against the wall, smiling a new smile she thought of as predatory. And maybe it was. "Oh, yes," she said. "I'll be there the first time. When Max and Kozyk run this thing and it turns them on. I'll be there. That's all I care to see."

He put his big hands on the wall on either side of her and leaned in. He smelled of sweat and liquor and his face was earnest with intoxication.

"I'll tell you something," he said. "As long as there's the real thing, it won't sell. They'll never buy it."

Angel thought so too. Secretly, because she wouldn't give him the satisfaction of agreement, she too thought they would not go that low. *That's right*, she told herself, *trying to sell it is all right—because they will never buy it.*

But they did.

A woman and a computer. Which attracts you most? Now you don't have to choose. Angel has made the choice irrelevant.

In Kozyk's office, he and Max go over the ad campaign. They've already tested the program themselves quite a lot; Angel knows this because it's company gossip, heard over the cubicle walls in the washrooms. The two men are so absorbed that they don't notice her arrival.

"Why is a woman better than a sheep? Because sheep can't cook. Why is a woman better than a Mannboard? Because you haven't bought your sensory add-on." Max laughs.

"And what's better than a man?" Angel says; they jump slightly. "Why, your MannComp touchpads, with two-way input. I bet you'll be able to have them personally fitted."

"Good idea," says Kozyk, and Whitman makes a note on his lapboard. Angel, still stunned though she's had weeks to get used to this, looks at them, then reaches across the desk and picks up her prototype board. "This one's mine," she says. "You play with yourselves and your touchpads all you want."

"Well, you wrote it, baby," said Max. "If you can't come with your own program . . ."

Kozyk hiccoughs a short laugh before he shakes his head. "Shut up, Whitman," he says. "You're talking to a very rich and famous woman."

Whitman looks up from the simulations of his advertising storyboards, smiling a little, anticipating his joke. "Yeah. It's just too bad she finally burned herself out with this one. They always did say it gives you brain damage."

But Angel hadn't waited for the punch line. She was gone.

Peterborough, Rouyn, Edmonton
1986–1988

TOWARDS A REAL SPECULATIVE LITERATURE: WRITER AS ASYMPTOTE

Candas Jane Dorsey

Candas Jane Dorsey is one of a handful of Canadian SF writers who had grown up seemingly overnight since the mid-1980's and who are beginning to gain recognition worldwide. She was first published in the small press in Canada and became a fixture of the *Tesseracts* anthologies, and her own first collection, *Machine Sex and Other Stories* (1988), was published in trade paperback in Canada and then printed in England by The Women's Press. As coeditor of *Tesseracts* (1990), she wrote an afterword to that volume which represents perhaps the most coherent and lucid statement on what it means to be a SF writer in Canada today.

Thinking back: thinking forward. Speculative fiction in Canada: how it used to be; how we define it; how it is going to be.

Used to be so simple. SF stood for science fiction and it was a Genre. Genres are formulaic, predictable, one thing or another, so it was easy to see SF as a strobe, a binary flash, on-off-on-off, beyond control. That kind of periodicity in lights can trigger electrical storms in the brain. But what is a state of speculation, "on" or "off"? "On," like a light, a current, a performer; "off," like a racer, a rocket or a firework? And what storms did it aim to generate in what brain? What was a preferable state, on or off? Binary, the dialectic, then seemed essential to modern scientific method—but now even computers are not binary, are based on neural nets and parallel processing: now a computer circuit can speak Sanskrit, encompass four valences (on, not on, maybe both, maybe neither). All this defines another kind of speculative prose.

What remains the same is that speculative writing is revolutionary, ghettoised, trivialised, falsely lionised, popularised and all those affixed words used by whatever fictions are speaking at the time to describe a simple phenomenon. Paul Tillich wrote: "The boundary is the best place to acquire knowledge." It has also been the best place to spin it off—the ragged edges of a jellyfish, the aurora at the earthly edge of the sun's corona, galaxies spinning out matter. Waiting: eventually, someone will look up.

Meanwhile—those cosmic rays tear through those of us who write, and some of the electrical storms in us are not very pleasant either.

What became clearer all the time was that truly speculative writing is always that asymptotic line on the graph which spends its career approaching, never arriving; always in transit between two imaginary points: take-off and destination; and therefore always beyond the binary, free to understand its fallacy. An impulse in progress is only the length of a synaptic gap, yet able to traverse light-years as quickly as any subatomic particle. But never the comfortable arrival, never the relaxed armchair and footstool at journey's end, never at home though always coming home. To live that way for a writer is not easy, even before the confrontation between what Guy Kay calls "practitioners seeking quality" and those whose idea of speculative fiction is a genre ghetto of adolescent wish-fulfillment and coming-of-age rituals.

(By the way, it is fine writing a groundbreaking literature if everyone knows it: if one knows one can be shot for it, or threatened with shooting, or, more happily, just lionised. Salman Rushdie is now a worldwide symbol of one collision of fixed boundaries. He is one of us, you know: saints don't fall from airplanes, and the fact that such fancies can threaten the raison d'être of nations is just what I'm talking about: here we are on the cutting, maybe even killing edge. Few pettinesses can withstand the onslaught of myth—they must either suppress it or be destroyed, c.f. Jung, William Irwin Thompson, and Harlan Ellison. If we accept we're rewriting humankind's essential stories, we risk hubris; but if we don't, we risk losing our value and our self-respect.)

Over the years the predicaments became clear, then were left behind. Once, Canadian SF writers' main problem was trying to live with one foot in and one out of the world of—pardon the expression—free enterprise: selling south of the border, and what happened to our work there. We saw that Gibson, Wilson, de Lint and Gotlieb made it into US print, but had garish space-girl covers on their books only slightly less often than Piers Anthony or a shared-world novelist. Those in the CanLit mainstream didn't know these names? Yes, and tens of thousands of SF fans in Canada, faces three-quarter turned to the glitter of the US pulp mass market, and in the main scarcely aware of the glimmer of brilliance at home, had never heard of the speculative writers of the Canadian tradition (which is mine, and so I always took it for granted): Sheila Watson, George Elliott, Robertson Davies, Rudy Wiebe, Marion Engel, Gwendolyn MacEwan, Jack Hodgins, Timothy Findley—and so many more. If one was lucky, one or two of them had already heard of Margaret Atwood before the movie was made of her *Handmaid's Tale*. C'est tout. (And as for the Québécois SF writers, find an anglo of any stripe who knew Élisabeth Vonarburg and already you had found a rarity. Welcome to multiculturalism—a rant for another time.)

There we were. Different countries. Couldn't get the average SF fan snob to even IMAGINE there was a Canadian literary tradition of speculation, alienness, exploration of frontiers in and outside self (a tradition by the way which did decades ago what US writers call postmodern in the SF world)—let alone read the stuff. Couldn't get the average academic CanLit snob to read anything with a lurid cover, or even in trade paperback format, let alone to admit an impressive body of great writing there in that "genre ghetto" SF. "Scifi," they liked to call it, very snotty and righteous; "mundane," the SFans liked to say, equally snide.

Yet out of this forest of mixed motives, out of this nation of enclaves, there has been coming for years now a fine, varied, growing, unique literature of speculation. Not monolithic or even binary, but full spectrum, multiplex, intense. And the boundaries we used to perceive, and along with which we used to range ourselves, are changing, are even—hurrah!—disappearing. Academics and fans meet at Canadian conventions devoted to reading the writers of home; all of them know something about the others' purview, and all of them know something about the synthesis: which is the land where we live, the land of Canadian speculative fiction, defined by all the influences and certainly not simply binary. One might almost call it multicultural, and happily so (for a change). Because meanwhile (circle round again), some of us have been simply writing. Ask us what. Those of us canny enough to have disguised ourselves in the garish face-paint of the American pulp tradition know all their labels and say things like "heroic fantasy" and "technowizardry" and "cyberpunk." Others of us keep our skirts closely gathered around us in that territory, not to become infected, and call it "magic realism" and "postmodernism" and perhaps in a daring moment "fantastic" or even, radically, "speculative." Then there are some of us with two names or two minds or with a kind of schizy double vision, who began to walk the strange land between. Walking the border, the boundary if you will, as if it were a tightrope, our toes clinging to the narrow line through the special soft shoes one must wear to do tricks on the high wire. The best of us, of course, are those flying up from the wire to do aerobatics above all categories. And in the last five years or so, all of us have been finding the boundary zone widening to become a whole country, comfortable enough to live in.

The Americans are catching up, learning an act we've practised for some time, as their SF writers find the boundaries with the mundane blurring, becoming frighteningly invisible, disappearing into a new landscape. They could take lessons from English-Canadian and Québécois SF writers—we know a lot about several kinds of cultural schizophrenia. Witness Albertan H. Hargreaves, whose scholarship of medieval French comes to light with his translation of Fontanelle's conversations on the Plurality of Worlds, while the fans know him only as a British-published senior SF writer yclept Hank.

Whether or not we are good at talking about what we write, though, we are writing it. Keeping in step just enough to get published, in US pulp SF mags or Canadian literary mags, it matters little so long as there's a chance to be read, to change the world, to make it count. Yet stepping as far outside the norms, the genre strictures, as we can, because changing the world, the changing world, is what matters most. We are reading each other's work, across boundaries which in the reading become invisible, and we are learning that we have common preoccupations.

For instance: *What for?* replaces *What if?* as the SF question at least half the time these days. David-Suzuki-fed question: will we make it in time? We have ten years. SF-fed belief: the work we do is as important to change as is recycling, cleaning up rivers, reforestation, or going to Neptune via Voyageur. Changing people's minds. Have we changed minds, ours or anyone's?

Okay, that's what we want to be doing, strobing those traditional values with a new light—sound like on-off potentiality, positive and negative, entropy and information again? The battle between good and evil, if you will? But in fact, we have no battles, nothing binary, just new vision, 20/20 for a change, telescopic even or wideangle, full-spectrum, holistic: lateral X linear = ? And "?" is our business. Our question. Our answer.

Now, just to confuse the issue, let me take this term speculative fiction which I have, with others of similar minds, adopted and which I encourage the Canadian community to adopt to distinguish our work and identify our own tradition. Let me take it and transform it yet again by saying: what fiction is not speculative? Is *Anna Karenina* documentary? Did Silas Marner exist? And Reil, though he certainly existed, did he speak the words Weibe gave him; did Big Bear think the thoughts likewise?

Give me a novel that is not set in a parallel universe—St. Petersburg or Manawanka—simply by virtue of being fiction. So we are not so different from mainstream swimmers after all, except that we made our worlds a little fancier—except that we like salmon moved more freely between salt water and fresh, while some like trout stayed in narrower streams. But both of us have to swim against the current to spawn, to create, to make the culture of the next generations possible. We just have more garish covers on some of ours. Think nothing of it. Like children dressed to impress grandparents, we didn't choose our clothes.

But we are not children, and the tracks we have followed to grandparents' houses have brought us into the dangerous realms of many forests, far from initial influences, under the yellow eyes of many wolves; like typical Canadians, we do not fight it: we map the forest, make friends with the wolves, and emerge from the woods subtly changed, having also transformed forests, wolves, and even our grandparents into something new, strange, wonderful.

All in search of new worlds, or new ways to define the old. Where did we begin? Everywhere, nowhere. By now, the beginning is lost, the change is constant, and the journey never stops.

APPENDIX

CANADIAN SF AWARDS

Canadian awards for science fiction or SF are, it seems, a complicated affair. In the early stages of compiling this anthology, the editors discovered that there is no single publication where the nominees and winners of the English-language or the French-language awards are listed. And so we set out to remedy that lack. What follows is the result of our best efforts to track down all the modern-day awards given in Canada for fiction by one or another segment of the science fiction community.

CANADIAN SCIENCE FICTION AND FANTASY AWARDS

This list was compiled by Dennis Mullen (current administrator of the Aurora Awards), Glenn Grant, Jean-Louis Trudel, Robert Runté, and Robert J. Sawyer.

THE AURORA AWARDS

Organised by the Canadian Science Fiction and Fantasy Association, the Auroras are Canada's only national "people's choice" awards. Ballots are distributed through Canadian SF specialty bookstores and periodicals. The readers nominate and then vote on the finalists (a small voting fee is levied on the second ballot), and the awards are presented at the annual national "Canvention."

A single "lifetime achievement" award was instituted in 1980. By 1986 it was officially known as the Casper, a play on the initials CSFFA, and the award was split into three categories, honoring outstanding work in English, in French, and contributions to fandom. Three categories later became ten categories, and the Caspers were renamed the Auroras in 1991.

—Glenn Grant

1980—Canvention 1 (HalCon 3, Halifax)
From 1980 to 1985, only one award, for work in English, was presented.
A. E. Van Vogt, Lifetime Achievement

1981—Canvention 2 (V-Con, Vancouver)
Susan Wood, Lifetime Contributions to the Field of Canadian SF and Fantasy

1982—Canvention 3 (NonCon 5, Edmonton)
Phyllis Gotlieb, Lifetime Contributions to the Field, and for *A Judgment of Dragons*

1983—Canvention 4 (MapleCon 5, Ottawa)
Judith Merril, Lifetime Contributions to the Field

1984—No Canvention held, no awards presented

1985—Canvention 5 (HalCon, Halifax)
Eileen Kernaghan, *Songs from the Drowned Lands* (Ace, 1983)

1986—Canvention 6 (V-Con, Vancouver)
From 1986 through 1988, three Caspers were presented each year, one for outstanding work in English, one for outstanding work in French, and one for contribution to fandom.

Judith Merril (English), Lifetime Contributions to the Field

Daniel Sernine (Français), "Yadjine et la Mort" *(Dix Nouvelles de Science-Fiction)*

Garth Spencer (Fan), for editing *Maple Leaf Rag*

1987—Canvention 7 (Ad Astra 7, Toronto)
Guy Gavriel Kay (English), *The Wandering Fire* (Collins, 1986)
Élisabeth Vonarburg (Français), "La Carte du tendre" *(Aimer)*
Élisabeth Vonarburg (Fan), for editing *Solaris*

1988—Canvention 8 (KeyCon 5, Winnipeg)
Charles de Lint (English), *Jack the Giant Killer* (Ace, 1987)
Alain Bergernon (Français), "Les Crabes de Vénus regardent vers le ciel" *(Solaris 73)*
Michael Skeet (Fan), for editing of *MLR*

1989—Canvention 9 (PineKone 2, Ottawa)
In 1989 the number of Awards expanded from three to nine. (Fiction nominees are listed here in alphabetical order, after the winning work. Some "Long-Form" nominees appear in successive years because novels remain eligible for a two-year period. The "Best Other Work" categories recognize anthologies, magazines, nonfiction books, and nonprint media.)

Best Long-Form Work in English (1987–88):
Mona Lisa Overdrive, William Gibson (Bantam)
Nominees:
Machine Sex and Other Stories, Candas Jane Dorsey (Porcépic)
Time Pressure, Spider Robinson (Ace)
The Silent City, Élisabeth Vonarburg (Porcépic)
Memory Wire, Robert Charles Wilson (Bantam)

Best Long-Form Work in French (1987–88):
Temps mort, Charles Montpetit (Paulines)

Nominees:
  Les Gélules utopiques, Guy Bouchard (Logiques)
  La Plage des songes, Stanley Péan (CIDICHA)
  Le Temps des migrations, Francine Pelletier (Le Préambule)
  Le Traversier, Esther Rochon (La Pleine Lune)

Best Short-Form Work in English (1988):
  "Sleeping in a Box," Candas Jane Dorsey *(Machine Sex and Other Stories)*
Nominees:
  "The Fruit Picker," Jo Beverly *(Writers of the Future IV)*
  "(Learning About) Machine Sex," Candas Jane Dorsey *(Machine Sex and Other Stories)*
  "The Paranoid," Spider Robinson *(Pulphouse* Issue 2)
  "Golden Fleece," Robert J. Sawyer *(Amazing,* September 1988)

Best Short-Form Work in French (1988):
  "Survie sur Mars," Joël Champetier *(L'Année de la SF et du F Québécois 1987,* Le Passeur)
Nominees:
  "L'Intrus," Jean Dion *(imagine . . . 43)*
  "SGV," Jean-François Dubé *(Solaris 78)*
  "Geisha Blues," Michel Martin *(L'Année de la SF et du F Québécois 1987,* Le Passeur)
  "Sans titre," Yves Meynard *(Solaris 80)*

Best Other Work in English: Gerry Truscott, Editor, Tesseract Books
Best Other Work in French: Luc Pomerleau, Editor, *Solaris*
Organisational Fan Achievement: Paul Valcour, Treasurer, PineKone I
Fanzine Achievement: Michael Skeet, *MLR*
Other Fan Achievement: Robert Runté, *NCF Guide to Canadian SF*

1990—Canvention 10 (ConVersion 7, Calgary)

Best Long-Form Work in English (1988–89):
  West of January, Dave Duncan (Del Rey)
Nominees:
  Barking Dogs, Terence M. Green (St. Martin's Press)
  Gate of Darkness, Circle of Light, Tanya Huff (DAW)
  The Sarsen Witch, Eileen Kernaghan (Ace)
  Rogue Emperor, Crawford Kilian (Del Rey)
  Gypsies, Robert Charles Wilson (Bantam)

Best Long-Form Work in French (1988–89):
  L'Oiseau de feu (Tome 1), Jacques Brossard (Leméac)

Nominees:

Berlin-Bangkok, Jean-Pierre April (Logiques)

L'Idole des inactifs, Denis Côté (La Courte Echelle)

Le Domaine des sans yeux, Jacques Lazure (Québec / Amérique)

Best Short-Form Work in English (1989):

"Carpe Diem," Eileen Kernaghan (*On Spec,* Fall 1989)

Nominees:

"Flaw on Serendip," J. Brian Clarke (*Analog,* November 1989)

"If You Go Out in the Woods," Paula Johanson (*On Spec,* Fall 1989)

"A Fertile Mind," Clélie Rich (*On Spec,* Fall 1989)

"Duty Free," Rhea Rose (*On Spec,* Spring 1989)

Best Short-Form Work in French (1989):

"Cogito," Élisabeth Vonarburg (*imagine . . .* 46)

Nominees:

"La Tortue sur le trottoir," Michel Martin (*C.I.N.Q.,* Logiques)

"Akimento," Claude-Michel Prévost (*Solaris* 87)

"Pas de dum-dum pour Mister Klaus," Claude-Michel Prévost (*C.I.N.Q.,* Logiques)

Best Other Work in English: Copper Pig Writers' Society, Publishers, *On Spec*

Best Other Work in French: Luc Pomerleau, Editor, *Solaris*

Organisational Fan Achievement: The Alberta Speculative Fiction Assn., ConText '89

Fanzine Achievement: Michael Skeet, *MLR*

Other Fan Achievement: Robert Runté, Promotion of Canadian SF

1991—Canvention 11 (ConText 2, Edmonton)

Best Long-Form Work in English (1989–90):

Tigana, Guy Gavriel Kay (Viking/Roc, 1990)

Nominees:

King of the Scepter'd Isle, Michael Coney

Gate of Darkness, Circle of Light, Tanya Huff

Golden Fleece, Robert J. Sawyer

Gypsies, Robert Charles Wilson

Best Long-Form Work in French (1989–90):

Histoire de la princesse et du dragon, Élisabeth Vonarburg

Nominees:

L'Oiseau de feu (2A), Jacques Brossard

Le Maître de Chichen Itza, Vincent Chabot

La Mer au fond du monde, Joël Champetier

L'Espace du diamant, Esther Rochon
Nuits blêmes, Daniel Sernine

Best Short-Form Work in English (1990):
"Muffin Explains Teleology to the World at Large," James Alan Gardner
(*On Spec,* April 1990)
Nominees:
"Wolfrunner," Mary Choo
"Freewheeling," Charles de Lint
"The Fair in Emain Macha," Charles de Lint
"Eternity, Baby," Andrew Weiner

Best Short-Form Work in French (1990):
"Ici, des tigres," Élisabeth Vonarburg (*Le Sabord* 25)
Nominees:
"À fleur de peau," Joël Champetier
"Coeur de fer," Joël Champetier
"Le Vertige des prisons," Roger Des Roches

Best Other Work in English: Copper Pig Writers' Society, Publisher, *On Spec*
Best Other Work in French: Les Compagnons à temps perdu, Magazine, *Solaris*
Artistic Achievement: Lynne Taylor Fahnestalk, Cover Painting, *On Spec*
Organisational Fan Achievement: Dave Panchyk, President, SSFS; Chair, Combine 0
Fanzine Achievement: Catherine Girczyc, *Neology*
Other Fan Achievement: Al Betz, Column, "Ask Mr. Science"

1992—Canvention 12 (WilfCon 8, Waterloo)

Best Long-Form Work in English (1990–91):
Golden Fleece, Robert J. Sawyer (Warner, 1990)
Nominees:
Blood Price, Tanya Huff (DAW, 1991)
The Difference Engine, William Gibson and Bruce Sterling (Bantam, 1991)
The Divide, Robert Charles Wilson (Bantam, 1991)
The Little Country, Charles de Lint (Morrow, 1991)
Kill the Editor, Spider Robinson (Axolotl, 1991)

Best Long-Form Work in French (1990–91):
Ailleurs et au Japon, Élisabeth Vonarburg (Québec/Amérique, 1991)
Nominees:
La Taupe et le dragon, Joël Champetier (Québec/Amérique, 1991)
Boulevard des étoiles, Daniel Sernine (Ianus, 1991)
Nuits blêmes, Daniel Sernine
À la recherche de monsieur Goodtheim, Daniel Sernine (Ianus, 1991)

Best Short-Form Work in English (1991) (tie):
  "A Niche," Peter Watts (*Tesseracts*[3])
  "Breaking Ball," Michael Skeet (*Tesseracts*[3])
Nominees:
  "Baseball Memories," Edo van Belkom (*Aethlon: The Journal of Sports Literature*, Vol. VII, No. 1)
  "The Man Who Would be Kzin," S. M. Stirling (*Man-Kzin Wars IV*, Baen)
  "Why I Hunt Flying Saucers," Hugh Spencer (*On Spec*, Fall 91)
  "Reaper," James Alan Gardner (*F&SF*, February 1991)
  "Raven Sings a Medicine Way, Coyote Steals the Pollen," Charles de Lint (*Author's Choice Monthly* 22)
  "The Water Man," Ursula Pflug (*Tesseracts*[3])

Best Short-Form Work in French (1991):
  "L'Enfant des Mondes Assoupis," Yves Meynard *(SOL)*
Nominees:
  "Rêves d'anges," Alain Bergeron (*imagine . . .* 56)
  "A't," Harold Côté
  "Jusqu'au dernier," Michel Lamontagne (*imagine . . .* 55)
  "Hôtel Carnivalia," Daniel Sernine (*Boulevard des étoiles*, Ianus)
  "Les Jeux de la paix et de la guerre," Jean-Louis Trudel (*imagine . . .* 55)

Best Other Work in English: TVOntario, Television series, Prisoners of Gravity
Best Other Work in French: Les Compagnons à temps perdu, Magazine, *Solaris*
Artistic Achievement: Martin Springett, Paintings
Organisational Fan Achievement: John Mansfield, Chair, Winnipeg 1994 Worldcon Bid
Fanzine Achievement: Larry Hancock, *Sol Rising*
Other Fan Achievement: David W. New, *Horizons SF*

1993—Canvention 13 (WolfCon 6, Wolfville)

Best Long-Form Work in English (published in 1991–92):
  Passion Play, Sean Stewart (Beach Holme, 1992)
Nominees:
  Children of the Rainbow, Terence M. Green (McClelland & Stewart, 1992)
  Blood Trail, Tanya Huff (DAW, 1992)
  A Song for Arbonne, Guy Gavriel Kay (Viking, 1992)
  Far-Seer, Robert J. Sawyer (Ace, 1992)

Best Long-Form Work in French (1991–92):
  Chroniques du Pays des Mères, Élisabeth Vonarburg (Québec/Amérique, 1992)

Nominees:

La Taupe et le dragon, Joël Champetier (Québec/Amérique, 1991)

Chronoreg, Daniel Sernine (Québec/Amérique, 1992)

Le Cercle de Khaleb, Daniel Sernine (Héritage, 1992)

Best Short-Form Work in English (1992):
"The Toy Mill," David Nickle and Karl Schroeder (*Tesseracts* [4])
Nominees:

"Blue Limbo," Terence M. Green (*Ark of Ice)*

"Couples," Eileen Kernaghan (*Tesseracts* [4])

"Farm Wife," Nancy Kirkpatrick (*Northern Frights)*

"Hopscotch," Karl Schroeder (*On Spec,* Spring 1992)

"Seeing," Andrew Weiner (*F&SF* September 1992)

"Ants," Allan Weiss (*Tesseracts* [4])

Best Short-Form Work in French (1992):
"Base de négociation," Jean Dion (*Solaris* 101)
Nominees:

"Revoir Nymphéa," Alain Bergeron (*Solaris* 99)

"Le Projet," Harold Côté (*Solaris* 101)

"Le Pierrot diffracté," Laurent McAllister (*Solaris* 99)

"Pluies amères," Daniel Sernine (*Solaris* 100)

"Suspends ton vol," Élisabeth Vonarburg (*Solaris* 99)

Best Other Work in English: Michael Skeet and Lorna Toolis, Editors, *Tesseracts* [4]

Best Other Work in French: Les Compagnons à temps perdu, Magazine, *Solaris*

Artistic Achievement: Lynne Taylor Fahnestalk, Cover, *MZB* and *On Spec*

Organisational Fan Achievement: Adam Charlesworth, Noncon 15

Fanzine Achievement: Karl Johanson and John Herbert, *Under the Ozone Hole*

Other Fan Achievement: Louise Hypher, SF2 show

1994—Canvention 14 / World SF Convention (Winnipeg)

The awards will be presented in September at Canvention 14 (the first not hosted by another SF gathering), which is also the 1994 Worldcon.

PRIX BORÉAL

Founded in 1980 by the organisers of the Boréal convention in Québec City, the Prix Boréal have been presented every year since then (except 1985), in spite of the current hiatus in actual Boréal conventions. Categories and rules have changed throughout the years. In 1986, at Boréal 8 in Longueuil, the nonprofit corporation Société du Fantastique et de la Science-

Fiction Boréal Inc. was set up to oversee the Boréal conventions and awards. In time for Boréal 11, in 1989, a set of rules for the Boréal Awards were drawn up by Luc Pomerleau and Jean-Louis Trudel, for SFSF Boréal Inc. According to these rules, all SF magazines and fanzines submit a list of dedicated SF readers from which a jury of about ten people is composed. This jury, in turn, selects five to six finalists in each category. Ballots are then distributed and all readers can vote, free of charge.

—Jean-Louis Trudel

Prix Boréal 1980 (Québec)

Meilleur livre (best book): *Un Été de Jessica,* Alain Bergeron
Meilleure nouvelle (best short fiction): "Jackie, je vous aime,"
Jean-Pierre April
Meilleur illustrateur (best illustrator): Mario Giguère

Prix Boréal 1981 (Montréal)

Meilleur livre (best book): *La Machine à explorer la fiction,* Jean-Pierre April
Meilleures nouvelles ex æquo (tied for best short fiction):
"TéléToTaliTé," Jean-Pierre April; "Le Geai bleu," René Beaulieu
Nouvelle sur place (on-site writing contest) "Le Retour des gueux," Francine Pelletier

Prix Boréal 1982 (Chicoutimi)

Meilleur roman fantastique (best fantasy novel): *Greenwich,* Michel Bélil
Meilleur recueil fantastique (best fantasy collection): *Déménagements,* Michel Bélil
Meilleur roman de SF (best SF novel): *Le Silence de la Cité,* Élisabeth Vonarburg
Meilleur recueil de SF (best SF collection): *Légendes de Virnie,* René Beaulieu
Meilleures nouvelles de SF ex æquo (tied for best SF short fiction): "Le Chemin des fleurs," Joël Champetier; "Le Cœur du monde bat encore," Jean-François Somcynsky
Meilleure nouvelle fantastique (best fantasy short fiction): "Un départ difficile," Jean-François Somcynsky

Prix Boréal 1983 (Québec)

Meilleur livre de SF (best SF book): *L'Enfant du cinquième nord,* Pierre Billon
Meilleur livre fantastique (best fantasy book): *Du Pain des oiseaux,* André Carpentier
Meilleure nouvelle de SF (best SF short fiction): "Les Virus ambiance," Agnès Guitard
Meilleure nouvelle fantastique (best fantasy short fiction): Pas de prix (No Award)

Nouvelle sur place (On-site writing contest): "La traversée d'Algir," Francine Pelletier

Meilleur chroniqueur (best SF column): Claude Janelle

Meilleur illustrateur (best illustrator): Jean-Pierre Normand

Prix Boréal 1984 (Québec)

Meilleur écrivain (best writer): Denis Côté

Meilleur critique (best critic): Luc Pomerleau

Meilleur dessinateur (best artist): André Côté

Personnalité de l'année (man of the year): Mario Giguère

Nouvelle sur place (on-site writing contest): Philippe Gauthier ex æquo (triple tie); Jean Pettigrew; Thierry Vincent

Prix Boréal 1985 (Québec)

No awards given.

Prix Boréal 1986 (Longueuil)

Meilleur roman (best novel): *L'Épuisement du soleil,* Esther Rochon

Meilleure nouvelle (best short fiction): "Compost," Agnès Guitard

Meilleur dessinateur (best artist): Sue Krinard

Prix Boréal 1987 (Montréal)

Meilleur livre (best book): *Coquillage,* Esther Rochon

Meilleures nouvelles ex æquo: (tied for best short fiction)

"Bonne fête, Univers," Alain Bergeron; "Une Chambre à l'Ouest," Jean Dion; "Contre-courant," Agnès Guitard

Meilleur essai (best essay): *Écrits sur le fantastique,* Norbert Spehner

Meilleur illustrateur (best illustrator): Mario Giguère

Nouvelle sur place (on-site writing contest): "Monde retapé: à vendre," Jean-Louis Trudel

Prix Boréal 1988 (Chicoutimi)

Meilleur livre (best book): *Le Temps des migrations,* Francine Pelletier

Meilleure nouvelle (best short fiction): "La Marquise de Tchernobyl," Claude-Michel Prévost

Prix Boréal 1989 (Ottawa)

Meilleur livre (best book): *Les Gélules utopiques,* Guy Bouchard

Meilleure nouvelle (best short fiction): "Geisha Blues," Michel Martin

Meilleur travail critique (best critical work): Luc Pomerleau

Prix Boréal 1990 (Laval)

Meilleur livre (best book): *L'Oiseau de feu (1-A),* Jacques Brossard

Meilleure nouvelle (best short fiction): "La Tortue sur le trottoir," Michel Martin

Meilleure production critique (best critical works): Luc Pomerleau

Prix Boréal 1991 (Rimouski/Laval)

Meilleur livre (best book): *La Mer au fond du monde,* Joël Champetier

Meilleure nouvelle (best short fiction): "Cœur de fer," Joël Champetier

Meilleure production critique (best critical works): Claude Janelle

Prix Boréal 1992 (Montréal)

Meilleur livre (best book): *La Taupe et le dragon,* Joël Champetier ex æquo (tie) *Boulevard des étoiles,* Daniel Sernine

Meilleure nouvelle (best short fiction): "À la recherche de Monsieur Goodtheim," Daniel Sernine

Meilleure production critique (best critical works): Luc Pomerleau

Prix Boréal 1993 (Montréal)

Meilleur livre (best book): *Chroniques du Pays des Mères,* Élisabeth Vonarburg

Meilleure nouvelle (best short fiction): "Convoyeur d'âmes," Yves Meynard

Meilleure production critique (best critical works): Élisabeth Vonarburg

Other Science Fiction and Fantasy Awards in Québec

The *Solaris* Awards

To the best of my knowledge, the award given to the winner of the *Solaris* writing contest is the oldest such literary award in Canadian SF. It was launched by Norbert Spehner of the publication *Requiem* in 1977 as the Prix Dagon. In 1981, after *Requiem* had become *Solaris*, the Prix Dagon became the Prix *Solaris*. A small monetary award, currently amounting to $300, is given to the winner, whose story is published in the pages of the magazine. Between 1981 and 1988 inclusively, the *Solaris* writing contest was open to European writers as well, until *Solaris* decided there were enough good writers in Canada to let them compete for the award.

Grand Prix de la Science-Fiction et du Fantastique

The Grand Prix de la Science-Fiction et du Fantastique Québécois arose out of discussions aiming to set up a regular award for Canadian SF in French that would not be tied to the Boréal conventions. It is an annual award, now worth $2,000, given to an author for the whole of his literary works in the previous year. (For two years, the award was split between a Best Book and a Best Short Fiction category.) It is presented in April of each year, alternating between Montréal and Québec City. The choice of winner is made by a jury that tries to involve personalities from the Québec literary and media milieus. Two software companies, Logidisque and then Logidec, have acted as sponsors for three years at a time, providing the money required for the award.

The Septième Continent Awards

In 1985 the Québec science fiction magazine *imagine . . .* established the "Septième Continent" writing contest to reward the writing of new short fiction exploring the "seventh continent." From the beginning, the contest was opened to all authors writing in French. Until this year, the winner received a monetary award of $300 and the winner's story was published in *imagine . . .* and a European periodical, which is currently the Belgian fanzine *Magie Rouge*. However, in 1994, with the tenth edition of the contest, this prize will climb to $500. Stories by finalists have also been published.

—Jean-Louis Trudel